Skylar

The Halversons: Book #9

by

KIMBERLY RAE JORDAN

THREE**STRAND**
P R E S S

A CORD OF THREE STRANDS IS NOT EASILY BROKEN.

A man, a woman & their God.
Three Strand Press publishes Christian Romance stories
that intertwine love, faith and family. Always clean.
Always heartwarming. Always uplifting.

Scripture taken from the New King James Version®. Copyright © 1982 by Thomas Nelson, Inc. Used by permission. All rights are reserved.

SKYLAR/ Kimberly Rae Jordan. -- 1st ed.
ISBN-13: 978-1-988409-85-6

We also glory in tribulations, knowing that tribulation produces perseverance; and perseverance, character; and character, hope. Now hope does not disappoint, because the love of God has been poured out in our hearts by the Holy Spirit who was given to us.
Romans 5:3 (NKJV)

CHAPTER ONE

Perched cross-legged on her couch, Skylar Halverson stared at the beat-up duffle bag sagging on the shiny surface of the coffee table in front of her. She narrowed her eyes at the bag, then looked down at the dark red liquid in her wineglass, swirling it before she lifted the glass to take a sip.

This isn't going to work. I can't be with someone who is so closed off most of the time. Like you never show any real emotions. At least not ones that are necessary for a solid relationship. Not sure why you are so locked down emotionally, but maybe you should go to a counselor or something.

The words played over and over in her head because it wasn't the first time she'd heard them.

She'd thought that Emmett might be the one who would finally give her the sense of security to trust him with her emotions. Unfortunately, it appeared that six months was too long for him to wait for her to open up, a test of patience he could not endure.

She couldn't quite say that she loved him, but she had cared for him deeply, more than most of the men she had been with. Yet, even her deep care and affection hadn't been enough to bridge the gap between them.

She lifted her glass again, intent on carrying out her plan of drowning her feelings about being dumped yet again.

When her phone rang, its screen lighting the dimly lit room, she glanced to where she'd set it on the end table. From where she sat, she couldn't see who was calling, and for a brief moment, she contemplated ignoring it. But then, on the off chance that Emmett had changed his mind, she leaned over and grabbed it.

Instead of Emmett's name on the screen, however, it was her supervisor's.

"Hello, Denise," she said as she swirled her glass again. "What's up?"

"Any chance you'd be available for work tomorrow?" she asked. "Regina is sick and can't take her New York flight. It's actually going to be a triple. Vegas to NYC to Miami, then back to Vegas."

"Who's the flight deck crew?" Skylar asked, because there were certain pilots she had no interest in flying with unless she absolutely had to.

"Jack Devons."

He was one of the good ones, and even if he had a co-pilot she didn't like, Jack did a good job of keeping everyone in line. The older man was well-respected and demanded a level of decorum on the flights he piloted that Skylar always appreciated. In a lot of ways, he reminded Skylar of her father.

"He's on all three flights?"

"Yep. You'll have an overnight in New York and Miami."

Maybe the distraction was just what she needed.

She unfolded her legs and got up. "Okay. I'll take it."

"Perfect. I'll owe you one."

"I like the sound of that."

"I owe you quite a few at this point," Denise said with a laugh. "I just wish everyone was as willing to step up when I need them to, the way you are."

Skylar was happy to accept any extra shifts that came up. At work, she could simply be a professional. No one cared how she felt. No one cared what was going on in her life. All they wanted from her was a friendly smile and her skill in making rich people feel at ease and catered to.

Her demeanor at work had made her popular among the people who frequently used their company for their private flight needs. Some of their regular clients even requested her.

All of that had made it possible for her to have a nice apartment with no need for a roommate, along with a robust savings account. What she was saving for, Skylar didn't know, but it gave her a sense of security, knowing that if something happened, she could take care of herself.

"I'll send you all the details in a minute," Denise said. "Once again, thank you."

"You're welcome."

After she ended the call, Skylar headed to the kitchen and emptied her wineglass into the sink. There was no way she wanted to work a flight while hung over. Been there, done that, didn't want to do it again.

As the dark liquid vanished down the drain, Skylar could only imagine what her mom would have said about her plan to drink away the upset of a breakup. And not for the first time.

She knew that drinking wasn't a solution for anything. Her parents had made sure all their children knew that they needed to develop healthy ways of coping with challenging situations.

However, with no one around her, she often turned to alcohol to deal with emotions and situations she'd rather not have to face head on.

Ignoring the duffle bag of her belongings that Emmett had dropped off, Skylar went to her bedroom to prepare her uniform and pack her suitcase. She'd need to pack more than usual since it was a multi-day trip.

Once everything was prepped, she went through her nighttime routine, then crawled into bed even though it wasn't very late. The info Denise had sent included the time when she had to be at the airport, and since she didn't like to be rushed in the morning, she needed to go to bed at a reasonable time.

At pre-departure the next morning, Skylar stood with the rest of the flight crew, preparing to greet the clients who were coming aboard the private jet. Though she was young, she had achieved seniority because of her experience and popularity, which meant she had a place right next to the co-pilot. Jack stood nearest the door, dressed neatly in the company pilot uniform.

"Good morning," Skylar said with a smile as she shook the hand of the first person to board the plane.

After they'd greeted each passenger, the pilots returned to the cockpit while Skylar and the other attendant went into the large cabin of the plane. Not every company plane required two attendants, but depending on the length of the flight and the number of passengers, there could be two of them serving the cabin.

All too soon, they were preparing for takeoff, and once they had reached altitude, she was up off her seat to take drink requests. That day, most of the passengers wanted coffee or tea, but occasionally there were flights where people wanted an alcoholic drink.

Slipping into professional mode was easy, and, in fact, a relief. Professional Skylar hadn't just been dumped by her boyfriend. Professional Skylar didn't have a duffle bag of assorted personal effects that her ex had returned to her sitting on her coffee table. Professional Skylar didn't have any personal problems.

As usual, her friendly approach to the clients on the plane brought a similar response from them. She was in her element, and very glad for it.

Three days later, she was back in Las Vegas, eager to get to her apartment. As much as she'd enjoyed the distraction of the flights and spending time in some nice cities, she was also ready to be home.

She had a couple of days off, with no firm agenda of activities planned. For the past six months, Emmett had been with her nearly every day that their schedules allowed, which was most of the time.

But now she was alone.

I like it that way.

However, no matter what she might tell herself, the quiet was heavy as she stepped into her apartment.

Standing just inside her door, Skylar pulled out her phone and sent a text to Denise.

Back from the triple. If you need me for any further shifts on my days off, just let me know. I've got no plans.

She slid her phone into her pocket, then carried her bag into her bedroom to empty it out. It didn't take long to put everything in its place. Dirty clothes into the hamper. Shoes onto the rack in her closet. Makeup bag onto the counter in the bathroom.

Though she had appreciated the distraction of the trip, she was also glad to be back in her apartment. Her sanctuary. Her haven.

She'd spent time and money decorating it the way she wanted to, using the interest she'd once had in interior design to create a cozy home for herself. She might not have everything she'd once thought she'd have at this point in time, but she'd built a life for herself that she cherished.

Once her bag was unpacked and she'd changed into her comfy clothes, Skylar made her way to the kitchen to get herself something to eat and drink. She eyed the wine bottle in the fridge, but passed it over, choosing instead to grab one of her fancy bottles of water.

She was in the process of trying to figure out what to make for her supper when the alert for a video chat sounded on her phone. Usually the only person who wanted to chat with her via video was her mom, so it didn't surprise her to see that was whose name was on the call request.

"Hi, Mom," she said as her mom's face filled the screen. When she saw a serious expression on her mom's face rather than her usual cheery smile, Skylar clutched her phone more tightly. "What's wrong?"

Her mom didn't reply right away, making Skylar's heart sink. "Just rip the band-aid off, Mom."

"So over the past few weeks, Shiloh has been having some health issues," her mom began, then paused again.

Skylar's breath caught in her lungs. Most days, she was able to not think about the child she'd given birth to, except in passing. However, it was as if her body knew that she was receiving bad news about something that had once been a part of her.

"What's wrong with her?"

"After doing some testing, they've discovered she has cancer."

"What?" Skylar felt like she'd been punched in the gut. "Cancer?"

She reached out to grip the counter, the bite of the sharp edge into her palm mirroring the sharp pain she felt in her heart. Her head spun as she struggled to draw breath into her lungs.

"How sick is she?"

"She's... not well, but she has a good chance of recovery with several treatment options available."

"So she's okay?"

"For the moment," her mom said. "But we're already thinking of possible future treatments should the initial ones not be as successful as we hope."

"So she's having treatment soon?"

"Yes. She'll be going into the hospital in Coeur d'Alene next week for chemo."

Skylar didn't know what to say. It was news she'd never even considered that she'd hear about Shiloh. And she had no idea what it meant long term for the beautiful little girl she'd chosen to carry to term, even though the baby's father had wanted her to *"get rid of it."*

"Is there..." Skylar paused, taking a deep breath and trying to swallow the emotions that threatened to choke her. "Is there anything I can do?"

"Yes. First, I think it might be good for you to come home," her mom said.

"What? Why?"

"It would mean the world for Charli and Blake to have you here."

"But no one knows I'm Shiloh's birth mom," Skylar reminded her. "So it would seem kind of weird if I came home, when presumably Cole won't be coming home."

"Well, that's the second thing."

"Cole is coming home?"

"No, but we would like you to contact Aiden," her mom said, rendering Skylar speechless. "And I think we need for you to consider letting the rest of the family know that you both are Shiloh's birth parents."

"Nope." The panic she felt rise at both those suggestions momentarily chased away the fear that had filled her at the news of Shiloh's cancer diagnosis. "No. Never."

She'd always held close the information that she was Shiloh's birth mom. No one but her parents and Charli and Blake knew the truth. And she'd wanted it to stay that way forever.

When her mom didn't answer right away, but continued to stare into the phone, Skylar said, "Please, Mom. Anything but that."

"It's important, Skylar Grace," she said. The use of her middle name made Skylar cringe. "It could make all the difference for Shiloh."

"What do you mean?"

"One option for possible future treatment is a stem cell transplant, which means we need to find someone who would be a match with Shiloh. Close family members are the best chance, but other relatives are also a good possibility. Which is why we need to test Aiden, his family, and ours. I think it would be impossible to do that and still keep her parentage secret."

Skylar closed her eyes and let out a heavy sigh. When she opened her eyes again, she stared out the window at the skyline of Las Vegas.

This was the last thing she wanted to do. The moment she'd handed Shiloh over to Charli was supposed to have been the end of her role in Shiloh's life beyond being an "aunt" to her.

She'd brought the baby safely into the world, but then it was Charli and Blake's job to guide Shiloh through her life, caring for and protecting her in Skylar's absence.

And she *was* absent. She only saw Shiloh once or twice a year, and for just a day or two at a time. It had been the only way she'd been able to distance herself from the feeling of being Shiloh's mom.

"Think about it, please, sweetheart." Her mom sighed, the weight of the situation clearly pressing down on her. "We are trying to do what we can to help Shiloh, Charli, and Blake through this."

Skylar still resisted agreeing to contact Aiden. All she could do was promise to think about it.

"Love you, sweetheart," her mom said. "Take care of yourself."

"You too, Mama."

"We'll be praying for you."

Her mom always said that, and Skylar never knew how to respond beyond saying, "Thank you."

After she hung up the phone, Skylar put the food and water back in the fridge and pulled out the bottle of wine. She couldn't deal with this news without a little fortification.

Her confusion over what to do held a huge amount of guilt. She was being selfish. She knew that.

Her own feelings should hold no weight in this situation. She needed to do what was best for Shiloh. For her daughter. Nothing else was important. Not her feelings. Not her fears. Not her plans to never reveal the pregnancy and its aftermath.

It looked like she was going to have to contact Cole to ask for details on his best friend, all the while hoping that he'd give them to her without asking why she needed them. But knowing Cole, she wasn't sure that was possible, especially considering that back when she and Aiden broke up, she'd told Cole she never wanted to talk about Aiden again.

Hopefully, a little alcohol would help give her the courage she needed. She knew her parents would recommend praying, but Skylar didn't believe as strongly as they did that God was paying attention to their lives.

So she'd leave the praying to them, while she turned to liquid courage to do what they wanted her to.

CHAPTER TWO

The chime of his phone's text alert drew Aiden McIntyre's attention away from the large monitor sitting on his desk. He was revising a design that he and his team had developed, attempting to incorporate the modifications the client had asked for.

It was a frustrating, but also challenging, situation, given that they'd thought they were nearing the end of the project. Unfortunately, the client had recently decided they wanted some things changed, leaving them to scramble to please the man.

Picking up his phone, he got to his feet and arched his back to stretch it out as he read the message that had come in.

Mom: *Hi darling! Hope your day is going well. Just a reminder that we're getting fast food for dinner. Willow wants to make sure you don't forget and work late.*

Blowing out a long breath, Aiden stepped over to the window. He had, in fact, forgotten. However, there was no way he was going to miss out. Spending time with his niece and mom was a priority for him, so he made sure to leave work promptly, even if it meant he had to finish tasks at home.

I'll be there. I plan to leave the office around five-thirty. Do you want to just meet at the restaurant?

Grateful for a bit of a break, he spent a few minutes messaging with his mom, sorting out the plans for their dinner date, then he returned to his desk. He hoped to get another solid hour of work in before he left to meet his mom and Willow.

He'd barely focused on his monitor when there was a knock on the door, then his assistant popped his head into the room.

"What's up?" Aiden asked, leaning back in his chair.

Tyler crossed his arms and scowled at him. "You forgot, didn't you?"

Aiden wracked his brain, then sat forward to grab his mouse and click it to bring up the calendar app on his monitor. "I have an appointment."

"Yep. And she's here."

"She?"

"Miss Grace. She's here for her appointment with you."

Aiden frowned. "What is the appointment for?"

"She said she has a project she wanted to discuss with you."

"Okay." Aiden sighed heavily. So much for his plans for the last hour of his day. "Send her in."

"Will do."

Aiden turned off his monitor, then angled himself at his L-shaped desk to face the chairs on the opposite side. He pulled his tablet toward him and opened the app he used to take notes. Sliding the pen free, he set it next to the tablet, hoping the meeting wouldn't take too long.

"Miss Grace," Tyler said.

Aiden looked up, then froze in the process of getting to his feet. "Skylar?"

"Hello, Aiden," she said as she stepped past Tyler into the office.

Tyler gave Aiden a questioning look but didn't say anything before pulling the door closed behind him as he left the office.

Aiden was thrown back in time to when he had last seen Skylar, and it was hard to reconcile that distraught teen with the poised woman standing in front of him.

She wore a navy pencil skirt that reached her knees and had paired it with a lilac colored short-sleeved silk blouse that looked stunning with her dark hair and eyes. Hair that was sleekly pulled back from her face, and eyes that were made up to highlight them.

All in all, she looked like a businesswoman, and it made him think she might be there in a professional capacity. Whatever that could be.

Her expression remained serene as she stepped closer to his desk. "Thank you for fitting me into your schedule."

"I had no idea it was you," he said, the words coming out more harshly than he'd intended.

"Would you have agreed to see me if you had?" she asked, coming to a stop behind one of the chairs opposite him.

He considered that for a moment, then shrugged. "I don't know."

Emotion flitted across her face at his honest response, but Aiden couldn't quite figure out what it was.

"It was important that I talk to you, so I couldn't take the chance that you wouldn't."

"Why don't you have a seat and tell me what's going on?" he said, gesturing to the chair she stood behind.

He waited until she'd taken a seat, gracefully lowering herself into the chair, then crossing her legs, before he settled back into his own chair.

"I would rather not be here," she said. "But I've been given no choice."

"Has something happened to Cole?"

"No. This has to do with our... daughter."

Shock locked Aiden's breath in his lungs as he stared at his ex-girlfriend. Their *daughter?* He was glad he was sitting down because he wasn't sure that his legs would have held him up if he'd still been standing.

"Our *what?*"

Skylar's chin lifted and her shoulders pulled back. "You may have told me that I needed to get rid of *it,* but I chose to ignore your terrible directive. Seven months after that horrible day, I gave birth to a baby girl."

"You really *were* pregnant?"

"What?" Skylar frowned at him, her eyes flashing with anger. "You thought I was *lying*?"

Aiden shrugged. "You wouldn't be the first woman who tried to hold on to an ex through a fake pregnancy."

Skylar's anger deepened, her brows drawing together over her furious brown eyes. "Maybe, but you knew I wasn't that type of person."

"Did I?" he asked. "You'd never gone through a breakup before, and you made it very clear that you didn't want things to end between us."

"Yes, because I thought I loved you," she said, anger heavy in her words. "But I also wouldn't have lowered myself to faking a pregnancy in order to keep you when it was clear that you didn't love me. Would you have told me to get rid of it if you'd known that I really *was* pregnant?"

"No." He hesitated. "I'd like to think I would have stepped up."

"Personally, I don't think you would have stepped up," she said. "You seem to think you would have known if I was telling the truth, only clearly you didn't because I *was* telling the truth. You didn't want me, and you certainly didn't want a baby, which would have stopped you from finding someone better than me."

Aiden did his best to firm his expression under the onslaught of her angry words.

Over the years since that conversation he'd had with Skylar following their breakup, he'd done his best not to think about what he'd said. In fact, he'd tried his utmost to not dwell on anything that had taken place between him and Skylar—good or bad.

"Are you here for money?" he asked, figuring there could be no other reason.

He hadn't thought Skylar could reach another level of anger. But it looked like they'd entered the highest level. Or at least he hoped it was the highest level.

The placid expression she'd arrived with was completely gone. Burned away by the anger she aimed at him. Anger she was probably entitled to, but he didn't plan to let her know that. At least, not yet.

"No. I'm not here for money." She spit the words at him. "You made it clear you had no interest in being a father, and I respected that. The last thing I wanted for her was to have a father in her life who had wished her dead, even if you weren't convinced that she was real. You didn't want her, and you didn't want me."

That was a stab to the heart, but he had thought he was doing the right thing for both of them back then. He'd told himself that they were too young to be tied to each other.

"So if you're not here for money, why are you here?" Aiden asked, desperate to move forward in this shocking meeting.

The anger slowly faded from Skylar's face, but it didn't disappear entirely from her gaze. "She has cancer."

"Cancer?" Shock greater than any he'd felt so far in this interaction overwhelmed him. Of all the things he'd expected her to say, that hadn't been it.

"Yes. My mom called me yesterday to let me know about her diagnosis."

"I don't understand," he said. "Why did you hear it from your mom? Is she her doctor?"

Skylar hesitated a moment before she said, "I'm not raising her. I gave her up for adoption. The adoptive parents... contacted my mom about the diagnosis."

Aiden stared at Skylar for a long moment, trying to piece everything together. "So you kept the pregnancy but not the baby?"

"Yes. I knew that I wasn't in the position to be a single mother, so I gave her to people I thought would be wonderful parents for her."

"So, why are you here today?" Aiden was determined to not let Skylar see how all this was impacting him.

"My mom said they need to test you to see if you're a match for her for a stem cell transplant."

She said it like there was no way he'd refuse to be tested, and she was right. He wouldn't. Mainly because his thoughts went to his niece, Willow. If she needed something from someone in order to live, he would have moved mountains and not accepted no for an answer.

Aiden could see the determination on Skylar's face, and he knew she felt the same way.

"Just me?" he asked, wanting to know if his family was going to have to get involved too.

Or rather, if he was going to have to reveal to his mom what had happened with Skylar nine years ago. He hoped he didn't have to because he really didn't want to see the look of disappointment that would surely appear on his mom's face when he told her.

"All of my family are going to be tested because even if I'm not a match, it's possible one of them might be."

"So, in other words, you want my family involved in this, too."

She hesitated for a moment, then said, "Yes."

Aiden pressed his fingers against his temple, trying to quell the pressure that was building there. This was just too much to deal with on top of the stress of his current project.

"I'll have to have a conversation with them, then let them know."

Skylar gave him a disgusted look. "As if your mom wouldn't help someone in need. Especially a child. And *more* especially a child who is biologically her granddaughter."

Aiden had forgotten how well his mom and Skylar had gotten along. His mom had been very upset when she'd learned that they had broken up.

"I haven't decided yet how I'll broach this with her," he said. "Or if I'll tell her who it is that needs the match."

Skylar's perfectly plucked eyebrows drew together for a moment before smoothing out. "You do you."

The anger finally disappeared completely from Skylar's face, but Aiden didn't think for a minute that it was gone. The placid expression had settled back into place, and while there was no anger showing, there was definitely no happiness there either.

It was so wild to see Skylar again. He'd figured that at some point in his life, their paths would cross, given that her brother was his best friend. However, he'd figured it would be at Cole's wedding or some other event where Cole was present. And that he'd have time to prepare for the encounter. This scenario had never crossed his mind.

"Let me know what you decide," Skylar said as she got to her feet. She opened her purse and pulled out a small piece of paper, which she set on his desk. "That's my number."

Aiden got to his feet as well. He followed her as she turned and walked toward the closed door of his office.

Tyler looked up as they exited the office, his brows lifted, but he didn't say anything until Skylar had stepped into the elevator.

"Meeting go okay?" he asked as Aiden stood by his desk, staring at the closed elevator door.

Aiden dragged his gaze from the elevator and looked at Tyler. "It ended up being personal in nature."

"Ex-girlfriend?"

"Yep."

"Hah." Tyler grinned. "That was just a wild guess."

"Wild and correct."

"She's back to tell you that you're a dad and owe millions in child support?"

Aiden just gave his head an exasperated shake at Tyler, not wanting to confirm or deny his question. "It was an interesting conversation that I need some time to digest."

"Good thing you have the weekend to do that," Tyler said, looking at his smart watch.

"You can go ahead and leave," Aiden said. "I'm sure you have a date."

"That I do. I'm taking her to a concert."

"Hope you have fun." Aiden had thought he'd have an enjoyable—albeit not very exciting—weekend. Now, he wasn't so sure. "See you on Monday."

Returning to his office, Aiden prepared to leave for the day. He also had a date, only it was at a fast-food restaurant with his mom and niece.

Somehow, he had to decide how best to approach this with his mom. He was still trying to grasp that he had a daughter, when all these years, he'd told himself that there had never been a baby.

The fact that Cole—his best friend and Skylar's brother—had never mentioned his sister being pregnant or having a baby had reinforced that for him. If Cole had gotten a whiff of Skylar being pregnant, he would have known it was Aiden's and come after him, perhaps with a punch or two.

So, in his mind, he'd been right. Skylar had only been trying to manipulate him into staying with her.

Except he'd been wrong. So very wrong.

When Aiden finally arrived at the restaurant a little while later, he still had no idea what to tell his mom. He left his suit coat in the car on a hanger, along with his work bag, and made his way inside.

He'd no sooner set foot in the restaurant when he heard his name called.

"Uncle Aiden!" Willow came running toward him, her curly, long, dark hair bouncing in a ponytail behind her.

He swung the little girl up into his arms and gave her a kiss on the cheek. "How're you doing?"

"I'm great!" She grinned at him. "Want to hear a joke?"

"You know I do," he told her as they walked to where his mom waited at a table near the play area.

"Why can't Elsa have a balloon?"

Aiden didn't have to ask who Elsa was. *Frozen* was very popular with Willow. "I don't know. Why can't she?"

"Because she'll let it go!" Willow laughed in delight as Aiden grinned at her.

"That's a good one." He held out his hand for her to give him a high five. "Probably your best one ever."

"You say that *allllll* the time," Willow said.

Willow's obsession with jokes always brought levity to his day, regardless of how dumb the joke was or how bad his day had been.

He set Willow down so she could climb into one of the chairs at the table. Aiden bent to kiss his mom's cheek.

She looked a bit tired, but that wasn't uncommon these days. She'd told him that she struggled to sleep at night.

"So what are we having for supper?" he asked. "Our usual?"

"I'm good with my usual," his mom said.

"Me, too!"

"Want to come with me, Willow?"

When she nodded, he held out his hand. With her tiny fingers tucked in his grasp, they walked to the counter to place their order. A big burger for him. A chicken burger for his mom. And nuggets for Willow. Each with fries and a drink.

After he had picked up the tray filled with their order, Willow skipped ahead of him to the table. His mom helped him clear the food off the tray. Then, knowing what was to come, he bowed his head and waited for Willow to pray.

It was a bit of an odd situation to find himself in. When he'd become a Christian as a teen, his parents hadn't been interested in Christianity. They'd been great parents and hadn't cared that he'd gone to church, but that hadn't been something they'd wanted for themselves.

However, his own faith had faltered when he'd gone away to college. During those years, his parents had become Christians and had done a much better job of embracing their faith than he had his. But in recent years, he and his mom were on the same page.

He was somewhat surprised that his mom's faith was still as strong as it was, considering the tragedies they'd suffered over the past couple of years. His dad's sudden death had been a challenge to accept, but as time passed, they'd made progress in their grief.

The grief had intensified just ten months later when his sister had died tragically in a boating accident, leaving behind her young daughter. That had been much harder to accept and had resulted in a life focus change for him.

His mom had still been struggling with her grief over the loss of her husband, so she'd needed a lot of support as she assumed responsibility of her young granddaughter, since Willow's father wasn't in the picture. It hadn't taken much thought for Aiden to decide to move in to help her.

The only thing he'd asked was that she consider a move to Coeur d'Alene so that he could get a job there and not have a long commute from Serenity each day. His mom had agreed, so he'd shopped around and bought a house with a suite in the basement. His Mom and Willow lived on the main floor so that he could have his own space while still being close enough to help them.

Thankfully, money had not been an issue as his dad had worked in finance and thus made sure to take care of all of them in the event of his death. His mom had refused to sell the house in Serenity, however. So it sat fully furnished but empty, with his mom going out every couple of weeks to check on it.

She'd hired a company to take care of the grass and snow, so Aiden didn't have to go with her, though he periodically did, depending on his availability when she chose to go. But it was sad to see the property without the colorful flower beds in both the front and back yards, since she hadn't planted anything there.

Thankfully, though, she hadn't abandoned her passion for gardening entirely, so their home in Coeur d'Alene now had beautiful landscaping.

"Is everything okay, honey?" his mom asked with a gentle touch on his arm. "You seem distracted."

That was very much an understatement. He was allowing his thoughts to go in the painful direction of the losses they'd suffered in order to not have to deal with the more pressing issue.

"Just had a meeting at work that is taking a lot of my attention."

"Something serious?"

"Kind of," he admitted. "But I'll work through it."

"If you want to tell me about it, I'm happy to listen."

He looped his arm around her shoulders and leaned to touch his head to hers. "I know, and I appreciate that. For now, let's just enjoy the evening."

"Can I go play now, Nana?" Willow asked, lifting the paper container that had held her nuggets to show them it was empty. "I'm all done."

"Yes, my darling," his mom said. "You can play. Remember to be gentle and kind to the other children."

Willow nodded, then ran off to the area next to their table where there was a tall structure with climbing ropes and slides. It was one of the places Willow liked to come to play. And that day, there were several other children her age already playing on the structure.

As his mom chatted about her and Willow's day, Aiden found himself only half-listening. The other part of his focus was now on the situation with Skylar. He had a hard time trying to figure out what to do.

He could be honest with his mom about who the little girl that needed his help was. *The little girl...* he didn't even know her name. But if he told her the truth about who she was, he'd have to give her the details about what happened nine years ago. And then deal with her disappointment in him.

The other option was to make up a story. To lie to his mom. To spare her the pain of learning that she had another grandchild, one she could lose if the treatments didn't help and the worst happened. She didn't need more grief in her life. Neither of them did.

But lying to his mom didn't sit well with Aiden.

So he was going to need to figure out how to reveal everything, and brace himself for the disappointment his mom was going to have in him because of his past actions.

CHAPTER THREE

Skylar set her silverware on her plate, finished with her lunch, even though she'd only eaten very little. Her appetite since finding out about Shiloh's diagnosis had been pretty much non-existent. Not to mention having had to see Aiden again. Both situations had robbed her of her appetite, and she only ate enough to keep her parents off her back.

"So you're definitely on board with us having a family dinner and meeting tonight?" her dad asked.

"Do I have a choice?" Skylar asked, trying to keep her true feelings out of her voice.

She'd agreed, but only because Charli and Blake had felt that it was necessary to inform the family when they asked them to consider being tested for the stem cell match.

Most of the time, Skylar refused to think about Shiloh being her daughter. However, that hadn't always been the case. In the days and weeks following Shiloh's birth, she'd had to train herself to only view Shiloh as a niece.

Now, she had to acknowledge that she was her birth mom and deal with the ramifications of that revelation. Her hope was that whatever happened, her interactions with Aiden would be non-existent. Unfortunately, she doubted that was possible.

Seeing him again after almost a decade had been jarring.

The last time he'd stood in front of her, he'd been clean shaven and boasting a longer-than-normal hair style. His tall, lanky body, clothed in faded jeans and T-shirt, had been tense with anger as he'd ended their relationship.

The man she'd seen in the office the day before hadn't shown much emotion at all. He'd been wearing a suit and tie and sported a professionally styled haircut. There was also the lightest bit of scruff on his face.

She'd heard from her mom, who'd heard from Cole, that a couple of years earlier, Aiden had lost his dad and sister over the course of less than twelve months. That no doubt accounted for the strain she'd seen on his face.

She didn't have much sympathy for Aiden, but she had a lot for his mom. She was such a sweet woman, and Skylar had loved her.

If the current situation had an upside, funnily enough, it was that she was no longer dwelling on her most recent breakup. The past and all its messiness were calling louder than the present and its heartache.

"What do you need me to do for the dinner tonight?" Skylar asked, even though she didn't want the meal to actually occur.

"We're going to have spaghetti, salad, and garlic bread," her mom said. "Zane told me he'd drop off the sauce, since he and Kelsey can't come because of work, though we'll make the pasta here. Kayleigh is bringing fresh bread from the resort, and Rori is bringing a salad. Oh, and Misha said she'd bring dessert."

"I guess my contribution will be setting the table," Skylar said. "And maybe pouring water."

Her mom chuckled. "Every job is an important job."

Skylar had heard that plenty while growing up. As she sipped her coffee, her mom continued to talk about the dinner. What tablecloth she wanted used. And if she'd have a centerpiece.

Skylar didn't give any input, but that didn't matter because her mom wasn't really looking for her opinion anyway.

Eventually, her mom got a phone call, which interrupted her chatter. Skylar finished her coffee, then rinsed out the mug and put it in the dishwasher.

"Going for a run," she mouthed at her mom, who nodded as she continued talking to the person on the phone.

Skylar went upstairs to her room and quickly changed into a pair of running shorts and a T-shirt, then put on her runners. It was only a matter of minutes before she headed down the front porch steps to the driveway.

She took a couple of minutes to stretch her legs, preparing to tackle the run she had in mind.

When she'd been in high school, she'd jogged outside. Now that she lived in Vegas, where it could be oppressively hot, she preferred the treadmill, usually watching a show or reading a book as she ran. That day, however, she was left with just her thoughts and a playlist of music with a beat that helped her keep her pace.

The road her parents lived on wasn't heavily trafficked, so she didn't have to deal with many cars. She didn't really expect to face any trouble during her run, but she had still brought a small canister of pepper spray with her, just in case.

Soon she left the long driveway and was out on the road, her feet pounding on the asphalt as she ran. The route she took was familiar since it was the one she and her parents had agreed on back in high school, and she didn't deviate from it even all these years later.

She hadn't gone far when she was reminded of how Aiden used to come on runs with her, insisting that he wanted exercise, though she'd thought his reason was to keep her safe.

Too bad he hadn't protected her from himself.

Anger fueled her, and soon her pounding steps on the asphalt were out of sync with the music and in sync with her emotions. Her life felt out of sync as well. Out of step with where it had been just days earlier.

The decision had been made to not just give all the details about the adoption to the family, but also to Shiloh. Skylar had hoped that wouldn't be revealed to Shiloh for years to come. Preferably when Shiloh was an adult, close to the age that Skylar had been when she'd delivered her.

But that was not to be.

And now Skylar had to accept that whether she liked it or not, her secrets were all going to come tumbling out.

When she returned to the house, she was dripping with sweat, and her muscles ached, but in a good way. She greeted her parents briefly, then went upstairs to take a shower.

As the afternoon progressed, the all too familiar flutter of nerves and anxiety grew. By the time her siblings arrived, Skylar was a mess, though she was trying her best to keep her emotions in check.

"Hey, sis," Wilder said as he wrapped her in a tight hug, then picked her up and spun her around before putting her back down. "I'm surprised you're here."

"Yeah. So am I."

His brows lifted at her response. "What's going on?"

"You'll find out a little later."

"That sounds... ominous." He glanced around. "Is something up with Mom and Dad?"

"No, they're fine."

"Nothing like keeping us in suspense," he said with a frown as he reached to take Lexi's hand. "I like that in movies and books, but not so much in real life."

"You'll survive," Skylar assured him.

The noise level in the house grew as more family arrived. With siblings and their spouses, there was almost twenty of them in total.

Though it was loud, once they were settled around the table, the conversation died down as their dad said grace. The food was delicious—especially the sauce that Zane had made.

Though a few of the siblings had tried to figure out why they were there, it wasn't until they were eating dessert that her dad finally asked everyone for their attention.

"I suppose you're all wondering if there's a purpose for our gathering tonight, and there is. You're probably also wondering why Skylar is here, when her visits rarely occur during this time of the year unless there's a wedding. There's a reason for that too."

"The same reason?" Gareth asked.

"Yes."

It felt like everyone looked at her, then back at her dad.

"What's going on?" Jay asked.

When her dad gave her a questioning look, Skylar gave a small gesture, indicating he should go ahead with the explanation. She wasn't sure she could get through it without a rush of emotions that she wouldn't be able to contain.

Over the next several minutes, her dad explained what had happened, though he didn't give all the details of the breakup. Skylar was grateful for that, but she had a feeling her siblings were going to ask all about it.

"Wait a second," Jay said, holding up his hand. "Shiloh is Skylar's daughter? And *Aiden*—Cole's BFF—is her father?"

"Yes," her dad said.

Jay turned to look at Skylar, concern on his face. "I can't believe he did that."

Well, in that regard, they agreed. "I couldn't either."

"Unreal." Jay shook his head. "Absolutely unreal."

"Does Cole know?" Gareth asked.

Skylar shook her head. "I never told him, though maybe Aiden has."

"If Cole hasn't been burning up the wire calling one of us, I would imagine that he doesn't know yet."

"I would really like to have a conversation with Aiden," Jay said darkly. "I spoke to the guys when I was coaching them, telling them how to treat girls and how to handle relationships."

"You'll get a chance to speak with him," their dad said, before he went on to explain what had brought Aiden into their lives, and how it related to Shiloh's diagnosis.

"So, is his family going to be tested, too?" Gareth asked. "Even though the likelihood of being a match is low?"

"Well, as you know, low is not no," her dad said. "Regardless of how we feel about what Aiden did, we need to find out if he or someone in his family is a match for Shiloh."

"So, how's this going to work?" Janessa asked.

As their dad explained everything that had been arranged for the coming Friday, Skylar looked around at her siblings. None of them were regarding her with judgment. Given that three of the ten of them had ended up with a child born outside of marriage, she supposed judgment wouldn't be their first response.

And from the sound of things, Jay was more unhappy with Aiden than with her.

After answering a few questions, the information portion of the evening was done. Several people got up and shuffled around to talk to those they hadn't been seated next to during the meal.

"I never thought you'd be so good at keeping secrets," Janessa said as she sat down in the seat next to Skylar. "You and Charli both."

"She kept this secret because I asked her to," Skylar told her. "From the start, she thought we should tell the family."

"I would have liked to know," Janessa said. "But I understand why you didn't want it to be public knowledge."

"And it still wouldn't be except for this latest turn of events and having to bring Aiden back into our lives."

"How has it been for you, seeing him again?" Janessa asked.

Skylar wrinkled her nose. "It's been difficult."

"Is he acting the same as he did when he broke up with you?"

"We've only had one conversation so far, so he hasn't had time to show too much of his attitude. But he didn't outright send me packing, so perhaps he's matured."

"I suppose losing your dad and your sister would cause a guy to have to grow up fast," Janessa said. "And rearrange your priorities."

"Hopefully it's had that effect on him."

"Too bad he wasn't that kind of man back when you got pregnant."

Janessa's statement echoed one of the thoughts Skylar had been struggling with. But it was irrelevant to where they were currently. They couldn't go back in time. They could only deal with the present, good or bad.

And once she had been tested, she'd head back to Vegas and put all of this behind her. She couldn't wait.

Soon, people began to leave. But before they did, each of her siblings came to her to give her a hug and offer her support. No one seemed angry at her for what had happened or for keeping the secret for so long.

"I think that went well," her mom said once it was just the three of them.

Skylar bent to put a few last plates into the dishwasher. "As well as could be expected, I suppose."

"You should give your siblings more credit," her dad admonished gently. "They love you, and they'd never attack you over something like this. Especially because they all know and love Shiloh."

Skylar had distanced herself from her family over the years, so it had been hard to know how they might react. "I hope that one of us will be a match for Shiloh."

"I hope so too," her mom said as she wiped down the counter. "It will be easier if we're dealing with a family member."

If Skylar didn't have to continue to deal with Aiden, that would be easier for her, too. But she had no idea what Aiden was going to do now that he'd learned that he really had fathered a child.

She was upstairs in her room, taking off her makeup, when her phone rang. Seeing Aiden's name on the screen made her want to ignore the call. Why couldn't he text like a normal person?

Maybe he was calling to say that he'd help, but then he wanted to walk away and never hear from her again.

"Hello?" she said as she answered the call and tapped for the speakerphone before setting the phone on the bathroom counter.

After they'd exchanged greetings, Aiden said, "I'd like to ask you a few more questions about the situation."

"Okay?"

"First, what is the baby's name?"

Skylar hesitated, not sure where Aiden was going. "I'm afraid that I'm not comfortable sharing that information at the moment."

"Why?" Aiden was direct in a way he hadn't been as a teen.

"Because I don't trust you." She could also be direct in that way. "Oh, and I also don't like you."

There was a long beat of silence before Aiden chuckled. "Well, you're certainly not pulling your punches these days."

"Why should I?" she asked. "You certainly didn't nine years ago."

She heard the heavy sigh through the speaker of the phone. "Fair enough."

"So, no name. Next question?"

As she dumped facial cleanser onto a cotton pad, she heard Aiden say, "What are the chances that I'd get to meet her? Should I decide I want that?"

Skylar's stomach sank, and her fingers squeezed the cotton pad until the liquid pressed against her palm. "Zero chances."

"Is that *your* answer or the adoptive parents' answer?"

She wanted to say it was both of theirs, but she honestly didn't know for certain how Charli and Blake felt about it. Charli had been after her for the last couple of years to let them tell Shiloh that Skylar was her birth mother.

So far, she'd resisted the idea. It was entirely possible that they might be open to the idea of telling Shiloh who her father was.

"It's mine, definitely," Skylar admitted. "But it's also possibly the adoptive parents' as well."

"I would like to know for sure that they feel that way."

She wanted to tell him she wouldn't ask them. Instead, she said, "I can ask them, but there's no guarantee they'll say yes."

"And no guarantee that you'd tell me even if they did."

She let her silence speak for her. "Next question. Or rather, last question."

"When do we need to come for testing?"

"I'll ask my dad for the specifics and text you the information."

Aiden might phone like some uncouth person, but she was polite enough to text.

"Appreciate that," he said. "Are you living in Serenity now?"

"You're not entitled to another question," she told him. "But I'll answer it, anyway. No, I don't live in Serenity."

She could tell he really wanted to ask where she lived, but to his credit—not that she wanted to give him credit for anything—he didn't.

"Well, I'll let you go," he said. "Look forward to your text. Have a good night."

"You too," Skylar replied, trying to be polite in a way she hadn't been earlier.

After she hung up, she puffed out her cheeks with a breath and stared at herself in the mirror. Tilting her head, she gazed into her own eyes.

What had Aiden thought when he'd seen her? Had he catalogued the changes in her the way she had in him?

She knew her appearance had changed over the years. Her hair wasn't as long as she'd worn it in high school. Her figure had filled out a bit more once she'd stopped cheering and because of the pregnancy. The thing that bothered her the most, however, were the slight lines that had appeared on her face in the past year.

They were nothing major, and it was unlikely that anyone else had noticed them. However, *she* had noticed them, and they bothered her. She wasn't even thirty years old!

With that in mind, she turned her attention back to her nighttime facial routine. She'd talk to her dad the next morning to ask about the plan for the testing.

And perhaps she'd give Charli a call to ask what they thought about Aiden knowing something about Shiloh.

Though she could probably put off making that call for a day or two.

CHAPTER FOUR

"Can I talk to you about something, Mom?" Aiden asked once Willow had finished her dinner, taken a bath, and was asleep in her bed.

His mom looked up from the embroidery hoop she held in her hand. After slipping the needle into the edge of the fabric, she set the hoop down on her lap, then pushed her glasses onto the top of her head and gave Aiden her full attention.

"What's going on, sweetheart?"

Aiden hesitated, knowing that what he said next was going to change things. He didn't want his mom to look at him with disappointment, but he knew she would.

"I need to tell you about something," he began, searching for a good starting point. He'd made the decision to be honest with her, but now that he was at that moment, he wanted to lie. "I didn't tell you the truth about why Skylar and I broke up."

His mom frowned. "Skylar Halverson?"

He nodded. "I know this seems out of the blue, but I promise you it will make sense."

Her frown morphed into confusion. "Okay?"

"I was the one who broke up with Skylar," he said. "I know I told you it was a mutual decision, but it really wasn't. Being in college had opened up a whole new world for me, and I wanted to be able to date other girls."

"Aiden..."

And there was the disappointment. Unfortunately, he hadn't even gotten to the worst part yet.

"The summer before I started my sophomore year at college, I broke up with her," he told her. "But then Skylar called me a couple of months later to tell me that she was pregnant."

"What?" His mom's eyes widened as she pressed a hand to her chest. "Skylar was pregnant?"

"That's what she said, but I didn't believe her."

"Why wouldn't you believe her?"

Aiden swallowed, then cleared his throat. "I thought she was just saying that to get us back together again."

"She wasn't that sort of girl," his mom said. "I don't think she'd ever have done that."

He wanted to tell her that emotional teen girls could do crazy things. Just like emotional teen boys could. But instead, he just nodded.

"So, was she really pregnant?"

"Yes. She was."

"What did you do?"

He sighed. "I didn't find out that she was until a few days ago."

"What did you say to her?" she asked. "Back when you thought she was faking it?"

His stomach felt sick as he lowered his gaze to the carpet. "I told her to get rid of it."

"Aiden... no." There was so much disappointment in her words that Aiden wasn't sure he'd ever be able to forget the sound of it.

"I didn't think she was really pregnant." Even as he gave voice to his reasoning at the time, he knew that his mom wasn't going to buy it anymore than Skylar had.

"Doesn't matter," she said, her disappointment having hardened into anger. "I didn't raise my son to view life so flippantly."

"I don't view it flippantly." That was true, especially now that he'd lost two loved ones. Life of any kind was worth fighting for. "At least not now."

"I just can't believe it," she said with a shake of her head. "Why are you telling me all this?"

Glad to be moving away from that part of the story, he told her why Skylar had shown up out of the blue at his office.

"So you have a daughter... I have a granddaughter... and she has cancer?"

He nodded. "And she needs our help."

"Well, of course we'll help."

Aiden had known that would be his mom's response. She never turned down someone in need, so she would have agreed even if the girl hadn't been related to them.

"Will we get to see her?"

"I don't know," Aiden said, relaxing back into the couch now that the worst part of their conversation was over. Or at least it was on the back burner for the moment. "I asked Skylar if I could meet her, and she initially said no."

"Big surprise there," his mom murmured as she picked her needlepoint up again and slid her glasses back into place on her nose.

"But she did agree to talk to the adoptive parents."

"So she knows who they are?"

"If not her, her parents do, as her mom told her what was going on with the girl's health."

"Skylar didn't tell you her name?"

"I asked. She said nope."

"How does Skylar seem now?" his mom asked.

Aiden stared blankly at the darkened television, remembering how Skylar had been during her visit. "Not happy."

"I suppose that's not a surprise."

"No, it's not."

There had been no glimpses of the woman he'd once loved.

His thoughts ground to a halt at that.

Had he really loved her?

Thinking back, Aiden wasn't sure he had. At least not with the love he should have had for a woman he was dating and talking about a future with. Because if he'd truly loved her, he never would have hurt her the way he had.

"I hope you can have a good conversation about what happened," his mom said. "Because you left things in a really bad way, I think."

"We did," Aiden agreed. "But I'm not sure she wants a conversation about it."

He wasn't sure that he really wanted to have another deeper conversation about it himself.

"You are sorry, though, right?" she asked, lowering her hoop once again.

Aiden wanted to be indignant in his response, but his mom had every right to ask, given how out of character she thought his actions had been. "I am."

"Have you thought of her over the years?" she asked. "Have you wanted to make amends before now?"

"I've honestly tried *not* to think of her," he said. It wasn't a confession he liked to make, but it was true.

His mom focused on her embroidery hoop again. "I think you know that I'm disappointed in how you handled things."

"Yeah. I know," he said with a sigh. "I'm disappointed in how I handled things as well."

"Why do you feel differently now?"

"Trauma and loss have a way of clarifying things."

"That they do." A sad smile crossed her face. "I wish your dad could have known he had another granddaughter."

Aiden felt a matching sadness, but his was tinged with guilt and regret. If Aiden had behaved differently, his dad could have had another granddaughter to love like he had Willow.

He'd inflicted so much pain because of his selfishness that continued well past the time during and after the breakup. It was a reminder that decisions made could impact more than just the people involved at the time.

Like ripples in the water after a stone is dropped into it, he could see the ripples of his long ago decision impacting the present and the future.

"I hope she's been with good adoptive parents," his mom said. "Though I suppose the Halversons would make sure she was in a good family."

Did his daughter even know that she was adopted? Would they tell her who her birth parents were?

They didn't know who Willow's father was. Bethany had never revealed his identity, and there had been nothing in her belongings to tell them who he might be. That void had left them with lots of questions, but at the same time, he didn't think that he or his mom would have been happy to lose Willow to her father, especially if he was someone Bethany hadn't wanted in her daughter's life.

In the short time he'd been fully present in Willow's life, Aiden had tried to be a father figure to her, in the absence of her own and in the loss of her grandfather.

By all accounts, his daughter had parents and grandparents, so they might not want him or his mom involved in her life. That would be a huge loss for them now that they knew of her existence, but he'd have no one but himself to blame.

Aiden let out a long sigh as he slumped down further into the couch. Though he wasn't doing much physically, he was exhausted. The shock of finding out about his daughter was taking its toll on him.

"Did I ruin Skylar's whole life, Momma?" The name he'd used for her as a child slipped out, letting Aiden—and probably his mom—know just how vulnerable he felt at that moment.

She lowered her hoop again and put her glasses on top of her head. The smile she gave him held an edge of sadness. "I don't know if you ruined her whole life, but it's true that you definitely had a negative impact on it. Only she can tell you how she truly feels, however."

"She's just so angry, so I feel like I ruined her life."

"The way you broke up with her would no doubt have impacted her," she said. "And I understand why she might be angry with you still."

Aiden nodded. He understood as well, but he wished that there was something he could do to make it up to her. But perhaps he'd done too much damage to ever be able to make things right with Skylar.

"I don't know what to do."

"There might not be anything else you can do, other than apologize," his mom said. "If you offer her a sincere apology, then that's all you can do. You can't force her to accept it."

Aiden sighed. How he wished he could go back to his younger self and smack him upside the head in hopes of knocking some sense into him.

He also wished he could go back and make sure that his dad was in the ER when his heart attack happened. And he'd make sure that Bethany never got on that boat with her friends.

But there was no way to change the past. He could only use it as a lesson for moving forward.

"Just apologize, then treat her with respect from now on," his mom said. "There's nothing more you can do. Treat her the way you should have treated her back then."

Aiden nodded, then sat forward. He'd had his moment of vulnerability, of weakness. Now it was time to focus on taking care of the people he loved and the people he'd wronged.

Getting to his feet, he said, "I think I'm going to go to the gym."

"Alright, sweetheart." She lowered her glasses back into place but peered at him over the top of them. "I'll probably be going to bed soon, so I won't be up when you get home. I'll see you in the morning."

He went to where she sat and brushed a kiss on her cheek. "Love you, Mom."

"I love you too, Aiden," she said. "Drive safe."

"I will."

Aiden went down to his apartment and packed up a bag for the gym, then headed out. Working out had always been a part of his daily routine, and he'd found it was a good time to mull over life and exhaust himself at the same time.

It was his hope that doing both would allow him to sleep when he crawled into bed later that night.

The next morning, he was at work when his phone let him know that a text had come in. When he glanced at it, he saw that Skylar was as good as her word. No call from her. Just a text.

Skylar: *Dad said that they've set up testing at the clinic for five o'clock on Friday.*

I spoke to Mom last night, and she is willing to be tested. Is Willow too young?

Skylar: *Who is Willow? And how old is she?*

Aiden realized that he hadn't told her about Willow during their confrontations—he could hardly call them conversations.

She is Bethany's daughter. She's five years old.

Skylar: *I'll ask Mom and Dad about that and let you know. Thanks. See you on Friday.*

Although, it was possible that Skylar wouldn't be present for the testing. She might choose to wait until he'd come and gone before showing up. He was kind of glad his mom and Willow were going to be there with him, since he hoped that would keep Skylar's brothers from decking him.

A couple of hours later, he got another text from Skylar.

Skylar: *Dad said that he wouldn't recommend Willow be tested since she's pretty young to give a donation for the transplant.*

Okay. We'll still have to bring her, however.

Skylar: *That's not a problem. There will probably be other kids there too.*

Aiden knew he shouldn't ask, but he couldn't help himself. *Will our daughter be there?*

He almost dropped his phone when it rang. Seeing that Skylar was calling made him pause before tapping the screen to answer it.

Before he could say anything, she jumped right in. "First of all, she is not *our* daughter. You need to stop thinking of her like that. She's the daughter of her adoptive parents."

"So, how do you refer to her?"

"I don't really refer to her at all," Skylar said. "But when I do, she's *their* daughter, not mine."

"Do you see her much?"

"Usually once or twice a year."

"Does she know who you are?"

"No."

"And you don't want her to?"

"Not really. I don't think it will improve her life in any way."

Aiden didn't know how to respond to that. He wasn't going to argue with Skylar that she would add worth to their child's life.

"So she won't be there on Friday?"

"No. They recommend she not be around a lot of people right now. They don't want her to get sick since that could impact her planned treatment."

"That's understandable."

"And no, I haven't asked about her meeting you yet, so you'll just have to be patient."

He knew there were more important things going on at the moment than him meeting his previously unknown daughter. "I understand why that's necessary, though I'm not usually one for keeping secrets."

"You're not a secret to everyone," Skylar said. "Just her. Everyone else now knows you're her birth father."

"They didn't know that before?"

"Of course not. I wasn't keen for Cole to find out and tell you. So I made my folks keep it a secret from everyone."

"I guess I understand that."

"How did your mom respond to the news?"

"A bit of a mixed bag," he said.

"What do you mean?"

"She was happy to hear that she has another granddaughter, but less happy with how everything ended between us."

"You told her the truth?" Skylar sounded a bit skeptical, and he couldn't blame her for that.

"Yes, I did."

"Why would you do that? I mean, it doesn't reflect well on you."

"I felt it was important she know the truth." He thought she might comment on that, but she remained silent. "Anyway, she expressed her displeasure and disappointment at how I treated you."

"I bet that was hard to take," Skylar said. "You always used to feel bad when you upset your mom."

"I still do. Honestly, these days, I'd rather not upset anyone, if possible. Though I realize you probably have a hard time believing that."

"A bit, yes."

Though he wanted to mention his mom meeting her granddaughter, he decided that that conversation was best left for a later time.

"Your mom doesn't live here in Serenity anymore?" Skylar asked.

"No, she and Willow are here in Coeur d'Alene with me, but she still has the house there. My dad left her financially secure, so she didn't have to sell the house to move here. I have an apartment in the basement."

"Nineteen-year-old you would have absolutely balked at the idea of living with your mom as a twenty-something man, especially in her basement."

Aiden sighed. "Nineteen-year-old me was wrong about a lot of things."

After a stretch of silence, Skylar said, "I probably should go."

"Okay. I guess I'll see you on Friday." He was disappointed to end the conversation but didn't press to continue it. It was enough that they'd talked for that long without any argument.

Once the conversation was over, Aiden tried to focus on his project. But it wasn't until the other team members showed up for a meeting that he was truly able to put the situation with Skylar and their daughter to the side.

And though Skylar had rebuked him for it, until he knew her name and who her adoptive parents were, Aiden felt like he had no other way to think of the little girl than as his daughter.

But it was weird to think that he could pass her on the street and have no idea who she was. Willow could have played with her at her favorite fast-food restaurant, and they wouldn't even have known who she was.

She was a total stranger.

Hopefully, that wouldn't be the case for much longer.

CHAPTER FIVE

The conversation she'd had with Aiden lingered in Skylar's mind throughout the day. She'd called him after initially texting because she'd wanted to lecture him about referring to Shiloh as *their daughter*. But somehow, they'd ended up having a full on conversation.

She'd gotten over her breakup with him and had even gone on to date other guys. And yet, seeing him again... seeing the man he'd become... was throwing her back into feelings and emotions she had never wanted to revisit.

Underneath the huge desire to flee Serenity and return to Vegas was the lingering desire to see Aiden again. It was a lesser desire, but the fact that it was there at all shocked Skylar. The last thing she should want was for the man who'd shattered her heart to be anywhere near her.

It was like her heart had separated the two in her mind. The person who had broken her heart was the boy Aiden had been. Who he was now seemed to be closer to the man she'd once imagined he'd become.

What was she supposed to do with that?

"Do you think there's a chance that Charli and Blake would let Aiden meet Shiloh?" she asked her mom as they sat together eating lunch. Her dad was out at a lunch meeting with an old friend.

"Definitely." The lack of hesitation before she responded had Skylar frowning at her.

"You don't think they'd mind?"

"Not at all. They've wanted to tell Shiloh about you, and now that Aiden is back in our lives, I think they'd be okay with him meeting her."

"Even with what he said when I told him that I was pregnant?"

This time, her mom seemed to consider her answer. "I think they'd like to meet him beforehand, to talk to him for themselves."

Skylar struggled with Charli and Blake's attitude toward Shiloh's adoption. If she'd had her way, Shiloh would never have known she was adopted. However, they'd told her a couple of years ago that she was part of their family through adoption.

Shiloh had seemed to take it all in stride and unsurprisingly, she'd asked who her birth parents were. At the time, Charli and Blake had simply told her that her mother was a special person who hadn't been able to raise her on her own.

Was now really the time to reveal who she and Aiden were to the little girl?

"I haven't told Aiden her name or who adopted her," Skylar said.

"Give Charli a call and see how they would like you to handle this."

Skylar dragged a baby carrot through the puddle of dip on her plate. "You don't think they have enough going on at the moment?"

"They do, but I think Charli would welcome a conversation with you."

Skylar's conversations with her older sister were few and far between, but that was because of Skylar, not Charli. She hadn't wanted to be in Shiloh's life because in her mind, it would be too hard to view her as Charli's daughter and not her own if she was around her too much.

"I'll text her and see if she has some time to chat."

"I really think she'd love to talk to you. After all, this is your daughter going through this health ordeal, too."

"She's not mine," Skylar said automatically.

Her mom stared at her for a long moment, then nodded. "I understand why you think that. However, she is yours. For nine months, you carried her. She is a part of you, just like she's a part of Charli."

Skylar had tried not to think too much about how it was her *daughter* that was facing cancer and not her *niece*. "I'll call her."

"Actually, she's coming here in a few minutes."

"What?" Skylar frowned. "Who's staying with Shiloh?"

"Julia said she'd spend the afternoon with the kids so that Charli could get a break," her mom said, referring to Blake's aunt. "Layla is also off work and will give her a hand."

"When does Shiloh have her first treatment?"

"She's going into hospital on Thursday, providing all the tests come back indicating it's okay to move forward with the chemo, then she'll have her first treatment on Friday."

Skylar didn't ask for clarification of what the treatment was. Medical stuff would just go over her head. It was enough to know that Shiloh was sick and that the treatment required to get rid of the cancer was going to be rough on the little girl.

Also, because of all the medical professionals in the Halverson family, she trusted them to tell her what she needed to know. They would understand what was happening with Shiloh's cancer and the treatment, and that was enough for her.

Once they finished their lunch, Skylar cleaned it up while her mom checked the meal she'd put in the crock pot earlier. Apparently, she'd been experimenting with crock pot recipes recently. In the few days Skylar had been there, the meals she'd had had been pretty good. Better than some of the ones she'd had growing up.

When the doorbell rang, Skylar froze. Neither of them moved to answer the door since they knew that if it was Charli, she'd walk right in. And if it wasn't, they'd ring the bell again.

Sure enough, Skylar heard the door open and turned to see her sister walk into the kitchen. Right away, she could see the toll Shiloh's diagnosis had taken on her sister.

But still, she smiled and came right to where Skylar stood. Reaching out, Charli pulled Skylar into a tight hug.

"I'm so glad you're here," she murmured against Skylar's ear. "I've missed you."

Skylar clung to her, feeling emotions threatening to rise and flow over the walls that usually held them back. She blinked back tears when she felt Charli take a breath that caught in her throat.

Soon, her mom joined them, wrapping her arms around both of them. They stood like that for several minutes, and when they stepped back from the embrace, they all had damp eyes.

"Why don't we go to the den?" her mom suggested, then led the way to the small cozy room at the back of the house.

The room wasn't big enough for the whole family, so it was only used by her parents when it was just the two of them, or when only two or three of the kids were there with them.

Charli let out a long sigh as she sank into their dad's favorite chair, pulling her legs up to rest her knees against the arm of the chair.

"How are you doing, darling?" her mom asked.

"I'm okay, I guess," Charli said. "Tired, though. I'm just not sleeping well."

"I'm so sorry that you're having to deal with this," Skylar said. "That should be me."

Charli held up her hand as she shook her head. "No. I believe that God works things out the way they should be. Shiloh has been a blessing to our family, and I know she's exactly where she should be."

That was always how Skylar had felt, but still... "Her being sick will take you away from your other kids."

"They will be fine," Charli said. "Plus, there are plenty of people who will step in and help with the kids and with Shiloh."

"Definitely," her mom agreed with a nod. "We have so many people in the family who are willing to pick up any slack."

But that wouldn't be her, and it should be. Of anyone in the family, she should be the one stepping up to help. She'd handed over the responsibility of Shiloh to Charli and Blake, and now they needed help.

Skylar pulled her legs up and wrapped her arms around them, hooking her heels on the edge of the seat cushion. "Do you want me to be here?"

Charli and her mom exchanged glances, then Charli said, "You need to decide that for yourself. We'd love to have you here, and not just because of what's happening with Shiloh. But you need to figure that out on your own. We're not going to pressure you."

Skylar glanced at her mom, who gave a soft chuckle.

"Okay. Maybe a little pressure from me."

"You've been trying to get me to move back for ages," Skylar said. "So I know it's not related to what's happening with Shiloh."

"I want to thank you for going to Aiden to ask him to be tested," Charli said. "How bad was it?"

Skylar shrugged. "It wasn't the best experience I've ever had."

"Was he shocked?"

"Oh yes. He told me that the reason he said I should "get rid of it" was because he didn't think I was actually pregnant. That I was just pretending so that he'd get back together with me. And the fact that Cole never mentioned me being pregnant or having a baby reinforced what he thought."

"I guess that could be understandable," Charli said. "But still... He should have known you better than that."

Skylar propped her chin on her knees. "It seemed that at the end, neither of us knew the other very well. The boy I thought I knew never would have done what he did."

"What does he seem like now?"

"From the look of the office he has, the company he works for is successful. He was wearing a suit, which was something he never really enjoyed doing as a teen."

"How did he deal with you?"

"Well, he didn't shoo me out of his office or anything," she said. "Since then, he's had more questions, and he'd like to meet Shiloh."

"Really?" Charli tilted her head. "What did you tell him?"

"That I would have to talk to her adoptive parents. I haven't told him anything about Shiloh beyond her diagnosis. Not her name, nor who adopted her."

"You can tell him," Charli said. "Blake and I wouldn't have a problem with that. I'd also like Shiloh to learn who you both are to her."

"Why?"

"Why what?"

"Why are you so willing to let Shiloh know who her birth parents are?" Skylar asked. "Wouldn't it be confusing for her?"

"When we told her that she was adopted, we talked about the different roles we played in her life. She knows that regardless of who gave birth to her, she is ours and belongs in our family. If her adoptive parents are in her life, their roles would be more like aunt and uncle."

"Kind of like how I already am in her life."

"Yep. So you can tell Aiden who adopted her, and maybe Blake and I can meet with him before he meets Shiloh."

Skylar didn't want any of that to happen. And though she didn't have total control, she was still going to try to limit any damage Aiden might do to their family.

She needed to make a couple of phone calls. One was to Denise, her supervisor, to request more time off. The second would be to the lawyer they'd used for the adoption. Before she gave Aiden any information, she wanted to make sure he wasn't going to mess things up for Charli, Blake, and Shiloh.

She didn't say any of that to Charli or her mom. They might be willing to give Aiden the benefit of the doubt, but Skylar wasn't. He'd hurt her a bit too much for her to ever give him that much trust again.

Skylar listened as Charli and her mom discussed the tests Shiloh had undergone and what the treatment would entail. It sounded like too much for the little girl to have to endure, and Skylar couldn't help but wonder why God would allow something like that to happen.

If she could switch places with Shiloh, she would. Anything to spare her little girl the pain she was enduring. But that wasn't an option.

Over the course of the next couple of hours, they chatted about all kinds of things. Skylar could see that Charli was glad to be able to focus on something else for a short period of time.

Before she left, Charli gave Skylar a tight hug. "Please come by and see Shiloh. I know she would love to see you."

Skylar didn't want to promise anything, but she nodded. "I'll try."

After Charli left, Skylar headed up to her room, while her dad joined her mom in the den.

She didn't know how long she'd be in Serenity, but she knew she needed to be there through the next weekend for the testing. Though she did have vacation time and some favors to call in, she couldn't take off time indefinitely.

But the more pressing call was to the lawyer to get that all sorted out.

Skylar stared out the car window at the two-story brick building as her dad turned into the parking lot next to it. Her stomach was a mess of nerves, and she was so glad her parents had come with her. At first, she hadn't been sure they should, but now, she was glad that they had.

"Let's say a prayer before we go inside," her dad suggested after he'd parked and turned off the car.

Though Skylar hadn't spent much time praying in recent years, she wasn't going to tell her dad no. If ever a situation needed prayer, it was this one.

After her mom and dad had both prayed, they got out of the car and headed for the entrance to the building. Her dad opened the door and held it for Skylar and her mom to walk in ahead of him.

The lawyer's office was on the second floor, so they headed up the stairs. When they stepped into the waiting room of the lawyer's office, she saw there was only one person there, aside from the receptionist. Aiden.

As soon as Aiden saw them, he got to his feet. His gaze swept over them as they approached him, and he held out his hand to her dad.

"Dr. Halverson," Aiden said with a nod, then turned to her mom and greeted her as well.

While he did that, Skylar observed Aiden. He wore a dark gray suit, with a white shirt and blue patterned tie. Aiden was still about the same height as he'd been in college, but his shoulders had broadened over the years.

The most striking difference from high school to then, however, was the confidence with which he held himself. In the past, he hadn't been super at ease around her parents, though he'd always been respectful and interacted with them whenever he was at their house.

But the way he held himself now was different, and it made Skylar wish he'd had that confidence back in high school and college. Maybe they would have gone down a different path if he had.

When Aiden turned his attention to her, Skylar willed herself not to show any emotion. She held out her hand, and as he took it, she felt a strength in his grip that she remembered from the past.

"Thank you for coming, Skylar," he said. "I really do appreciate it."

Skylar was prevented from giving a—no doubt snippy—response when her mom spoke first. Perhaps she knew what was on the tip of Skylar's tongue.

"I was sorry to hear about your dad and your sister," her mom told Aiden. "I'm sure it's been very difficult."

Aiden's jaw clenched, and his Adam's apple bobbed as he swallowed. "Yeah. It has been."

"How's your mom doing?"

Aiden slid his hands into his pockets as he shrugged. His gaze had dropped to the floor. "About as well as can be expected, given everything that's happened."

Before they could say anything more, the door to the office building opened again, and a tall man in a black pinstripe suit stepped through the doorway. His dark brown gaze swept the room, and when he spotted Aiden, he offered a smile and a nod.

"Hey there, Dennis," Aiden said as the man approached them. After he shook his hand, Aiden said, "This is Dennis Ulrich. He's my lawyer."

Skylar frowned at Aiden. He hadn't said he was bringing a lawyer. Was this about to get messy?

"Not here to create any issues," Dennis said, as if reading her mind. "I've just drilled into him that if there's anything legal involved, he needs to call me."

"Hello, everyone." A female voice interrupted them, and the woman who had helped with the adoption eight years ago joined them. After greeting each of them, she gestured to a hallway. "Why don't we go to the boardroom?"

Their group migrated down the hallway to a room with big windows and a table surrounded by several chairs. Lynda Cartwright took a seat at the head of the table, while Skylar and her parents sat on one side, with Aiden and his lawyer opposite them.

"I'm glad you're here, Dennis," Lynda said. "I planned to suggest that Aiden take the document to a lawyer before signing it."

"Good to hear," Dennis said. "So what's going on? Aiden shared a bit about it, but you know I'll need more details."

Lynda grinned. "Of course."

It didn't take long for Lynda to recap the situation that had brought them there that day.

"You're okay with this, Aiden?" Dennis asked when Lynda was done.

"Maybe the two of you should discuss it," Lynda suggested. "We'll just step outside."

Skylar almost asked why, but instead, she got up and followed her parents out of the room. They returned to the waiting room and settled into seats to wait for the side meeting to end.

"Do you think this is going to create any problems?" her dad asked.

"It shouldn't," Lynda said. "But if it does, it's better that they come up now rather than later."

Skylar supposed that was true, so she didn't protest it. But if this didn't go the way she hoped, she had no idea what would happen. Worst case would be if his fancy-dancy lawyer filed for a custody agreement so that Aiden had a permanent role in Shiloh's life. Or worst case, he'd fight the adoption because he'd never terminated his rights to Shiloh.

Oh, how she hoped that wouldn't be the case.

Her parents chatted with Lynda while they waited, but Skylar kept her thoughts to herself. It felt like forever before Dennis appeared to tell them they were ready. In reality, it had probably been less than twenty minutes.

They gathered back around the table, and Dennis slid the file that Lynda had given him before they'd left the room, back across the table to her. The file that would make sure that Aiden could never challenge the rights of Charli and Blake to raise their daughter.

"Any questions, comments, or concerns?" Lynda asked as she took the folder and flipped it open. Her gaze skimmed the page before looking back up at Dennis.

"I had a few, but Aiden assured me that this was what he wanted to do. That it was the right thing."

Relief rushed through Skylar. She'd thought he might refuse to sign it until they allowed him to meet Shiloh. That he hadn't done that gave Skylar another glimpse of the man he'd become.

Unless there was an angle she wasn't seeing.

However, even if that was the case, Skylar trusted that Lynda or her parents would have figured it out.

Usually, she didn't rely on other people to pick up the slack for her. However, this whole situation with Shiloh had been stressful and confusing for her from day one. She didn't trust her own judgment when it came to anything pertaining to the child she'd given birth to, then placed in her sister's arms.

For a moment, she was back in time, listening as the doctor announced that she'd had a healthy baby girl.

If Aiden had been there with her, they would have had a daughter. Now, they only had memories of a horrible time of heartache and betrayal, and she'd had to watch their daughter grow up from a distance. And now she'd have to watch her fight for her life from a distance.

As her gaze held Aiden's, she saw regret in his eyes. It should have made her feel better, but it didn't. His regret did nothing to change the circumstances they found themselves in. There was no going back.

She'd accepted that a long time ago. And with the stroke of a pen, Aiden had now accepted it.

Skylar was glad of that, but there was something within her that wished with all her heart that he had been the man she'd thought he was back when they'd been dating. At least at the start of that teenage romance.

When the meeting came to a close, Aiden turned and said, "Can I speak to you for a couple of minutes, Skylar?"

She glanced at her parents, who were both looking at her with raised eyebrows. They didn't say anything though, clearly leaving it up to her. She didn't want to speak with him. Not really. But she couldn't deny she was curious about what he wanted.

"Sure."

"Is it okay if we use the room for a few more minutes?" Aiden asked Lynda.

"Definitely," the woman said with a nod.

"We'll be in the waiting room," her dad said before they all filed out of the room, leaving her alone with the man who'd broken her heart so spectacularly.

And he was slowly drawing her back in, whether she wanted that or not.

CHAPTER SIX

Aiden didn't quite know what had compelled him to request a conversation with Skylar, but he was glad she'd agreed. The roller-coaster of emotions over the past hour or so had been crazy.

The first time he'd laid eyes on her in his office, he'd been so stunned by her sudden return to his life that he couldn't truly take her in. Now, he had the chance to observe her more attentively. He looked for traces of the woman he had once loved, but it was difficult to spot any.

She held herself with a sophistication and elegance that she hadn't shown as a teenager. Her dark hair was styled in a sleek twist away from her face, and her makeup was understated.

As a teenager, she'd preferred jeans or leggings paired with a sweatshirt or T-shirt. Her hair had usually been pulled back in a ponytail, and she'd rarely worn much makeup.

That day, however, she stood before him in black slacks, heels, and a red blouse, giving off a professional vibe. It made him curious about her occupation.

"Thanks for agreeing to speak with me," Aiden said, sliding his hands into his pockets. "You'd be well within your rights to refuse."

She shrugged. "I figured that maybe it was time."

"Will you tell me more about our daughter now that I've signed the papers?" he asked.

"Again... she isn't *our* daughter. She's the daughter of the couple who adopted her. You really need to start thinking of her like that."

Aiden nodded, though it pained him to have to accept that. "Sorry. This is all so new to me."

"The sooner you accept that, the easier it will be."

"Do you have a picture of her?" he asked. "Will you tell me her name?"

"Her name is Shiloh," she said after a brief hesitation. "I can show you a picture. I don't have a really recent one, though."

Aiden was willing to accept anything at that point. He just wanted to be able to put a face to the daughter he'd never known. Given what he'd told Skylar to do with the baby years ago, he was grateful for even an older picture of her.

"This was her when she was around three," Skylar said, holding her phone out so he could see the screen.

Aiden stepped closer, bending his head to look at the phone without taking it from Skylar. On the screen was a toddler with a big grin, her face framed by dark curls. Her brown eyes weren't quite as dark as Skylar's, but they sparkled with delight. Clearly, she was a happy child.

He searched for something of him in her features, but he couldn't pinpoint anything.

"Here's one taken a couple of years later," Skylar said as she showed him another photo on her phone.

In that picture, Shiloh looked to be a bit younger than Willow was now, and he could see a resemblance between them. So perhaps there was something of him in Shiloh after all.

It was hard seeing her healthy and happy, knowing that wasn't the case anymore. His heart clenched at the idea of her in pain and suffering.

"So you've spoken to her adoptive parents about me?" he asked, looking up at Skylar.

"Yes." She stared at him for a long moment, her brown gaze unreadable. "Just so you know, all of this is pretty much my worst nightmare. Not just Shiloh's health, but also you being back in my life and hers."

Shame and regret flooded Aiden. He'd spent most of the days since their breakup trying *not* to think about Skylar. Given what he'd done to her, it was actually a surprise that she'd agreed to any of this.

He slid his hands into his pants pockets, dipping his head a bit, though he still held her gaze. "I really am sorry for all of that."

Her eyes narrowed briefly, and in that moment, he understood that she might never forgive him. And he couldn't blame her for that. She owed him nothing, while he owed her everything.

"Anyway... Her parents are Charli and Blake," Skylar said.

Aiden straightened in surprise. "Like your sister, Charli?"

"Yes. She and Blake agreed to adopt her when I asked them to, once I realized you weren't interested in being a part of my life or hers."

The relief he felt at knowing who had been raising his daughter was immense. "I bet they've been great parents to her."

"They have. When I made the decision to give Shiloh up, I knew I could only do it if it was to someone I already knew and trusted."

"I'm glad they stepped up," he said. "When I didn't."

"I don't want to disrupt her life anymore than the cancer already has," Skylar said. "But Charli and Blake don't seem to have a problem with telling her who we are."

"So she doesn't know who you are?"

Skylar shook her head. "I've always just been Auntie Sky to her."

"Have you spent a lot of time with her over the years?"

"No. I've just seen her at Christmas and if there was a family wedding during the year. It was the only way I could separate my feelings about her being their daughter and not mine."

Aiden could see the toll that had taken on her in the haunted expression in her eyes. "Are you going to try to keep your distance even after she knows who you are?"

"That would be my preference, but I doubt that I'll be able to."

"Are you going to be in Serenity for awhile?"

"I'm not sure. At the moment, I have another week off, with the option of taking more, if needed."

"So I'll see you again?"

Aiden wasn't sure why he'd said that. He was probably the last person she wanted to see again.

"Probably." Naturally, she didn't sound enthused by the idea. "We'll see how things go."

Aiden understood that the family was dealing with more than his desire to get to know his daughter. They had a fight on their hands.

"I'd better go," Skylar said as she turned toward the door.

They joined the others in the waiting room, then the five of them left the building. After saying goodbye to the Halversons, Aiden and Dennis walked to where he'd parked earlier.

"Everything else okay?" Dennis asked once they were at his car. The man had been a family friend, and he'd done his best to take care of them legally and more since Aiden's dad had passed away.

"Yep. Things are going fine."

"Well, keep me posted about this situation," Dennis said. "And give my regards to your mom."

"I will." After shaking the man's hand, Aiden got into his car and left the parking lot.

Rather than head home, he went to the park near Harrison Slough, not far from downtown Coeur d'Alene. He needed to have a few minutes to process everything.

After taking off his suit coat, Aiden headed for a bench near the sand. The water sparkled in the sunlight, making him wish he'd grabbed his sunglasses.

Given it was the middle of a workday afternoon, the area wasn't very busy. Willow loved coming to the beach, so maybe he'd bring her on the weekend and give his mom a few hours to herself.

Letting out a long exhale, Aiden leaned forward, bracing his elbows on his thighs. He let his head fall forward and stared at the ground between his feet.

"Missing you a whole lot today, Dad," he murmured. "I hope I'm doing the right thing, and that you'd be proud of me."

Even as he said the words, Aiden knew that he wouldn't be proud of Aiden's behavior with Skylar back when they'd been dating. His parents had been very disappointed when things hadn't worked out between them. His dad had asked him what he'd done, but Aiden had brushed it off as a mutual decision, made because a long distance relationship was too hard to maintain.

His parents had met in high school and, by all accounts, had been happily married up until the day of his dad's death. They wouldn't have understood Aiden's need to see if there was life beyond Serenity. Beyond Skylar.

Yeah. They would have been very disappointed at the time if they'd known the truth. Looking back at his actions, Aiden was disappointed in himself.

His current life would probably be a whole lot different had he made better decisions in the past. But there was no going back. Only moving forward and doing what he could for Skylar now. Which included getting tested.

It was nearly five by the time he pulled into the parking lot behind the clinic. There were a few cars there, but he suspected others would come once it was past five.

He and his mom got out, then he helped Willow out of the car seat in the back. They each took one of her hands and walked along the sidewalk that ran beside the building to the front.

Though he felt nervous about seeing more of Skylar's family, he tried his best to keep his nervousness hidden, especially from his mom and Willow. As they reached the front door, he pulled it open and allowed them to precede him into the building.

The small group of people standing at the reception desk turned as they walked in.

"Aiden?"

While he didn't know them all, he did recognize Janessa. "Hi, Janessa."

"Come to get your blood drawn for the testing?"

"Yep. Both Mom and I are here for that."

"Hi, Mrs. McIntyre," Janessa said as she approached his mom and gave her a hug. "I was sorry to hear about your husband and Bethany."

"Thank you." His mom smiled at her. "It's good to see you again."

"You too." Janessa turned her attention to Willow. "And who is this beautiful little girl?"

"This is my granddaughter, Willow."

Janessa held out her hand. "Hi, Willow. My name is Janessa. It's nice to meet you."

Willow smiled up at Janessa as she took her hand. "Nice to meet you too!"

"Well, we're closed for the day, so let's head back to the staff room," Janessa said as one of the women locked the front door. "The technicians are set up there. Dad pulled some strings or greased some palms or something to have this testing done here after hours."

Aiden trailed behind his mom, Willow, Janessa, and the other women as they walked down the hallway to the back of the building. They preceded him into the break room, and Aiden heard Skylar's mom greet his.

Before he stepped into the break room, the back door opened, and Wilder walked in with a beautiful woman at his side.

When Wilder's gaze landed on him, he came to a stop, his eyes narrowing. "Aiden."

Aiden gave him a nod. "Wilder."

"Does Skylar know you're here?"

"Of course. She's the one who told me the time and place."

Wilder advanced on him. "If I had known what you did back then, you'd have been sporting a shiner."

"You can give me one now if it'll make you feel better."

"Well, since you're offering..."

Wilder pulled his arm back, eliciting a startled yelp from the woman at his side. She clutched at his arm. "Wilder!"

"I wasn't really going to hit him." Wilder grinned at her. "I just wanted to scare him a little."

"Well, you scared *me*."

He pressed a kiss to her head. "Sorry, babe."

"You should be," the woman said. "That wasn't nice."

"What Aiden did wasn't nice," Wilder told her with another glare at Aiden. "In fact, what he did was far worse. He deserves quite a few scares."

"He's right," Aiden told the woman. "I do."

"While I understand Wilder's sentiment, let's move along," Janessa suggested from the doorway, then turned to lead the way into the staff room.

As soon as he stepped through into the room, Aiden glanced around to see if Skylar was there. He spotted her talking to his mom, but he'd only taken one step in their direction when someone said his name, stopping him in his tracks.

"Aiden." The all-too-familiar voice made Aiden wince.

He'd tried not to think about coming face to face with the man who had spent so much time not just coaching him and his teammates on basketball, but coaching them on how to be gentlemen. How to treat people respectfully. Especially the women in their lives. The women they dated.

Turning, Aiden came face to face with the tall figure of Jay Halverson. "Hi, Coach."

"Don't *hi coach* me, Aiden."

Aiden pulled his shoulders back to keep them from slumping under the weight of the man's disappointment and anger. It was all he could do to hold the imposing man's stare. He could manage disappointment and anger from most people, but there were a few it was harder to stomach it from. Jay Halverson, being one of them.

"Sorry about that, Coach."

Jay placed a hand on each of his shoulders. "I thought I taught you better than that. And even if I didn't, I *know* your dad and mom did."

Aiden nodded. "They did. And you did too. I just... Well, there's really no excuse beyond immaturity and selfishness for what I did."

"It was definitely both of those things," Jay agreed. "I can't believe that you didn't tell Cole. I mean, he knows now, but he was clueless back then."

Aiden's stomach sank. It had been stupid of him not to think that someone would let Cole know. He should have told him himself, but he'd been worried that he'd lose his best friend. Cole might have other people he considered his best friend now, but he was still Aiden's number one.

"Jay, it's your turn."

Aiden turned to see Cathy gesturing for Jay to come to where the technician was set up at the table.

"I'll talk to you more in a minute," he said.

Whether that was a threat or a promise, Aiden wasn't sure. But he wasn't going to run off, even if it was a threat. He knew he deserved everything that Jay dished out to him.

While the man went to do his test, Aiden made his way to where his mom, Cathy, and Skylar stood talking. Skylar was dressed in a pair of black shorts and a white T-shirt with a floral pattern on the front. She wore flat black sandals, and her hair was pulled back in a braid.

The small diamond studs in her ears reminded him of the pair of earrings he'd given her for her birthday one year while they were dating. He wondered what she'd done with them and the other things he'd bought her.

He kind of hoped that she'd thrown them away, because that's what he'd done with her gifts to him back when he was being immature and selfish.

Her gaze met his for a moment, and his heart skipped a beat. It shocked him enough that he lifted a hand to rub at his chest before he realized what he was doing.

"Hey," he said, giving her a small smile as he tried to get his heart to behave itself.

Was he having this reaction to her because of their past relationship? Or was there something about her now that resonated with his heart?

"Hi." She shifted closer to her mom to give him space to join their group.

Cathy greeted him with a smile, and when Willow lifted her arms to him, Aiden picked her up with ease, settling her on his forearm as she hooked her arm around his neck.

He saw that Skylar's gaze was on Willow, and he was once again left to wonder what was going through her mind. Cathy, however, smiled at Willow, her feelings clear.

Aiden wished they could see Shiloh, but she'd been admitted to the hospital and had had her first treatment earlier that day. He didn't expect that any of Shiloh's family would show up at the clinic.

"How did Shiloh do today?" Aiden asked.

Cathy's smile slid away. "Charli texted me a little while ago and told me that she was feeling quite sick after the treatment."

"I'm sorry to hear that," Aiden said, his heart sinking at the news of his daughter suffering like that.

"It was expected," Cathy explained. "But it's still hard to see in reality."

"Oh, Blake made it after all," Skylar said, her gaze going to the door.

Aiden turned to see a tall, solidly built man holding the hand of a young boy. There were three other children with him, and he assumed that the dark-haired teen was Layla. The last time he'd seen the girl, she'd been just a few years older than Willow. She might even have been the age that Shiloh was now.

Thinking about that was kind of depressing. Time passed so quickly. And so much had changed since he'd last been surrounded by the Halverson family.

It made him realize just how many years he'd missed of his daughter's life. Even if he'd only seen her once or twice a year like Skylar had, it would have been something. By his own actions, he'd robbed himself of that.

Of course, if they'd stayed together, it was unlikely that they would have given the baby up for adoption. He would have been in Shiloh's life all these years.

Blake gazed around the room, and when he saw their group, he headed in their direction, the other kids following him.

"Hi, darling," Cathy said, as she gave Blake a hug. "I'm glad you made it."

She greeted each of the children with a hug before gesturing at Aiden. "This is Aiden, his mom, and niece, Willow."

Blake greeted Willow and Aiden's mom, then turned to Aiden. Aiden held out his hand and Blake took it. The man looked like he could crush Aiden's hand, but while his grip was firm, Blake didn't squeeze only hard.

"Aiden," Blake said with a nod of his head. "Good to meet you finally."

Though Blake and Charli had been dating back when he and Skylar were together, Aiden had been away at school most of the time, so he hadn't met Blake then.

"Good to meet you too," Aiden said, meaning every word of it.

Blake laid a hand on each kid's shoulder as he introduced them to Aiden.

"I know him already," Layla said. "I used to hang out with him and Skylar all the time. And Cole too."

"You've grown up," Aiden told her.

"You've gotten older."

Aiden's mouth quirked at the starchiness in her voice. She was definitely on Skylar's side. As she should be.

"I definitely have," he agreed with a nod.

Layla went to Skylar and gave her a hug. The other kids followed, and after they'd all greeted their aunt, they headed off to talk to the others in the room.

Blake crossed his arms as he braced his feet. Aiden prepared himself for what was to come. He had no idea what Blake's reaction to him and his request was going to be.

"I understand that you'd like to meet Shiloh," Blake said.

Aiden nodded. "I would, and my mom and Willow would too. If you'd be okay with that."

Blake regarded him for a long moment. "With her being in the hospital, I think it would be best if it's just you for now."

"That's understandable," Aiden said, trying not to show his excitement at the prospect of finally meeting Shiloh.

"Perhaps you and Skylar could come together," Blake suggested. "I think Shiloh would like that."

Aiden glanced over at Skylar. She didn't look like *she* would like that.

"We can talk about it and let you know," Aiden said, not wanting to upset Skylar by agreeing to something she may not want.

Blake glanced over at where the technicians were just finishing up with a couple more people. "I'm going to see if they're ready for us."

When it was just the four of them, Cathy said, "I think it would be a great idea for the two of you to see her together."

"She already knows me," Skylar said.

Cathy gave her daughter a gentle smile. "Yes, but she doesn't know you as her birth mom."

Skylar's lips tightened, then she gave a single nod. Looking at Aiden, she said, "We'll talk about it."

Aiden knew this meant that even when Shiloh was ready for visitors, Skylar's mood was still going to have to be considered.

She looked a bit ruffled by it all.

He was sure that she hoped to keep most of her emotions under wraps, just like he did, but there were moments when things slipped through. And in those moments, he just wanted to do something to soothe her.

However, he knew any such efforts would be totally rebuffed.

"Have they told Shiloh about us?" Aiden asked.

"Yes. They told her last night. They wanted to give her something positive to look forward to."

"Did Charli say how she took the news?" his mom asked.

"Oh, she was surprised," Cathy said. "But also excited. And she was happy to hear she has another grandma and a cousin close to her age."

Aiden's mom smiled. "That's good. I look forward to meeting her someday. In the meantime, I will be praying for her."

Cathy's smile trembled a bit. "We sure appreciate that."

Janessa came over to them. "You four ready?"

They had to wait for the technicians to finish up with the kids, then Cathy and his mom had their turn. Willow watched intently as the woman inserted the needle into her grandma's arm.

Her arm tightened around Aiden's neck. "Does it hurt?"

"A teeny tiny bit," he said. "Kind of like a mosquito bite."

Willow didn't seem reassured by his words. Her eyes widened as she saw the blood flow into the tube. Meanwhile, his mom was chatting with the technician, not paying any attention to what was happening with the needle in her arm.

"Are they going to do that to you too?" Willow asked, turning her wide-eyed gaze towards him.

"Yep, but it'll be fine."

Willow encircled his neck with both her arms and pressed her cheek to his. "I hope it doesn't hurt you."

"I'll be fine, princess," he said, rubbing a hand up and down her back to reassure her. "Look, Grandma is all done, and she didn't cry. I won't either."

He moved around the table to take his mom's seat, while Skylar settled into the seat vacated by Cathy. Aiden tried to set Willow down, but she insisted on sitting on his leg with his arm around her.

The technician pushed his sleeve up and began the process of prepping his arm for the needle. Another person in a lab coat was labelling vials and putting them into a stand.

Aiden didn't focus on the needle, not really being a fan of them himself. However, Willow kept a close eye on what was happening. And not just with Aiden, but with Skylar as well.

When it was done, Aiden got to his feet, keeping Willow with him.

"Did it hurt her?" Willow asked, pointing to where Skylar still sat.

It appeared that the tech was having a bit of trouble finding a vein, but Skylar didn't look upset, so he felt safe saying, "No. She's fine."

When the tech finally had things working, Skylar looked up and nodded. "Yep. I'm fine."

Her gaze lingered on Willow before meeting Aiden's briefly.

"All done," the tech said to her after she'd put a strip of tape over a cotton ball on the needle prick.

Skylar got up and moved away from the table. Aiden moved to follow her, but a hand on his arm stopped him.

Jay again.

"Out of respect for your niece, we won't have a conversation here," he said. "But I'd still like to have a chat."

"Okay. Skylar has my number, so you can get it from her."

"I will." Jay smiled at Willow, then looked back at Aiden. "Regardless, it's been good to see you again."

"You too, Coach."

Though Aiden might have liked to talk more with Skylar, she didn't seem inclined to have a conversation with him. Instead, he went to where his mom was, and the two of them said goodbye to the Halverson family members gathered there.

It had gone pretty well, in Aiden's estimation, and it seemed that his mom felt the same way. Before heading back to Coeur d'Alene, they went to the house and checked it over, then went to the local diner for dinner.

No one had punched him. They'd gotten tested. All in all, it had been a good day for him.

However, his thoughts kept going to Shiloh and how this was most likely not a very good day for her. He hoped that she would have a restful night, and that the treatments she was undergoing would be what led to her regaining her health.

CHAPTER SEVEN

"I'll be praying for you," Aiden's mom said as he prepared to leave for the hospital. "That everything goes smoothly."

"Thanks, Mom." He gave her a kiss on the cheek, then walked to where Willow sat at the table with a coloring book and pressed a kiss to the top of her head. "Take care of Grandma, okay?"

She smiled up at him. "I will."

"You'll probably be asleep when I get home, so you can tell me two jokes tomorrow when we're eating breakfast, okay?"

She held out her hand. "Deal."

After they shook on it, Aiden left the house and climbed into his car. He was full of nerves as he anticipated meeting his daughter for the first time. Willow and his mom had gone out and bought a coloring book, a bunch of crayons, and a stuffed unicorn for him to give Shiloh.

He kept waiting for the other shoe to drop and for the Halverson parents to chew him out for what he'd done to their daughter. Skylar certainly had. Maybe they figured that was enough.

There were still ten minutes to spare when he pulled into a parking spot at the hospital. Rather than get out and go wait in the hospital, he sat in the car for a few minutes. He wished he had someone to talk to about all of this, but the one person he usually confided in was Cole.

He hadn't heard from his friend, but then he hadn't called him either. The silence between them was rather deafening and made him worried that this would impact their friendship to the point where it would no longer exist. He didn't think it would come to that... but anything was possible in this mess he'd created.

But he'd get that sorted out after this meeting with his daughter.

Picking up the gift bag, he left the car and headed into the hospital. It took him a bit to locate the waiting room where Charli and Blake had told him to go, and when he found it, he saw Skylar was already seated there.

"Hi," he said as he sat down, leaving a chair empty between them.

She glanced at him as she uncrossed her legs and crossed them again in the opposite direction. "Hey."

It was hard not to recall the times when she had greeted him with much more enthusiasm. But he couldn't claim to miss those times since he'd been the one to toss them away.

He wanted to ask her if she was nervous. From the way her foot tapped the air, and how she crossed her arms tightly across her waist, it seemed like she might be. She wasn't meeting Shiloh for the first time like he was, but she was seeing her for the first time after Shiloh had learned Skylar's true identity.

"Are you doing okay?" he asked.

It took her a long moment to respond, which Aiden figured was an answer in itself.

"I guess. I just hope this is the right thing for Shiloh."

"Charli and Blake seem to think it is."

She nodded. "And maybe I'm scared to see my little dau—my little niece sick with cancer."

"Yeah." Aiden sighed as he leaned forward, bracing his elbows on his thighs as he stared at his hands. "I wish there was more I could do for her. But there's nothing beyond getting the test and hoping I'm a match."

"She's such a sweet kid," Skylar said, her voice tight. "She doesn't deserve this."

"I felt that way about what happened to Willow. She lost her mom and her papa in such a short period of time."

"You're good with her," Skylar told him.

"After Bethany died, I moved back to Coeur d'Alene to help my mom out," he said. "Since we've been living together for almost awhile now, we've gotten close."

"You're like a dad to her."

Aiden shrugged. "I suppose. Her father wasn't in her life, but my dad did his best to fill that role. Now, with him gone, I've tried to step up."

Skylar didn't respond, and when Aiden glanced back at her over his shoulder, he noticed her looking at the entrance to the waiting room. Aiden straightened and saw that Blake had entered the room.

Aiden got to his feet as the man approached them. He rubbed his suddenly damp palms on his pants.

"Thanks for coming," Blake said as he shook Aiden's hand. "She's excited and having a pretty good day."

Hearing that was a relief, as Aiden had been uncertain about how he'd deal with seeing her in pain.

Looking over at Skylar, who had also stood up, Aiden saw her lift her chin and purse her lips. He had the overwhelming urge to assure her that everything was going to be okay.

Of course, that wasn't anything he could guarantee, and even if he could, she probably didn't want to hear it from him.

As they reached the door of what he assumed was Shiloh's room, Blake disappeared inside. When Skylar hesitated, so did Aiden.

He glanced at her and found her watching him. This was it. He was meeting his daughter for the first time. Not as a baby, like most men would have, but as an eight-year-old.

Stepping closer to Skylar, he gently laid a hand on her back. "We need to go in. She's waiting."

He could have stepped in by himself and let Skylar follow when she felt comfortable doing so. However, he felt it was important to do it together.

She gave a nod and moved toward the door, leaving his hand to fall from her back. Aiden took a deep breath, then followed, bracing himself for what was to come. Good or bad.

His gaze swept the room, taking in the large windows, the medical equipment, and the furniture before settling on the little girl laying in the bed. She was quiet, her wide brown eyes moving between Aiden and Skylar.

"Hello again, Aiden." Charli gave him a smile, then went to where Skylar stood frozen in place and gave her a hug. She didn't let go and appeared to whisper in Skylar's ear.

Skylar bent her head to rest her forehead on her taller sister's shoulder, then nodded.

"Are you my dad?"

Aiden had been momentarily focused on Skylar, but his attention was drawn back to the little girl. She gazed at him with curious brown eyes.

Smiling at her as he took a step closer to the bed, he said, "I'm your birth father."

He wanted to claim the role of dad, but he knew he didn't have that right. For the past several years, Blake had loved and raised Aiden's daughter as his own. The other man owned that role one hundred percent.

"So I have two dads?" she asked. "And two moms?"

Aiden glanced past Shiloh to where Blake and Charli stood. "I guess you do."

"Come sit down," Charli said, gesturing to the chairs that were clustered close to the bed.

Charli's chair was closest to Shiloh, while Aiden and Skylar sat beside each other.

Reaching out, Charli ran her hand over Shiloh's hair. "Do you remember what we talked about yesterday?"

Shiloh glanced at Aiden and Skylar, then nodded. "You said that Auntie Sky had me in her tummy, like you had the boys, but then she gave me to you to take care of because she couldn't."

"That's right," Charli said. "Sometimes a mommy and a daddy can't take care of a baby, so they give that baby to someone that can take care of it. Auntie Sky loved you enough to want the very best for you, even if she couldn't give that to you herself."

"You loved me?" Shiloh asked, directing her question to Skylar.

"Yes. Very much." A tremulous smile crossed her face. "I still do."

"So you didn't give me away because you didn't like me?"

"No. Definitely not. I loved you very much, but I knew that Charli and Blake would love you very much too, and that they'd be great parents for you."

"What do I call you?"

"You call me what you've always called me," Skylar said.

"Auntie Sky?"

"Yep."

"What about him?" Shiloh asked, poking in Aiden's direction with a small finger.

"You can call him Uncle Aiden," Skylar said, not even giving Aiden a chance to say anything else. Not that he would have. "And Aiden has a niece, so she's a cousin to you. Just like Timothy is."

Shiloh turned her attention to Aiden. "What's her name?"

"Her name is Willow," he said. "She's five years old."

"What does she look like?"

"I have a picture on my phone if you'd like to see that."

Shiloh seemed more interested in Willow than in Aiden, but that was fine. He pulled out his phone and searched for a good picture of Willow. The best one was of her and his mom, so he chose that, then held out his phone so she could see the picture.

Shiloh bent her head to look at it closely, then she looked up at him with a gaze that was so like Skylar's. So far, like with the photos Skylar had shown him, he didn't see much of himself in her.

"She's pretty," Shiloh said. "Who's that with her?"

"That's my mom."

"She's your grandmother," Charli said.

Shiloh turned to look at her mom. "I have another grandma?"

"You do."

"And another grandpa?"

Aiden felt a pang of grief at the question. Charli gave him a sympathetic look before addressing her daughter.

"Sadly, Aiden's dad died," Charli said. "So though you do have two grandpas, only one of them is here with us now."

"Is he in Heaven now?" Shiloh asked.

Charli looked at Aiden with lifted brows, clearly leaving it up to him to answer that question. She might be remembering that his family hadn't been Christians when he'd been a teen.

"Yes. He's in Heaven now," Aiden told her, grateful that it was actually the truth.

"When do I get to meet Willow and my new grandma?"

Shiloh was certainly taking everything in stride. She was a confident, inquisitive little girl, and he knew that it was most likely because of the loving and stable home she'd grown up in.

But none of that could hide the fact that she was also a very sick little girl. She might have a bright sparkle in her eyes, but her skin was pale, and she looked frail sitting in the bed, surrounded by machines and hooked up to things that were there to help her make it through this horrible stretch of her life.

If he'd been thinking about trying to get custody of her, this meeting would have dissuaded him. He could no longer deny that she was exactly where she needed to be. The home she would have had with him and Skylar if they'd been forced to get married after they'd broken up, wouldn't have been anywhere near as loving and stable as Charli and Blake's.

"We'll talk to Aiden and see when it works for them," Charli said. "It might have to wait until you're out of the hospital."

Shiloh frowned. "That might be a long time."

"We'll see how you're doing," Charli said as she took Shiloh's hand. "Maybe we can do it before then."

"I hope it's soon," Shiloh told her. "I want to meet them."

Aiden couldn't help but smile at her. His mom was going to love her, and so was Willow.

"What does Willow like to do?" Shiloh asked. "Does she do ballet or figure skate?"

"She loves to paint, color, and read. She also likes to swim," Aiden said. "One of her favorite things is to tell jokes. She thinks it's fun to tell me a joke whenever she sees me."

"I like to color too," Shiloh said. "And paint, but Mommy doesn't let me do that very much because the boys get into it and make a mess."

Aiden lifted the gift bag he'd set on the floor. "Willow helped pick out a few things for you from us."

"Really?" Shiloh's face lit up as she took the bag and tipped it toward herself so she could pull the items out. "Oh, a new coloring book. I like this one, and a stuffed unicorn! I love her. I'm gonna keep her right here next to me."

"Do you want to name her?" Charli asked. "Then Aiden can tell Willow and her grandma what it is."

Shiloh hugged the stuffed animal. "Let me think."

"What does Willow call your mom, Aiden?"

"She calls her Nana."

"Maybe Shiloh could also call her that."

Warmth filled Aiden. "My mom would love that."

Charli smiled. "It will make it easier since my mom is Grandma."

"I'm going to name her Sparkle," Shiloh announced as Shiloh slid the unicorn under the blanket that covered her legs so just her head and horn showed. "Because she's got sparkly stuff in her fur."

"That's a great name," Aiden told her. "I'll be sure to tell Willow."

"Could you do a video of me, Momma?" Shiloh asked. "Then I can say thank you to them, and Uncle Aiden can show it to them."

Charli glanced at Blake, then nodded. "That's a great idea, lovey."

Blake grabbed her phone off the nearby table and handed it to Charli. After a few minutes adjusting the bed and pillows, Charli lifted her phone to video Shiloh.

Aiden felt his heart swell with emotion as Shiloh thanked his mom and Willow for the gifts. He knew that his mom was going to be happy to see her newest grandchild. But it would also be hard for her to look at her and see her frailty.

After the video was done to Shiloh's satisfaction, Aiden gave Charli his phone number so she could text it to him.

"Do you like to read?" he asked, eager to know more about his little girl.

Shiloh wrinkled her nose. "Not for school. Those stories are boring. I like to read books from the library."

"Maybe you and Willow have read some of the same books."

"Momma, I want to buy a book and a stuffed animal for Willow. Maybe a coloring book so we can color together. Can we do that?"

"We certainly can."

Aiden felt the tension he'd been carrying about the meeting slip completely away. Did Skylar feel the same way?

When he looked over at her, he saw her watching Charli and Shiloh, but her expression was unreadable. The open emotions from her teen years were a thing of the past, apparently.

"Can you take a picture of me, Momma, and Daddy to show Willow and Nana?"

Aiden nodded, then waited for them to arrange themselves next to the bed. Shiloh smiled widely, and it lit up her whole face. Charli and Blake's smiles were a little more strained.

"Can we take one of me with Uncle Aiden and Auntie Sky, too?"

Aiden looked at Charli, since he found he was loath to overstep his bounds. They'd been so accepting of his appearance in Shiloh's life. He wasn't going to repay that by making things difficult for them.

"Let me take that for you," Charli said, holding out her hand for the phone. "Get over here, Sky."

Skylar was a little slow to move, but soon Charli was organizing them for the shot. She had them on opposite sides of the bed, then they bent closer to Shiloh. Without any prompting, Shiloh wrapped her thin arms around each one of theirs. "Cheese!"

Aiden grinned, appreciating Shiloh's enthusiastic approach to things. He was glad to see that she hadn't completely lost her child-ish enthusiasm to all the medical procedures she was going through.

He needed to figure out how to address Shiloh's health with Willow. They'd told her that her cousin was sick, but beyond that, they hadn't given her many details. The video and the photos would show how fragile and unwell she was, and Willow might have questions. He'd just have to be honest with her.

He didn't like to think about it, but the reality was that Shiloh was a very sick little girl. There was no guarantee that the treatments would work. And there was every possibility that he'd just met his daughter, only to have to say goodbye.

Aiden swallowed against the emotion that thickened in his throat. He couldn't think about that. Couldn't allow himself to grieve before he needed to. He needed to focus on her in the pre-sent, cherishing each moment he had with her.

Over the next little while, Shiloh entertained them all with stories about school, her friends, and the figure skating lessons she'd been taking with Wilder's wife, Lexi, before she'd gotten sick.

As he continued to observe her, Aiden finally saw glimpses of himself. Much like Willow had dark hair and eyes that must have come from her father's side, Skylar's genes had definitely dominated in that department with Shiloh.

Her enthusiastic approach to things reminded him so much of how Skylar had been as a teen, and he wondered if, outside their current situation, she was still that way.

That hadn't been apparent in any of their interactions so far. But given how unhappy she'd been when he'd come back into her life, he wasn't surprised.

Soon though, Shiloh began to fade, exhaustion revealing itself in her eyes' weighted blinks.

"Well, sweetie, I think it's time for Skylar and Aiden to go," Charli said around seven-thirty.

"Will I see them again soon?" Shiloh asked, gesturing to him and Skylar.

"Of course. Skylar is your aunt, so she'll be around, and Aiden lives nearby, so you'll see him too, I'm sure."

"Auntie Sky hardly ever comes to visit, though," Shiloh said with a small pout.

"Maybe she'll come more," Charli said with a glance at her sister who sat expressionless in her chair.

Shiloh looked at Skylar. "Maybe you should move here, then I could see you all the time."

Skylar's expression tightened. "I don't know if I could do that. But I'll try to visit more often."

For a moment, Shiloh just stared at her, then she nodded. "Okay."

With that settled, Aiden and Skylar said goodbye to Shiloh, as well as Charli and Blake. It was hard to step out of the room, and even harder to walk down the hallway to the elevator that would take them to the main floor and exit. Skylar was silent through it all.

As they stepped out of the hospital, they moved to the side, and Aiden stopped and stared up at the sky. Though it had been hard to see Shiloh struggling with her health, he was relieved that the visit had gone so well. He glanced at Skylar to see what she thought.

She stood with her arms crossed, her gaze distant, leaving him to wonder what was going through her mind.

"I think that went pretty good," he said. "Didn't it?"

Her lips tightened, then she turned her gaze to him, and Aiden felt like he'd been stabbed in the heart. The absolute devastation on her face took his breath away.

"Skylar?" He didn't know what to say or do at that moment.

She took two steps toward him and thumped her fists on his chest. "Why couldn't you have been the man you were supposed to be? Why couldn't you have loved me enough to build a family and a future with me? She could have been ours. She could have been... mine..."

Her voice cracked on the last word as her devastation spilled out all over Aiden.

She thumped his chest again as tears flowed down her face. "I hate you for what you did to me. What you did to *us.*"

Aiden wrapped his arms around her, trapping her hand between them. It was all he could think to do.

Lowering his head to rest his cheek on her hair, he said, "I'm so sorry, Sky. I'm so sorry for everything. I'm sorry for robbing you of the chance to be a mother to Shiloh." His own voice cracked with emotion, and he swallowed against the tightness in his throat. "I'm sorry for everything."

"Why couldn't you have been the man your parents raised you to be?"

Her words were like a knife to his heart.

"I don't know. I thought I needed to be different than that," he said. "But I was wrong."

They stood in silence for a long moment, then Skylar suddenly jerked free of his embrace, and she stepped back from him. Anger and hurt spilled off her in waves, but Aiden was helpless to do anything about it.

He knew he deserved every bit of her anger, but he wished that he could ease it for her.

She glared at him, then turned and marched away from him. He watched her go, wondering if there was anything at all he could do to help her. It was hard to see her so upset.

Aiden stood there for a moment, frozen by the guilt and grief he felt for his actions in the past. Over the years, he'd come to realize how wrong he'd been. But in that moment, he felt the depths of that wrongness more than ever before.

Skylar was right. He was the reason she hadn't been able to keep her daughter and raise her in a family like Charli and Blake had. She probably could have kept the baby and raised her, but who he'd been then wouldn't have been happy about being saddled with a child and tied to the woman he'd dumped. So it wouldn't have been a happy or stable life for any of them.

With an aching heart, he went to where he'd parked earlier and climbed into the car. He sat behind the wheel for a few minutes, trying to deal with the emotions Skylar's words had brought to the surface.

The whiplash of the high of meeting Shiloh and the low of Skylar's words left him floundering and helpless. He could do nothing to help Shiloh, and it felt like there was nothing he could do to help Skylar, either.

He had no idea what that exchange with Skylar meant for the future. It didn't feel like it would mean anything good.

CHAPTER EIGHT

After an emotionally tumultuous hour's drive back to Serenity, Skylar walked into the house. She heard the murmur of her parents' voices in the kitchen, but she didn't want to see them. She didn't want to see anyone, so she went right up to her room without making any detours.

Her emotions were pressing so hard against her chest she felt like it was going to explode and every ugly feeling would spew out over everything. Once in her room, she locked the door, then went into the bathroom and locked that door too. She turned on the exhaust fan to try to block out the world.

Sinking down onto the floor, Skylar stared blankly at the floral shower curtain that her mom had chosen to match the sage green walls.

Surely, this was just a bad dream.

That's what the thought of Aiden finding out about Shiloh—and Shiloh finding out she was her mother—had always felt like. A nightmare waiting to happen.

But now it was a reality, and all the emotions she'd tried to suppress for the past eight years had burst forth from the deep pit she'd buried them in.

Never in her wildest dreams had she imagined that Aiden would be back in her life—and that she'd be the reason he was—or that he'd actually *want* to get to know his daughter. And yet... here they were.

Being with him, together with the daughter they'd given up, taking pictures together, watching him smile as he interacted with Shiloh had destroyed her.

If only he'd had the same desire to be a part of their child's life eight years ago.

Her plan going into all of this had been to just tolerate Aiden. To never let him know exactly just how much he'd hurt her. But that had all gone out the window after spending time with him and Shiloh.

Skylar felt like her whole world had been ferociously shaken and then tipped upside down, and she had no idea how to set it right once again.

Shiloh seemed glad to know that she and Aiden were her parents, and she even wanted Skylar to live closer so she could see her more. It seemed her eight-year-old daughter/niece who was battling cancer was more emotionally stable than Skylar was.

Her phone rang, interrupting her spiraling thoughts.

Skylar let out a sigh before she leaned over so she could pull it from her pocket. Her mom's name was on the screen, but Skylar wasn't in any shape to talk to anyone right then.

She declined the call, then sent a text to her mom to let her know she'd talk to her later. Hopefully, her mom understood she just needed a little time to herself.

Turning her phone off, Skylar reached up and put it on the counter. She didn't want to know if anyone else was trying to contact her. She just needed to be alone.

Once she'd been tested, she should have caught the first flight back to Las Vegas and her calm, solitary life there.

It wasn't that she didn't want to be there for Shiloh and her family. It was just so hard to not be there as the mother to the child she'd given birth to. And she didn't know how to deal with that.

And it had been so hard to look at Shiloh and see only a shadow of her previous vibrant personality and healthy body. Her baby was in the fight for her life, and Skylar didn't know how to help her.

Out of the blue, tears flooded her eyes, making her equal parts angry and sad. The wall she'd worked hard to put up around the deep emotions she'd felt in the weeks and months after Shiloh's birth had been shattered.

That was not good. Especially if she was going to have to continue to interact with Aiden and Shiloh.

If Skylar had realized how much revealing Shiloh's parentage to her would devastate her, she would have fought harder against that happening. But it was too late now.

Anger flooded her then. Anger at Aiden for how he'd treated her. Anger at herself for not being strong enough to keep her baby, the way Charli had kept Layla. Anger at cancer for invading her child's body. And anger at cancer for having brought Aiden back into her life.

How could she get rid of the anger and regret? The guilt and the hurt?

The words she'd thrown at Aiden came back to her as she sat there, and part of her regretted them. But another part of her felt like he needed to know exactly how much he'd hurt her.

Though he'd seen her hurt when he'd broken up with her, she'd had to tell him about the baby over a text because he refused her calls. He'd needed to know the pain she'd felt at having to give up their child. How shattered she'd been, not just by the breakup but by his words when she'd told him about the pregnancy.

The fact that Shiloh knew who they were now didn't magically make everything better. In fact, right then, it felt like everything was worse.

Skylar had no idea how long she'd sat there when she became aware that her behind was going numb from the hard floor. Her emotional outburst had drained her energy, and it took a lot of effort to get herself up off the floor.

When she was finally on her feet, Skylar decided that she was just going to go to bed. She didn't have the emotional capacity to have a conversation with anyone.

Grabbing her phone from the counter, she left the bathroom without removing her makeup or even brushing her teeth. She peeled off her clothes, leaving them strewn across the floor in a manner that was very much unlike her. Then, clad in just her underwear, she climbed under the covers.

Once she was settled, she turned her phone back on and sent a message to her mom that she was going to bed and would talk to her the next day.

Skylar saw there was a missed call from Charli, as well as a text message, but Skylar didn't read it or call her back. She would deal with everything the next day.

Hopefully, a good night's sleep would help her shore up her defenses.

After a restless night, Skylar dragged herself out of bed just as the sun was rising. Though she was exhausted on every level, she dressed in her running clothes and shoes. She didn't fix her messy braid or wipe away her smeared mascara before grabbing her phone and earbuds and leaving her room.

The house was quiet as she headed down the stairs on light feet. She went into the darkened kitchen to get a drink of water, then let herself out of the house.

The early morning hour was cool and quiet, which her mind most definitely still wasn't. She stretched a little, trying to limber up her legs before setting out.

When she was finally running, she tried to let the music in her ears and the rhythm of her stride soothe her. And for the most part, it worked.

Twenty minutes into her run, she was so in the zone that when a bird flew across the road in front of her, it scared the life out of her. Her instinct was to step away from the bird, and without watching where she was going, her foot landed on the edge of the asphalt.

A tearing pain shot through her ankle as it twisted sideways, and she landed on her hip on the packed dirt mixed with gravel that ran alongside the road. Panting, she rolled onto her back and stared up at the sky that had lightened to a clear blue while she'd been running.

"Ahhhhhhhh!" She pounded her fists on the ground. "Ahhhhhhhhhhhhh!"

It felt like the rotten cherry on top of a wretched sundae. Tears filled her eyes, blurring the sky.

"Why, God?" The question was yelled at the sky, and had anyone been in the area, they probably would have thought she was crazy.

It felt like the world was conspiring against her lately. Nothing was going right.

And even though she wasn't the one in the family with a medical degree, she was fairly certain that her ankle was pretty messed up. If it wasn't broken, it was likely badly sprained.

Either way, she wasn't going to be able to escape back to Vegas or go back to work as soon as she'd hoped.

How was this her life?

It felt like everything had fallen apart, starting with her relationship with Emmett. From that moment on, things had just gone downhill.

She stayed on her back, trying not to focus on the unrelenting pain in her ankle. Finally, the tears stopped, and she lifted her hands to brush the moisture away.

Rolling over to her hands and knees, she used her good leg to balance herself as she straightened. Once she was up, she put her foot down and tried to take a step.

Immediately, the pain had her crying out and sinking down onto her butt. She stretched her leg out and glared at it. There was no way she was going to be able to make it home on her own.

She was going to have to call her parents.

When she reached for her phone in the arm strap she usually wore it in, she realized it wasn't there. She'd been so distracted that she hadn't realized it had fallen out.

Looking around, she saw it laying on the ground face down. Using her good foot, she scooted over to where it was and picked it up.

She stared down at the shattered screen. "Are you *kidding* me?"

Her frustration climbed as she tried to figure out what to do. Hoping the phone still had service, even with a smashed screen, she looked at her smart watch.

Relief flooded her when she saw that her watch was still connected. She tapped on the small screen, bringing up her contacts. It was still early, not quite seven, but she hoped that her dad would be up.

"Skylar?" he said when he answered.

Tears sprang to her eyes again, and she had to swallow hard to clear her throat enough for her to talk. "Dad, I need help."

"What's wrong, honey?"

His voice sounded distant through the watch. "I was out running, and I twisted my ankle. I can't walk on it."

"Okay. I'm on my way," he said. "Where are you?"

And just like that, her dad was on his way to rescue her. Just like he'd picked her up when she'd tripped and skinned her knee as a child. She'd always known he would be there for her if she needed him in a way no other man had ever been.

With rescue on the way, Skylar kept her injured leg stretched out but drew her other leg up. She wrapped her arms around it and bent to rest her forehead on her knee.

She tried to just blank out her mind, afraid that if she thought too much about everything, she would start to cry again. She didn't want her dad to arrive and find her sobbing.

It didn't take long for the rumble of a car engine to sound in the distance. As it neared, she looked up and watched as her dad's car slowed to a stop not far from her.

He got out and came around the hood to where she sat. Lowering himself to one knee, her dad looked at her.

He gave her a gentle smile. "Let's get you home, then we'll check over your ankle. Everything's going to be okay."

She appreciated his optimism, but she didn't share it. Right then, it felt like her life had been torn apart, and she wasn't sure how she was going to put it back together and move forward.

With careful movements, her dad helped her up and then wrapped his arm around her waist and guided her as she hopped toward his car. She let out a long sigh as she settled back in the front seat.

Though she'd been running for a while before injuring her ankle, it didn't take long to get back home. Once there, her dad helped her into the house and guided her to the kitchen.

"What happened?" her mom cried when she spotted her. She still wore her pajamas, which consisted of a pair of shorts and a T-shirt, and she was standing with the coffee carafe in her hand.

"I twisted my ankle," Skylar said as she settled into a chair at the table.

Her dad bent down on one knee and carefully worked off her shoe and sock. She hissed out a breath of pain as he gently rotated it. "We're going to have to get an x-ray of it. I'll call Gareth to see if he can come in early to check it over, too."

That was the benefit of having several medical professionals in the family. They always managed to fit her in when she needed their help.

"Here." Her mom handed over an ice pack from the freezer. "Put this on it to help with the swelling."

Her dad moved a chair over so she could prop her leg up, then he put the ice pack on it. Unfortunately, it didn't help with the pain, which was pulsing strongly in her ankle.

"What happened?" her mom asked again as she brought two mugs of coffee to the table, then returned to the carafe for a third.

She settled across the table from Skylar as she recounted what had led to her injury. Skylar took a sip of coffee, feeling her rattled nerves begin to settle now that she was home with her parents.

"How are you feeling?" her mom asked. "Other than your ankle."

Skylar had kind of hoped that her mom would forget about the fact that she'd shut herself off from everyone the night before. Her mom, however, never forgot things like that when it came to her kids.

Keeping her gaze on her ankle, Skylar said, "I'm okay. It was hard seeing Shiloh looking so sickly. The last time I saw her, she was so full of energy."

"Yes. That's really difficult," her mom agreed. "I know the other kids are struggling with her being in the hospital."

Skylar again felt bad that Charli and Blake were having to shoulder this burden that should have been hers. Their children were having to take on an emotional burden they might not have had to if their relationship with Shiloh had been that of a cousin.

"But Shiloh is getting the best care," her dad said, reaching out to touch her shoulder. "And Charli and Blake don't view what's happening as a burden they could have avoided had they not adopted Shiloh. That's not in their thoughts at all."

It was like her dad could read her mind. "But I feel like I should be the one going through this with Shiloh. That Charli and Blake shouldn't have to deal with this when they have a large family who needs them."

"You can still go through this with Shiloh and with Charli and Blake," her mom said. "If you considered moving closer, you could do that."

Skylar gave a huff. Her mom just wasn't going to give up on her efforts to get her to move back to Serenity.

"Not sure what I'm going to do about work," she said, then gestured to her ankle. "Since this makes it pretty much impossible to do my job."

"You're welcome to stay here as long as you want," her mom said. "It's nice to have someone else with us in this big old house."

Staying with her parents hadn't been as bad as Skylar had thought it would be. Aside from all the subtle—and not-so-subtle—comments about her moving back to Serenity, her parents had kind of just let her be. Which she greatly appreciated.

Right then, however, she wanted her parents. She needed her parents. And she knew with one hundred percent confidence that they would be there to support her.

"Let me make you some breakfast," her mom said, getting to her feet. "And then we'll go to the clinic."

As her mom went to the fridge, her dad pulled out his phone. "I need to call Gareth."

Skylar listened as he explained the situation to her oldest brother, while her mom fried up some eggs.

"Okay. We'll be there at eight-thirty."

When her dad hung up, Skylar asked, "Am I going to be able to take a shower before we go? I'm sweaty and dirty."

"As long as you can balance on one leg," he said.

"I think I can do that. I really don't want to be out in public like this," she said, gesturing to herself.

"You've got a few scrapes, too," he told her, pointing to her leg.

Skylar bent over to look and frowned. "I guess I didn't even feel those since my ankle hurts so bad."

"A shower would help clean them up," her mom said.

Once she'd finished her breakfast, her dad helped her up the stairs to her room. It took some effort, but she made it into the shower. The scrapes and bruises were more evident without her clothes on, revealing that she'd landed hard on her thigh and hip on the same side as her hurting ankle.

Though she would have liked to linger under the warm water, she didn't take too long in the shower. Since Gareth was making the effort to get to the clinic early, she didn't want to make him wait.

Still, everything seemed to take forever. It was a pain to move around, but finally, she was all cleaned up and in clothes more appropriate for going to the clinic.

She maneuvered down the stairs on her bum, then stood at the bottom of them, waiting for her parents.

"Ready to go?" her dad asked as he came out of the kitchen, her mom trailing him.

"Are you coming too, Mom?"

"Of course!"

Skylar laughed, in spite of her frustration and pain. "Anything medical, huh, Mom?"

"You know it," she said. "And lucky you, getting three doctors' opinions for the price of free."

Skylar knew that sometimes having three doctors available for opinions wasn't all that great. There had been heated discussions among her parents and brother sometimes. Not usually of a patient of theirs or a family member, but rather some medical case that one of them had read about and had passed on to the other two.

As they drove to the clinic, her mom talked about the people she was messaging with news of Skylar's mishap. Thankfully, it was just family members.

Her accident and the meltdown that followed had served to shock her out of the emotional tailspin she'd been in since the previous night. Not that she thought those emotions were gone. But at least, for the moment, she had something else to focus on.

CHAPTER NINE

His co-worker immediately followed up his knock on Aiden's door by opening it and stepping inside his office. Normally, that would have aggravated Aiden, but he had been expecting this visit, and he and Devon always operated with an open-door policy between them.

Aiden watched as the man he was closest to in the company—and considered a close friend—walked toward him, then took a seat on the opposite side of the desk.

"So, what's up?"

He and Devon had started at the company around the same time, with Aiden beating him for seniority by two weeks. While some people might be competitive with someone who was at their same level within a company, he and Devon had chosen a different approach.

They'd been assigned to a couple of projects together, and they'd worked super well as a team. It was something the project manager had also noticed, and that had led to them both being assigned to most of the same projects over the past couple of years.

When the owner of the company decided to promote them to managing their own projects, he'd talked with them to see if they'd be willing to co-manage the projects. In the end, they'd agreed and decided to alternate taking the lead on projects.

Their current project was their biggest one yet, and Aiden had the responsibility of taking the lead on it. Except he was preparing to pass that lead to Devon.

"I have a bunch of stuff going on in my personal life that is demanding a lot of my time and attention. I've talked to George, and he agreed that I could pass the lead to you so I could step back a bit."

Devon frowned. "Are you sure?"

"Yes. Very sure." He'd been thinking a lot about it as the situation with Shiloh and Skylar had begun to take up more of his time and thoughts.

Normally, he'd still work on—or at least think about—the project during evenings and weekends. But since everything had unfolded recently, he'd spent relatively little time working on the project outside of work hours, which wasn't going to lead to the success of it.

Aiden shared what had been going on, and Devon listened patiently and with a concerned expression. He didn't usually talk a lot about his personal life at the office, but Devon was someone he'd spent time with outside of work hours.

"I'm sorry to hear about your daughter," Devon said. "I can't even imagine what you're feeling."

"It's been quite the experience, that's for sure," Aiden told him. "I'm just glad that they're willing to let me have a role in Shiloh's life. They certainly didn't have to do that."

"You're fortunate, because I'm not sure that everyone would have reacted the way they did."

"I'm pretty that Skylar doesn't agree with what her sister and brother-in-law have decided regarding me knowing about Shiloh."

"Sounds like she hates you," Devon said.

Aiden couldn't really blame her if she did, but his heart hoped that she didn't. For some reason, it felt as important to have some sort of relationship with Skylar as it did with Shiloh.

"She's certainly not happy with me," Aiden agreed. "But she's still talking to me, so that's something."

"Well, I'm happy to take the lead if you need to step back."

"I really appreciate that."

"Of course, this has been our most difficult client yet, so maybe you're just trying to get out of dealing with them."

Aiden chuckled. "I'd never do that to you."

"You better be available for venting sessions," Devon said as he leaned back in his chair.

"I'm always available for that," Aiden assured him. "And I'll still be at all the meetings. I'm not leaving the project completely."

It was a relief to shift the responsibility for the project to Devon, and he was glad that his friend didn't mind stepping up to help him. The man's reaction to Aiden's request was a true reflection of the working and personal relationships they had.

"I guess I'll see you at our next meeting," Devon said as he got to his feet. "Take care of yourself and give my regards to your mom. And of course, say hi to the little princess for me."

"Will do," he said. "And you tell Glory I'm sorry for adding to your workload."

"She's busy with school," Devon said of his wife of a year. "So we can sit on the couch together in the evenings and work. At least we're together."

He envied Devon and Glory's marriage. They were what he would like to have in a relationship. They were supportive of one another, and though they were both busy, they made time for just the two of them.

In a lot of ways, they reminded him of his parents. The way they worked in partnership, loving and respecting each other.

He was happy for his friend, but the desire to have something like that for himself had grown over the time he'd known the couple.

After a brief discussion about what parts of the project Aiden would continue to have responsibility for, Devon left. Aiden tried to focus on those aspects of the project for the remaining hours of the workday.

His phone rang as he was driving home once he was done work, and since he had it running through the Bluetooth of his car, he answered it without looking to see who it was.

"Brooooo." Cole's voice coming through the speakers made Aiden wish he'd looked. "What on *earth* is going on?"

He was actually surprised it had taken Cole this long to call him. Although Aiden knew that he probably should have been the one to reach out.

"What do you know?"

"That you and Skylar are Shiloh's parents," he said. "Like what? How did that happen?"

"After we broke up, she told me she was pregnant," Aiden said, then swallowed hard before continuing on. "I told her to just get rid of it."

"What?" Confusion was gone, replaced by anger. "You told her to get an abortion?"

"To be honest, I didn't think she was actually pregnant," he told Cole. "I thought she was trying to get us back together again. She really hadn't wanted the breakup."

"You had to know that Skylar would never do that," Cole scoffed. "She isn't that sort of girl."

"You're right, I did know that," Aiden admitted. "But at that time, I told myself she was, to justify brushing her off. When you never said anything about her being pregnant, I just thought that I'd been right."

"Why did it even come up now?" Cole asked.

"So you know that Shiloh is sick, right?"

"I'd heard that Charli was concerned about something."

"Cole, Shiloh has cancer," Aiden said. "You didn't know that?"

There was a long stretch of silence before Cole said, "I must have missed that message in the family chat."

"Good grief, bro," Aiden said. "You need to pay more attention to your family."

"I know. I know." Cole sighed. "It's just... life."

"You mean how you're not living the life your parents would want you to?"

"Yeah. That."

"Well, right now, you need to be more aware of what's going on," Aiden said. "For your niece's and my daughter's sake."

"That is just so weird," Cole said. "I really can't believe you're Shiloh's birth father. I don't know how to feel. I mean, I'm mad at you for how you treated Skylar, but I'm also mad at her for not saying anything. I'm speechless actually."

"Be great if you stayed that way," Aiden said.

"Hah," Cole replied. "Don't think you're going to get off that easy."

"Jay and Wilder have both lectured me already."

"And what did Skylar do?"

"Well, even though she contacted me to see if I'm a match for a stem cell transplant for Shiloh, I think she actually hates my guts."

"You can't be surprised by that."

"No, I'm not."

"Have the two of you managed to have any conversations about what happened back then?"

"None that have felt positive."

"This explains so much," Cole mused.

"What do you mean?"

"She's just changed a lot from how she was in high school. Since then, she's refused to talk about you, and I always just assumed it was because you two broke up. I'm going to guess that's not the case."

"It was definitely partly because of that. Our breakup was... not so great."

"Why?"

"I told her that we were young, and we would probably meet people who were better suited for each of us."

"Hmmm. So essentially, you told her that you thought you could do better than her, because I doubt she thought she could do better than you."

"You're right," Aiden said. He had to start taking accountability for what had happened with Skylar, and everything that followed. "I was immature and convinced that the best of my life was yet to come."

"I suppose I can't blame you for feeling that way," Cole said. "We all kind of did."

"You were just smart enough to not get into relationships in high school when we really weren't mature enough to handle them. Or rather, I wasn't mature enough."

"I'm still just a little shocked by everything," Cole said. "And I'm surprised *you* didn't say something to me."

Aiden pulled his car to a stop in the driveway of his house. "I'm sorry. Honestly, I'm ashamed of what happened back then, and I didn't want to chance losing you as a friend. I seem to have precious few of them these days."

"You're never gonna be able to get rid of me, bro. I might have people in my life I consider friends now, but no one knows me like you do. Given how things have gone for me, I don't take our friendship for granted. I always know you're not after my money."

Aiden chuckled. "Nope. Definitely not that."

He had such a sense of relief over the conversation with Cole. The reassurance of their friendship was what he needed, though he wouldn't have blamed his friend if he'd taken his sister's side.

Not that Aiden thought Cole had taken his side over Skylar's. Just that, as in the past, he was taking the role of Switzerland, not really choosing to get involved.

They talked for a bit more as Aiden let himself into the house and headed down to his small apartment to change and put his work bag away.

"Are you planning to come back to Serenity at some point?" he asked as he hung up his suit coat and began to unbutton his shirt.

There was a long pause before Cole said, "Maybe. I don't know."

"Now might be a good time to come," Aiden told him. "Skylar has stuck around longer than I thought she would."

"I got the feeling she wasn't any more interested in returning to Serenity than I am."

"I think circumstances have made it somewhat impossible for her to leave."

"What do you mean?"

Aiden sat down on the edge of his bed. "Well, though we are not legally Shiloh's parents, we're still biologically related to her, and it's hard to walk away when Shiloh's facing the cancer fight that she is. Though she might deny it, I think Skylar is emotionally engaged enough that she can't run away."

"And you?"

"I'm definitely unable to walk away. I would like to be *more* involved. But so far, I'm taking Skylar's advice—which is more like a demand—that I not overstep my boundaries."

"I have to say it's a bit weird to think that you have a daughter, and Skylar has a daughter, and that they're the same person."

"You and me both, bro," he said. "You and me both."

"I don't know Shiloh well."

"Or at all," Aiden said as he stood and made his way to the chest of drawers to pull out a pair of shorts and a T-shirt.

"Or at all," Cole agreed.

"Maybe you should change that."

"Maybe."

Cole was definitely not going to commit to anything. They'd never really touched on his reluctance to return to Serenity, mainly because it hadn't mattered one way or another to Aiden. Several times during the year—usually through the basketball season—Cole would send him tickets to home games, along with a ticket for him to fly to where Cole lived, to attend the games.

Now, however, he wanted his friend to consider coming home. Skylar had ended up coming home for more than just a couple of days, so it was possible that Cole might too.

As their conversation ended, Aiden realized how glad he was that he'd had the chance to chat with Cole. And that even though he'd had to deal with his friend's anger at finding out what had happened, they'd gotten past it and come out the other side, still friends.

When he got upstairs, he found his mom stirring a pot on the stove, while Willow set the table.

"Uncle Aiden!" Willow cheered as she skipped over to greet him with a hug.

Aiden swung her up into his arms. "Gotta joke for me?"

Willow nodded, her pigtails dancing, then said, "What do you call a bear with no socks on?"

Aiden bounced her a couple of times. "I don't know. What do you call him?"

"Bearfoot!"

Aiden chuckled. The jokes weren't always funny to him as an adult, but Willow's joy was infectious and always brought laughter, regardless.

As they ate the dinner his mom had prepared for them, Aiden recounted the phone call he'd had with Cole. His mom and dad had always liked Cole, and his mom had expressed more than once that she was glad that they'd kept in contact, regardless of their lives moving in different directions.

"Have you heard anything about Shiloh today?" his mom asked.

"No, but I think I'll text Skylar to see if she knows anything. I don't really feel comfortable going directly to Charli or Blake."

"That's understandable," his mom said with a nod. "But hopefully with time, you'll be able to communicate directly with them."

"That will come in time," he agreed. "But only if they want me to have more involvement in Shiloh's life. I'm still not sure what they're thinking."

"You might need to initiate a conversation about it if they don't."

Aiden didn't want to do that, but he also didn't want to miss out on the opportunity to get to know his daughter better. Considering the current state of Shiloh's health, he had to face—whether he wanted to or not—the very real possibility that things might not go well for her.

Pushing those thoughts aside, he made himself focus on only a positive outcome for Shiloh. Just like he prayed for every day.

Once dinner was over, he helped his mom clean up, then spent a couple of hours with Willow. His mom used that reprieve to have some time by herself after spending all day with the little girl.

He and Willow started out their time by putting together a puzzle, then moved on to doing some coloring before he read her a story. After that, he filled the bathtub with warm water and some bubbles so that she could take a bath before getting ready for bed.

Once she was in her pajamas and had brushed her teeth, his mom came out to tuck Willow in and pray with her. His mom already wore her favorite robe—one his dad had given her for her last birthday before he passed—but instead of going back to her room, she went to the kitchen.

They chatted for a couple of minutes, then Aiden said goodnight and headed down to his space. He wanted to get hold of Skylar before it got too late to see if she had an update she'd share with him.

He sat down in his recliner and, after considering his words, tapped out a message.

Hi Skylar. Hope you had a good day. Just wondering if there's been an update on how Shiloh's doing after her treatment today.

He waited for a minute, watching to see if a response came back right away. When nothing appeared, he closed the app and opened his work email. He might not be in charge of the project anymore, but that didn't mean he wasn't going to pay attention to it, even after hours.

After checking through the emails and finding nothing needing his attention, he moved on to his social media. He wasn't very active on any of it, but he usually checked out the one where there were more newsy posts.

It took about ten minutes before his phone alerted him to a new text message.

Skylar: *She had a treatment today, so it's been a rough day. Hopefully, she'll feel a bit better tomorrow.*

Aiden hated to hear that Shiloh was struggling. He wished there was something he could do to make things easier for her. But there wasn't.

However, perhaps he could help with the weight Charli and Blake carried.

Do you think we could stay with her for a couple of hours to give Charli and Blake a break sometime?

Skylar: *We? We, who?*

You and me.

He could see that she was writing a message, but then it stopped. And started up again. Then stopped. And started up again. Then stopped.

Aiden had pretty much given up on a response when one finally popped up on his screen.

Skylar: *I'm not sure that's a good idea.*

Why not?

And, once again, the starting and stopping of a message began. He knew it would probably be a hard sell, but he doubted that Charli and Blake would agree to just him hanging out with her, since Shiloh didn't know him very well. He needed to do his best to sell the idea to Skylar.

Skylar: *I'm not sure that Charli would want to leave Shiloh when she's feeling so bad.*

I'm not saying we have to go when she's feeling poorly, but maybe on a day when she's not doing too badly.

Skylar: *I'll ask Charli, but don't hold your breath.*

Aiden smiled, even though he knew that it was possible she was just saying that to get him off her case. And it was possible that she'd tell him that Charli didn't want them to go, without even talking to her sister.

Still...

Thanks so much. Let me know what she says. Also, thanks for the update on Shiloh. Mom was also wondering how she was doing, and I know she's praying for her.

Skylar: *You're welcome, but still, don't hold your breath.*

I won't.

Aiden would have liked a longer conversation but decided not to push for it since he'd basically asked her for a favor. Ticking her off wouldn't help achieve that.

If they were able to spend some time with Shiloh, he'd be able to talk to Skylar more then. He really hoped that it worked out because, beyond being able to spend time with Skylar, he thought it would be good for the two of them to spend time together with Shiloh.

CHAPTER TEN

Skylar gritted her teeth as she used the crutches to make her way into the hospital and up to Shiloh's room. It wasn't her first time on crutches in her life. When she'd been a cheerleader, she'd sprained her ankle on a badly performed cartwheel. But she wasn't any happier about using crutches this time than she'd been that time.

"Hi, Sky." Charli greeted her with a smile and a hug. "How's the ankle?"

"It's throbbing, reminding me it's still attached." Skylar glanced over at the bed to see that Shiloh was asleep.

"How long will you be on the crutches?" Charli asked as they sat down on the chairs by the window.

"Too long." Skylar leaned her crutches against the wall. "Gareth said probably for four weeks or so."

They chatted quietly for several minutes before Blake showed up. The man smiled at them, but he went to the bed and leaned over to brush a light kiss on Shiloh's head.

Seeing Blake treat Shiloh with such love and affection was always so reassuring to Skylar that she'd done the right thing. Blake might be rough around the edges and on the stoic, silent side, but she could see that he was fiercely protective and loving of those close to him.

After kissing Shiloh, he came over to greet Charli. She stood up and moved into his embrace. They shared a brief kiss, but then Blake continued to hold her when she tucked her head against his shoulder.

Skylar looked away, feeling like she was intruding on an intimate moment between her sister and her husband, even though it was just a hug.

"Have you decided where we're going?" Blake said as they stepped apart.

"I think so."

"Do you want to go now?" he asked.

"Sure. Skylar's here if Shiloh wakes up."

Skylar felt a frisson of alarm at being left alone with Shiloh. "Will she be upset if she wakes up and you're not here?"

Charli shook her head. "She'll be fine. I talked to her about the plan, and she was excited about it."

Skylar wasn't sure *she* was going to be fine. But she was this far into things, so she couldn't back out now.

Before Charli and Blake had a chance to leave, Aiden showed up. Skylar felt her heart skip a beat as he walked into the room. He was wearing a suit, so had probably come from work. He carried several things, including a drink tray with two large cups and a smaller one.

"Hi, Aiden," Charli said with a smile. "Good to see you again."

"You as well," he replied. "Thanks for agreeing to let me spend some time with Shiloh."

"Well, it works out all around." She smiled up at Blake. "I'm looking forward to a couple of hours alone with my husband."

Aiden set the drink tray and bags he carried down on the small table next to Skylar. He stared at her wrapped ankle with a frown. "What happened?"

"We're going to leave you guys," Charli said. "Have fun!"

When it was just them, Skylar said, "I twisted my ankle while I was out on a run."

"You weren't watching where you were going?"

She gave him a withering look, which prompted a grin from Aiden. "I was doing just fine until a bird shot out of the trees and scared me."

"A bird?"

"Yep. And I had to call Dad to come rescue me."

"Are you going to be able to work with your ankle like that?"

"Nope. I had to let them know that I was going to be out of work for at least four more weeks."

"Where do you work?" he asked as he removed the drinks from the tray, setting one in front of her.

"I'm a flight attendant for a company that rents out private jets."

He paused for a moment before turning his attention to the contents of a bag with a fast food company logo on it. "You decided not to pursue interior design?"

"No. There was too much going on back then. I got through my first year, but after Shiloh was born... Well, it was just a difficult time. Charli's friend Melissa, who was a flight attendant, eventually helped me get a job with an international airline. Then, from there, I got the job at this place."

He set a wrapped burger and a container of fries next to her drink. "And you enjoy it?"

"I do," she said, then pointed to the food. "What's this?"

"I took a chance that you still like chicken burgers and fries." He looked up at her. "Do you?"

She wanted to tell him that she hated both items, but the reality was that she did still really like them. With having to watch her weight so she'd fit into her uniform, it wasn't a meal she indulged in very often, however.

"And the drink?"

"It's diet."

Skylar didn't want to be touched that he'd remembered what she liked nine years after they'd last shared a meal like that.

Seeing this version of him was really a struggle for her.

"Did you get food for Shiloh as well?" she asked, gesturing to the smaller drink.

"Yep. I asked Charli if I could bring something for her. She said there was no guarantee that she'd eat anything, but her favorites are nuggets and fries."

Skylar nodded. That seemed to be a favorite with most of the kids in the family. It had been her favorite at that age, too. It was a quick food that her mom couldn't mess up since it involved pulling bags of nuggets and fries from the freezer and dumping them on a tray and putting them in the oven.

"Auntie Sky?"

Hearing Shiloh's voice, Skylar reached for her crutches and got herself up on her feet. She made her way over to the bed to find her niece awake and smiling at her.

Skylar reached out to tuck a strand of hair behind her ear. "Hey, sweetie."

"Is Uncle Aiden here too?"

Aiden joined her at the side of the bed. "I'm here."

"Momma said you were going to stay with me while she and Daddy went on a date."

"Yep. And Aiden brought you some supper."

Her eyes lit up. "Nuggets?"

"Yep," Aiden said with a grin. "Do you want them now?"

At Shiloh's nod, Aiden went to get the food while Skylar rolled the over-the-bed table into position in front of Shiloh, then moved so that Aiden could set the food and drink on the table.

When Shiloh held out her hands to them, Skylar knew immediately what she wanted. With a glance at Aiden, she took Shiloh's hand. He did the same, then she bent her head, waiting for Shiloh to pray.

Only silence followed, however, so Skylar looked up to find Shiloh sitting with lifted brows as she stared at them.

"What's wrong?" Skylar asked.

"We *all* have to hold hands."

"Oh." Skylar looked at Aiden again.

The man didn't hesitate or blink an eye as he reached out to take Skylar's hand. "You're quite correct, Shiloh."

The moment his fingers tightened around hers, Skylar was thrown back in time, and it was all she could do not to cling to his hand. She tried to focus instead on Shiloh as she prayed for their meal.

The prayer was actually short, but it felt like it had stretched on unreasonably long. When Shiloh ended her prayer with an amen, Skylar echoed it, then pulled her hand from Aiden's. She waited until Shiloh released her hand, pulling it back to clasp it together with her other one.

Shiloh pulled a nugget from the container and took a small bite. Skylar felt a bit sad at the thought of how little Shiloh might eat of the meal Aiden had brought.

"We have some food too," Aiden said as he went to sit at the table.

The room was small enough that they could still talk with Shiloh even when they were at the table. Skylar's appetite had dipped, but she didn't want the food to get cold. Or colder than it already was.

Shiloh took small bites of her nugget as they talked, and she ended up eating two of the four, plus half the fries. Skylar had no idea if that was good or bad considering her current circumstances, but she supposed that any amount of food that Shiloh took in was a good thing.

It appeared that Shiloh might be discharged in the next couple of days since her first round of treatments was almost done. It all depended on how she was doing after the final treatment.

It wasn't long before the little girl started to fade again. Skylar got up to move the table out of the way. As she did that, Aiden approached with a decorative bag in his hand.

"My mom and Willow picked up a few more things for you," he said as he set the bag on her lap.

Shiloh's face lit up, and she reached out to tip the bag toward her. Aiden helped, holding it in position so she could reach into it with the hand that wasn't currently hooked to an IV.

Over the next few minutes, she pulled out a selection of books, a thick coloring book, some colored pencils, and another small pink stuffed unicorn that looked like the baby of the one they'd given her previously.

"I love all of it," Shiloh said as she smiled up at Aiden. "Thank them for me, please."

"I will," Aiden assured her as he reached out to rest his hand briefly on Shiloh's shoulder.

In his words and actions, Skylar could hear love and affection for Shiloh. She still wasn't sure that allowing Aiden into their lives—or her life—was a good thing. However, it was clear he did. And she was sure that Shiloh did too.

Watching them together was yet another harsh reminder of what had been lost. Even if Shiloh had still ended up with cancer, at least they would have been a family.

A nurse came into the room while Shiloh and Aiden were looking at the books. Shiloh greeted her by name, then showed her the items Aiden had brought her.

"You got another unicorn! What's this one's name?" the nurse asked as she stood at Shiloh's bedside opposite Aiden.

"Rainbow?" Shiloh held the unicorn in front of her face. "Yep. Rainbow."

"Rainbow the Unicorn," the nurse said. "I like it."

The nurse spent some time chatting with Shiloh, casually asking her questions that Skylar realized would help the woman gauge how Shiloh was doing without asking her directly. Soon, the nurse left, giving Skylar and Aiden a smile as she headed for the door.

"Did you want to nap a bit more?" Skylar asked Shiloh.

The little girl hesitated, then nodded. Aiden returned the books to the bag, then set it on the floor next to the table. He left the stuffed animal with Shiloh, as she didn't seem inclined to let it or the other stuffed unicorn out of her sight.

"Will Momma and Daddy be back soon?" Shiloh asked.

When Aiden glanced at her, Skylar said, "I think they'll probably be here not long after you wake up from your nap."

Shiloh nodded, appearing fine with the news that her parents wouldn't be back right away. The little girl shifted on the bed, then wrapped her arms around the stuffed animals.

Skylar stared at Shiloh as her eyes closed, wishing there was something she could do to take away everything Shiloh was struggling with physically. She imagined that Charli and Blake felt the same way.

"She looks a lot like you," Aiden said as he sat down across from her again.

Skylar flicked her gaze in his direction before looking back at Shiloh. "Which means she also looks a lot like Charli. That was why I thought they could get away with not telling people that Shiloh was adopted."

"Did you really not want Shiloh to know?"

They'd talked about it before, but it was clear that Aiden really had no idea how much she hadn't wanted that.

"No, I didn't," she said. "I didn't want her to be confused by my presence in her life. Even though they told her she was adopted, I didn't want her to know I was her birth mom."

"Was it just for her sake?" he asked.

"What do you mean?"

"I mean, perhaps you didn't want her to know because it would be easier for you."

Skylar glared at him, hating that he'd focused in on that. "Her not knowing didn't mean that I didn't know. I'd never forget giving birth to her and then giving her away."

"True. But Shiloh not knowing allowed you to keep your distance from her."

His words, unfortunately, hit close to home. She hadn't known how to be around Shiloh and not want to take her into her arms and run away with her. Her emotions had been—and apparently, still were—a mess.

"So you think I didn't want them to tell her about me because I was selfish?"

"I don't think that at all," Aiden said.

Maybe he should, because it was partly true. She'd kept her distance because it was easier for her. Emotionally, she had thought it would be too difficult to be so close to Shiloh. So yes, she'd been selfish in the decision to keep herself apart from Shiloh after the adoption.

She'd been so young—two years younger than Charli had been when she'd had Layla—and she'd feared ruining Shiloh's life if she tried to raise her on her own. In her mind back then, Charli would be a better mom to Shiloh, and through Blake, Shiloh would also have a father, which she wouldn't have with Skylar.

Regardless of her motivations for giving Shiloh up, it was clear that she'd made the right decision. Charli and Blake had been better parents to Shiloh than she and Aiden would have ever been, even if they'd stayed together. She was sure of that.

"I know you did what you thought was right," Aiden said. "And given the circumstances you found yourself in, I can't blame you for what you did."

Skylar wanted to be angry at him, but it was getting harder to hold on to the anger she'd had towards him for so long. She wasn't sure why, because she didn't think she could say that she'd forgiven him for how he'd hurt her in the past.

Perhaps it was because she'd been able to vent to him all the hurt and anger she'd carried from what had happened between them.

Aiden sighed. "I'm sorry that my desire to know Shiloh has forced you into a situation you really didn't want to be in."

"Three times now you've forced me into situations I didn't want."

"Three?"

Raising her hand, she lifted her index finger. "First, when you broke up with me. Second, when you told me to get rid of the baby. And third, when you wanted to meet her, when all I wanted from you was a little blood."

Aiden's shoulders slumped. "I've let you down in a lot of ways, and I'm sorry for that."

Skylar didn't want his apologies. Except she kind of did. But what she didn't want was to talk about the past all over again.

"Do you have a girlfriend?" she asked.

The question had been in her mind since they'd reconnected, and she'd been curious where he was in his personal life. If he did have a girlfriend, did he plan to introduce her to Shiloh?

Skylar didn't like that idea at all.

"Nope. Ever since my sister passed away, I've had other things to focus on." He hesitated, then said, "Do you have a boyfriend?"

It was weird that not that long ago, she'd had one. It felt like she'd lived a lifetime since the breakup. She hadn't thought at all about Emmett since the day she'd gotten the call from her mom.

As she thought of him, she felt nothing. Apparently, a family health emergency was the cure for the breakup blues.

"No." She didn't tell him that recently she'd had one. Or that the guy had broken up with her because she hadn't let him get close.

Aiden looked at her expectantly, as if waiting for her to expand on her answer. He could wait from then until eternity because she wasn't going to. The last thing she wanted to do was tell him that she'd just been dumped. Again.

She could only hope that he would move on or allow himself to be guided in a new direction for their conversation. "Have you met any of Cole's girlfriends?"

Aiden gave a huff of laughter. "A couple."

"We haven't met any of them."

"That's because he would only bring someone home that he was really serious about."

"And he hasn't felt that way about any of them?"

"Nope. He said he didn't really have the desire to commit to marriage while he was at the height of his career."

"So why bother dating?"

"It looked good, I suppose," Aiden said with a shrug.

"Did he lead them on?"

"No. They know what the score is. The relationship lasts until the ladies call it off."

"So weird," Skylar said with a shake of her head. "I'd have never imagined that Cole would end up like that. The pair of you and relationships. So messed up."

She waited for him to defend himself and Cole, but he didn't.

"You're probably right," he said. "But hopefully it's not too late to change our ways."

"Even though Cole is still at the height of his career?"

"Maybe he'll meet someone who'll make him reconsider his stance."

"Mom would like that," Skylar said. "She's determined to get all her children married."

"Even you?"

"Oh, I think Mom's given up on me."

"You've never brought anyone to meet the family?"

And now they were back to her dating life. "Not a chance. Never got serious enough about anyone to risk bringing them home to Mom."

This time it was Aiden who redirected the conversation, asking about the grandkids in the family. Though Skylar didn't spend much time with any of them, she still knew who belonged to who and their relative ages.

"Cole didn't tell you about them?" Skylar asked after she'd given him the rundown.

That got a laugh out of Aiden. "I think the guy has trouble remembering the spouses of his married siblings, let alone all the kids."

"Yeah, Cole wasn't here for most of the weddings."

Aiden's expression turned sad as he stared out the window. "Having lost my one sibling, I wish Cole had more appreciation for what he has."

Skylar had to admit that she wasn't as appreciative of her siblings—beyond Charli—as she could have been. But distance and lack of communication wasn't conducive to building strong relationships.

As she took in Aiden's profile, Skylar had a momentary thought, wondering if she'd be attracted to Aiden if this was the first time they were meeting.

Frowning, she looked away. Why would she even think about something like that?

Regardless of how he was now, he'd betrayed her in the past. And he was only back in her life because she'd sought him out for Shiloh's sake. Not for hers, and certainly not for his.

So there would be no thinking about him like that. None at all.

CHAPTER ELEVEN

Aiden couldn't believe that it had worked out for him to spend time with Shiloh. Even though he'd asked Skylar to check with Charli about giving them a break for a couple of hours, he really hadn't expected her to do it.

But thankfully, she'd spoken to Charli and had shown up herself, even though it had meant spending time with him. And she hadn't even protested when he'd come bearing the meal he'd remembered as being her favorite from back when they were dating.

As he sat across from her, it became harder and harder to not remember the times they'd sat like that on their numerous dates. They'd often eaten fast food because it was what he could afford at the time on the pay he got from delivering pizzas or from one of the other part-time jobs he'd held.

Her smiles didn't come as readily, and she didn't laugh as easily, but she was still just as beautiful as she'd been back then. It surprised him that she didn't have a boyfriend, because she'd always garnered male attention, even back when they were dating.

But even with all that male attention, she'd never given him any reason to think that he couldn't trust her. Even after he'd left for college, he hadn't worried. Unfortunately, he had been nowhere near that trustworthy.

Which was undoubtedly why there was a lot of wariness in her gaze whenever they interacted.

It was his hope that over time, she'd see that she could trust him to be a better man than he'd been nine years ago. He wanted her to know that he wouldn't do anything to hurt Shiloh. And though he wished he could play a bigger role in her life, he was going to respect the roles and responsibility Charli and Blake had in Shiloh's life.

Alongside Skylar's beauty and wariness was a hardness that might be partly due to becoming an adult and the difficulties that could bring. Unfortunately, he had a feeling that what happened between them and with Shiloh had added to it.

"I think Shiloh is supposed to go home in the next few days, following her last treatment," Skylar said, her gaze on Shiloh.

"I'm sure she and Charli and Blake are looking forward to that."

Skylar nodded. "I would imagine so. Although, for me personally, I think I'd find being in the hospital reassuring, to some extent."

"Yeah. Is there a concern with them being over an hour's drive from the hospital?"

"I think they might have been more worried if we didn't have so many medical professionals in the family to help them should something come up."

"Will they be limiting visitors for her?"

"I don't know," Skylar said. "Are you thinking of your mom and Willow?"

"Yes. I know they'd love to meet her, but I don't want to push."

"I'm sure Charli understands that," Skylar said. "And I'm sure that Shiloh would also like to meet them."

He knew his mom was happy that, after losing two members of their small family, they had added one. Of course, his mom wished the circumstances were different. But at the end of the day, Shiloh was another grandchild for her, and she was thrilled about it.

Charli and Blake ended up coming back before the two hours were up. As soon as they came into the room, they both walked over to Shiloh's bed. Charli bent to press a kiss to her head.

"How was everything?" Blake asked as they came over to the table. "Did she wake up at all?"

"Yes." Skylar gave a brief recount of the time they'd been there, including the small amount of food she'd eaten.

"Oh, I'm glad she ate," Charli said. "Hopefully, her appetite is returning a bit."

"Aiden brought her some gifts from his mom and Willow," Skylar said.

"That's lovely." Charli took the bag Aiden had picked up and held out to her. "She loves to color and read. Please thank your mom and Willow for us."

"I'll pass that on," Aiden said.

"I know your mom and Willow would like to meet Shiloh," Charli said. "And Shiloh would definitely like that as well. I'm hoping that once she's home, we'll be able to set something up."

"Will you prepare Willow with information about Shiloh's diagnosis?" Blake asked. "I would prefer that Shiloh not have to discuss it. She knows what's going on, but I think it would be good if the two of them could just be a couple of kids hanging out together."

"I'll make sure she knows what's going on," Aiden assured them. He'd already talked a bit about it with Willow, and he'd make sure she had more information before she met Shiloh.

"Thank you for coming here, so Blake and I could go on a date," Charli said as she gave Skylar a hug, then held out her arms to Aiden.

It felt a bit weird to hug Charli, as that had not been part of their dynamic when he'd last been around her. But he'd take a hug over a punch in the gut, which was what he was on the watch for whenever he was around Skylar's family. Well, mainly her brothers.

"I'm happy to come back any time to babysit," Aiden said.

As he said the words, a memory of his dad came to him. Bethany had asked their dad if he'd babysat her and Aiden a lot when they were little. His dad had said that he'd never babysat them.

Bethany had been indignant, insisting that she remembered at least one time when he'd stayed with them.

He'd corrected her, stating that he hadn't been babysitting them. He'd been taking care of them, as a father should.

Unfortunately, in Aiden's reality, he wasn't a parent taking care of his child. He *was* a babysitter.

"I'm going to head for home," Skylar said as she shuffled onto her crutches.

Charli gave her another hug. "Thanks for coming, sis."

Aiden followed her out of the room, then kept his stride short as they made their way down the hallway, maneuvering around people and medical equipment. When they reached the elevator, they didn't have to wait long.

Thankfully, there was only one person on it when the doors slid open. However, it stopped on the next floor down and several people joined them. Aiden positioned himself between Skylar and the others in the elevator car so that no one bumped into her or her crutches.

When they reached the main floor, he let the others exit before placing his hand on the door to keep it open so Skylar could leave the elevator.

The sun hadn't completely set yet since the summer days were long, and warm fresh air embraced them as they stepped from the air-conditioned building.

"Thank you again for setting this up," Aiden said. "I'm sure it wasn't what you wanted to do."

Skylar leaned on her crutches as they stood off to the side, out of the way of the doors. Last time they'd had a more emotionally intense moment standing there, and Aiden hoped there wouldn't be a repeat of it. He wasn't sure he could handle it.

"I did it more for Charli, Blake, and Shiloh."

"I know," Aiden told her. "But I still appreciate it."

"I don't suppose we'll be doing it again," Skylar said. "If they're going to be going home soon."

Aiden wanted to be able to spend more time with Shiloh, but he had a feeling that if he did, Skylar would not be part of it. That made him sad because it felt like they should be building this relationship with Shiloh together. He was well aware, however, that she didn't feel the same way.

"Why don't you give me your car keys," he said, holding out his hand.

"Why?"

"I'll go get your car and bring it around so you don't have to use your crutches all the way to the parking lot."

"It's not that far."

Aiden lifted his eyebrows and kept his hand out. He remembered how she'd been in high school when she'd ended up on crutches, so he was sure that she would actually like to not have to walk on the crutches any further than necessary.

"C'mon, I know you don't like walking on those things," he said. "I suppose I could carry you like I used to, or... I could just take the keys and bring the car around to you."

She glared at him. Her expression was so familiar that it brought a smile to his face. "C'mon, Sky. Hand them over. You know you want to."

"Fine." Rolling her eyes at him, she dug into the pocket of her jeans and pulled out a key ring with a fob. Holding it above his hand, she sighed, then dropped it into his palm.

After telling him what she was driving and approximately where she'd parked, he turned and headed for the parking lot. The smile over the exchange didn't fade as he walked away from Skylar.

The exchange... her reactions... it had all been so familiar and a poignant reminder of the past. Not just of the time when they'd dated, but also of all the years they'd known each other. Which had basically been their whole lives.

He and Cole had met in kindergarten, and it hadn't been long after their meeting that he'd met Cole's little sister. She'd had long, wavy brown hair and big brown eyes, just like Shiloh had, and she'd become a fixture in his life as well.

As he neared the area where Skylar had said she'd parked, he pressed the fob and listened for the chirp. Soon, he found the vehicle and slid behind the wheel.

It didn't take long to circle around and pull up to where he'd left Skylar. There were other cars there also picking up people, so he quickly hopped out and waited by the door for Skylar to circle around the car.

"Thank you," she said, leaning in to put her crutches on the passenger side, then she hopped around to angle herself to slide into the driver's seat.

"Talk to you later," Aiden said, then closed her door and moved out of the way of the vehicles.

Once she'd pulled away, he headed for his own car to make the short drive home to his mom and Willow.

Over the next few days, Aiden found himself revisiting the exchange he and Skylar had had. And along with the exchange, memories of their time together growing up and dating.

There had been a time in his life when he'd believed that he'd do anything to protect Skylar. First as his best friend's sister, then as his girlfriend.

They'd grown up together, sharing many moments of laughter and joy. Even when he and Cole had found her to be a pain sometimes, especially when they were newly turned thirteen years old. Skylar had just been eleven, but they'd still tolerated her and let her tag along.

The two years' difference in their ages hadn't meant as much when he was seventeen and noticing that Cole's little sister was actually a beautiful young woman. When he'd asked her out on a date, her parents had made it clear the only reason they were allowing her to date him at fifteen was because they knew him and trusted him to treat her well.

He'd promised that he would take care of Skylar and be a good boyfriend to her.

Only he hadn't been.

He'd been terrible to her.

During the years since he'd last seen her, thoughts of that time had come to mind more than he would have wanted. There had been times he'd wanted to ask Cole how Skylar was doing, but he'd bitten his tongue.

Cole had stuck to Aiden's request that they not talk about Skylar, and Aiden hadn't been sure how to change that. Or if he wanted to open that door for Cole to ask for more details about the breakup.

Initially, when guilt had tried to edge its way into his emotions, he'd managed to tell himself that the breakup had been for the best. But as he'd matured, and then experienced the trauma of losing his dad and sister, the guilt had surfaced more and more.

However, he hadn't known what to do with it.

Would he have ever contacted Skylar if she hadn't appeared in his office?

Maybe when their paths had crossed, which he'd assumed would happen at some point. Though he hadn't known exactly when or where that would be, it had seemed inevitable because of their connections to Cole.

But that's not what happened. And now she'd had to accept him back into her life when it seemed to be the last thing she wanted. Which wasn't a surprise at all. And he also couldn't blame her for how she might feel.

Now that he'd spent some time with her, Aiden really wanted to find a way to make things up to her. Unfortunately, absolutely nothing came to mind.

That evening, after he'd spent time with Willow before she went to bed, he decided to call Cole again. He was hoping that his friend had talked to Skylar and could give Aiden some idea of where her mind was at.

"How's it going, bro?" Cole asked when he answered Aiden's call. "Guess Skylar hasn't offed you yet, huh?"

"I don't think she's even tried," Aiden told him.

"Well, I have a feeling she's thought about it."

"Have you talked to her?" he asked.

"I have," Cole said. "And she is not your biggest fan."

"Tell me something I don't know."

"You don't blame her for not liking you, do you?"

"Of course not," Aiden said. "I deserve how she feels about me."

There was a beat of silence before Cole said, "Do you wish that she didn't feel that way?"

"Well, no one wants someone to dislike them, even if they do deserve it," Aiden told him. "And it would make things easier, for Shiloh's sake, if we got along."

"That would be true if you were actually co-parenting, but you're not. You don't have to spend time with Shiloh together," Cole said. "Unless that's what you want."

Aiden realized that he *did* want that.

"Dude..." Cole said when he didn't answer right away. "Don't tell me you think you have a second chance with Skylar. I hate to tell you that I'm not sure that's even remotely possible."

"I understand that." Unfortunate, but true. "But if we could at least be friends again, I think it would be the best thing all around. It's not going to be good for Shiloh if she thinks her birth parents hate each other or can't get along."

"I wish you the best of luck with that," Cole said. "Truly I do, but you hurt Skylar pretty badly."

Aiden slumped forward in his seat. "I am aware of that. I just want to know if there's *anything* I can do to help make it easier for her to get along with me."

"I have a feeling she'd say you staying away from her would help her get along with you."

Not exactly what he wanted to hear, but completely understandable. "Don't suppose you'd care to go to bat for me."

"You want me to play matchmaker?" Cole asked, skepticism heavy in his voice.

"No. Not a matchmaker. Just maybe help her to see that a friendship between us isn't the worst thing in the world. I'm not even asking for us to be best friends. Just... friends."

"I'll see what I can do," Cole said. "But I make no promises."

"Any chance you're going to come home anytime soon?"

"Serenity isn't home to me anymore, bro," Cole said.

"You know what I mean. Family is home for us, regardless of where we might actually live."

"I am kind of curious about everything going on with the family at the moment," Cole said. "And you're not the only one trying to get me back to Serenity."

"Who else?"

"Jay and Will have both told me I should come home for a bit. Maybe get myself tested for Shiloh."

"That's an excellent reason for you to come back," Aiden said.

"Yes, it is," Cole agreed. "I'll see."

Conversation moved—as it often did with them—to basketball. It was the off-season, so Cole wasn't actively practicing, but he was never one to slack, even then.

It was hard to believe that he'd been playing pro for almost six years already. They'd both ended up with the careers they'd hoped for.

Early on in his teen years, Aiden had thought that he wanted to play pro as well. However, it soon became clear that he could never play at the level Cole did.

Aiden had been good, but Cole had been amazing. So by the time he made it to college, Aiden had known he needed another career path. Which was how he'd ended up in architecture, and he was happy with that.

By the time their call ended, Aiden thought maybe he had a chance of Cole helping him with Skylar.

But he could also help himself by going places where she might be, to see if she could get used to him being around, even in just a peripheral way.

CHAPTER TWELVE

Skylar looked out at the manicured yard and the woods beyond it as she sat on the back deck, her leg propped up on a chair in front of her. It was a lovely warm, sunny day, but the most she could do to enjoy it was to sit outside and stare at the nature that surrounded her parents' home.

The alternative was to be sitting in her apartment in Vegas. Which wasn't a bad alternative, necessarily. But her view there certainly wasn't as nice as the one she was currently enjoying.

It had been a couple of days since she and Aiden had babysat Shiloh for Charli and Blake, which had left her with a lot of emotions that she wasn't sure how to handle.

Seeing Shiloh in that hospital bed, looking so frail, had cemented in her the need to stay in Serenity. It felt like it was important for her to stay close by.

It was getting easier to be around Shiloh. The confusion of emotions when it came to her—and Aiden—was still there, but the longer she was around them and Charli and Blake, things were slowly gaining clarity.

Well, the clarity came more regarding the situation with Shiloh, Charli and Blake. There was little clarity regarding Aiden and how she felt about him and what had happened.

It seemed that the more she was around Aiden, the more confused she became. That was not what she wanted. During the years since their disastrous breakup, her feelings and emotions concerning Aiden had always been very clear.

She hated him for what he'd done to her. The breakup and his reaction to the pregnancy. But now that she'd spent some time with him, that clarity had devolved into confusion.

Though she told herself that she still hated Aiden for what he'd done, it wasn't as easy to hate him when she was around him. Like the exchange they had outside the hospital the other night.

His offer to get her car had been thoughtful, but it was his mention of when she'd last been on crutches and how he'd helped her that had made it difficult to ignore the good moments in their past. Which is what she'd tried to do for the past nine years.

There had been no point in thinking about the good times. They weren't together anymore, and that wasn't going to change. Sticking with anger and hate had been easy.

Now, however, it was much harder.

Being around him was hard enough, but having him treat her well and bring up fun memories from the past made it even harder. She wasn't sure how to deal with him as a mature man instead of the younger version of him who'd treated her so callously.

He seemed to be very different from the person who had dumped her, and she really struggled with that. It would have been so much easier if he'd been willing to do the blood test but had no interest in Shiloh. Easier for her, but she was coming to understand it wouldn't have been good for Shiloh.

She'd not just gained an uncle, along with the knowledge of who he truly was, she'd also gained another grandmother and cousin. It was selfish of Skylar to wish that away, just so things would have been easier for her.

She needed to stop thinking about just herself. To stop being selfish.

Skylar sighed, wishing she could escape the conflicted feelings. But she had a feeling that even if she went back to her apartment in Las Vegas, they would follow her there.

Her phone rang, interrupting her thoughts. She reached out and picked it up from where it sat on the small table beside her chair. Also there, was a tall frosty glass of sweetly tart lemonade that her mom had made earlier.

Seeing Cole's name on the screen, Skylar frowned. She'd already heard from him once a couple of days earlier, so she wasn't sure why he'd be phoning again.

"Hey, Cole," she said when she answered the phone.

"How're you doing, sis?"

"I'm okay. Just sitting on the back deck, enjoying the nice weather."

"Sounds nice."

"It's not bad. At least it's not as hot as Vegas."

"Are you planning to stick around Serenity for awhile?"

"Probably until my ankle has healed enough for me to go back to work."

"I'm surprised you're willing to stay there," Cole said. "Considering Aiden is living around there now."

Skylar didn't need to be reminded of that. "Have you spoken to him?"

"Yes. A couple of times."

She doubted that he would tell her what they talked about. But despite everything she'd told him about what had happened in the past with her and Aiden, she was pretty sure that they'd continue to be best friends.

They had been friends for most of their lives, so it stood to reason that they would continue to be best friends. Even when they were teens, Skylar had realized that if Cole had to choose between her or Aiden, he'd most likely pick his best friend.

It was one of the reasons she'd never told him about what had happened.

But now he knew, and Skylar was sure that his friendship with Aiden was still intact.

"Was there something you needed from me?" Skylar asked. Her tone of voice was probably harsher than it should be because of her thoughts about the friendship her brother and ex-boyfriend shared.

There was a long pause before Cole responded. "I was just wondering how you were doing. How you felt about Aiden and the situation with Shiloh."

"I don't think how I feel about any of that is relevant to anything."

"What do you mean?"

"My feelings about all of it haven't mattered to anyone."

"Tell me how you're feeling."

"Why?"

"Because I care about you," Cole said. "I love you and feel bad that you didn't think you could confide in me."

"You're best friends with the man who hurt me very badly."

"That's true, but that doesn't mean I wouldn't understand and support you."

"Would you have supported me not wanting Aiden to meet Shiloh?" she asked. "Or me not wanting Charli and Blake to tell Shiloh about me and Aiden?"

Another long pause confirmed what she'd assumed would be his position.

"Sky, it's not as black and white as that."

"Of course it's not," she said. "For you and everyone else. But for me it is. No one else was there at the end of our relationship. No one else was there when he told me to get rid of the baby."

"He said he told you that because he thought you were trying to trap him."

Instead of anger, Skylar felt sad and a little sick. "You know I'm not like that."

"I do know that," Cole said. "But I also know how much you loved Aiden, and how much you hoped to have a future with him."

"But not enough to lie about being pregnant," she told him. "You know that. Plus, why would I want to be with someone who clearly didn't want to be with me?"

"You're right," he said. "You never would have done that."

"And Aiden knew that, too. He just chose to believe I *would* do something like that in order to justify what he said."

"He knows that what he did back then was wrong," Cole told her. "Both the way he broke up with you and how he reacted when you told him you were pregnant."

Skylar didn't respond to that. Aiden had expressed the same sentiment to her. She'd heard his apology, so she knew he was sorry.

She stared at the birds flying in the sky high above the trees in the distance. Suddenly, she felt weary. Weary of fighting for what she'd thought was right. Weary of being made to feel bad about not wanting what everyone else wanted.

"Sis, I'm sorry," Cole said. "I'm not trying to make you feel bad about what you wanted in this situation. I know this all must have been really hard on you."

"It is hard," Skylar agreed. "But nothing I'm dealing with is as hard as what Shiloh is facing, and what Charli and Blake are experiencing. The focus just needs to be on them, and what is best for them."

She truly believed that. So even though she struggled with what was going on, it was something she needed to keep to herself. This conversation with Cole would be the last time she addressed it.

Maybe she should go back to Vegas. That way, she'd be able to escape the weight of everything.

Shiloh can't escape what she's going through.

The thought slipped into her mind and made her pause.

"Skylar?"

She realized she'd missed something that Cole had said. "What?"

"Are you going to be okay?"

"Of course," she said without hesitation. She'd survived plenty over the past several years, so she'd survive this too.

"I know you probably don't want to hear this, but I think you should try for a friendship with Aiden."

His suggestion didn't surprise her. "I'll take that under consideration."

"Not going to argue with me about it?"

"Nope."

"But you're probably not going to do it, are you?"

"I don't know. I'll just have to see how things go and how I feel."

"Fair enough."

With that, their conversation died out, so Skylar told him she needed to go, and they said goodbye. She set her phone back on the table and picked up her glass of lemonade to take a drink.

Everyone seemed so willing to welcome Aiden back into the fold. Cole's feelings about Aiden weren't a surprise, but the rest of the family's were.

Perhaps she'd done herself a disservice by not telling people what had happened in the past. She'd kept her pain over the breakup to herself, and she'd been alone as she'd tried to heal her shattered heart.

Unfortunately, that hadn't happened before she'd given birth to Shiloh, which had meant that her heart was broken even further as she handed her baby over to her sister and walked away. No one had been there as she'd wept over the loss of the man she loved and the baby they'd created.

So no one truly knew the depth of the hurt she'd experienced because of Aiden's actions, and she wasn't inclined to parade it out for them now.

When Skylar heard the back door open, she looked over to see her mom step out onto the deck with a glass in one hand and a bowl in the other. She wore a pair of dark blue shorts and a light green and white striped tank top in deference to the warmth of the day.

As she joined Skylar, she set the glass and bowl on the table, then settled into the Adirondack chair on the other side of it. Skylar saw that the bowl held a mixture of berries.

"Cole called me," Skylar said after she'd eaten some of the fruit.

"Really?" Her mom turned toward her. "What did he want?"

"To check on me, I guess," she said. "And to tell me I should become friends with Aiden."

"That would be a good idea, I think," her mom said.

Skylar stared at her for a long moment, then shifted her gaze to the yard once again. "Why?"

"It would make things easier for you and for everyone else too, especially Shiloh."

Like with Cole, her mom's words weren't a surprise. "Can you explain to me why you and everyone else are so willing to accept Aiden after what he did?"

"I can only speak for myself," her mom said. "I learned a hard lesson about how I treated people when Kelsey came into the family."

"What do you mean?" Skylar hadn't been around when Zane and Kelsey had come to live in Serenity. "What happened with Kelsey?"

"I wasn't as welcoming to her as I should have been."

"Why weren't you? Was there something wrong with her?"

Her mom shook her head. "I had a hard time with her relationship with Zane, especially because he'd changed after things had ended with his previous girlfriend. We hardly knew Kelsey, and then they eloped, so we weren't even included in the wedding. It was the first time someone had come into the family that we didn't know at all, and I didn't handle it like I should have. I reacted badly, I know that. I didn't show God's love the way I should have."

"She came home with Zane for Christmas one year, though, didn't she?" Skylar seemed to recall meeting her on one of her quick visits home over the holidays.

"Yes, but you know how chaotic that time of year is," her mom said. "They were only here for a couple of days, so I didn't have any chance to get to know her."

"So you didn't treat her well?"

"I wasn't as welcoming as I should have been, and God really convicted me of my attitude. I'm just grateful that Kelsey was gracious and accepted my apology."

"What does that have to do with Aiden?"

Her mom didn't answer right away as she took a sip of her lemonade, then held the glass between her hands in her lap. "I know he did some wrong things in the past. I know he hurt you... badly. But I see the man he is now. Someone who seems regretful and apologetic for what he did."

Skylar couldn't argue with that. Aiden did seem to regret what had happened.

"I'm going to give him the benefit of the doubt," her mom said. "Charli and Blake are willing to give him a chance to prove he's changed. So I am too."

In order to not have to respond, Skylar put a strawberry in her mouth. Her mom hadn't told her anything she hadn't already known. Because they were Christians, she'd been aware that they would be more likely to give Aiden a second chance if he seemed apologetic for what happened than to condemn him.

"How do you feel about Aiden being back?"

"You know I'm not happy about it," Skylar said. "I might have been the one to tell him about Shiloh, but I didn't want him to come back into our lives. I'd really hoped that he'd take the blood test but keep his distance."

"But he didn't."

"Nope. He didn't." She took a blueberry from the bowl, but didn't eat it right away. Rolling the smooth fruit between her fingers, she said, "And now everyone thinks we should be friends."

"I'm sure that wouldn't be easy, darling," her mom said, her tone gentle. "And no one thinks you have to be close like you once were. But a friendship of even a casual nature would make things easier."

Skylar tried to picture how that might work with Aiden. So far, when they'd been around each other, she'd made a concerted effort to keep her negative feelings about him under wraps. Some times more successfully than others.

There was a part of her that worried that if she let go of the hurt and pain of the past, what would take its place would open her up to more hurt.

"Maybe you should start praying for Aiden," her mom suggested.

Skylar managed not to laugh at the suggestion.

Prayer hadn't been a part of her life for a long time. Though she prayed for Shiloh, it was hard to imagine praying for Aiden.

"When you pray for someone, it becomes more difficult to hold onto your anger or hate towards them."

Skylar figured that that was probably true. Because of that, she wasn't sure she wanted to pray for Aiden, even if she had been a praying person.

There was a light touch on her arm. "Have I told you how glad I am that you've stuck around?"

Looking at her, Skylar covered her mom's hand with her own. "It's not been as difficult as I thought it might be."

"I'm glad to hear that." Her mom smiled. "Are you going to stay until your ankle is better?"

"Probably. No sense in going back to Vegas just to sit in my apartment."

"Maybe you'll decide that Serenity is a great place to live."

"I already know it's a great place to live," Skylar told her. "It just doesn't work for my job. There's no airport here."

"There's one in Coeur d'Alene," her mom said. "And I know private jets fly in there. Hudson flies in and out of there whenever he uses one of Alexander's planes."

Skylar didn't know that she'd be able to get a job there as a flight attendant, but she could probably find a job doing something else. She wasn't sure she wanted to do that, however.

She liked her job. Though she wasn't thrilled about living in Vegas, she liked her apartment and the opportunity to visit lots of places around the world. Moving back to Serenity hadn't been part of her plan for her life.

Her mom squeezed her arm, then let go. "Okay. Moving on."

Skylar chuckled softly. "Moving on."

They discussed the latest news on Shiloh, which indicated that the little girl would be discharged soon. Then they'd have to wait. Wait to see if the treatment had been effective in getting rid of the leukemia. If not, the next step might be the stem cell transplant and all that that involved.

There had been no results from the blood tests yet. Though she knew it was a long shot, Skylar really hoped that there would be a match from among the ones who had been tested. She didn't care who it was, just so long as it was someone. Even Aiden.

As she sat there thinking about her birth daughter, Skylar realized that if she was going to purposely pray for anyone, it should be for Shiloh. But the thought her mom had planted in her mind about praying for Aiden wouldn't leave her alone.

But she wondered if God would hear her prayers for either of them.

CHAPTER THIRTEEN

Aiden guided his car into an empty spot in the church parking lot. He still wasn't entirely sure why he was there, but a large part of what had propelled him that day was a sense of gratitude.

Gratitude that he'd had the opportunity to meet and get to know his daughter. Even though he couldn't take on the role of father to her, he was still in her life. And for that, he was grateful.

That gratitude had led him to make the decision to seek out the church where he'd first made a profession of faith and also the family who had played a role in that.

Aiden pushed open his car door, then reached back for the Bible he'd placed on the passenger seat. It was his dad's, given to him by his mom when he'd told her that he was planning to go to Serenity for church that morning. His mom and Willow hadn't come with him because they regularly attended a church near their home in Coeur d'Alene.

He had gone with them on occasion, but his attendance was sporadic. Perhaps his mom had sensed that him deciding to go to the church in Serenity was something different and special, which was why she'd chosen that day to give him his dad's Bible.

Aiden didn't like that tragedy was what had ended up bringing him back to God and opening his eyes to his failings in the past. But he felt like God was giving him the strength and desire to take accountability for his past actions.

With broad strides, he crossed the parking lot to the large front doors. The day was already warm, so it was a relief to step into the coolness of the building.

Glancing around, he spotted Wilder first, but he didn't approach him. Aiden still wasn't sure how the man felt about him, and he wasn't really feeling up to a confrontation before the morning service.

Instead, he headed for the doors that led to the sanctuary. Once through them, he stepped to the side, taking in the sight of the space that looked much the same as it had the last time he'd been there.

Memories flitted through his mind as he stood there. First, of him and Cole and the other friends they'd had at the church, attending youth group together when they'd gone into ninth grade. Then Skylar had joined them, and as she'd blossomed from best friend's annoying little sister to beautiful teen, he'd been drawn to her.

Any time there had been a service, he'd been there to sit beside her. Any time there had been a youth event, he was there with her.

Most of their dates had been as part of a group. They'd gone bowling together. They'd skated hand in hand at the roller rink. In the winter, they'd bundled up and gone ice skating with their friends. And afterwards, they'd sat around a fire built near the outdoor rink, pressing close to keep warm as they drank hot chocolate.

So many memories of that happier time bombarded him.

"Good to see you here, Aiden." Jay's voice dragged him from the past as the man's hand landed on Aiden's shoulder.

He turned to see Jay standing there with his wife, Misha, and a young girl he assumed was Ciara, who'd been just a toddler when he'd last seen her. "Good to see you again, too."

"Are you planning to take a seat?" Jay asked.

He glanced at the pews. "Yep."

Aiden's intention had been to just sit at the back. However, he soon found himself following Jay and Misha down the aisle to the front. Several of the Halverson siblings and their spouses arrived right behind them, including Skylar, who made her way carefully down the aisle on her crutches.

When they were all settled in their seats, Aiden somehow found himself next to Skylar. He hadn't intended to make things uncomfortable for her by showing up at the church, so hopefully she didn't think that.

There was plenty of space between them, though. It was space that would never have been there when they were dating. But that was the past. He had to keep reminding himself of that.

The service format had changed little, though some of the songs were new. He didn't recognize the people on the stage playing the instruments. Previously, members of the Halverson family had been part of the worship team.

When Pastor Kennedy stood up, Aiden smiled. The older man still looked much the same as he had when he'd last seen him. The pastor had the older kids that were in the service come to the front. After chatting with them for a couple of minutes, he said a prayer before dismissing them for their children's program in the basement.

The familiarity of the format of the service made Aiden feel at ease. Skylar, on the other hand, didn't seem to be relaxed at all.

She stood when everyone else did, but she didn't sing along. Which was odd, because in the past, she'd loved singing. When they sat down, she crossed her injured leg over her other one and kept her hands folded in her lap, her spine straight and stiff.

Why was she coming to church if she didn't want to be there? He doubted that her family would have forced her to attend. However, she might have felt like she didn't have a choice.

He couldn't deny that he enjoyed seeing her again, though her expression hadn't changed at all when she'd spotted him.

The more time they spent around each other, the more he struggled with how to be in Shiloh's life without constantly wondering how things might have been between him and Skylar had he not messed up so badly. He thought that perhaps they'd be living a completely different life as parents to Shiloh and possibly more children.

Even though she said she didn't currently have a boyfriend, he wondered if she'd had any serious relationships over the years. If there had been any man she'd been tempted to settle down with.

Immediately following their breakup, he'd casually dated a lot of different women. It had been fun at first, and he'd also relished the freedom once he hadn't been tied to just one woman anymore.

But within about six months, it didn't feel like much fun anymore. And the one-time dates no longer held the appeal he'd thought they would.

Near the end of his junior year, he finally found someone he'd enjoyed spending time with. They'd been together for six months before she'd broken it off. At that point, he'd chosen to focus on finishing college, then getting a job. Only dating sporadically.

But when his dad died, Aiden had felt like his world had crashed and then narrowed in focus. Not long after that, his sister's death changed the trajectory of everything once again, and any thought of a relationship had vanished from his mind.

Aiden wished that he'd recognized what he'd had with Skylar. That he hadn't thought he needed to date a bunch of women before he could settle for just one.

He should have gone to his parents for advice on how they'd handled going from high school sweethearts to something more serious. He should have asked his dad how he knew with certainty that his mom was the one he wanted to spend the rest of his life with when he'd been so young.

The reality was that if he had loved Skylar enough, he wouldn't have wondered if there was a better woman for him. He could see now that his maturity level then hadn't allowed him to love and understand Skylar enough to cherish a relationship with her.

But now... for some strange reason, Aiden couldn't help wondering if there was a way to breach her walls and find something with her. Even if it was just a friendship.

Pulling his thoughts back to the service, Aiden tried to focus on Pastor Kennedy as he spoke, knowing he was probably going to have a discussion with his mom about it later that day.

When the man gave a reference, Aiden opened his dad's Bible. The pages were thin, but his dad had highlighted several passages and written in the margins. It was all he could do not to be distracted by them. The familiar scrawl brought tears to his eyes, but he blinked them away.

His dad had highlighted the very same passage that Pastor Kennedy had read.

Romans 12:3: *Do not be conformed to this world, but be transformed by the renewal of your mind, that by testing you may discern what is the will of God, what is good and acceptable and perfect.*

Aiden wondered if his dad and mom had talked about the verse. Had she highlighted it in her Bible, too?

His dad hadn't been a Christian his whole life, the way the Halverson parents had been. But regardless, his mom and dad had been good and loving parents. Them becoming Christians hadn't meant a significant change for him, since he'd been an adult and out of their house by then.

It had felt, however, that their love for him and Bethany had deepened, and had been a significant catalyst to Bethany becoming a Christian too, shortly before their dad had passed away. In the end, his family had become more active in their faith than he was in his, even though he'd been a Christian longer.

Skylar shifted beside him, and Aiden glanced over at her. There was tension in her profile, and Aiden wondered what he'd missed.

As if sensing his gaze, she turned her head, and their eyes met. For all that her body conveyed control, the emotion in her eyes suggested that perhaps that control was only an outward illusion.

He'd never dealt with that depth of emotion from Skylar before. Not to say her emotions had been shallow, particularly at the end of their relationship. However, he hadn't been interested in emotional depth at that time.

Skylar blinked and turned her attention back to the stage, effectively shutting him out.

Aiden hoped that his mom didn't ask too many questions about the sermon. His thoughts had been scattered in a few too many directions, making it hard to focus on what Pastor Kennedy was saying.

Aiden hadn't planned to linger once the service was over, but he found himself invited to the home shared by Lee, Zane, and their wives.

When he looked at Skylar to see how she felt about the invitation, she met his gaze but didn't indicate what she thought. Not that he really needed her to reveal anything. Aiden had a pretty good idea of what she would want him to do.

In the end, he accepted the invitation.

"Can I bring anything?" he asked Jay, who had, surprisingly, been the one to issue the invitation.

"Pretty sure they have it all in hand," he said. "Unless you have a specific type of soda you like to drink."

"They live where Janessa and Charli used to, right?"

"Yep. We're keeping the house in the family, it seems."

"Okay. I'll see you there in a bit."

In his car a few minutes later, Aiden pulled out his phone to call his mom.

"Are you on your way home, sweetie?" his mom asked. "Willow and I have eaten already because she was hungry, but there's a plate in the fridge for you."

"Actually, that's why I'm calling. Jay invited me to lunch with the family."

"Oh, that's nice. I take it you accepted, and that's why you're calling?"

"Yes. So I'm not going to be home until later unless you need me home before that."

"I absolutely do not need you home sooner," his mom said. "You enjoy yourself and say hi from us."

"I will," Aiden told her. "See you later."

After they said goodbye, Aiden dropped his phone into the cup holder. He glanced around and saw that the parking lot was about half empty, so he started up the car and left.

By the time he got to the house, several cars were already parked in the driveway and along the curb. That meant he had to park partway down the block and walk.

Which was fine because it gave him time to prepare to see Skylar again.

As he climbed the stairs, he realized how weird it was to be joining a Halverson gathering without Cole. For as long as he could remember, Cole had been his connection to the family. He had never attended any of their gatherings without his best friend also being there.

That day, Cole wasn't there. Instead, Aiden's connection was through a little girl and her birth mom.

When he reached the house, Lee answered the door. He gave Aiden a smile as he held out his hand. Once he had hold of Aiden's hand, he pulled him in for a quick bro hug.

"Good to see you again, man," Lee said. "Glad you could join us."

"Hope it's not a problem that I've shown up."

"It's not at all. Jay let me know he'd invited you."

Lee led the way into the kitchen, where he slowed to let Aiden greet Zane and the women there before heading on out to the back deck. Hudson was there, along with Wilder and a young boy whose parentage Aiden had no clue about.

Aiden approached Wilder warily. It seemed that Jay had gotten over his upset with Aiden, so perhaps Wilder had as well.

"Guess I gotta be nice to you," Wilder said.

The words might have stung if Aiden hadn't been able to see the humor on the guy's face. "I guess so."

"Lexi's still ticked at me over the last incident."

"Somehow I doubt that," Hudson said. "You have the ability to annoy people into not being mad at you anymore. Honestly, I don't know how you do it."

"It works the best on Lexi, to be fair."

"Well, the one person it never works on is Kayleigh."

Wilder grinned. "True. When I try to cajole her into not being irritated anymore, her irritation only intensifies."

"One would think you'd have learned not to do it anymore," Hudson said.

"Life's always more fun when you don't learn all the lessons you're supposed to."

"Tell that to Kayleigh."

Aiden felt himself relax with the familiar banter of the Halverson family. Charli and Blake weren't there, but Layla and Amelia had come together, and there was some talk about Layla having gotten a new-to-her car.

By the time Skylar arrived with her parents, he felt at ease enough to have held a couple of conversations with different people. When Skylar walked out onto the deck on her crutches, her gaze met his. However, she didn't move in his direction.

Shifting from one foot to the other, Aiden felt a bit of doubt that they'd ever be able to build a friendship. One where they'd be able to chat comfortably and be at ease in each other's presence, especially when they were also with Shiloh.

The awkwardness currently between them was almost bad enough to make him want to leave. Not because of how it made him feel, but because it undoubtedly made her feel stressed and unhappy to be around him.

He was so desperate to find a way to be part of his birth daughter's life that he wasn't giving as much consideration to Skylar's feelings as perhaps he should.

He also wanted to be on good terms with the Halverson family at large. Like it or not, their lives were all now intertwined beyond more than just his friendship with Cole.

"How's the ankle, Sky?" Wilder asked as she approached him and Aiden.

"Getting better every day," she said.

"Does that mean you can go back to work soon?"

Skylar frowned. "Nope. I still can't wear anything but a supportive runner, and that doesn't cut it for my uniform for work."

"No exceptions?" When Skylar shook her head, Wilder turned to Hudson. "Is that normal for those flights you rich dudes take?"

Hudson shrugged. "It wouldn't be an issue with the attendants on our planes. At least not anymore. Alexander has made things a little less formal over the years unless we have someone we really need to impress on board. Then we're all dressed a little more formally."

"We have a pretty strict dress code," Skylar said. "Since we deal with people who rent our planes, we have to give them the experience they pay for."

"So you'll just hang around here for the time being?" Wilder asked.

"Perhaps. I haven't decided yet."

"Is there a *reason* you have to be back in Vegas?"

"A reason besides my job?"

"Yeah. You know..." Wilder shrugged. "Like a boyfriend?"

Skylar's eyes narrowed at her brother. "I'm not sure I'd tell you if I had one or not."

"So, in other words, no." Wilder turned to Aiden. "How about you?"

"How about me what?"

Wilder crossed his arms. "You got a girlfriend?"

"Nope." He could have been vague like Skylar, but why? It didn't make sense to avoid answering the question.

"Why not? Something wrong with you?"

"Not according to my mom."

Wilder laughed. "Gotta love moms. So if you're perfect—according to Mom McIntyre—what's the problem?"

"You are aware of how my life has gone over the past few years, right?"

Wilder's expression sobered. "Yeah. Sorry about your dad and sister, bro."

"Thanks. Unfortunately, dealing with their passings and trying to help Mom and Willow have filled my hours."

"I can only imagine how that's been," Hudson said. "Losing a parent is terribly difficult, and then losing a sibling on top of that must have been crushing."

It sounded like Hudson might have lost a parent at one time, though Aiden didn't know his history. "It hasn't been easy, that's for sure."

"Excuse me, everyone," Lee said loudly as he clapped his hands. "Let's gather around to pray, then we can dig in."

Aiden stepped closer to the others and closed his eyes. When the prayer was finished, the kids had help to fill their plates first, then the adults gathered around the food-laden table.

Glancing around, Aiden noticed that Skylar was hanging back, probably because holding a plate while being on crutches wasn't very doable.

"Here you go, Aiden," Janessa said as she held out a paper plate for him.

He almost asked for a second one so that he could help Skylar get her food. However, a glance in her direction showed that her mom was with her, holding a couple of plates.

As Aiden waited for the others to get their food, he pondered why he felt such a strong urge to help Skylar. Was he wanting to prove to her that he was a different man than he'd been back when they broke up? Or was he just falling back to how he'd treated her before he'd lost his mind and dumped her?

Back then, when she'd been on crutches, he'd helped her get her food, so he supposed it was natural that his inclinations would go in that direction.

Aiden watched Skylar as she pointed to different foods, which her mom then placed on her plate. As the crowd thinned, he moved closer to the table and chose from the array of foods set out.

When he looked around to see where Skylar was seated, Aiden realized that maybe there was another reason for his desire to help Skylar. It wasn't exactly upsetting to come to that realization. At least not for him.

He had a feeling that Skylar wouldn't feel the same way.

CHAPTER FOURTEEN

After her mom had set her plate on the picnic table, Skylar maneuvered herself onto the bench, then propped the crutches up on the end of the table. Janessa, Will, Jay and Misha were also seated there and greeted her with smiles.

"Hey, Aiden," Jay called out. "Come sit here."

Skylar frowned at her brother as Aiden headed over and put his plate down on the table next to Jay.

"I'm going to get a drink," he said. "Anyone else need one?"

Janessa nudged Skylar's arm. "You don't have a drink."

"Want me to grab you one, Skylar?" Aiden asked.

"Uh, sure."

After she told him her preference, he gave her a nod, then headed toward the large cooler that held cans of soda packed in ice.

"Stop scowling," Janessa said. "Your face is gonna stay that way."

"From what I've seen, that's already happened," Wilder commented drily.

Skylar rolled her eyes at her brother while Lexi elbowed him. "That's not a nice thing to say to your sister."

"You know that teasing my siblings is how I express my love for them," Wilder told his wife.

"You could just say you love us, like a normal person would," Janessa told him.

"But where's the fun in that?"

"Here you go, Sky," Aiden said as he approached her.

She looked up at him as she wrapped her hand around the can he held out to her, the condensation on its smooth surface chilling her fingers. "Thank you."

A quick smile crossed his face as he said, "You're welcome."

He headed back to the other end of the table where he'd set his plate. Settling down on the bench by Jay, he cracked his soda open and lifted the can to take a sip.

Skylar shifted her attention to her meal, taking a bite of the potato salad as she tried not to focus on Aiden.

It hadn't been a big surprise to show up at the house and find Aiden there. In fact, once she'd seen him at church, she would have been more surprised if he hadn't been invited.

She *was* curious as to why he'd shown up for the morning service. At the end of their relationship, she'd known that he had moved away from his faith, and she was sure that Cole had as well. Not that she was pointing fingers at them because she'd basically done the same thing.

It had been hard to find a church to plug into when she'd left Serenity for college. And when she'd discovered she was pregnant, finding a church had dropped completely off her priority list. Since then, she hadn't even attempted to grow in her faith.

She was attending church in Serenity simply to appease her family. It wasn't as bad as she'd thought it would be. In fact, there had been something comforting about being back in the familiarity of her childhood faith.

Glancing down the table, she did another quick category of Aiden's appearance. It was hard not to compare him to the young man she'd fallen in love with.

Though he smiled easily enough as he conversed with her family, she could see that he didn't have the carefree attitude he'd had as a teen. There were dark smudges under his eyes, and he'd lost the glow of youth. The responsibility of caring for his family in light of the tragedy they'd endured seemed to weigh him down.

Sadly for her, none of that had diminished his attractiveness.

It was one of the things that had sparked her initial crush on him. He'd also always treated her well, even when Cole was frustrated with her. Around the time she turned fifteen, their interactions had turned mildly flirtatious as they'd each put out feelers toward the other.

And then there had been their first date. Their first kiss. Holding hands. Hugging.

All of those moments played through her mind in great detail, and familiar butterflies came to life in her stomach. It was like the period of time around the breakup didn't exist. The man he was now was most similar to the one she'd fallen in love with. Not the one who'd broken her heart.

"How're you doing, Sky?" Jay asked. "Ankle doing better?"

"Not better enough." Skylar took a sip of her soda, grateful for the distraction from her thoughts. "I still have pain if I'm not careful."

"I've sprained a few ankles in my day, and they can be so annoying. Almost worse than a break because mentally, it feels like it should heal faster, and sometimes it doesn't."

"Sprained muscles can take a while to heal," Misha said. "It really depends on how badly the muscle and ligaments are impacted."

Conversation flowed easily around the table. Even Aiden was participating, sharing about his life and his career. She was a bit surprised at how well he interacted with her family.

In the past, he would never have shown up without Cole being there. Even when they were dating, he was most at ease when Cole was present, too. The way he conversed with Will and Jay spoke to the maturity he'd gained over the years.

When the guys began talking about basketball and how Cole had done in the most recent season, Janessa and Misha started up their own conversation, centered on the kids. Skylar just listened as she ate, since she had nothing to contribute.

"How are you finding things with Shiloh now that she knows about you?"

Skylar glanced at Janessa before lifting the hotdog her mom had fixed for her. "So far, so good."

"Is it weird?" Misha asked.

"Yes." She didn't really need to ask Misha to clarify. "It was challenging enough when no one else knew. But it feels worse now."

Janessa frowned at her. "What do you mean?"

"Everyone, including Shiloh, just viewed me as her aunt. Now, everyone knows she's my biological daughter, and it just feels... weird. Harder."

"Do you wish she was yours and Aiden's now?"

Skylar shook her head. "Not in the way you mean. I think Charli and Blake are better parents to her given the circumstances, especially with what's going on now. Had the situation been different, sure, it would have been nice to raise her, but that's not how things worked out for us."

Misha nodded. "You seem very determined to live in the moment and not dwell on what might have been."

Well, that all depended on the moment, to be honest, but Skylar decided not to tell her that. She had a feeling that Misha was aware of that.

Was anyone ever able to live completely in the moment? Without any regrets for past decisions?

She didn't think it was too likely.

"I just wish you hadn't thought you had to keep it a secret from us all these years," Janessa said.

"I thought it was for the best at the time."

"Do you still think that?"

"Yes."

"Well, I think you all have handled it quite well," Misha told her. "Shiloh seems to be doing fine with it, from what Charli says."

"She does seem to be taking it all in stride quite well," Janessa agreed.

"It probably helps that they told her she was adopted early on, but then didn't tell her who her birth parents were until later. It gave her time to get used to the concept."

Skylar didn't bother to tell them that had Aiden not agreed to show up for the blood test, Shiloh probably still wouldn't know. She glanced over at Aiden and found him watching her.

The fluttering in her stomach was reminiscent of the past, and she wasn't sure she wanted to be reminded of that time. But the reality was that he was the last man who'd brought those butterflies to life in her in that way.

After what happened with Aiden, she hadn't let herself feel that anticipation or excitement over a man. She viewed the relationships she'd had as friendship with a side of intimacy. Which was probably why all of them had ended.

Apparently, Aiden didn't have a serious relationship going on either. That didn't mean he hadn't had one in the time since they'd been together, however. It was ironic that he'd dumped her to find someone better, and yet he still hadn't found that perfect woman.

If she hadn't been perfect for Aiden before, she was definitely not perfect for him now. The thought sent a pang of hurt through her, but she ignored it. She wasn't in the market for a relationship, let alone one with her ex.

At some point, the kids came to ask their parents if they could have ice cream. The two couples got up to help them, leaving Skylar with Aiden, Wilder, and Lexi.

"I want ice cream too," Wilder said, swinging around on the bench. "How about you, love?"

"I shouldn't..."

Wilder held out his hand to her. "C'mon. Help me choose what flavor I want, and I'll let you share it with me."

Lexi let Wilder help her up from the picnic table, then they wandered hand in hand to where Lee and Rori had ice cream and all the fixings for cones or sundaes.

Skylar watched them go, then turned back to Aiden. He was looking at her expectantly, a small smile playing on his lips. She felt a pang of nostalgia wash over her as memories of their past flooded her mind. She quickly pushed them away, focusing on the present moment.

"Are you getting ice cream, too?" Skylar asked, trying to sound casual.

Aiden nodded. "Yeah, I think I'll indulge a little." He stood up, then picked up his empty plate. Motioning to hers, he said, "Want me to toss that out for you?"

"Sure. Thank you."

She watched him as he walked to where they were dishing up the ice cream, pausing to toss their used plates into the garbage can that was set up for the trash from the meal.

Dragging her gaze away from him, Skylar looked down at her phone, checking to see what was new on her social media. She didn't have large numbers of people on her accounts, but she had a few co-workers who posted a lot.

One co-worker in particular had posted tons of pictures from a recent work trip to Rome. As she looked at the photos, Skylar found herself missing the trips she'd taken. She hadn't been to Rome, and that flight might have been hers if she'd still been working.

She'd been resigned to the fact that she wasn't going to be taking any flights for at least a couple more weeks. Maybe more if she gained weight while she was basically unable to exercise and wasn't watching what she was eating very closely. If she didn't fit into her uniform, she might end up sidelined for longer.

She'd never had it happen to her, but others in the company had. Some might say such a rule was sexist, but it actually applied to all flight attendants, regardless of gender. If they didn't fit their assigned uniform, they needed to do what they could to rectify that.

Movement on the other side of the table had Skylar looking up. Aiden was now seated opposite her with two dishes of ice cream. He slid one across the table to her.

Skylar stared down at it, taking in the choices Aiden had made for her. Vanilla ice cream. Walnuts. Bananas. Mini marshmallows. Chocolate syrup. Everything she would have chosen for herself. Everything she'd chosen back when they'd been dating, which is how he'd known what to get her now.

"I assumed your tastes hadn't changed too much over the years," Aiden said as he dipped his spoon into the chocolate ice cream in his bowl, which he'd covered in peanuts, caramel, and marshmallows. He never mixed fruit with his ice cream.

Given what she'd been thinking about right before he set the ice cream down in front of her, she should probably not indulge. But... "Thank you. I do still like all of this."

Aiden flashed her a grin that was so familiar that it hurt her heart. "You're welcome."

Skylar took a spoonful of the ice cream, making sure to get a little bit of everything. The ice cream was rich and creamy. Obviously, they'd bought the good stuff, unlike what her mom had used to buy them when Skylar was a kid.

"How are you doing, Sky?" Aiden asked after they'd been eating in silence for a couple of minutes.

Frowning at him, she said, "I'm fine."

One of his brows lifted. "Are you? I'm not asking flippantly. I'm serious. How are you?"

Skylar took another bite of her ice cream before answering. "Let's see. I hear that the girl I gave birth to has been diagnosed with cancer. Then, in order to help her, I have to contact her birth father, who didn't treat me very well. And on top of that, I sprained my ankle so I can't go back to work. So yeah, I'm doing just fine."

"I wish I could tell you that I'd walk away to make it easier on you, but I can't."

"I know that," she said. "And I wouldn't expect that you would because it would upset Shiloh."

"I would like for us to become friends," he said. "I understand that might be a bit of a stretch at the moment, but I really hope that eventually, we could reach that point."

Skylar wasn't sure how she felt about it. Her conversation with Cole had put the thought into her mind, but she hadn't dwelled on it too much. Part of it was because she didn't want to think about how she was apparently good enough to be a friend, but hadn't been good enough to be something more.

"I don't think it matters if we're friends or not," she told him. "Once my ankle is better, I'll be gone."

"But surely you'll be back to see Shiloh," he said as he lifted another spoonful of ice cream to his mouth.

"Definitely, but I won't be here for extended stays. Not like this time."

"I think that being friends would also be beneficial as we relate to Shiloh," he said. "She would probably pick up on the fact that we're uncomfortable around each other if we can't be friends."

"We don't have to see her at the same time, so she won't know how we do or don't relate to each other."

Resignation settled over Aiden's features. "I do understand why you don't want to be friends. I treated you badly, and I am very sorry for that."

"Not sorry enough to approach me to apologize," she said, trying to keep her emotions from her voice. "You could have asked Cole where I was, or you could have asked him for my phone number. If you'd really regretted what you did, you would have found a way to contact me."

"You're right." Aiden stirred his ice cream, keeping his gaze lowered. "I should have apologized before now."

Skylar waited for him to give excuses for why he hadn't.

"I was a coward," he said with a shrug. "I didn't like being confronted by what I'd done to you. I didn't like to think about that time."

Skylar thought he might have used what had happened with his dad and sister to excuse why he hadn't pursued making amends with her. So for him to admit it was because he was scared to do it surprised her.

Right then, she wasn't sure if there was anything he could do to bridge the chasm that had grown between them because of what had happened. But she also knew that it would be better if the two of them were on friendly terms, even if they wouldn't ever be friends the way they once had been.

"I agree that it might be best if we could be around each other without tension," she finally said. "Let's just leave the past in the past."

He tilted his head. "Just like that?"

"Just like that," she said.

It wasn't like they hadn't discussed the past. They'd touched on what had happened, and she'd had an epic meltdown about it right in front of him. That was enough for her. She had no desire to have an in-depth conversation about it all.

Though he didn't look thrilled, he gave a single nod.

If things went the way she planned, any time they spent together would be when others were around. And it wouldn't be for long periods. So there was really no need to rehash the past more.

She wasn't sure what her future held, but she'd come to the place of accepting that Aiden was going to be a part of it to varying degrees. Whether she liked it or not.

CHAPTER FIFTEEN

Aiden noticed a car parked in front of the house as he pulled into the driveway after work one day and wondered if it was someone visiting his mom. Though she didn't have a lot of friends in Coeur d'Alene, she still had several in Serenity who came to visit.

Sometimes he felt guilty about having had her move to Coeur d'Alene, rather than him driving an hour or more each way to commute to work. However, his mom had assured him that it was fine. That she needed a little separation from the life she'd shared with his dad in Serenity.

There was a strong possibility that she'd move back to Serenity one day because she'd kept their house there. But for now, Coeur d'Alene would be their home.

Opening the side door, Aiden immediately heard the pitter patter of little feet.

"Uncle Aid!" Willow came running towards him, and Aiden reached out to grab her and swing her into his arms.

He gave her a kiss on her cheek, which she returned to his. "How was your day?"

"Great! A man brought me a new tablet with a pretty cover."

Aiden frowned. "What?"

He walked out of the kitchen to the living room at the front of the house. There he found his mom speaking to said man.

"Cole?" Aiden bent to set Willow down, then gave Cole a brief but tight hug when he approached Aiden. "What are you doing here, bro?"

Cole shrugged as he put his hands on his hips. "I thought I'd come and get myself tested. Say hi to the fam."

That surprised Aiden. Cole had come back to Serenity even less than Skylar had over the years. "You're not dying, are you?"

"Aiden James!" his mom exclaimed.

Cole chuckled as he turned in her direction. "It's fine, Miss Tracy. I know why he's asking that."

"It's been an age since you showed up."

"It has, but I think it's for a good reason."

"You staying in Serenity?"

"Probably," he said. "My folks will most likely want me out at the house with them."

"Most likely," Aiden agreed.

"You want to go out and grab a bite?" Cole asked. "I plan to head out to Serenity later."

Aiden glanced at his mom, who waved her hand. "You go on. Willow and I will be just fine. I'll take care of her for bedtime tonight."

"Thanks, Mom," he said, then turned to Cole. "I'm just going to get changed, and we can go."

It didn't take him long to swap out his suit for a pair of jeans and a T-shirt, then he jogged back up the stairs to join Cole in the living room.

"Hey, Willow," he said, moving to where his niece was seated on her favorite little child size recliner. "You didn't tell me a joke yet. Whatcha got for me?"

Willow's face lit up. "What do you call cheese that's not yours?"

Aiden once again made a show of trying to think of the answer. "I give up, what."

"Nacho cheese!"

As he grinned, Aiden heard Cole chuckle. "That's a great one, kiddo."

He held out his hand for a high five, which Willow gave him with great gusto. Cole also held his hand out, and Willow didn't hesitate to smack his hand, too.

"Let's take my car," Aiden said as they walked toward the side door. "What are you in the mood for?"

As Aiden backed out of the driveway, they had a brief discussion before deciding on a nearby steakhouse. Once there, it wasn't long before they were seated, and as usual, they garnered some female attention.

It was mainly Cole who drew the attention, but occasionally—like that day—the waitress flirted with them equally. Probably hoping that one of them would bite. Aiden didn't know if Cole would, but he certainly wouldn't.

He had enough going on in his life at the moment. Getting involved with a woman was nowhere near the top of his current priority list. Truth be told, it wasn't even on it.

"You didn't have any other plans now that basketball season is over?" Aiden asked once they'd given their orders. "I wouldn't think Serenity would be where you'd want to go for a break."

Cole shrugged. "I thought maybe it was time."

"Really?" Aiden was still perplexed by his friend's appearance.

"Yep. I figured that if Skylar could do it, so could I," he said. "Plus, if she's around, the attention won't be solely on me."

Aiden could understand why Cole felt that way. He probably didn't want his family asking too many questions about his life.

Not that they were oblivious to what was going on with him. He made the gossip news often enough. Either because he was seen with a woman, so the dating speculations exploded, or something happened with his career.

"I think you might not be in luck with that," Aiden said. "She's been here for a little while now, so they've probably gotten all the information out of her that they're going to."

Cole grimaced. "Perhaps I made a mistake."

"You haven't. You're here to help your niece."

"Your daughter."

Aiden shook his head. "I'm trying not to think of her that way."

"Is it getting any easier?"

He didn't answer right away, as their server had returned with their drinks and a basket of fresh rolls. When it was just the two of them again, he said, "Maybe. I correct myself all the time about Shiloh being my daughter. It helps that I don't see her a lot, though I wish that wasn't the case."

They talked a bit more about Shiloh, with Aiden sharing what he knew about her current condition. She had gone home, and from what he'd heard, she was doing well. He hoped that meant that his mom and Willow could meet her soon, but he didn't want to push.

As they ate their steaks, they talked about what had been happening with Cole and his team. He had one more year on his current contract and seemed confident that he'd be offered another one, given his performance over the past few years. He'd only gotten better and better, and his team had gone to the playoffs every year he'd been with them.

Aiden hadn't realized how much he'd missed hanging out with Cole. Though Devon was a good friend, Cole was more than that. More like a brother than a friend. They knew everything about each other. Well, almost everything. He'd never shared with Cole that Skylar had told him she was pregnant.

It dawned on him then that there might be things Cole hadn't told him since they'd gone in different directions in their lives. However, even if Cole did keep some things to himself, it didn't seem to affect the ease Aiden felt when they were together, and their conversation flowed like it always had.

It was too bad that he probably wouldn't get to hang out with him much if he was only going to be there for a few days, during which Aiden had to work.

When they finally left the restaurant, it was close to nine. The sun had set, casting the evening in shadows.

"So you plan to head out to Serenity tonight?"

Cole shoved his hands into the pockets of his jeans. "Yeah. I guess so."

"If you want to crash at my place, you're welcome to," Aiden said. "As long as you don't mind sleeping on the couch."

"How big is the couch?" Cole asked, then waved his hand. "Doesn't matter. I'll sleep on it."

Aiden wondered why Cole had even come to Idaho if he didn't really want to go to Serenity. But rather than ask him, Aiden said, "It's a pretty good size, and I've napped on it plenty of times."

When they reached the house, Cole detoured to his car to grab a suitcase and a duffle bag.

Aiden sent Cole downstairs while he went to check in with his mom. The upstairs was already dark, which meant Willow was in bed, and his mom was in her room.

He rapped lightly on her door, and when she called for him to come in, he opened the door just enough to stick his head in. "We're home, and Cole is going to stay the night and bunk down on my couch."

"Okay, sweetheart," his mom said with a smile. She was seated in an overstuffed rocker-recliner, a tablet in her hands. "It was so nice to see him. And he brought such lovely gifts."

"What did he bring you?" he asked, opening the door a bit more to lean against the doorjamb.

"A brand new tablet with a pen," she said, holding up the tablet in her hand. "And a gift card for me to buy apps I might like."

"Well, that was sweet of him."

"I thought so," she agreed. "Though Cole should know he never has to worry that I'll turn him away if he shows up empty-handed."

"I'm sure he knows that, Mom. He just likes to buy things for those he cares for."

"In return, I shall cook him a breakfast that I know he'll like."

Aiden grinned as he straightened from the doorjamb. "I'm sure he'll enjoy every bite."

He crossed the room to kiss her cheek, then said goodnight before leaving her to her tablet and the quiet of her room. On the way back downstairs, he stopped by the hall closet to grab some bedding and a pillow for Cole to use.

When he walked into his apartment, he found Cole stretched out on the couch. He grinned at Aiden. "Looks like it will do."

Aiden tossed the bedding on top of him. "I told you it would."

Wrapping his arms around the pillow and blanket, Cole sat up and swung his feet to the floor. "Appreciate you giving me a place to crash for tonight."

"You're welcome to stay as long as you want," Aiden told him as he dropped into his recliner.

"I might take you up on that," Cole said. "Do you want to come out to Serenity with me tomorrow?"

"Unfortunately, I have to work for a living."

Cole chuckled. "Maybe I should hire you."

"To do what?" Aiden asked. "If you were a pro golfer, I could caddy for you. But not much I can do for a pro basketball player."

"You could design me a house."

"Sure. I could do that," Aiden agreed. "Where are we building said house?"

"Not sure yet."

"You could probably find some land around here." Now that Aiden had resigned himself to living in the area for the foreseeable future, he wouldn't mind if his best friend ended up back in the area, too.

Cole didn't immediately shoot down his suggestion, but he didn't jump at it either. He sat forward and reached for his suitcase. "I brought you something that could help with your designing."

"You didn't have to bring anything for me, bro," Aiden said. "Or for my mom or Willow."

"I know." Cole unzipped the suitcase and flipped the lid open. "But I like to buy stuff for you guys."

Cole had always been very generous, but sometimes it made Aiden uncomfortable. He never wanted his friend to think they expected anything from him. They weren't poor. However, he and his mom were both frugal in their day-to-day lives.

"Here you go." Cole held out a flat box.

Aiden hesitated, then took it from him, feeling its heft. "Seriously, bro. You didn't have to get me anything."

"I know." Cole shrugged as he sank back into the couch. "I just wanted to."

Aiden set the box on the coffee table and opened it, staring in shock at the expensive laptop it revealed.

"Figured you could make good use of that. I ran into some big wig architect and asked him what the best laptop was for someone in his profession. He gave me the info, and there you go."

"Thanks so much, Cole," Aiden said. "I really appreciate this."

"You don't have one like it already?"

Aiden gave a huff of laughter. "No. I certainly don't."

"Hope you can put it to good use."

"I'm sure I can," Aiden assured him. "This is really great."

He didn't bother to unpack the laptop right then, figuring he'd tackle setting it up another night.

"Have you had much luck with Skylar?" Cole asked as he propped his feet on the coffee table.

"I suppose that depends on your definition of luck." Aiden also propped his feet on the coffee table. It would drive his mom batty, but he'd chosen a style of furniture that would stand up to such use. "She's agreed that it would be best if we got along, but I don't think she wants us to be friends."

"She can be stubborn," Cole pointed out.

"Or maybe she's just trying to protect herself from someone who has hurt her in the past."

"Yeah. Maybe that too."

"I think it's a given that's why she doesn't want a friendship," Aiden said. "And I'm not sure anything will change her mind."

"Are you going to try?"

"No. I mean, I'm not going to keep bugging her about being friends. I will treat her better than I did before, because that's the right thing to do."

"How do you feel about her?" Cole asked.

Aiden narrowed his gaze at his friend. "I don't hate her or anything, if that's what you're asking."

"It's not." Cole crossed his arms as he slumped further back into the couch. "I just remember thinking when the two of you started dating that you'd be the real deal. In it until the end."

"You didn't feel that way at first," Aiden pointed out.

"True. But you were the one that convinced me that it was serious. You said your parents had been childhood sweethearts, and it had worked out for them. I just came to accept that in addition to being my best friend, one day you'd be my brother-in-law."

"Life doesn't always work out the way we think it's going to."

Aiden felt that was a bit of an understatement when it came to his life. At no point had he thought he'd lose both his dad and his sister while still in his twenties.

"That doesn't mean that you can't have a second chance at something if the opportunity presents itself."

"But it hasn't," Aiden said. "That would mean that both Skylar and I were interested in trying again. And unless she's been telling you something different, that is definitely not the case."

"But would you be if she was interested?"

Aiden didn't have an answer for that. He'd changed. She'd changed. Their current circumstances were challenging.

It would take determination and commitment on both their sides to make something work, and nothing she'd said or done had hinted that she was inclined to make that sort of commitment to a friendship, let alone something more serious.

"I think I've learned that you shouldn't close the door on any possibilities in life," Aiden said slowly. "However, in this situation, I just don't see how that could work, given Skylar's rightful anger with me over how things played out in the past."

There was a part of Aiden that wanted to say that if it was God's will, it would work out. But while he knew that Cole would understand what he meant, he probably wouldn't agree with that approach.

"I wish I'd asked more questions about the situation when the two of you broke up," Cole said. "Maybe you'd be in a different position now."

Aiden shook his head. "I think Charli and Blake have been better parents than Skylar and I would have been if we'd tried to make things work back then."

"What do you mean?"

"She told me she was pregnant after we'd been broken up for almost two months. It had been a nasty break up, and by that point, I'm sad to say, I'd already been with a couple of other girls. I'd definitely moved on, and if people would have tried to force us together because of the baby, we would have really struggled. I don't think that would have been a good environment for Shiloh. Or Skylar, for that matter."

"I suppose that's true."

The reality that Aiden would admit to no one was that he was still drawn to Skylar. He didn't know if that was just because he knew that she was the mother of his child, or if he was being drawn in by the memory he had of their relationship before it ended.

Maybe he'd feel differently if he'd been the one hurt in the breakup. Which was undoubtedly why Skylar held no fondness for him.

"You need to just steer clear of this topic with Skylar," Aiden cautioned. "We're both dealing with a lot right now, given Shiloh's situation."

"I understand that," Cole said. "But while I might not pester Skylar about a relationship with you, I'll definitely encourage her to consider a friendship."

The last thing Aiden wanted was for Skylar to become annoyed with him. More than she already was. But at the same time, he couldn't control what Cole did. Aiden just hoped that Skylar didn't think he'd put her brother up to it.

Although maybe she wouldn't believe that he could actually be interested in rekindling anything, given the way he'd dumped her. It was a very complicated situation all around, and thinking about it too much exhausted him.

They stayed up later than Aiden normally did, but he didn't regret taking the time to chat with his friend in a way that they hadn't had the opportunity to in quite a while.

Aiden thought Cole might be back on their doorstep in a day or two, but he kind of hoped he was wrong. Selfishly, he wanted Cole to be okay with spending more time with his family because a successful visit now would mean he'd come back to Serenity more.

CHAPTER SIXTEEN

After a leisurely start to her morning, which included a bath, shaving her legs, and doing a face mask, hunger finally drove Skylar to leave her room and head downstairs. Her ankle was doing better, but Gareth felt she still needed to have it supported. Though she didn't want to be restrained in using her foot, she knew she needed to err on the side of caution so that she was ready to return to work sooner rather than later.

As she reached the main floor, she heard the rumble of a man's voice that wasn't her dad's coming from the kitchen. Pausing, Skylar listened, convinced that it wasn't really her brother she was hearing. Why would Cole be in Serenity?

When she walked into the kitchen, she did, in fact, find her brother sitting at the counter talking to her mom and dad. He looked over as she approached and gave her a wide smile as he got to his feet.

"Hey, sis," he said as he bent down to gather her into a tight hug. "Good to see you."

"What are you doing here?" she asked as he stepped back from their embrace. "Are you dying?"

He laughed and shook his head. "Funny. Aiden said the same thing when I stopped by to see him last night."

For a moment, Skylar was reminded of the banter that the three of them had shared back in their teens. "So I guess you're not?"

He settled back on his stool. "Nope. No death on the horizon for me that I know of."

"So what brings you to Serenity, then?" she asked as she joined him at the island counter.

"I thought maybe I should come and give my blood to see if it will help my niece."

"Oh. That's great." Skylar hadn't expected him to show up for that, but she was so grateful that he had.

"Have there been any results yet?" Cole asked as he lifted the mug sitting in front of him.

"Not yet," her dad said. "But we could hear any day now."

"So, are they having to wait for treatment until the results are in?"

"No. They want to see the effect of this first round of treatment before deciding if they need to move on to the stem cell transplant," her mom explained. "We just want everything in place if we get to that point."

Skylar stared at her brother, taking in the changes she saw in him. Like Aiden, he had filled out over the years. His broad shoulders and muscular build spoke of his athleticism.

She'd watched a lot of his games, but seeing him in person revealed how much he'd changed over the years. His arrival was still a bit of a mystery. Like her, he wasn't one to come to Serenity without good reason, like a wedding or a holiday. And sometimes, not even then.

"So you saw Aiden?" her mom asked.

"Yep. I went by there after I picked up my rental car yesterday, then we went out for dinner. He offered to let me crash on his couch, and I took him up on his offer since it was late."

"How is he doing?" Her mom set a mug of coffee down in front of Skylar. "And his mom and Willow?"

"They're doing great," he said. "His mom made me a huge breakfast this morning before I left."

"I hope that we can see them again soon."

"Aiden said they haven't had a chance to meet Shiloh yet, but they're looking forward to being able to do that."

"I think that will happen soon," her mom said. "I talked to Charli earlier this morning, and she said that Shiloh is doing better every day. The nausea and other side effects from this initial round of treatment are slowly abating."

"That's great to hear," Cole said. "I hope I can see her. I've brought a gift for her."

"You have?" Skylar asked.

"Yep. It's not every day I find out my best friend and sister have a daughter."

Skylar frowned at him. "You can't think of Shiloh like that."

"Why not?"

"Because she's Charli and Blake's daughter. She's no different from any of your other nieces or nephews. She's not more special than any of them, just because Aiden is her birth dad."

Even as she said the words, Skylar knew that they weren't true in her heart. Shiloh would always be different from her other nieces and nephews. Definitely more special.

"I beg to disagree," Cole said. "Even aside from who her parents are, Shiloh is going through a lot right now. She is a very special girl and deserves to be treated as such."

Skylar felt tears sting her eyes, and she looked down at the mug and wrapped her hands tightly around it. Would Cole have felt that same way back when she'd first found out she was pregnant?

"You're right, son," her dad said. "Shiloh is a very special girl. However, Skylar is also right. I know you all haven't had as much time to adjust to the knowledge of her parentage, but it is best to think of her as Charli and Blake's daughter, and not Aiden and Skylar's."

"How has Shiloh taken the news?" Cole asked.

"That little girl has taken everything in stride," her mom said with a smile. "She's known for a while that she was adopted, but only recently found out her birth parents are Aiden and Skylar. I think she was really excited about that because she already knew and liked Skylar."

"That's great," Cole said. "It wouldn't have been very good if Shiloh hadn't liked Skylar. Especially since she can be really difficult to like."

Skylar glared at her brother. "I beg your pardon?"

Cole grinned at her as he sat back on his bar stool, crossing his arms over his chest. "Just kidding. You're my favorite sister."

"Well, at the moment, Gareth is my favorite brother, since he's taking care of my wounded ankle."

"So what would it take to get back into the top spot?" Cole asked. "A new luxury bag, by any chance?"

Skylar lifted her brows at him. She wasn't a luxury bag collector, but she would never turn one down. So far, the bags in her small collection had all come from Cole.

Every birthday since he'd started playing professionally, an elegantly wrapped package would end up on her doorstep, and inside would be a lovely luxury purse or small bag. In fact, she had one upstairs that she'd brought with her. And now, it sounded like she was about to gain another one for her collection, for no apparent reason.

Cole pulled his long legs in and got to his feet. He went to the bags sitting beside the entrance to the kitchen and opened one up. After removing several items, he returned to where they sat. "Here you go."

He handed nearly identical packages to Skylar and her mom, and a smaller cube size one to her dad.

"You didn't have to bring us anything, son," her dad said as he took the box. "We're just so glad to have you here."

"I know." Cole gave a shrug. "But I wanted to bring a few things."

Skylar could only shake her head as she opened her gift to reveal another Hermes bag. It was beautiful, but really unnecessary. None of the bags Cole had bought her had been necessary.

"This is lovely, Cole," her mom said as she lifted her bag from the box. "It's so soft."

While her mom's was a more basic black, Skylar's was a deep burgundy.

"Yes, this is beautiful," Skylar agreed. "Thank you."

"This is incredible," her dad said, drawing Skylar's attention to the watch his box had contained.

"I thought it would be useful," Cole said, leaning close to his dad to show him all the features of the watch.

Skylar set her bag back in the soft covering it had come in and then into the box. Lifting her mug, she took a sip of the coffee her mom had prepared for her.

She was still trying to figure out Cole's real reason for showing up. It was possible that he really had come just to give blood for the test. Skylar wasn't convinced of that, however.

Was he that excited about the fact that Shiloh was her and Aiden's daughter?

Everyone else had just taken the news in stride, with no one making a big deal about learning who Shiloh's birth parents were. The only difference between Cole and the rest of her siblings was that Cole was super close to Aiden. So maybe it was possible.

"How long are you here for?" Skylar asked.

"Not sure. Probably through to the weekend."

"Really? Wow."

"We need to have a family dinner while you're here."

"Could we have something on Friday or Saturday and include Aiden and his mom and Willow?"

"Sure, we could do that," her mom said with a nod. "I'll see if Charli thinks Shiloh would be up for joining us so that they could meet her."

Just one big happy family, Skylar mused. The way they had once imagined their future would be.

Sure enough, the plan came together for them all to get together on Friday evening. And from what Cole had said, it sounded like Aiden and his mom and niece were actually going to spend the weekend at their house in Serenity.

"I'm going to talk to Jay and see if he can get the high school gym for a couple hours for us to play some basketball or volleyball."

It was like Cole was rewinding time to his teen years when he'd gone to the high school gym with Jay whenever he could. He'd put in hours and hours of practice to become the best that he could be. And it had paid off.

"I'd say you could come be a cheerleader for us," Cole said. "But you went and hurt your ankle. So now you'll have to cheer from the bleachers."

"If I decide to go," Skylar told him.

"You'll go," Cole replied with a grin.

"Why would I do that?"

"Because there's not much else to do in this town on a Friday night."

He wasn't wrong about that. There hadn't been much to do on Friday nights back in the day, especially in the summer, when there hadn't even been church youth group meetings. She doubted that it had changed much in the past several years.

"I think we'll just do a barbecue," her dad said. "That works well when we're all together."

"Sounds like a plan," her mom agreed. "I'll post it in the group chat and see if we can get this all arranged."

"And you'll set up for me to get the blood test?" Cole asked.

"Yep. I'll give Gareth a call," her dad said. "He'll set it up for you."

Skylar had two days to prepare herself for seeing Aiden and his family again. Not that she thought it would go badly. The opposite, in fact. She knew that Aiden would be fine, and his mom would be sweet and friendly, just like always.

It was almost harder for her when they were nice, since her feelings about Aiden were still so turbulent. However, it was easier for everyone else that they weren't making things difficult.

When Friday morning rolled around, they were busy preparing for the gathering later that day. Everyone but Zane and Kelsey were able to make it. With Friday being a busy night for Zane's restaurant, he would be there working. And Kelsey kept her schedule similar to Zane's, so she would also be at her job at the hospital.

Skylar walked around in the boot that Gareth had given her permission to use. While it was nice to be off the crutches, the boot wasn't exactly easy to maneuver around in either. Cole had taken to calling her Hop-Along, and she couldn't grab hold of him to make him stop because she couldn't catch him with her hop-along...

Still, she managed to help out wherever she could. Over their many years of growing up, her mom had become a pro at assigning tasks, even to the littlest or the wounded of them. So Skylar had been given the task of cutting up lettuce and tomatoes for the hamburgers.

Even Cole was pitching it and helping their dad set things up in the back yard, preparing for the influx of children. Though they'd talked about not having the kids come, in the end, it was decided that it might be best to have other children for Willow to play with if Shiloh got tired. Plus, the cousins had all missed seeing Shiloh, and it would probably do her good to be with them again.

Everyone was contributing something to the meal, so they were mainly responsible for the meat, the buns, and the fixings for the hamburgers. The others were bringing salads, desserts, chips, and drinks.

Around five, Wilder and Lexi showed up, and over the next little while, the rest of the family trickled in. The plan was to eat at six, so as the time neared, Skylar had to keep herself from constantly checking her watch.

She wasn't surprised that Aiden and his mom had accepted the invitation, and while Skylar was happy that Shiloh would have another grandparent and cousin, she wished they didn't come part and parcel with Aiden.

Layla and Amelia arrived first, then a few minutes later, Charli and Blake arrived with Shiloh and the boys. Blake had Shiloh in his arms and carried her over to the counter to set her down on the stool next to Skylar.

Skylar was so glad to see Shiloh free of all wires. The little girl looked up at Skylar, a smile growing on her thin face.

"Hi, Auntie Sky."

"Hi, sweetie." Skylar slid an arm around her narrow shoulders and gave her a hug, resting her cheek lightly on the hat covering her head. Her hair had begun to fall out, so she kept her head covered now. "How was your day?"

"It was good! Momma made strawberry popsicles for us, and we sat outside on the swing eating them."

Such a small thing, really, but Skylar could see how much Shiloh had enjoyed it. After being cooped up in the hospital for so long, sitting outside probably was a wonderful thing.

The rest of the family greeted them, then filed out into the backyard, leaving just her parents, Charli, Blake, Shiloh, and Skylar in the house. They'd agreed that it might be easier to introduce Aiden's mom and niece to Shiloh with fewer people around.

The ringing of the doorbell had them all turning toward the front door, but it was her dad who went to answer it. Skylar slid off the barstool she'd been perched on, wanting to greet Aiden and his family on her feet. She kept her weight on her non-injured ankle as she held onto the counter.

When her dad reappeared, Aiden followed him, carrying his niece and with his mom at his side. The little girl had dark curls and eyes that made her look surprisingly like Shiloh. Her eyes were wide as she took them all in, kind of like how she'd been when Aiden and his mom had come to get tested.

"Hi, Tracy," her mom said as she approached Aiden's mom to give her a hug. The two women embraced for a long moment, then separated. "It's so good to see you again. I'm sorry our contact has dropped off over the years."

"It happens," Aiden's mom said with a gentle smile.

The woman had lost significant weight, which Skylar supposed resulted from losing a husband and daughter in a short amount of time. And having to care for her young granddaughter in the midst of her grief.

Back in the day, Tracy McIntyre had been a full-figured woman with light brown hair that she'd worn long. Smiles and laughter had come easily to her, and Skylar had imagined that she'd make a great mother-in-law.

And while that was probably true, it had turned out that she wasn't destined to be Skylar's mother-in-law.

Tracy's gaze swept the room, and when it landed on Skylar, a smile lifted the corners of her mouth. She made her way over to where Skylar stood.

"Skylar, my dear, it's so good to see you again."

Skylar accepted the woman's hug, a familiar scent greeting her as she did. "It's good to see you again, too."

And though she might not have thought that was the truth initially, it turned out that it was. Skylar was glad to see the woman who'd been so good to her when she had been Aiden's girlfriend.

"Hi, Shiloh," Aiden said. "This is Willow."

Skylar and Tracy turned to watch as Shiloh approached Aiden and Willow. Aiden went down on one knee to set Willow down. The two girls stared at each other, then Shiloh said, "Your hair looks like mine." She lifted a hand to touch the head covering she wore. "Well, when I have hair."

"You're pretty," Willow said with a smile.

A smile bloomed on Shiloh's face. "So are you!"

Skylar knew that Aiden and his mom had chosen to share with Willow that Shiloh was sick. As the two girls stood next to each other, Skylar could see that even though Shiloh was a bit taller than Willow, they were about the same size. Willow was a slender little girl, looking like she was a bit on the small size for her age. It just reinforced the toll illness had wreaked on Shiloh's body.

"I brought something for you," Willow said, then turned to hold out her hand toward Aiden. He gave her a gift bag, which she then held out to Shiloh. "We got you another coloring book. Uncle Aiden said you liked the other one."

"I did," Shiloh agreed. "Coloring is one of my favorite things."

Watching the two little girls bond over their love for coloring let Skylar know that, regardless of the personal cost, seeking Aiden out had been the right thing to do.

"This is my nana," Willow said, motioning to Tracy. "And she's your nana, too."

Tracy stepped closer to the two little girls, a gentle smile on her face. She didn't attempt to physically interact with Shiloh as she said. "It's good to meet you, Shiloh."

Shiloh smiled at her, then glanced at Charli and Blake. The couple stepped over to greet Tracy themselves.

As they chatted, Aiden approached Skylar. "How are you doing?"

"I'm fine," Skylar said as she sat back on her stool. "You?"

"I'm good." He put his hands on his hips, and she noticed that he was wearing a pair of black slacks along with a short-sleeved button-up shirt in a shade of blue that made his eyes stand out. "Happy to be here for the weekend."

"I didn't realize your mom had kept her house here."

"Yep. And it's coming in handy." He glanced down at her leg, then gestured to the boot. "Is that an upgrade or downgrade?"

"Gareth tells me it's an upgrade, and I'm inclined to agree, since I don't have to use the crutches anymore."

"That's good. You've always hated having to use them."

"Not sure anyone likes using crutches."

Aiden grinned. "True."

How was it that Aiden seemed to be perfectly at ease with her, while she was a mess of nerves and emotions? It was only her experience of putting forth calm when dealing with a difficult passenger that allowed her to keep her feelings under wraps.

It was possible that Aiden was doing the same, but she really doubted it. There was just something in his smiles and laughs that made her feel like they were genuine. Like he truly enjoyed being around her.

Cole came in with their dad and immediately greeted Willow and Tracy, then bumped fists with Aiden.

"Time to eat," her dad announced. "The burgers and hotdogs are ready to go."

They made their way outside, then when they were all there, her dad said, "Why don't we all hold hands as I pray for the meal?"

It wasn't an unusual request, since they'd always held hands for the prayer before meals. But that day, holding hands meant she was going to have to hold the hand of the man she'd once loved.

It wasn't the first time recently, since Shiloh had made a similar request when they prayed with her at the hospital. But that didn't make it any easier.

Looking down, she saw Aiden curl his fingers into a fist, then relax them. He held his open hand toward her, palm up. When she glanced up at him, he lifted his brows, as if daring her to take it.

Well, she wasn't one to back down from a dare, especially from him, and there was no way she could let him know that inside she was a bit of an emotional mess at the thought of holding his hand once again.

She slipped her hand into his, fighting a swell of emotion when his fingers tightened around hers.

She'd always loved to hold hands with him. In some ways, it was a claiming. He was with her. She was with him. They were together. And her heart had always skipped a beat when he'd hold out his hand to her, waiting with a smile on his face for her to take it.

And every single time, she had.

CHAPTER SEVENTEEN

Aiden drove with his mom and Willow back to the Halversons' home the next afternoon. Charli had said she'd bring Shiloh over so the two girls could hang out together a bit more. His mom would stay there for a couple of hours with Willow while he headed to the high school gym with Cole.

Jay had let them know that—at Cole's request—he'd invited a group of guys to play some basketball there. Apparently, he'd recruited enough people for two teams, including one made up of any high school varsity players who were currently around Serenity. They had all agreed without knowing that they'd be playing with Cole.

Aiden hadn't played basketball in awhile, so he was probably going to be a bit rusty. Hopefully, it all came back once he had a ball in his hands. Back in the day, he and Cole had been a team within the team.

Every team they played knew that if Aiden got the ball, it was going to end up in Cole's hands. That meant that they tried to make sure they were guarding them both closely throughout the game. But the funny thing was that it didn't matter. He and Cole could read each other on the court without having to say anything.

"I can't wait to see Shiloh again," Willow said.

"I think you're going to make cookies with her and her grandma," his mom said.

"My grandma too," Willow reminded her. "She said that since I call you Nana, I can call her grandma."

"That's right, she did," his mom said. "So now you have a grandma and grandpa and a nana and papa."

"Except my papa is gone. Just like my mom."

There weren't a lot of times that Willow talked about their passings. She'd been quite young when they'd each died, so their memories were rather fuzzy for her. However, they'd shown her pictures of both of them, and she'd seen from those photos how much they had loved her.

"Yes. They're both gone." His mom's voice was soft. "But they'll always live in the memories in our heart."

"Which is where all our special memories are," Willow said.

"Exactly."

Aiden hoped Willow wouldn't have to say goodbye to yet another person in her life, but Shiloh's diagnosis meant there was always that possibility. It was a possibility he tried his best not to think about.

When he got to the house, he discovered Cole and Skylar were both waiting to go to the gym. He hadn't thought that Skylar would join them, but he couldn't say that he was disappointed that she was.

"Hi, Shiloh," Aiden said as he bent down on one knee so he was closer to her level. "How are you doing today?"

"I'm fine," she told him, then stepped forward to wrap her arms around his neck.

Emotion rushed through Aiden as he carefully put his arms around her. He should have memories of a lifetime of hugs from her. But instead, the number of hugs they'd shared could be counted on one hand.

When the hug ended, Willow joined them and gave Shiloh a hug as well. Aiden got to his feet, then turned to greet Charli and Cathy.

"We gotta go, bro," Cole said as he dropped his arm on Aiden's shoulders.

"I would have thought you'd want to hang around and make cookies with the girls," Aiden said to Skylar as the three of them made their way to Cole's car after saying goodbye to the others at the house.

"I already spent some time with Charli and Shiloh," she said as they neared the car. "Now I'll let Willow and your mom have some time with her."

Aiden would have liked to hang out with her himself, but this weekend had been more about his mom and Willow spending time with her. He welcomed the chance to hang out with Cole and others, playing a sport he loved.

"You drive, Aid, and you sit in the front, Sky," Cole said as he opened the front passenger door. "I think there's more room for me in the back seat."

Skylar gave him a skeptical look but didn't say anything, just angled herself into the front seat. Cole grinned at Aiden across the top of the car before disappearing inside.

Aiden glanced back at him as he slid behind the wheel. His friend didn't look super comfortable, but then his height meant that most normal vehicles didn't have a lot of leg room for him. Of course, he'd had no problem with the front seat of Aiden's car when they'd gone out for dinner a couple of nights ago.

As he drove to the high school, Aiden was reminded of all the times the three of them had arrived together for basketball games, whether they were home or away. Since Skylar had been a varsity cheerleader, she'd travelled with the team to most of their games.

They'd celebrated many of their wins by going for ice cream afterwards. Her parents hadn't protested them hanging out together because Cole was often with them. Those had been wonderful times, and as he parked the car, Aiden felt a strong yearning for the past and the innocent joy he'd had then.

As they walked toward the large doors of the high school, Cole's long strides took him out in front of them. Aiden kept his pace slow as he walked beside Skylar. Her walking boot gave her a bit of a limp.

Cole was waiting at the doors, holding one of them open for them. "Being back here is a bit crazy."

"It sure is," Aiden agreed as they walked down the wide hallway, Skylar in the middle. "Not much has changed."

Their footsteps echoed in the hallway as they headed toward the gym. As they neared the door, Aiden could hear the thump of several basketballs as well as the squeak of rubber shoes.

Jay was standing just inside the wide doorway of the gym, hands on his hips as he watched several people on the floor.

"Hey there," Jay said as he turned toward them. He gave quick hugs to Aiden and Cole, and a more careful one to Skylar. "Come to cheer us on?"

"As long as all I have to do is yell," she said, motioning to her boot.

"If you weren't in that boot, could you still do all the cartwheels and stuff?"

"Yep. Once a month, I try all of them. If I can't do it well, I practice it more."

"Too bad you can't show us," Cole said.

"Next time."

The action on the court had stopped, and Aiden glanced over to see that the young men who'd been practicing now stood clumped together, looking over at them. He had a feeling that they'd recognized Cole.

Jay turned back to the group and asked, "What's going on?"

"That's Cole Halverson, right?" one teen called out.

"Sure is," Jay agreed. "And you're going to be playing against him this afternoon."

"*Against* him?"

"Yep. So keep warming up."

The teens quickly began to dribble and shoot.

"Are you two ready to go?" Jay asked. "Or do you need to get changed?"

"Just got to swap my shoes," Aiden told him.

Cole nodded. "Me too."

Skylar pointed to the bleachers. "I'm going to sit over there."

"You're not going to be on your own," Jay told her. "I think there are a couple wives and maybe some kids showing up, too."

Cole followed Skylar, then sat down on the lowest bleacher, putting his bag on the foot row behind him. Aiden sat next to him, while Skylar settled on the row above them.

As he was tying his second shoe, Wilder and Lexi arrived, and not long after that, Will showed up with his oldest son, Liam. Wilder joined them on the bench to swap his shoes as well, and Lexi climbed up to sit next to Skylar.

Once he was done, Aiden stretched out his feet and leaned forward, stretching out the muscles in his calves. He was looking forward to playing, but he hoped he didn't regret it when he woke up the next day.

After some stretching, he and Cole got to their feet.

"Let's see if we still have that old high school magic," Cole said as he easily caught the ball that Jay slung at him.

For the next little while, he and Cole passed the ball between them, then jumped for baskets. Cole made every shot he took, but Aiden only made about one out of three. He was so out of practice.

When Wilder and Will joined them, Cole said, "Are you playing these days, Will?"

"Yeah. I decided that now I have age as an excuse for why I'm not great at the sport. When I was younger, I had no excuse except that I sucked."

"Okay, guys," Jay called out as his son, Peyton, walked into the gym, dressed to play. "Gather round and let's figure out how we're going to do this."

"Since we're short a player for the adult team, we'll randomly choose one of you teens to join them."

The teens shared nervous but excited glances at Jay's pronouncement.

They decided on playing to twenty, figuring that there were enough handicaps on the adult team to offset Cole's skills.

"Are we playing shirts and skins?" Wilder asked, then lifted his arms to flex. "I think my wife would like skins for me."

"Well, Lexi is in for disappointment, I'm afraid," Jay said. "We have jerseys."

Soon they were suited up and ready for the jump ball. Jay was refereeing the game, but Aiden didn't expect they'd get any special treatment from him.

It was a pretty even game, which Aiden attributed to Cole not playing as aggressively as he might have if he'd been playing with his peers. At one point, he noticed another teen boy come in, followed by a young woman who climbed the bleachers closest to the door and sat down. The boy made his way around the outside of the court and went to the bench where a couple more teens were sitting.

While he waited for one of the teens to complete their free throws as a result of a foul called by Jay against the adult team, Aiden looked to where Skylar sat with Wilder's wife. He remembered in the past that he'd often sneak looks at Skylar when there were lulls in the game. If she caught him looking, she'd always given him a small wave with her pompoms.

That day, their gazes met, but she didn't wave or smile. Aiden was glad when the guy took his second free throw, and the game continued, so he had an excuse to look away.

The next time he looked in that direction, he saw that Layla and Amelia had joined the women. He wondered if the older teen was there to support her family or one of the teen boys on the opposite team.

In the end, the adult team won. Before the next game started, there was some discussion about mixing it up. Will decided to sit the next game out, and Wilder went over to the other team. They ended up with two teens on their team because Jay said their handicap would now also include only four players on their team.

Aiden was more tired than he'd thought he'd be, considering he worked out regularly. Cole, on the other hand, showed no signs of tiredness at all.

The teen who'd showed up later than the rest was on their team. He seemed in awe of Cole, and Aiden wasn't sure how effective he'd be. However, once they started to play, the kid focused in and actually played quite well.

They won again, but no one really seemed to care. After the second game, the teens circled around Cole, and soon, the group was going through some exercises with him.

Aiden took the chance to go sit on the bench in front of Skylar and the other ladies. Wilder also joined them.

"Good job, sweetie," Lexi said as she leaned forward to accept Wilder's kiss.

"I tried to play skins for you, but Jay said no."

"Skins?" Lexi asked. "What's that?"

"It's when one team plays without shirts and the other team wears shirts," Aiden said. "It's useful in casual play when you don't have uniforms."

"You wanted to play without your shirt?" Lexi asked.

"For you, babe. Wouldn't you have liked to see that?"

Lexi lifted a brow at her husband while Skylar made a gagging sound. Layla and Amelia giggled as Wilder turned a frown on his sister.

"I understand that you might rather see Aiden without his shirt, but I'd thank you not to interrupt me as I'm attempting to flirt with my wife."

"You're already married, bro," Skylar said. "I don't think you need this level of flirting anymore."

"Flirting keeps things fun," Wilder told her. "You should try it sometime."

Aiden waited for Skylar to respond, but all she did was roll her eyes at her brother.

"Are you girls here to support the family or cheer on a couple of cute boys?" Wilder asked as he turned his attention to his nieces.

"Can't it be both?" Layla asked.

"Ooooh." Wilder rubbed his hands together. "Does your dad know about this?"

"You are such a troublemaker, Wilder," Skylar said. "I don't know how Lexi puts up with you."

Wilder batted his eyes at his wife. "She loves me. Just like I love her."

"Do you really, Lexi?" Skylar asked.

A smile lit up Lexi's face as she gazed at Wilder. "More every day."

At her words, envy shot through Aiden. He hoped that some day he'd have the chance to experience that.

About a year ago, his mom had started to more aggressively hint that it was time for him to open himself up to the possibility of dating once again. He'd put it on the back burner following his dad and Bethany's death.

He couldn't deny that finding out about Shiloh and having Skylar back in his life had brought it to the forefront for him. The only problem was, with what was going on with Shiloh currently, he didn't feel like he wanted to add one more thing to his life.

As he listened to Wilder tease Layla and Amelia about what boys they were interested in, Aiden felt old. It felt so long ago that he'd been that young, even though it really wasn't.

Oh, the things he'd tell his younger self if he could go back in time. But would he have listened to himself? Back then, he'd thought he'd known everything.

The truth that had become apparent over the years was that the only thing he'd really known was how to mess up. Because he'd done that spectacularly.

"Hi, Amelia."

Aiden looked up to see the teen who'd arrived late standing in front of the bleachers where Layla and Amelia sat. Amelia's cheeks were pink as she returned the young man's greeting.

"How are you doing?" The teen came across as very polite and respectful as he interacted with Amelia.

Aiden glanced at the woman who'd come with him. She was still seated a short distance away, but she was watching the interaction without expression.

Aiden was sure there were going to be questions for Amelia later. And possibly Layla too, as another older teen approached them and greeted her.

"I want to go for ice cream," Cole announced as he came to stand beside Aiden. "You up for that?"

Aiden shrugged. "Sure."

"You okay with that, Sky?"

She seemed to consider it for a moment before she nodded. "Anyone else coming?"

"Can we come?" Layla asked. "And Dawson and Benjamin?"

"Of course," Cole said. "The more the merrier."

The teen who'd been talking to Amelia stepped over to where the woman he'd arrived with sat. "Can we go with them to get ice cream?"

The woman's gaze travelled over them, then she nodded. "I'll just have to let them know."

The boy grinned, revealing a mouthful of braces. "Thanks, Annie."

After confirming where exactly they were going, Aiden changed his shoes, then put them into the duffle bag he'd brought. He took a long drink from his water bottle before returning it to the bag as well.

Thankfully, it hadn't been an intense workout, so he wasn't too sweaty. Previously, they would have showered and changed after a game, but the games that day hadn't made him sweat too much.

"That was fun," Cole said as they walked out to the car. "Been awhile since I've just played for the heck of it."

"I keep forgetting you're famous," Skylar told him. "Until people go a little crazy around you."

Cole chuckled as they got in the car. "They weren't too bad. I've had some real crazy encounters."

It was only a short drive to the ice cream parlor. It looked the same on the outside, but the inside had changed a bit. The place had always had an old-timey feel to it, but they'd redone it to really lean into that aesthetic.

"Wow," Skylar said, coming to a stop just inside the door. "This is amazing."

Alongside the glass case, which contained many ice cream flavors, there was a long counter with round red cushioned bar stools, while the floor was made of large white and black tiles. Tables were lined up in the remaining empty space with similar red cushions on wrought-iron chairs that had been painted white.

Cole led the way to the counter, then motioned for everyone to gather around before speaking to the employee waiting behind the counter. "This is all going to be on one bill."

They told the teens to go first, but the boy, who seemed interested in Amelia, hung back. He turned to say something to the woman who had brought him. They held a brief conversation before the woman pulled a wallet from her bag and gave him a card from it.

"This is my treat," Cole said as the teen made a move to speak to one of the other employees. "You don't need to pay."

"There's no need for you to pay for us," the woman said, her voice soft but firm. She reached up to push her glasses back up her nose. "You don't even know us."

"That's easily remedied," Cole said with an engaging grin.

The woman stared at him, her gaze narrowed. Her response to him made Aiden want to laugh. Cole was most likely used to girls falling over themselves to gain his attention. Aiden had seen that happen himself, and he would bet that not one of those girls would have turned Cole down if he'd offered to buy them ice cream.

Cole stuck out his hand. "Hi, I'm Cole Halverson."

The woman hesitated a moment before she shook it. "I'm Annie, and this is Benjamin."

"It's wonderful to meet you, Annie. I'd love to buy you some ice cream and have you join us."

Annie still didn't appear swayed by Cole's charm, but she finally nodded her head. "Thank you."

"You're very welcome."

By this time, the teens had placed their orders. Cole waved for Annie to go first, then Skylar and Lexi followed. Aiden, Cole, and Wilder were the last ones to place their orders, then Cole took care of the bill.

"Come sit with us," Cole said once Annie had her ice cream. "That way, you'll be more willing to accept when I want to pay for something next time."

"Will there be a next time?" she asked, her brows lifted.

"You never know," Cole said, one corner of his mouth lifting as he winked at her.

"Good grief," Skylar muttered from were she stood next to Aiden. "Cole, you're going to scare her off."

Cole lifted his hands. "Just making friends."

Aiden looked over and met Skylar's gaze. He couldn't help but grin when she shook her head.

The woman must not have been too freaked out by Cole because she ended up joining them. The teens sat at one table, while the adults clustered around a couple of others nearby.

Aiden ended up sitting next to Skylar, while Cole was seated on Skylar's other side. Their new friend, Annie, had taken a chair on the opposite side beside Lexi.

"By the way," Cole began, then motioned to Skylar. "This is my sister, Skylar, and my best friend, Aiden. That guy is my brother, Wilder, and you're sitting next to his wife, Lexi."

Annie gave them a small smile. "Nice to meet you all."

Lexi shifted a little in her seat, then said, "Have I seen you at church?"

Annie nodded. "I recognize you and your husband."

"Small world," Cole said.

"Small town, more like," Wilder added.

"Have you lived around here long?" Cole asked.

"Pretty much my whole life," she said before taking a bite of her ice cream.

"Really? What class were you in?"

"I didn't go to school here," she told him. "I was taught at home."

"Your brother isn't, though, is he?" Cole asked.

"No. He really wanted to go to school, so our parents relented."

Aiden found Cole's interactions with the woman intriguing. While Cole wasn't a stranger to flirting, usually it was after a woman had expressed an interest in him.

He leaned closer to Skylar and, pitching his voice low, he said, "Do you find this a little odd?"

She looked over at him, then tilted her head a little closer and said, "Just a little."

Back when they'd been dating, they'd teased Cole anytime a girl would try to flirt with him. He'd been adamant that he wasn't going to date for a long time. Cole had been determined to reach his career goals before getting serious with anyone.

"Are you two together?" Annie asked, drawing Aiden's attention from Skylar.

An immediate denial jumped to his tongue, but he didn't blurt it out. Instead, he glanced at Skylar. She had a frown on her face as she shook her head.

"They're not now," Cole said. "But they used to be."

"And could be again," Wilder added.

"Wilder!" Skylar's voice held a considerable amount of exasperation.

Annie's gaze bounced around at all of them before settling on Skylar. "Sorry to bring up a touchy subject."

"It's fine." She waved it off. "We don't live here, so you wouldn't know."

Aiden wasn't sure what had made him hold his tongue, but he had a feeling that Skylar noticed and would have some thoughts about that.

CHAPTER EIGHTEEN

Skylar slowly made her way down the stairs to the main floor, taking them one at a time. She had to be careful how she moved because twisting it wrong still sent a pang of pain through her ankle, even with the boot on

Her parents were already in the kitchen, dressed for the church service they'd be attending shortly. As was she.

There was no sign of Cole, which wasn't a surprise. Skylar doubted that he'd show before they left in an hour.

The smell of coffee drove her to hitch her way across the kitchen and reach for a mug.

"Good morning, darling," her mom said, brushing a kiss across her cheek. "You look very nice."

"Thanks, Mom. So do you."

Her mom had chosen a white denim skirt that reached to her knees and paired it with a dark blue floral blouse. Her dad had on a light blue polo shirt and a pair of black slacks. Given how well they matched, Skylar was certain her mom had picked out both of their outfits.

In deference to the warm summer day, Skylar had chosen a light lavender sundress. It had wide straps and a fitted bodice that had an empire waist. The skirt fell to just below her knees, and it was light and flowy.

Pancakes were stacked on a plate on the counter, so Skylar picked up a plate and took a couple. She spread some peanut butter on them, then added a light drizzle of syrup.

Her parents chatted as they ate their breakfast. Skylar was always a bit surprised at how her parents—who spent so much time together—still found stuff to talk about.

When Cole walked into the kitchen a few minutes later, Skylar stared at him in surprise. He was dressed in a pair of dark jeans and a plain green short-sleeved T-shirt, which made her think he was going with them.

"Are you going to church with us, darling?" her mom asked as she got up to fill a mug with coffee for Cole. There was no pressure in her mom's voice, but there was definitely hope.

"Yeah. I thought I would. Aiden said he'd be there since they stayed in Serenity again last night."

"Excellent." Her mom got a plate from the cupboard and handed it to him. "Get yourself some breakfast."

"Yes, ma'am."

Once they were done eating and had cleared away the breakfast dishes, they prepared to leave for the church. Though her parents offered to drive them all, Cole said he was taking his own car, so Skylar decided to go with him.

"Surprised you're coming this morning," Skylar said as Cole pulled away from the house.

"You and me both," he replied with a laugh. "But I figured it couldn't do any harm. Have you gone on the Sundays you've been here?"

"Yep."

"Why?"

She shrugged. "Not sure. I guess I just thought it would keep everyone from pestering me about it if I didn't go."

"Yeah. That's kind of how I feel."

"When are you leaving?"

"I don't have a definite departure date," he said. "What about you?"

"I'm waiting for the blood test results to come back and my ankle to heal."

"How long will that take?"

"I expect we'll have results within the week, and I hope my ankle will be good to go not long after that."

"Are you going to be happy leaving?"

Skylar pressed her finger against her lower lip. Over the past few days, she'd purposefully tried *not* to think about leaving. It pained her to think of not seeing Shiloh for long stretches of time.

Aiden's face came to mind, but she quickly refocused on Shiloh. She was doing better, and Charli said she was gaining strength every day. It was possible that she wouldn't even need a stem cell transplant.

If that was the case, Skylar tried to convince herself that she wished she hadn't gone to Aiden already. But that wasn't entirely the truth.

Though she hadn't wanted to, she believed him when he'd said he hadn't really thought she was pregnant.

It still hurt that he'd thought her the type of person to try to trap him that way. Or maybe he'd convinced himself of that in order to abdicate responsibility. That alone might have made her think that he was lying.

But when she had combined that information with seeing how he was acting now, she thought that there was a good chance he was telling the truth.

She was glad that Cole didn't mention anything about Aiden, since she was feeling very conflicted about the man.

Because Cole had mentioned that Aiden was going to be at church, she wasn't surprised when she saw him and his family there. And by the time the service started, she was in a pew, sitting between Cole and Aiden.

It was a seating arrangement they'd used many, many times in the past. Although, back then, she'd definitely sat closer to Aiden than to Cole. This time, she was equidistance between them, and she was not holding Aiden's hand, nor was his arm around her.

The memory of that opened up a hole in her emotions. A yearning for that time when everything had seemed so simple. When she'd trusted that they would be there for each other.

She was glad when the worship leader led the rest of the team up onto the stage, distracting her from her thoughts wandering down memory lane.

Skylar felt movement as Aiden leaned a little closer to her. "Is that Jay's son on the drums?"

"Yep. Gareth taught him, and now he's taken over." Her tall, lanky nephew, Peyton, sat behind the drums, a spot that Gareth had occupied plenty over the years.

"Incredible. Where has the time gone? He's like a young adult now."

"He is, and it sounds like he's following in Misha and Gareth's footsteps to become a doctor. He's helping out some at the clinic over the summer."

The conversation ended there as the man behind the podium led them in an opening prayer, and then moved into a song. The worship leader encouraged them to stand, which meant Skylar had to maneuver herself up to her feet, keeping most of her weight on her good ankle. That meant she edged closer to Aiden, since it was her right leg that was good.

Though she hadn't sung along on previous Sundays, that morning, the music seemed to be drawn out of her soul. Familiar melodies accompanying familiar words.

They sang several worship songs, their words projected up onto the screens at the front of the sanctuary. She knew all but one, so it felt like no time at all had passed since she'd last been in a service.

After they sat back down, someone got up and read off several announcements. There wasn't a lot going on since it was summer, and most programs at the church had been suspended until the fall.

Soon enough, Janessa's father-in-law, Pastor Kennedy, took his place behind the podium. He gave the congregation a warm smile as he gazed out over them. The pews weren't as full as she remembered them being in the past, but that was probably due to it being summer and people being away on vacation.

She'd downloaded the Bible app a couple of Sundays previously, so when Pastor Kennedy gave them a reference, she was able to look it up. As a teen, she'd never been allowed to use a Bible app on her phone. She'd had a physical Bible that her parents had bought her, but it was probably still in a storage box somewhere in Vegas.

"So earlier this week, I decided to do something romantic for my lovely wife. I had Reese help me prepare a picnic lunch. I made reservations for a boat so we could spend time on the lake. I even picked up a bouquet of flowers. I did everything except check the weather, so I didn't realize there was a rainstorm in the forecast."

A ripple of chuckles flowed through the congregation.

"So there we were, sitting out in the boat, enjoying our picnic, when the sky suddenly darkened and spit out a few raindrops. That didn't last long, however, because soon it was a torrential downpour. Needless to say, I wasn't happy about how my plans had been derailed.

"Too often in life, we rush ahead with our plans, not even checking the weather. Then, when it rains, we get angry and frustrated with God." He lifted his Bible. "Let's turn to Romans 5, verse 3."

Skylar opened her Bible app and found the verse.

We also glory in tribulations, knowing that tribulation produces perseverance; and perseverance, character; and character, hope. Now hope does not disappoint, because the love of God has been poured out in our hearts by the Holy Spirit who was given to us.

After Pastor Kennedy read the verse out loud, he said, "When trials come our way, we are presented with two options. We can glory in those tribulations, or we can rebel against them."

There was no doubt in Skylar's mind which choice she'd made when faced with the trials that were a result of her own actions. She'd never viewed that time as a stepping stone to a deeper faith. Instead, she'd run from everything that could have guided her to a place of peace as she'd moved through that difficult time.

Skylar shifted on her seat, the pastor's words as he shared examples of people who had chosen to be thankful for their trials convicting her. Over the past few Sundays, she'd been able to block out most of his sermons, letting her thoughts wander far from the church in Serenity.

That wasn't the case that Sunday, however. Even sitting next to Aiden wasn't enough to distract her.

When Pastor Kennedy mentioned that it was never too late to learn and grow in one's faith from the trials of life, it really sank deep. Just because she rejected that path nine years ago didn't mean she had to continue to reject it now.

As they stood to sing the final song, she glanced at Aiden, wondering if he'd been paying attention to the sermon the way she had. He was staring at the pastor, his expression tense.

Skylar fought the urge to reach out and take his arm the way she had in the past. Instead, she gripped the pew in front of her as she bent her head. She sang along to the hymn, not needing to see the words since it was one she was well familiar with.

My hope is built on nothing less
than Jesus' blood and righteousness;
I dare not trust the sweetest frame,
but wholly lean on Jesus' name.

On Christ, the solid Rock, I stand;

all other ground is sinking sand;
all other ground is sinking sand.

When darkness veils His lovely face,
I rest on His unchanging grace;
in every high and stormy gale,
my anchor holds within the veil.

His oath, His covenant, His blood,
support me in the whelming flood;
when all around my soul gives way,
He then is all my hope and stay.

When He shall come with trumpet sound,
O may I then in Him be found:
dressed in His righteousness alone,
faultless to stand before the throne.

On Christ, the solid Rock, I stand:
all other ground is sinking sand;
all other ground is sinking sand.

As the song ended, Pastor Kennedy once more stepped up to face the congregation. Bracing his hands on the sides of the large pulpit, his gaze swept over the audience.

"I know that there are those in our congregation today who are surrounded by darkness or are facing that whelming flood. It might be job loss, illness, relationship troubles, money troubles, family troubles or any number of other things. We are not promised a life of ease as Christians, but we are promised that we will not face those difficulties alone. We as brothers and sisters in Christ are here for you, but more importantly, God is here. His grace is never changing, and He is our hope and stay. I pray you choose to stand on that solid rock, so that one day, you will also stand faultless before His throne. Let's pray."

Once the final prayer had been spoken, the pastor dismissed them, encouraging everyone to enjoy the beautiful day that God had given them.

Skylar was quiet as she followed Cole up the aisle, moving more slowly than him. Between his long strides and her being inhibited by the walking boot, she wasn't able to keep up with him. Aiden, however, didn't seem to be in the rush that Cole was because he fell into step beside her.

"Are you heading back to Coeur d'Alene this afternoon?"

"Yeah, but I think my mom and Willow might be back out here in the next couple of days."

"Really?"

Aiden nodded. "I think she's missed living here."

"It's good she's kept the house."

"Yes. I think she figured that at some point, she'd be able to handle living there again. That she'd *want* to be there again."

"How do you feel about it?"

They'd entered the foyer by then. Aiden stepped clear of the doorway, and Skylar followed him.

"I'm glad that she's feeling like she can find joy in the memories instead of pain. If she decides to move back here with Willow, I'd support that, though I'd miss having them with me in Coeur d'Alene."

"You wouldn't move here?"

"I don't really want to have an hour plus commute each way. Just makes a long day even longer."

"Hey, bro," Cole said as he looped his arm around Aiden's shoulders. "You stickin' around this afternoon?"

"Yeah. We'll probably head back around five or so."

"You sure you have to go?"

"Of course. I have to work."

"I still think I should hire you," Cole said as they moved away from the sanctuary. "Then you wouldn't have to work all the time."

Aiden laughed. "I'm not sure I'd want you as my boss."

"I'd be a *great* boss," Cole replied indignantly. "Just like I'm such a great friend and brother that I rented a boat for the afternoon."

"A boat?" Skylar asked.

"Yep. I rented a pontoon boat for us."

"Who all is going?"

"Wilder said he and Lexi would come, and Kayleigh was going to talk to Hudson." He thumped Aiden on the shoulder. "And I hope you'll come too."

"Of course. I think my mom was planning to spend some time with a couple of her friends. They have some grandchildren around Willow's age, so I think they're going to the park together."

"Were they going to see Shiloh?" Skylar asked.

"I talked with Charli this morning about spending some time with her," Aiden said. "But she said that Shiloh had a bit of a rough night, so they were just going to give her a low-key day today. She did say we could stop by before we head back to Coeur d'Alene to say goodbye, though."

Before discovering that Shiloh had cancer and doing some additional research of her own, Skylar had thought that once chemo was over and indications were that the treatment had seemed to work, that everything would go back to normal. Unfortunately, that was not the case. So it was possible—probable even—that Shiloh would continue to suffer with the negative effects of the treatment she'd received so far.

"Well, let's head out and get on that boat," Cole said. "Do you have a swimsuit, Aid?"

"I'm sure I've got a really old one at the house."

"How about you, Sky?"

"Yeah. I'm not sure why I stuck a couple in, but I did."

"Perfect." He turned back to Aiden. "Do you want us to swing by and pick you up so your mom can have the car?"

"Sure. That would be great. I'll just need to head to the house first with them."

"Okay. We'll be there in an hour," Cole said. "Is that enough time?"

"Should be."

A few minutes later, she and Cole were in his car, headed to the house.

"Is there anyone you'd like to invite to join us?" Cole asked. "We've got the room. The boat I rented accommodates fifteen people."

"Who would I invite?"

"Is Allie still living around here?" Cole said, naming her best friend from high school.

"No clue."

"You guys fell out?"

Skylar shrugged. "I guess you could say that. She didn't approve of a couple of my decisions."

"Like?"

Skylar wasn't sure she wanted to delve into all that with him, but it might help him understand some of what she'd gone through.

"When I was worried that I was losing Aiden, I decided that the best way to keep him was to sleep with him."

"Really?" Cole's tone was incredulous. "Pretty sure we were told in our youth group to *not* do that."

Skylar sighed. "I know. It wasn't the right thing to do, and Allie felt the same way. She told me not to do it, but I ignored her. When she found out what I'd done, she was furious that I'd gone against everything we'd been taught."

"Wow. I mean, she always was very focused on her faith, even at a young age, so I guess her reaction kind of makes sense."

"When I found out I was pregnant, I never told her," Skylar said, remembering how hard that time had been. She'd been away at college, dealing with a breakup, the loss of her closest friend, and finding out she was pregnant. "When I went to her, upset that Aiden had ended things, she basically said I told you so. That was the last conversation we had."

"I'm sorry, sis."

"Yeah, well. It's all in the past now."

"Is it though?"

"As far as I'm concerned, it is," Skylar told him. "I haven't spent the years since bemoaning the loss of her friendship. I know what I did was wrong, but I don't think it warranted ending a friendship the way she did. If that's the type of friend she was, I am better off without her."

"I know you probably wish Aiden weren't still in my life, but I've been incredibly grateful for his friendship. I've needed someone who I know I can trust not to have ulterior motives in their dealings with me. I feel like what we have is genuine."

"I'm sure it is," Skylar said. "Aiden seems to have gone back to being the person he once was."

"I guess I wasn't the best friend or brother back then."

"You had a lot going on." Skylar had wished that she could confide in Cole during that time, but she hadn't been sure that he'd take her side in things.

"Still, I'm sorry for not being there for you."

"I forgive you." Of course, it was far easier to forgive Cole for what had happened back then than it was Aiden.

"Well, let's try to have fun this afternoon," Cole said as he pulled up the driveway to the house.

"What are we doing for lunch?" Skylar asked as they made their way to the front door.

"I placed an order at the deli, and we'll swing by and pick it up before we get Aiden."

"You've been busy," Skylar said. "When did you do all of this?"

"Yesterday afternoon. I didn't want to just sit around today."

"Did you want to ask Annie to join us?"

Cole shrugged. "I did consider it when I saw her at the church, but doubt she'd have accepted."

"Her brother might have," Skylar said. "Why don't you invite Layla and Amelia, and tell them they can bring friends?"

"I might do that. Though that doesn't mean Annie would come with her brother."

"True, but you might learn more about her from her brother if you're truly interested."

"I'm not sure if I am or not."

"Well, then I'd suggest you leave her alone," Skylar said as she headed up the stairs.

"Don't take too long," Cole called after her. "We need time to pick up the food before we get Aiden."

Up in her room, Skylar wondered if she really wanted to go. Did she want to hang out with Aiden even more? Once again doing something they'd done as teenagers? Back then, the family had owned their own boat, so they'd spent a lot of time on the nearby lake.

She'd brought both a two piece and a one piece swimsuit, but she decided on the one piece as she liked it more than the other one. After she put it on, she pulled on a pair of shorts and a T-shirt and one sandal.

Staring down at her feet—one booted—she grabbed her phone and shot a text off to Gareth to make sure she could take the boot off to go into the lake. She took it off for showers and baths, but that was slightly different from swimming in the lake.

She quickly French braided her hair, then grabbed a towel from the bathroom to take. It had been a long time since she'd done anything like this, and she found she was looking forward to it, even if Aiden was going to be there.

CHAPTER NINETEEN

Aiden slid into the back seat of Cole's rental car, putting his duffle bag with his towel and a change of clothes onto the seat beside him.

"Should I have grabbed lunch at the house?" Aiden asked. "If yes, can we swing through a drive-thru so I can get something to eat? I'm starving."

"No worries," Cole assured him. "I picked up a bunch of stuff from the deli, along with some drinks, chips, and treats I had ready for pickup at the store."

"You've planned quite the party, bro," Aiden said.

Aiden was a bit surprised to see Skylar in the front seat next to Cole. He'd thought that she might decide not to come because he'd be there, too.

He would have liked to think it meant that she was starting to be okay with him being around. However, he wasn't sure that was the case. It was likely that she was there because going out on the lake was something she'd always enjoyed.

They were the first ones to reach the place where Cole had rented the boat. He and Skylar waited at the car while Cole went to check in with the rental place.

"Are there others coming?" Aiden asked.

"Yeah. Wilder and Lexi, and Kayleigh and Hudson. I think Layla and Amelia might join us, too."

"And their boyfriends?"

Skylar gave a soft huff of laughter. "Don't let Blake hear you call them that, or he might ban you from ever seeing Shiloh."

Aiden grinned. "Well, I definitely don't want that."

"Poor girls," Skylar said. "Their dad keeps pretty tight tabs on them, I think."

"Isn't Layla eighteen already?"

"I think her age is irrelevant to Blake. She could be thirty, and he'd still probably be protective of her."

Aiden didn't bring up how her parents had felt when they'd first moved past the best friend's little sister/brother's best friend relationship they'd had to something more serious. It wasn't a time he really wanted to revisit.

"Okay, you two, let's grab the food," Cole announced as he strode up to them where they stood next to the car. They'd left the confines of the vehicle since it had been getting a little warm.

After grabbing their bags from inside the car, they helped Cole gather up everything in the trunk, then made their way down the dock to where the boat was moored.

"This looks great, Cole," Skylar said as she climbed onto the boat.

"I thought so from the pictures online."

Aiden followed Cole on and set his bags down on the bench seat that ringed the area beneath the canopy. Cole took the things Skylar held, so Aiden held out his hand to help her onto the boat.

She hesitated, and Aiden slowly closed his hand and began to lower it. But then Skylar reached out and grasped his arm. Aiden automatically tightened his forearm so that he could support her as she stepped onto the boat.

"Thank you," Skylar said as she released her grip on him.

"You're welcome."

Even with her boot on, she maneuvered around the boat quite well, helping Cole empty the bags onto the small table.

"You remember how to drive something like this?" Aiden asked.

"It's like riding a bike," Cole said. "I'm sure."

Aiden wasn't so sure that was how it worked, but he figured his friend probably remembered enough that he'd be able to navigate a pontoon. If it was a speedboat, Aiden might have had a different feeling about Cole piloting them around.

It wasn't long before more people arrived, including Layla and Amelia. When they said that their friends—who happened to be boys—would be joining them, Cole walked with them to the parking lot.

Aiden watched as Cole stood with his arms crossed, his tall form towering over everyone else.

"What's he doing?" Kayleigh asked as she came to stand beside Aiden.

"I think he wants to see if the one boy's sister drops him off."

"A sister?"

"Yeah. He seemed rather..." Skylar looked at Aiden. "Enamored with her?"

"Intrigued for sure," Aiden said. "She joined us for ice cream following the basketball games yesterday."

"Is she nice?"

This time, Aiden looked at Skylar. He wasn't sure why, but he didn't want to be the one giving an evaluation of the woman.

"She seemed nice," Skylar said. "A little on the quiet side, but that could just have been because she was hanging out with a bunch of people she didn't know."

"Is he going to ask her to join us?"

"Probably, but I don't think she'll accept."

Kayleigh turned to look at Skylar. "Why not?"

"I got the feeling she wasn't sure what to make of Cole. Or the rest of us, for that matter."

Aiden watched as Cole strode toward a vehicle that had just pulled to a stop, Amelia at his side. He approached the driver's door, then lowered himself to a knee. Meanwhile, the lanky boy from the day before got out of the passenger side and greeted Amelia with a smile and a wave.

"It looks like perhaps he's going to try to charm her into joining us," Kayleigh remarked.

"Well, if there's one thing that Cole has aside from the skill to sink a basket from half-court, it's the ability to charm people," Aiden remarked.

"We'll see," Skylar said. "She didn't seem to fall under his charm much yesterday."

Soon, Cole straightened, resting his hand on the roof of the car. He bent and said something more, then stepped back. He stood with his hands on his hips, watching as the car drove off.

"Guess you're right, Sky," Aiden said.

Layla's friend had arrived as well, so the four teens made their way to the dock leading to where the pontoon boat was still tied up. Cole trailed behind them, looking at something on his phone.

"Are we all here?" Skylar asked as Cole stepped onto the pontoon.

He glanced around at the people on the boat, then nodded. "Yep. We can head out."

"Did Annie not want to join us?"

He shrugged. "She said she had something else to do."

"My sister doesn't really like to be around people she doesn't know well. She mainly stays home."

"And that's perfectly fine," Skylar assured Benjamin with a smile. "There are times I prefer to stay home and away from people, too."

The teen gave Skylar a small smile. "She's really great, though."

Aiden could see the boy was trying to defend his sister, but he didn't have to do that. Not with this family.

"She seemed very nice when we had ice cream yesterday," Skylar said. "Maybe someday we'll get to know her a little better. Especially if you're hanging around Amelia."

"She usually just needs to know ahead of time if she's going to be going out with people," Benjamin said, then looked at Cole. "If you give her advance notice next time, she might say yes."

"I'll keep that in mind," Cole said.

With that settled, Aiden helped Cole prepare the boat to leave the marina, and soon they were headed away from the dock.

There was hardly a cloud in the sky, and the sun sparkled off the bright blue water. Though the day was hot, there was a slight breeze which kept it from being oppressively so.

Skylar sat on one of the benches with her legs crossed. Kayleigh and Lexi sat beside her while their husbands stood with Aiden near the pilot's seat where Cole sat, guiding the boat out into the expanse of the lake.

The teens were clustered near the back of the boat, using their phones to take photos. It was so odd to see the next generation living a part of their lives that Aiden remembered so clearly. It made him feel old.

After a little while, Cole slowed the boat to a stop. They dropped anchor, then sorted out the food, opening the cooler bag that contained everything Cole had ordered from the deli. There was far more food than they'd probably eat, but when Cole did something, he did it big.

Once the food was all set out, Cole turned to Hudson. "Would you say grace for the food?"

Hudson nodded, and everyone bowed their head as he prayed. Though Cole didn't practice the faith he'd been raised with, he was still respectful of it.

After the prayer, they loaded their plates, then found seats on the long benches. The boat had a Bluetooth speaker system and soon Cole had some music playing.

They weren't alone on the lake. Given how beautiful a day it was, it was no surprise that there were a variety of watercraft out on the water.

Once they had finished eating, the teens quickly stripped down to their swimsuits and jumped into the water. There were some inflatables which Cole tossed out for the teens to use. The adults didn't seem to be in any hurry to join them as they continued to sit under the canopy of the pontoon, out of the sun.

"Alright," Cole said after they'd been talking for a bit. He slapped his thighs, then got to his feet. "I think I'm going to join the kids."

Aiden stood up, and he was a little surprised when Skylar did, too. She'd loved to swim when they'd been younger, and it seemed that perhaps she still loved it.

Cole took his T-shirt off, then dove off the back of the pontoon. He popped up beyond where the teens were using some of the inflatable tubes. When he splashed them, they shouted and splashed him back.

Skylar came to stand next to Aiden on the platform at the front of the boat, then carefully removed her walking boot. She set it to the side, then grasped the handle of the ladder that could be used to climb up onto the boat from the water.

"It looks very refreshing," she said.

"Want me to throw you in?" Aiden asked with a grin.

"I think not," she said, but then she reached out with both hands to shove him.

Without thinking, Aiden grabbed onto her, and they both fell into the water with a mighty splash. As they sank, he wrapped his arms around her and kicked hard to get them to the surface. As soon as they broke through the surface of the water, he let her go, anticipating that she was going to be less than thrilled about what had just happened.

Surprisingly, Skylar was grinning as she used her arms to stay above the water. "Well, I suppose I deserved that."

"So I don't have to apologize for pulling you in with me?" Aiden asked as he grabbed one of the large tubes and hooked his arm around it. He moved it closer to Skylar so she could also grab it.

"Well, if I insisted on that, then I'd have to apologize for pushing you." With one arm hooked around the tube, she leaned back, her feet floating to the surface. "Let's just call it even."

Aiden was happy with that. He leaned back in the water, his position mirroring Skylar's. Contentment swirled inside Aiden, marred only by the uncertainty that lingered over Shiloh's health.

He looked up at the sky, his gaze taking in the splendor of it. He knew that the God who had created the spectacular beauty surrounding them could heal Shiloh. He could erase the cancer from her body and allow her to gain health and strength once again.

But was that God's plan for their little girl?

Aiden looked across the tube and saw that Skylar had closed her eyes as she floated there. He thought of the years he'd wasted by not approaching her to admit that he'd been so wrong in how he'd treated her and to apologize. But he'd been too much of a coward.

He hated to admit it, but it was only because of Shiloh's cancer diagnosis that he was back in their lives. Without that, he wouldn't even know that he had a daughter. Nor would he have Skylar in his life once again.

Had God used Shiloh to bring him back to this family? But more than that, had He used Shiloh's illness to bring Aiden fully back to Himself?

Whatever the reason, Aiden wanted healing for his daughter. He might never be able to play the role of father in Shiloh's life, but forever in his heart, she would be little girl.

Please, God, let the treatment have worked for Shiloh. She's such a strong little girl. Precious beyond words. Please heal her.

"Are you okay?"

Skylar's soft question had Aiden blinking away the moisture that had suddenly swelled in his eyes. As he felt a tear slip down his cheek, he lifted his hand to splash himself.

Dragging a hand down his face to wipe away the tears and the lake water, Aiden shifted to rest his chin on the edge of the tube while he wrapped his arms around it from underneath it.

"I'm fine."

Skylar shifted so she was in the same position as him, facing him directly. "You didn't look fine."

Aiden glanced around, noting that they weren't too close to others, then said, "I'm just thinking about Shiloh."

"She's doing fine," Skylar said. "Charli said that even though she still has some residue effects from the chemo, she's doing better each day."

Aiden nodded. "It's just so hard to see her like that and not be able to do anything to help her."

"Yeah. It's a very helpless feeling."

"I'm just very grateful that Charli is letting us have a relationship with her. I know my mom has been so happy to welcome another member of the family after having lost two. And Willow loves her already."

"Charli and Blake are better people than I am," Skylar said. "I'm not sure I would have been as welcoming."

"Yeah. Me either, to be honest."

They drifted quietly for a few minutes, then Aiden said, "Do you know when you're leaving yet?"

Aiden didn't want her to leave. Now that he had her back in his life, he didn't want her to go back to Vegas. However, he understood why she might find it difficult to stay in Serenity. She'd already stayed longer than he'd thought she might. Of course, the main reason was probably her inability to work because of her foot.

Skylar took her time answering. "I don't know. Probably in a week or so. I see Gareth tomorrow, so we'll see what he says. Once

I can wear my work shoes again, I'll have to get back to my job. I doubt that they'd hold my position for much longer."

"Too bad you couldn't get a similar job flying out of Coeur d'Alene," Aiden said, trying not to add on that he really wished that could be.

"Yeah. Unfortunately, that's not really a possibility for me."

"Have you ever considered another type of job?"

"Sure. I've thought about what I might do if this didn't work out. But so far it has, so I haven't really given much thought to it."

"I wish I could move back to Serenity," Aiden mused. "But there's no company here for me to work at, and I don't really want to drive an hour every morning to get to work."

"You could start one," Skylar said. "Your plan was always to start your own business."

"Our plan," he reminded her. "We were going to open that company together."

Skylar's expression saddened, and her gaze went distant, as if recalling all the moments they'd spent talking about that future. "Yeah. Guess that wasn't what life had for us."

It hurt him that his actions had derailed the future she'd planned for herself. Because of everything, she'd abandoned her schooling and moved in a completely different direction.

"Are you happy at your job?" If she was, that would help to ease the guilt he carried over what he'd done to mess up her life.

However, the long pause before she answered caused his guilt to increase.

"It's not a bad job, and I've had the opportunity to visit places I might not have otherwise. So I enjoy that, but sometimes I feel like I'm missing something that satisfies the creative side of me."

"Do you have any hobbies that help with that?"

"Not really. These days, if I want an outlet for my creativity, it usually comes in the form of coloring in an adult coloring book."

212 · KIMBERLY RAE JORDAN

"My mom has a couple of those," Aiden said. "We use them when Willow wants us to color with her."

"You color in them too?"

Aiden shrugged. "Yep. It's not something I ever thought I'd do, but it's pretty hard to say no to my mom or to Willow. I've become pretty good at staying in the lines."

Skylar laughed. "You should have learned that in kindergarten."

"Guess I'm a late bloomer."

All of a sudden, Cole shot up through the hole in the tube, startling them. Skylar let out a shriek, then reached out to shove Cole's shoulder.

"You're going to give us a heart attack."

Cole grinned as he leaned back against the tube, hooking his arms around it. "What's happening?"

"You mean aside from you so rudely interrupting us?" Skylar asked.

"Well, yes. Aside from that. What are we chatting about?"

"Our jobs," Aiden said as he treaded water.

"Oh really? That sounds rather boring."

"It's not our fault that we don't have an exciting career like you do," Skylar told him. "Us lowly peasants sometimes have to work in dull jobs in order to pay the bills."

"You know I'd hire all of you," Cole said. "I've already made an offer to Aiden."

"I don't want to work for you," Skylar said. "You bossed me around for too many years when I didn't have a choice. No way am I going to willingly give you that position in my life."

Cole grinned at her. "I'd be a fantastic boss."

"Well, I'm not about to find out," Skylar said. "Given the way you're tossing around job offers, I hope you have a good financial advisor."

"I do. And I give everything to Jay so that he can look over all of it. He's better at numbers than I ever was."

"How much longer are you going to play?" Skylar asked.

A shadow crossed Cole's face. "I'm not sure. Maybe until my body has reached its limit. I have a year left on my current contract, so we'll see what happens after that."

"The team would be foolish to not re-sign you," Aiden said. "You're their top performing player."

Cole shrugged, making the tube shift with the movement. "You just never know where life will lead. Things happen that can change the trajectory of our lives."

Aiden gave a huff of laughter. "You're kind of preaching to the choir here, bro."

Cole grinned and nodded. "I suppose that's true."

"What's your interest in Annie?" Skylar asked, voicing the question that had been in Aiden's mind.

"I don't know." Water splashed beyond the circle of the tube as Cole kicked his feet. "There was just something about her."

"But you don't know anything about her."

"I know."

"Also, she's very, very different from the women you usually date." Skylar shifted on her side of the tube so she was higher up on it and stared right at her brother. "Are you trying to tell me this is a love at first sight situation?"

"I'm not sure about love," Cole said. "But there's... interest."

Aiden had to admit that he was slightly confused by his friend. Everything he'd seen from Cole since he'd shown up in Serenity had been slightly... off. He had no idea what it meant, but maybe it was time to have a serious conversation with the man.

"Well, it looks like you've chosen to get interested in someone who might give you a run for your money."

"We'll see."

"Cole!" Layla's voice carried across the water to them. "Can you pull us on the tubes?"

Cole slid under the water and popped up a few feet away. "I suppose I could. Let's get it rigged up. It's not going to be like getting pulled by a speedboat, though."

"That's okay. We don't want to go too fast."

"And you have to wear life jackets."

"We will."

The teens swam toward the boat, and they followed, with Cole and Aiden pulling the tube while Skylar hung on. When they got there, they climbed the ladder to get onto the platform.

"Need a hand, sis?" Cole said when Skylar approached the ladder.

"Maybe."

"Come over here." He motioned to a part of the platform away from the ladder. "Help me out, Aid."

When Aiden joined them, they bent over and each took hold of one of Skylar's arms. On the count of three, they straightened, pulling Skylar up out of the water onto the platform.

She grinned as she balanced on her good foot. "Thanks. I appreciate the hand up."

The joy on her face in that moment, combined with the beauty he'd always seen in her, made Aiden's heart trip over itself.

As a teen, he would have been more interested in how she looked in her swimsuit than the joy on her face. However, he'd since learned that focusing strictly on outward beauty led him down a path he shouldn't go with someone who wasn't his wife.

Of course, Skylar was a beautiful woman. After they'd broken up, he'd never been able to date a woman with dark hair and eyes without comparing her to Skylar. Comparing and finding them lacking in some way.

"Here's your towel, Sky," Kayleigh said as she came over with it.

"Thanks."

Skylar bent to dry off her leg before putting her walking boot back on. She then tied the towel around her waist and moved out of the way of the others, who were busy putting on life jackets, while Cole hooked the tubes up to the ropes that had been provided by the rental company.

Aiden was drawn to follow her to the bench seat where she settled, but instead, he stayed to help Cole get everything ready for the teens. Then, as the boat began to move, he stayed at the back so that he could keep an eye on the four who were on the tubes.

It struck him like a punch to the gut that this was what he'd thrown away. He and Skylar could have had more days like this. He could have gone to sit with her, putting his arm around her like Hudson had done with Kayleigh.

He could have had everything, but he'd thrown it all away because he hadn't accepted that he'd found the person he could spend the rest of his life with as a teenager. And now he had to live with a persistent ache of that loss and the realization that he might have been wrong.

CHAPTER TWENTY

"There was a match?" Skylar asked her dad. He'd announced that he had good news, and that, as far as she was concerned, was the only good news that would put that smile on her dad's face.

"Yes, indeed. There was a match."

Skylar felt a rush of relief as she sank back into her chair, covering her face with her hands as emotions overwhelmed her. She felt the couch dip beside her and an arm go around her shoulders.

Had that happened in different circumstances, she would have pulled away from Aiden. She knew it was him because of his cologne, and for once, she allowed herself to take comfort in his closeness.

"That is just the greatest news," Aiden said, his voice thick with emotion. "I know it was a long shot, but I've been praying that God would allow there to be a match for her."

"We've all been praying," her mom said. "And I'm so thankful for this answer."

Skylar wiped the tears from her cheeks as she looked up. Blake and Charli were also showing emotion over the news. In fact, Skylar wasn't sure she'd ever seen that much emotion on her brother-in-law's face. He had his arm wrapped around Charli just as Aiden did with her.

"Who is the match?" Blake asked.

Skylar expected her dad to say her or Aiden, given they were closest to Shiloh genetically. However, she knew there was a chance it could be someone else in the family or even a stranger.

Her mom and dad had tried to explain how that might happen, but there was a reason Skylar had struggled a lot with science and biology. She just couldn't grasp it.

"I've already spoken to the person, and he gave me permission to share the news with everyone."

Well, that ruled out her or Aiden, because, surely, if it had been Aiden, he would have shown some indication about it.

"He?" Aiden asked.

"Yep. The test results revealed that Cole is a good match for Shiloh."

"Cole?" She and Aiden spoke in unison, their shock was reflected on Charli and Blake's faces as well.

Her dad smiled. "I guess it's a good thing that he decided to come home and be tested."

Skylar turned to look at Aiden. He was close enough she could see the flecks of dark blue in his light blue irises. She could also see the emotions he was trying to keep in check.

"I can't believe it's Cole," he said with a grin. "He is never going to stop spoiling her now."

Skylar smiled. "This is just wild."

She leaned against Aiden for a moment, then realized that perhaps people would read more into their interaction than was there. She didn't jerk away from him, but as she straightened, his arm fell away.

"Will they do the transplant right away?" Aiden's mom asked.

Her dad shook his head. "Doing the transplant will be the step they'll take if it appears that this first treatment hasn't worked. So for now, we won't do anything with this information, but pray that we don't need it. However, if Shiloh does, then we're ready to go."

It seemed timely that this news came just as she was preparing to leave. Cole had stayed for a week before he'd flown off again. And now it was her turn.

Her ankle was much better and barely gave her any pain, even when she walked around in her work heels. She'd let Denise know that she was prepared to go back on the schedule, and her first shift was just four days away. She would be flying back to Vegas in two days' time.

It was time to get back to her job. To Vegas. To her life there. It was what she'd wanted when she'd first come back to Serenity. She hadn't intended to stay this long, so she should be looking forward to leaving.

But she wasn't.

The thought of leaving her family. Of not being able to see Shiloh for long stretches of time. Of not seeing Aiden... All of it left her with a very heavy heart. And a reluctance to return to the life she'd left behind in Vegas.

She'd come to Serenity nursing a bruised heart from a breakup, only to have her heart further broken by having to see the man who'd hurt her so badly in the past.

But somewhere along the way, healing had begun within her. Healing not just from the hurt inflicted by men, but healing from the hurt, guilt and anger she'd carried from believing that God had abandoned her. That He'd allowed Aiden to take so much from her.

Her time in Serenity, being with family, attending the church where she'd committed her life to God, seeing the changes in Aiden, spending time with Shiloh... There was no way she could be surrounded by all of that and not experience some change herself.

Her heart may have been hardened to some extent, but being around those who knew and loved her most had reached beyond the shell she'd erected around herself and her emotions. It was what Emmett had complained about when he broke up with her. That he didn't feel like she was emotionally connecting with him.

Leaving was going to be so hard.

Tears pricked at her eyes, but she refused to let them fall. There would be time for crying later. This was her life, and she needed to get back to living it.

The conversation continued on around Skylar as she tried to keep her emotions from spilling out in front of everyone.

"Sky," Charli said, drawing her attention from her thoughts. "Did you want us to bring Shiloh over tomorrow afternoon so you and Aiden can spend some time with her before you leave?"

"Yeah." The word came out strangled, so Skylar cleared her throat and tried again. "That would be great."

Willow and Shiloh were currently out in the backyard with Amelia, who had come with her parents and Shiloh for the meeting. It wasn't a full family gathering, but Skylar imagined that the news would be posted in the family group chat soon enough.

"We're still not taking her to church, but we'll come by around two," Charli said.

"Why don't you all come for lunch?" her mom suggested.

"That would be nice," Charli said. "But that's a lot of people to feed."

"We'll just do burgers and hotdogs again. That's easy enough." Her mom turned to Tracy. "And you and Willow are welcome to come with Aiden as well."

"Thank you for the invite, but I think that this time, it's best for us not to be here. If we come, Willow won't want to leave, and I think it's important that Aiden and Skylar have that time with Shiloh."

"We'll come for lunch, but then we'll take the other kids home so they're not a distraction either," Charli said.

With the plan settled, Charli and Blake decided it was time to go. Shiloh and Willow were disappointed when they were brought inside and told that they had to part ways.

As Shiloh came to say goodbye to her, Skylar had to once again hold back her tears as she wrapped her arms around Shiloh's frail body. "I love you, sweetie."

"Love you too, Auntie Sky."

She moved on to Aiden, and gave him a hug, then high fived his hand when he held it up for her. It was interesting to see how Aiden interacted with her. He was gentle with her, just like he was with Willow, but he was also willing to do whatever it took to coax a smile or laugh from her.

He would have made a great dad.

Pain spiked again, and she crossed her arms over her waist and turned away from Aiden and Shiloh.

"This was such great news," Charli said as she slid her arm around Skylar. "Are you doing okay?"

"I am," she assured her. "Just a little emotional with it all. I kind of didn't dare hope that we'd have a match since the chances were so slim. And yet here we are with a match, and it's Cole."

"I can't wait to talk to him to find out how he took the news."

"I'm just so grateful that he came to be tested. I didn't pressure him, because it seemed unlikely that he'd be a match."

"Something prompted him to come," Charli said. "Or maybe I should say some*one* prompted him. I believe God has been at work in all of this."

"You're not mad at God for allowing this to happen to Shiloh?"

"No. I don't understand why, but there's no way Blake or I could have made it through this if not for our faith that God has a purpose in everything that's happened. We might never know what that is while we're on this earth, but I trust that God is at work. Whatever happens, He's in control and working this out for His glory."

Skylar had heard those words plenty of times over the years, but they struck deeper now. As an adult, she had an understanding of life that she hadn't had as a teen. Back then, things working out for

God's glory hadn't held a lot of meaning. Her life had been relatively simple. She hadn't faced any huge tragedies.

But then she'd gotten pregnant and had to give up her baby. From that point on, she could understand more about the complexities of life and the situations people faced. Some of it she'd also seen in her own siblings' lives.

Life wasn't black and white. Families didn't always get along. People like Rori and Lexi had family issues that were deep and hurtful. And yet, they'd risen above them and had come to love God in spite of those circumstances.

Could she do that? Could she give her life fully to God, as she'd once pledged to do? Now that it might require difficult things of her?

The question lingered in her mind as they said goodbye and the house emptied out until it was just her and her parents. When they headed to the family room at the back of the house, Skylar went up to her room.

Once there, she pulled out her work heels and slipped them on again. The idea of going back to wearing them for hours on end did not appeal to her at all. Wearing them had never bothered her before, but now, putting the heels back on represented something that left her an emotional mess. It represented her leaving behind her family, and those she loved the most.

After wearing them for a while with no pain, she slipped them off and put them beside the suitcase that now sat open on the loveseat near the window. She needed to pack soon, but not right then.

The next day, when they got home from church, Skylar went to change into something more comfortable before returning to the kitchen to help her mom and dad with the meal. As she worked alongside her parents, she realized that this would likely be the last time she did that for the foreseeable future.

When her mom bumped her hip playfully to get her to move out of the way, Skylar just about burst into tears. She was going to miss them so much.

Given that she'd lived apart from them for so long, she wouldn't have thought that she'd find it difficult to leave. But she was really struggling with being away from her family in a way that she never had before.

It wasn't too much later when Charli and Blake showed up with their kids, followed shortly after by Aiden. They gathered around the tables on the back deck, delving into the food that had been prepared.

The meal was lively since Charli and Blake had brought their two youngest. A pair of boys who had more energy than Skylar could ever remember having.

But Charli and Blake were very patient with them, correcting them when necessary. It was clear that the boys loved all three of their older sisters, but they were especially gentle and loving towards Shiloh. The youngest had insisted on being able to sit next to her and had offered to share his food with her, even though she had her own plate.

It was a good reminder that Shiloh was part of a wonderful family. If there was one thing that had gone right in that whole situation in Skylar's estimation, it was that she'd asked Charli and Blake to adopt Shiloh. Even though her feelings were still a mess over all the things that had transpired back then, she had peace in knowing that Shiloh had been well-loved by her family.

Once the meal was finished and cleaned up, Charli, Blake, and the other kids left, promising to come back in a couple of hours to pick Shiloh up.

Since it was such a nice day, they stayed in the backyard while her parents went inside.

"What would you like to do, Shiloh?" Skylar asked once it was just the three of them.

"Mama brought a bag of things," Shiloh said, pointing to a large tote that sat near the back door.

Aiden went to get it, then set it on the table and unzipped it for Shiloh. "What all did you bring?"

"Stuff to color with and some books."

"Looks like you have a couple of games in here too," Aiden said as he set out the items from the bag onto the table. "What would you like to do first?"

"Can we color?" she asked, then looked at Skylar. "And maybe you could read to us while we do."

"I can do that," Skylar said. "What book are you reading?"

Shiloh picked up a book with a familiar title on it and handed it to her. "We're reading this one."

Skylar stared at the cover for a moment, recalling when she'd read the books of the *Little House on the Prairie* series for herself. It struck her as surreal that here she was, preparing to read it to her daughter.

Skylar's gaze went to Shiloh as she and Aiden decided on the pictures they wanted to color—Aiden's in an adult coloring book that Charli had thoughtfully included.

Once that was decided, Skylar opened the book at the bookmark, then lifted it and began to read.

After she'd read a chapter, Skylar paused to ask Shiloh some questions about the story and what she thought of what was going on. She had clearly been paying attention to the story because she didn't hesitate to answer.

"You read really good," Shiloh said. "Just like my mama."

"Does your dad read to you, too?"

"Sometimes. But he doesn't like it as much as Mama does."

"How about I read another chapter, then Uncle Aiden can have a try?"

Shiloh glanced at Aiden, then nodded with a grin. "I'd like that."

Skylar's gaze met Aiden's, and she thought he might protest, but he just shrugged. It dawned on her then that he probably had more experience reading out loud, thanks to Willow.

When she finished the next chapter, she handed the book over to Aiden and took possession of the coloring book. Aiden had only half-finished his picture, so she decided to finish that while he read.

"You read good too," Shiloh said after Aiden had read a chapter. "Almost as good as Mama and Auntie Sky."

"I get lots of practice, since Willow likes me to read to her sometimes."

"Is Willow your daughter?" Shiloh asked, placing her elbow on the table and leaning her cheek against her hand.

"No. She's my sister's daughter. My sister died. That's why Willow lives with me and Nana."

"But why isn't she your daughter, too?" Shiloh asked. "Like Auntie Sky couldn't take care of me, so her sister became my mom. If Willow doesn't have a mom or dad anymore, why aren't you her dad?"

The question showed that Shiloh had given her own situation some thought, and it was a logical conclusion when she applied the framework of her situation over Willow's.

"To be honest, I'm not sure. My mom was named Willow's guardian, and she wanted to take care of her, so that's how it's worked out."

Shiloh shrugged, then focused on her coloring again. "Maybe Willow would like to have another mom and dad. I have two moms and dads. It doesn't seem fair that she doesn't have any."

"Well." Aiden cleared his throat. "Perhaps that's a conversation we need to have with Willow to see what she'd like."

Shiloh made a lot of sense, but it appeared that it wasn't something that Aiden had spent much time considering.

Rather than pursue that topic of conversation, Aiden started to read the next chapter. But Skylar had a feeling that it was still in his mind, just like it was in hers.

When Shiloh had finished her coloring, she declared that she wanted to play a game. They were sorting out the cards for *Go Fish* when her mom came out with a pitcher of lemonade and three glasses.

"I thought you might be getting thirsty," she said as she poured juice for each of them.

"We are," Skylar replied, picking up her glass. "I've been reading out loud, so my throat is parched."

"It sounds like you've been having fun out here."

"We're going to play *Go Fish,* Grandma." Shiloh held up her handful of cards. "Want to play too?"

"Not today, darling," she said, bending to press a kiss on the top of Shiloh's head. "I'm spending some time with Grandpa. Next time though."

After she went back inside, Skylar had Shiloh explain the rules to them just to make sure they were all on the same page. At some point, Shiloh began to show some tiredness. Skylar had her come sit on her lap and they played one hand together against Aiden.

Skylar took in the feel of her daughter on her lap. The scent of her shampoo. The little laugh she'd give each time she told Aiden to go fish.

She packed away every little detail to pull out later when she was back in Vegas and missing Shiloh and the rest of her family.

By the time Charli returned to pick Shiloh up, she was definitely showing signs of being exhausted, and Skylar hoped she hadn't overdone things by hanging out with her and Aiden. Charli didn't seem overly concerned, however. Just commenting that they'd take a nap when they got home.

After Skylar had hugged Shiloh, she turned to Charli, her eyes flooding with tears as her older sister gathered her into her arms.

"Thank you," Skylar whispered. "Thank you for being such a great mom to her. I love you."

Charli's embrace tightened. "I love you too. I know it was hard to give her up, but just know that you gave Blake and me the best gift ever. We love her with all our hearts, and I'm glad that she knows about you now and the sacrifice you made so that she could be part of our family."

They stood together for a couple of minutes as Skylar silently wept on her sister's shoulder. When she finally felt the swell of emotion ebb, Skylar took a deep breath, then stepped back, reaching to wipe her cheeks with the sleeve of her T-shirt.

"Here you go, darling," her mom said, pressing a wad of tissues into her hand.

"Thanks." As Skylar dried her eyes and blew her nose, she noticed that Shiloh wasn't there. Nor was her dad or Aiden.

"They went out onto the front porch to see the bird feeder Dad put in last week."

Skylar was glad that Shiloh hadn't been there to witness her meltdown. "I guess we should go see it, too."

Charli led the way, while her mom looped her arm through Skylar's and followed Charli.

Aiden was holding Shiloh in his arms while Skylar's dad showed off the bird feeder that hung from a branch of a tree in the front yard. Emotion once again threatened to choke her, but Skylar swallowed hard and refused to let the tears spill yet again.

At Charli's urging, she gave Shiloh one more hug, then a few minutes later, waved as Charli drove down the driveway.

Once they were gone, her parents went back into the house. Skylar and Aiden remained on the porch. Skylar wanted to turn to Aiden for support in that emotional moment, but that wasn't how things were between them.

"Do you need a ride to the airport tomorrow?" Aiden asked, breaking the silence.

"Uh, I think my dad was going to take me."

"If you want, I can give you a ride to Coeur d'Alene."

Skylar shifted to look at him. "Don't you need to work?"

"I can go in a little late. I'll just stay at Mom's tonight."

Where the idea would have been abhorrent not that long ago, Skylar now found herself considering it. "If you're sure."

"I'm positive."

"In that case, I'll take you up on that offer."

She gave him the details of when her flight was scheduled to depart and from there, they decided on the best time to leave Serenity.

"I'll see you in the morning," Aiden said. "Thanks for letting me hang out with you and Shiloh this afternoon."

"I think it went well." She hesitated, then asked, "Would you send me pictures of her when you spend time with her? And when she's with Willow, too?"

"I'd be happy to do that."

"Do you think you'll see her a lot?"

"I'm not sure," Aiden said. "But I plan to come home on the weekends to spend time with Mom and Willow."

Skylar wished that her life would accommodate such regular visits, but it didn't. And she had no idea when she'd next be back in Serenity. After Aiden said goodbye, Skylar watched as he drove away, then went inside to spend some time with her parents.

The countdown was on, and she wasn't happy about it at all.

CHAPTER TWENTY-ONE

Skylar was ready to go when Aiden showed up the next morning. He loaded her bags into the car while she said goodbye to her parents.

"I hope it won't be too long before we see you again," her dad said as he gave her a tight hug. "It's been wonderful having you here with us the past few weeks."

"Yes, it has been," her mom agreed as she moved in to take her husband's place. "It was nice to have a not-so-empty nest for a little while."

"Sprained ankle aside, I had a nice time," she told them. "And I'll be back when I can."

"Thanks for taking her to the airport, Aiden," her dad said as Aiden joined them, holding out his hand to the man.

"I figured I was going that way anyway," he said as he shook her dad's hand. "Though I have to admit I'm a bit surprised she agreed to go with me."

Her dad chuckled. "You and me both."

Skylar glared at them. "Hey, now!"

Her mom laughed as she slipped her arm around Skylar's waist. "You have to admit that had he made this offer when you first came home, the answer would have been a resounding no."

"True, but this is now. Things change."

"That they do," her mom said with a nod. "And for the better this time."

"Well, we'd better go so I don't miss my flight."

"Let us know when you get to the airport and when you get home."

"I will."

After another quick hug for each of her parents, she told them she loved them, then followed Aiden to where he'd parked. He opened the passenger door for her before going around to slide behind the wheel.

As soon as he started the engine, Skylar rolled down her window and waved at her parents.

"Safe travels, darling," her mom called out.

As they drove down the winding driveway to the road that would take them to Coeur d'Alene, Skylar let out a long sigh.

"You doing okay?" Aiden asked.

"I guess." She leaned her head back against the head rest and stared out the window at the familiar scenery that slipped past. "I just didn't expect that leaving would be this hard."

"Like you said, things change. From what I understand, a lot more went down on this trip than usually does on your visits home."

"That's true," Skylar said, turning her head to look at him. "In the past, Shiloh was perfectly healthy. It was easy to slip in and slip out again without too much emotional turmoil."

"I know it can't be easy to leave when Shiloh's still not one hundred percent, but she's headed in that direction."

Skylar took in his profile as he spoke. He had a strong jawline with a nose that had a slight bend to it thanks to him having it broken by a collision with a guy's elbow when playing basketball in high school. His clean-shaven cheeks as a teen had disappeared, as he seemed to prefer a bit of scruff. A five o'clock shadow is what her dad would likely call it.

She hated to admit that she found him as attractive now as she had when they were teens. For a moment, she wondered if the reverse was true. However, as quickly as that thought came into her mind, she shoved it away.

Skylar already knew that he'd thought he could do better than her as a teen, and that probably hadn't changed. It was a moot point, regardless.

They'd reached a point where they could be around each other without anger and hurt raging inside her. It wasn't completely gone, but she could manage it in a way she'd struggled to when they'd first reconnected.

"Are you getting used to living in a place on your own, rather than in your mom's basement?"

Aiden gave her an exasperated glance before he said, "I wasn't living in my mom's basement. I actually own the house, so I was living in *my* basement while my mom and my niece lived on the main floor."

"So, are you going to move up to the main floor now that she and Willow have moved back to Serenity?"

"I don't think so. At least not yet," he said. "I think there will be times when they come to spend time in Coeur d'Alene, so then they can stay in their old rooms. Plus, I've got the basement set up like I want it, and I don't need all the extra space that's on the main floor."

"Were you surprised when your mom decided to move back to Serenity?"

Aiden didn't answer right away, his attention on the traffic as they came to a stoplight. As he accelerated through the light when it turned green, he said, "Yeah. A little, but I was pretty sure that it would happen at some point. I'm actually happy about it though, even if it means I'm living on my own."

"Why are you happy about it?"

"One of the reasons my mom was so willing to move in with me was because that house was just too hard for her to be in. She'd been doing okay after Dad's death, but when Bethany died, it was like Mom couldn't handle being in the house anymore. She just walked away from it, not wanting to bring any of the furnishings or anything to the house in CDA."

"I can't imagine how difficult that has been for her."

"I remember so clearly what my mom said as we stood over Bethany's casket, her staring at her daughter for the last time." Aiden hesitated, then cleared his throat. "She said no parent should ever have to bury their child. That a parent wasn't supposed to outlive their children."

The words sank deep into Skylar's heart as she considered the battle Shiloh was fighting for her life. She couldn't imagine how she'd handle it if Shiloh lost that battle.

Her breath caught in her throat as her heart began to pound. Her world narrowed as she struggled to take a breath because of the vice that had tightened around her chest.

"Skylar?" Aiden's voice was distant, but she could hear the alarm in it. "Hang on, baby. Just hang on."

She felt the car come to a jerking stop and reached out to grab the dashboard, hanging on to it like a lifeline. The door beside her opened, and she felt a touch on her back, then Aiden took her hand, which was fisted against her chest.

"Skylar, I want you to breathe with me." Aiden's voice was closer, calming her with its steadiness. "Deep breath in. Now let it out."

Skylar unfisted her hand to grab onto his as she focused on his voice, fighting to draw in a breath to fill her lungs when it felt like there was a vice around her chest.

Was she having a heart attack?

Or was this just a panic attack?

Aiden continued to guide her breathing, and slowly but surely, her breaths got deeper and more fulfilling. Then her heart rate slowed, and everything around her came back into focus.

"Aiden?" she said as she turned to look at him.

He gave her a gentle smile that filled his eyes with something that almost looked like affection.

"Are you feeling better?"

She nodded. "I'm sorry. I think that was a panic attack."

"You've never had one before?"

"No."

"What brought it on?"

Skylar swallowed and tightened her grip on his hand, even though she knew she should let go. "It was when you said that bit about parents shouldn't have to bury their children. All I could think of was how close we are to that with Shiloh. The treatment might fail. The transplant might fail. We might... we might have to..."

Aiden put his arm around her and gently pulled her close. "She's doing better. She's strong. We have to believe that she'll come through this."

This time, Skylar's fears came out in tears, which frustrated her, even as she found a sort of cathartic release in them. She'd cried more in the past few weeks than she had since the time following her giving Shiloh up for adoption. She didn't want to shed any more tears.

But first, she had to get through that crying spell.

Aiden continued to hold her, surrounding Skylar with his strength, his gentleness, and the scent of his cologne, which she'd forever associate with him.

"I'm sorry if I triggered that for you with what I said. I didn't mean to upset you."

"I know." Skylar took a deep breath and let it out, trying to send the lingering emotions out into the world. Anywhere but deep in her chest where they hurt so badly.

Finally, she straightened, giving him a sideways glance as he let her go. "We should probably go. I don't want to miss my flight."

After a long moment, Aiden closed her door, then circled around to get behind the wheel. Starting the engine back up, he gave her a quick glance. "I'm beginning to think maybe you *should* miss your flight."

"What do you mean?" Skylar asked as she pulled a tissue out of her purse. "I need to get back to work. I can't stay here."

"I understand that you need to leave for the sake of your job," he said. "But for the sake of your heart, I think you should stay."

With that, he pulled back out onto the road and continued the drive to Coeur d'Alene. It was a drive made in silence, but for the music softly drifting from the speakers.

The silence wasn't angry or hostile, but it was weighted and tense. Like it was holding its breath, waiting for the next word to be spoken. It didn't come from Skylar, though, because she didn't know what to say. And perhaps Aiden had the same problem, since he too didn't break the silence.

When they pulled up in front of the airport, Aiden said, "I'm sorry I can't go in with you, but I need to be at work for a meeting."

"You don't have to worry about that. I think I'll probably be going through security pretty quickly."

Aiden gave a nod, then got out to retrieve her bags from the trunk of the car. Once she had them, he closed the trunk. He stood, his hand resting on it, staring at her and seeming to have some sort of battle with himself.

Finally, something broke his indecision, and he crossed the space between them and took her into his arms. Skylar froze for a minute, then wrapped her arms around him.

"Take care of yourself," he murmured. "And don't be gone too long."

Skylar's hands gripped the back of his shirt. "I'll try not to be. And you take care of yourself too."

Flooded with unfamiliar emotions, she pulled away and grabbed the handles of her check-in and hand carry bags to pull them into the airport. She didn't glance back until right before the glass doors slid closed, and she caught a glimpse of Aiden still standing there.

The doors slid open again as someone else walked in, and she saw him lift his hand. After a brief hesitation, she waved back at him. When she turned around that time, she didn't look back again.

But as she stared out at the plane that would take her away from Serenity Point and those she loved, Skylar knew that Aiden was right. Her heart didn't want to leave.

Skylar pulled her flight bag into the apartment and set it off to the side. She let out a groan as she slipped off her shoes. Grabbing the handle of the bag, she pulled it into her bedroom. After she took off her uniform and hung it up, she unpacked the bag she'd taken for the five-day trip to New York, London and Paris.

Jumping time zones was never easy, and she was exhausted. Thankfully, she had three days off before her next trip.

She took a long shower and did a bit of pampering before climbing out. After drying off, she dressed in a pair of loose cotton shorts and an oversized T-shirt.

Feeling more refreshed than when she'd walked in the door, Skylar went to the kitchen to make something to eat since lunch had gotten forgotten in the busyness of the plane's arrival in Vegas, completing the end of flight jobs, and then getting home. But before she pulled the stuff out to make a sandwich, she checked her phone for messages.

On the way home in the ride share she'd called at the airport, she'd texted all the usual people. A habit she'd gotten into over the past two weeks since returning home.

Mom: *Glad you made it home, darling. Did everything go well? It went smoothly. Glad to be home again, though. Love you!*

She backed out of that text conversation and into the next one.

Charli: *Yay! We need to set up a chat for you and Shiloh sometime in the next couple of days. She wants you to read to her again.*

I don't have anything going on, so any time you want will work for me. Looking forward to it. Hugs and kisses to you all.

She had bought a copy of the book that she'd read to Shiloh that last time they'd been together, and she'd continued to read from it with her every couple of days. Charli had said that Shiloh had asked that Skylar be the one to keep reading that book, so Charli had chosen a different book for them to read at home.

After that message, she went to the next one.

Aiden: *Back on American soil, huh? Hope you didn't have any cranky passengers or ones that got air sick.*

Skylar chuckled, unable to keep the smile from her face.

No cranky or sick ones, thankfully. But glad I don't have to deal with people for a few days.

She didn't bother to mention that this flight had had a couple of flirty and slightly handsy men in the group. It always seemed like there was one or two on flights like that who thought they'd shoot their shot with her.

On most flights, she was far more likely to deal with drunk and flirtatious men than she was cranky or sick people.

How was your project presentation?

He'd mentioned that he was putting on what they hoped would be their final presentation for a client before they would sign off on the project.

Somehow, in the two weeks since she'd returned home, they'd fallen into texting each other fairly regularly. At least once a day, if not more. Skylar wasn't exactly sure why she encouraged it, though she tried to convince herself it was because he was sharing things with her about Shiloh.

Except she actually got most of her information on Shiloh from Charli. Aiden only passed stuff on to her after his visits with Shiloh on the weekend.

Aiden: *It went really well. We should hear within the next couple of days if this is the accepted version of the design. This has caused me and my partner to gray prematurely, I have to say.*

Well, they say men with gray hair are distinguished, so I think you'll be okay.

Aiden: *LOL But no one wants to look like a grandfather when they're not even a father yet. Well, I mean, not a full-time father yet.*

Is that something you want?

Aiden's response was slow to come, and Skylar didn't even realize she was holding her breath until his reply popped up on the screen, and it rushed out of her.

Aiden: *Definitely. I'm just not sure when it will happen. For now, I'm happy to have Shiloh and Willow in my life, and to have a father/uncle role with them.*

Skylar shifted to lean her hip against the counter as she stared down at the reply. In the past few weeks, she'd imagined what Aiden would be like in a fatherly role, but now the image that came to her was of Aiden having children of his own with some unknown woman.

Putting her phone face down on the counter, she moved to the fridge to pull out some deli meat, tomatoes, and cheese, as well as everything else she needed to make her favorite sandwich. Her phone chimed with an incoming text message, but she waited until she'd laid two pieces of bread on her plate and spread mayo on them to check it.

Aiden: *What about you?*

I'm not sure kids are in my future, and I think I'm okay with that.

Aiden: *What? Why?*

Skylar could picture him frowning at his phone as he typed out the message.

Let's just say my attempts at relationships have been unsuccessful, and I'm not in a place at the moment where I want to devote that much time and energy into someone else.

Aiden: *I guess I understand that, but you always hoped to have kids, so I hope it works out for you.*

We'll see.

I need to get a few things done here, so I'll chat with you later.

Or maybe they wouldn't. This conversation was the most serious and personal one they'd had to date, and she wasn't in a hurry to change that.

After that last interaction at the airport, Skylar hadn't been sure how it would impact things between them. Neither of them had mentioned it, but the memory of it lingered in her mind and in her heart, leaving her wanting... more. Not more panic attacks. More closeness with Aiden.

Aiden: *Sure thing. Have a good rest of the day.*

You, too.

Skylar set her phone down again and finished getting her lunch ready. Once it was made, she filled a glass with water, then carried the plate and glass to the table that was set out on the balcony. It was fiercely hot outside, but she didn't mind dealing with it for the short time it took her to eat.

She was back in the kitchen cleaning up when her phone chimed again. After drying her hands, she checked the screen, frowning when she saw the message.

Emmett: *How's your day going? Denise mentioned you were back from your latest trip. Could we meet up for coffee?*

This wasn't the first time he'd texted her since she'd returned to Vegas. Skylar wasn't sure what to make of his attempt to get together with her.

Why?

Emmett: *I thought it would be nice to catch up.*

Things are over between us. You ended our relationship, so I'm not sure what you're wanting now.

Emmett: *I've missed you. I think perhaps I was hasty in ending things.*

You were right to break up with me. Unfortunately, if you thought I was emotionally unavailable before, I'm even more so now.

Plus, there was no way she could get back together with someone who gave up so easily.

Are you dating someone else already?

Unbidden, Aiden came to mind as he'd been the moment she'd turned back to look at him at the airport.

No. But I have a lot of stuff going on with my family, and I'm just not prepared to be in a relationship. And I'm sorry, but you had your chance. I don't feel strongly enough about you to want to try again. You were right to end things.

Emmett: *Well, I'm sure if we could just meet, you'd remember how good we were together.*

He wasn't wrong that they'd had some good times together, but the thought of being in a relationship with him again twisted her stomach. A big part of their relationship had been physical, and she knew she couldn't go back to that.

Something had stirred in her spirit that now had her rejecting parts of how she'd previously lived her life.

I'm sorry. But it just won't work out.

Not wanting to get any further text from him, Skylar quickly went through the process of blocking his number. Next, she went through social media and blocked him on all of those accounts. She didn't want to have to deal with him again.

It was unfortunate that he was friends with people she worked with, which was how they'd met. But Skylar hoped they could understand why she just wasn't interested in dating him again.

Tiredness swamped her as she finished up in the kitchen. She didn't sleep super well when she was away from her own bed, so the tiredness wasn't a surprise.

She went to her room and dropped down on the bed. After setting her alarm for two hours, she curled up with her pillows and closed her eyes.

As she did, an image of Aiden and Shiloh came to her mind. It was them posed as they'd been in the picture she'd taken of them as they'd bent over coloring books on their last time together.

Now, Aiden was able to still spend time with Shiloh and color with her, but Skylar was relegated to virtual interactions with her. Her heart hurt that each time they said goodbye, there was no hug or kiss. Just a small wave as the screen went dark.

She wanted more. She didn't want to take Shiloh from Charli or Blake, but she wanted more of those interactions with her. To be close enough to celebrate the special moments in her life—and Skylar refused to believe that there would be anything but lots of special moments to come.

If God answered her prayer, she'd be there to witness the big events. Graduations, her wedding, her baby or babies. Skylar wanted to be there for all of that.

But she also wanted to be able to tell her what a good job she'd done coloring a picture. She wanted to watch as she learned to ride her bike. As she improved in her skating. Skylar wanted to be in the audience when Shiloh searched the crowd. She wanted to see the smile bloom on her face when she spotted her.

She wanted as much as she could have in her role as Shiloh's birth mom.

Unfortunately, she wouldn't be able to have hardly any of that if she stayed in Vegas.

If the ache in her heart was anything to go by, it was perhaps time to consider that change lay in her future.

CHAPTER TWENTY-TWO

Aiden leaned back in the booth he was seated in, patting his stomach as he did. "That was delicious."

Devon nodded and mirrored Aiden's position from his spot across the table. "I thought we deserved a celebration after what we've had to deal with in this project."

"I can't believe they finally signed off on it," Aiden said with a sigh. "I was beginning to wonder if we were going to end up with our first stalemate."

"I'm just glad they finally accepted that they couldn't have everything they wanted. We're not above the regulations of the city and state."

"And now we move forward."

The past week had been stressful, and yet also fulfilling with regards to his career.

He couldn't say the same about things between him and Skylar. For some reason, after they'd texted earlier in the week, he hadn't heard anything further from her. Which was odd since they'd been texting pretty much every day prior to that.

Unfortunately, she was off on another trip, and he didn't feel comfortable bothering her while she was working.

On Monday, it would be three weeks since she'd left. It honestly felt like the longest three weeks of his life. Perhaps time would be going faster if he knew when he'd see her again, but Skylar had given no indication of when she planned to come back to Serenity.

He knew he should be worried about his desire to see her... to be with her... again. But he wasn't. Being around her again had drawn something to the surface of his heart that he couldn't ignore.

Over the weeks that she'd been in Serenity, he'd gotten to know the woman she'd become, all the while getting glimpses of who she'd once been. It hadn't happened right away, since she'd been determined to keep distance between them and had erected a glass wall around herself. One that he could see her through but left him with no access to her emotions.

It had happened gradually. But on the boat, he'd finally felt like that wall was cracking and that she didn't hate him like she had at the start.

He'd thought he'd be happy with friendship between them. But as time passed, his heart was telling him that he wanted something more. Something deeper and lasting. Something more than they'd previously had.

"Are you heading to Serenity tonight?" Devon asked as he picked up his coffee and took a sip.

"I'm not sure yet. I may just go out tomorrow morning."

"How has it been not having your mom and Willow around?"

"It's quiet, and I have to cook all my own meals now."

Devon chuckled. "So you miss your mom's cooking?"

"Sure do," Aiden said. "Wouldn't you?"

"Definitely not. I grew up on burnt ramen and mac and cheese. My mom is a terrible cook. She tries, bless her heart, but she rarely succeeds."

"My mom's a great cook," Aiden said. "So without her, my diet has narrowed to some pretty basic stuff."

"How is Shiloh?"

Aiden thought of the conversation he'd had with Charli the night before. "She hasn't been feeling very well the last day or so. Charli wasn't sure if it was just more residual effects from the last round of treatment or if it was something more."

Aiden had been praying hard that it wasn't something more. The idea that the initial treatment might not have worked was scary and almost induced a panic attack similar to what Skylar had experienced on the way to the airport.

Shiloh not feeling well was one of the reasons he didn't feel compelled to rush to Serenity that night. Usually, he spent some time with Shiloh on Saturday mornings, but with her feeling ill, Charli had said it would probably be best if he didn't come by.

His worry over Shiloh was high, but he was trying to do as Pastor Kennedy had said during his latest sermon. He needed to place this current situation with Shiloh fully into God's hands. He needed to trust that God would work this all out for His glory.

It was the hardest thing to do, and it made him feel incredibly helpless.

As their meal ended, Devon and Aiden settled the bill then left the restaurant. As they walked out into the August evening, Aiden took a deep breath. The sun hadn't quite set yet, but the night shadows were beginning to encroach on the day.

"I'll see you Monday," Devon said as he stuck out his hand. When Aiden took it, Devon pulled him in for a quick hug, thumping him on the back. "Hope you have a good weekend."

"You too. Tell your lovely wife I said hi."

"Will do." He gave a two fingered salute, then turned in the direction of his car.

As Aiden drove home, he contemplated going to Serenity. Normally, he wouldn't even be debating it, but something was giving him pause, and he didn't know why.

Please God. Give me guidance.

It didn't seem to be something that should require this much prayer and thought. But it just didn't feel like an easy decision that night for some reason.

When he got home, he called his mom.

"If you feel like you should stay there for the night, then you do that," his mom said when he explained that he was feeling unsure what to do. "Willow is already in bed, so she won't know that you're not here."

"Okay. I'll try to get out there first thing in the morning."

"If you still don't feel you should come then, don't. We're fine."

The unsettled feeling continued to grow in Aiden even after he hung up the phone. Sitting on the edge of his bed with his phone grasped between his hands in his lap, Aiden bent his head and prayed.

Heavenly Father, I lift this whole situation before You, asking You to guide and direct me. I also pray that You will place Your hand of healing on Shiloh so that whatever might be plaguing her body goes away.

Aiden paused, swallowing hard. *Please God, don't let it be related to the cancer. Don't let her be relapsing, please.*

A vice tightened around his chest as he thought of that possibility, and with that thought came one of Skylar. *I don't know why she's not responding to me, Father, but I really feel like she should be here. I'm going to text her again, so I pray that she'll be receptive to hearing from me. And impress on her heart the importance of coming back to Serenity.*

Aiden wasn't sure why he felt so strongly about Skylar being back in Serenity, but there was no denying that he did. And it wasn't just because he wanted her close by. He felt it would be good for Shiloh and Skylar's family, too.

He gripped his phone more tightly as he fought against the feeling of helplessness that he just couldn't seem to get rid of. There was some solace in knowing that he wasn't the only one feeling that way. He had a feeling that Blake and Charli also fought against the helpless feeling that came with being unable to control Shiloh's health.

When his phone rang, Aiden jerked, and it fell between his feet on the carpeted floor. As he reached for it, he prayed that it wasn't Charli.

Aiden's heart sank when he saw Blake's name on the screen. Blake was never the one to contact him, so he knew this couldn't be good news.

"Hi, Blake," he said. "What's up?"

"We've had to bring Shiloh into the children's hospital," Blake said, his deep voice rough. "She spiked a fever. Gareth came with us, and he's with Charli and Shiloh now. But Charli wanted me to tell you what's going on."

"Thanks for letting me know," Aiden said. "Should I come up to the hospital?"

"Probably not tonight, but you could possibly come in the morning, depending on what they say about her condition."

"Have you let Skylar know?"

"Not yet." Blake cleared his throat. "But Mom or Dad might have called her."

"Okay. Maybe I'll get in touch with her to see if she knows already."

For some reason, Aiden wanted to be the one to tell her since the two of them were the only ones who truly understood the difficult position they found themselves in as parents to a child who already had parents.

Blake sighed. "I'd better go."

"Could you let me know how she does through the night? Text or call me at any time."

"We'll do that."

"And I'll be praying."

"Thanks. We'll be praying hard too."

After the call ended, Aiden felt a rush of emotion. Fear, anger, worry. It swamped him like a tsunami, and he didn't know how to deal with it, so he just let it come out.

At one time in his life, weeping would have made him feel emasculated, but right then, all he felt was broken with helplessness. But in the midst of the storm in his heart there was one bright unwavering light.

He may be feeling helpless and broken, but he was not without hope.

Wiping the tears from his eyes, Aiden took a deep breath, then lifted his phone. For a long moment, he pondered what to say. It took several attempts to get out the simple message to Skylar.

Have you talked to your parents? If not, give me a call when you can.

As he waited for a response, he prayed that she was in a place where she could have a difficult conversation with him. If she was in the middle of a flight, he probably wouldn't hear from her for several hours.

While he waited, he called his mom back and let her know what was going on. Her silence after he told her that Shiloh was back in the hospital told him that she was finding the news as difficult to process as he had.

"I'll fast and pray for her healing tomorrow," she said finally, her voice tremulous.

Fasting was something he'd learned recently that his mom frequently did, especially in combination with praying for a specific situation.

"Pray also that Skylar will be strong enough to hear this news on her own."

"I will, sweetheart," his mom assured him.

"Speaking of Skylar, she's calling," he said when his phone vibrated in his hand and her name popped up on the screen. "I'll call you back later."

When he answered her call, her first words were, "What's going on, Aiden?"

"Shiloh spiked a fever earlier today, and they've had to take her back to the children's hospital," he told her, deciding that ripping the bandage off was the best way to go.

"Noooo." The word came out as a soft wail, piercing deep into Aiden's heart. "She wasn't supposed to get sick again."

"They don't know for sure what's causing the fever," he told her. "It might be something that just requires antibiotics."

"Or it might be something more."

Aiden sighed. "Yes. It might be something more."

There was silence from Skylar for a long moment.

"Where are you?" he asked.

"I'm in Miami at the moment," she said, her voice wavering. "I'm supposed to fly back to Vegas tomorrow."

Aiden wanted to tell her that she should come to Serenity, but he had no right to do that. It was a decision she needed to make for herself. She had the information, now it was up to her to decide what to do.

"I'll keep you updated on what's going on," he said. "Blake was the one to call me earlier, and he said he'd keep me in the loop."

"Blake called you?"

He knew that would seem as strange to her as it had to him. "Yes. He said Charli and Gareth were with Shiloh as they were getting her admitted. I guess he was given the task of calling people."

"Gareth was with them?"

"Yes. Blake said he'd come with them from Serenity."

"She must really not have been doing well if they wanted a doctor with them for the trip."

A similar thought had flitted through his mind earlier, but he hadn't wanted to dwell on it.

"I knew she wasn't feeling well because I'd spoken to Charli earlier today and she'd mentioned Shiloh probably wouldn't be up to a visit from me in the morning."

"When I was on my last video call with her she seemed more tired than usual."

"I think we may have to prepare ourselves that this could be a recurrence of her cancer."

"It shouldn't have happened so soon." Skylar's voice cracked with emotion. "She should have had more time to gain strength so she could fight it again."

"It's good that Cole's offseason, because if this is a recurrence of her cancer, we're going to need him."

"I don't know what to do." The words were spoken softly. "What should I do, Aiden? Should I come now?"

She may have been asking his advice, but it was a decision she needed to make for herself. Still, he couldn't help but point her in the direction he thought she should go.

"If I were in your position, I think I'd come," Aiden said. "But I know you have to take your job into consideration."

"I'll book a flight for after I get back to Vegas tomorrow. Hopefully by then they'll have a better idea of what she's dealing with."

"Let me know when you're arriving, and I'll pick you up at the airport."

"I need to call my parents," she said.

"I have a feeling they're helping out with the other kids."

"Yeah. Probably."

Aiden could see the benefit of having a large family in a situation like this one. There were many people to call on for help. Like Gareth coming with them to the hospital in Coeur d'Alene.

"I'd better go and make some calls myself," she said. "I'll talk to you soon."

"Take care of yourself," he told her. There was more he wanted to tell her, but that had to be all he said for the time being.

After the call ended, Aiden tried to sort through his thoughts over everything and what it would mean for him over the next few days. He wouldn't be going to Serenity, that was for sure.

He realized he should probably let Devon know the latest development, since he'd always shown concern for Shiloh after Aiden had explained the whole situation to him.

For the next couple of hours, he tried to fill his time as he waited for an update. It was nearly eleven when his phone finally chimed.

Charli: *Shiloh has been admitted, and they're going to be running some tests. Gareth and Blake are headed back to Serenity. I'll send more updates in the morning, unless something happens during the night.*

Thanks for the update. Will be praying for a quiet night for you both. If there's anything I can do, let me know. I didn't go out to Serenity, so I'm close by.

Charli: *Thanks. Have a good night.*

He'd wanted to ask more questions about Shiloh or to request that Charli send him a picture, but he just set his phone aside. She had enough to deal with.

When he climbed into bed a short time later, he made sure his phone's volume was turned all the way up so he wouldn't miss any calls or texts.

He had a rough time falling asleep, but he used that time to pray for Shiloh and everyone else involved. Then he recited all the verses he knew about trusting God.

Finally, he drifted off and managed to sleep until eight the next morning. He woke to a text from Skylar saying she had booked herself a flight into Coeur d'Alene that would arrive around nine o'clock that evening and asking if it was still convenient for him to pick her up.

The answer to that was an immediate yes.

The problem came when he tried to figure out what to do with her after that. He wanted to be in Coeur d'Alene near to the hospital, and he suspected Skylar would too. However, he didn't feel comfortable having her at the house with him when it was just the two of them.

Nothing inappropriate would happen, he knew that. But he also knew that it wouldn't look right to their families. He wondered if Cathy would consider coming in and staying at the house with them.

He took the time to get himself out of bed and dressed with a mug of coffee in his hand before he called Cathy.

"Hello, Aiden," she said when she answered. "How are you doing?"

"Alright, all things considered."

"Yes, all things considered."

"I was calling because I just got a message from Skylar that she is flying in tonight and she asked me to pick her up."

"Yes, she also let us know of her plans," Cathy said. "Thank you for being willing to pick her up."

"It's definitely not a problem," he assured her. "But I'm wondering what to do with her afterward. I'm sure she's going to want to stay close to the hospital. However, I don't feel comfortable having her stay here with me."

"Oh, that is an issue, because I'm sure you're correct that she'd rather stay there than come on out here to Serenity."

"What I was wondering was if you'd be willing to come stay here at the house with her for the next couple of nights, until we can get everything sorted out. I have a suite in the basement, but there are three bedrooms on the main floor that you and Skylar can choose from."

"That would be wonderful, actually. I'd love to be close by to help Charli. Could I bring Dan too?"

"Certainly. There's plenty of room."

"Let me chat with Dan, then I'll get back to you. Even if he doesn't come, I will."

"Okay. Thank you for considering my suggestion."

"It's absolutely no problem," Cathy said. "If anything, I should be thanking you for giving us a place to stay, closer to the hospital. We really appreciate that."

After they said goodbye, Aiden went upstairs to make sure that the rooms were ready. His mom's had a queen size bed in it, and she always made sure the sheets were washed after she was there, so he wouldn't need to remake the bed. In addition to Willow's room, which had a twin size bed, there was a double bed in the third room.

It hadn't been used recently, since it was set up mainly for his mom's friends who came to stay for the weekend, which wasn't all that frequent an occurrence. That room didn't currently have sheets on the bed, so he went to the linen closet and pulled out what he needed to make it.

For the rest of the day, he was in a restless state as he waited for updates on Shiloh. Unfortunately, they seemed to be in a holding pattern as they waited for results from the initial tests, and while continuing to conduct other tests.

Charli had said that Shiloh had seemed a bit better after having been on an IV overnight that had included some drugs, based on the team's preliminary examination of her. Aiden knew that Charli was hopeful that they would be able to take Shiloh home soon, and while Aiden hoped that too, he was also tempering his hopes with reality.

When he reached the airport later that night, he parked his car and went in to meet Skylar, rather than wait out in front of the terminal. Her flight was on time, so it wasn't long before passengers began to appear.

He kept his gaze on the passengers, looking for that one special face. After several people had walked past where he waited, he spotted Skylar coming toward him. Her head was bent as she looked at her phone, pulling a bag behind her.

"Sky!" he called out as she almost walked past him.

She looked up, her eyes widening when she spotted him. Though she looked like she still wore her hair and makeup done up from her flight earlier that day, he could see the strain on her face.

Almost immediately, he could see that she was near to tears. As she approached him, he couldn't help but open his arms to her. There was barely any hesitation before she stepped close and allowed him to gather her into a hug.

He didn't say anything, just stood there holding her as her body trembled with silent weeping. Though he was sure she would rather have comfort from anyone but him, he was grateful that she did accept what he offered. Because it came from his heart.

"Sorry to cry all over you," she said when she finally stepped back. "I can't seem to stop crying."

"I've shed some tears of my own," Aiden told her. "So I understand."

"Hopefully I can get myself under control before I see Charli or Shiloh." Turning away from him, she pointed at the conveyor belt where suitcases were beginning to circle. "I have two suitcases to pick up."

They moved closer to the baggage claim, and when Skylar pointed out her bag, Aiden hefted it off the conveyor belt.

"Wow. This is heavy," he said. "Did you bring the kitchen sink?"

"Almost."

After her second bag had arrived, they left the terminal and walked to where he'd parked. The sun had set so it was dark as he loaded her bags into the back of the car.

As he guided the car out of the lot, Aiden said, "I hope you don't mind but we made some preemptive decisions regarding where you'll stay."

"What do you mean?"

"We figured that you might want to stay in Coeur d'Alene to be close to the hospital this time."

"Yes. I would."

"I have space at my place, but I didn't feel comfortable with just the two of us staying there, so your parents are also going to come in and stay for a few nights. Once we have a better idea of what's going on, then you all can decide what to do next."

"That sounds good. Thank you for putting us up in your home."

"I wouldn't have it any other way."

He meant that with all his heart, but he doubted she grasped that. And she might never come to understand the depth to which his feelings for her had grown of late.

This time, he might be the one left hurting.

CHAPTER TWENTY-THREE

Skylar felt an incredible sense of relief as Aiden drove her to his house. She'd felt very alone since hearing the news about Shiloh being readmitted to the hospital, but now she wasn't.

She probably shouldn't have fallen into his arms like she had, but she'd needed his support to know that she wasn't alone. Hopefully, he brushed it off as friends who happened to be co-parents, consoling each other.

Unfortunately, she was now an unemployed co-parent. When she'd asked Denise about taking more time off, the woman had said that they'd already stretched what they could allow her to take. That had left her with no option except to quit.

She'd hated to do it since she enjoyed her job. But right then, Shiloh was more important. Skylar couldn't stomach being far away from the little girl when her health was once again hanging in the balance.

She wouldn't have done it for any other niece or nephew, but Shiloh wasn't just a niece. She was her daughter, even if she'd given up those rights to Charli and Blake. She felt compelled to be by her side, even if it meant losing her job.

As they drove, Aiden shared what they knew so far—which was very little. It sounded like Cole had been notified, however, and it was possible he'd fly in again, just in case he was needed for the transplant.

When they arrived at the house, her parents were already there, having used the door code to let themselves in. Skylar greeted them with tight hugs.

"It's so good to see you again," her mom said, cupping Skylar's face in her hands. "I just wish it was under better circumstances."

"Me too. I much preferred when my visits home were for weddings or holidays."

Aiden had taken her suitcases into the room she'd be using, then showed them around the kitchen, revealing he'd made a trip to the store to stock up on food for them.

"Thank you for allowing us to crash here," her dad said. "It's good to know that we're closer to the hospital in case Shiloh's condition worsens."

"Who's staying with the other kids?" Skylar asked.

"Blake's aunt and uncle said they'd stay with them for a few days," her mom said. "And after that, we'll reevaluate how things are and go from there."

"I wish I had more room for all of them to stay here, but we're just about maxed out."

"It's not a big problem," her mom said. "We have plenty of people willing to step up. Denise, Misha's mom, has also stayed with them in the past and would gladly step in to do so again. All the adults have helped where they could as well. We'll get it sorted. I'm not too worried about that."

There might be some downsides to having a big family, but in her estimation, having a lot of people to help circle the wagons when a family member was going through a rough time was a benefit that outweighed all the negatives. And they had that not just in their family, but in their community also.

"I hate to put an end to this get-together so soon," Skylar said. "But I've been up since three-thirty this morning. Our flight out of Miami left at eight, which was five Serenity time. It's been a long day."

"Oh, that is a long day for you." Her mom moved to give her a hug. "Sleep as long as you need to tomorrow. We'll wake you if there's news."

"Are you going to Serenity for church?" Skylar asked.

Her mom shook her head. "We'll just watch the service on the internet."

After getting a drink of water, Skylar turned to Aiden, who was leaning back against the counter in the kitchen, arms crossed over his chest. "Thank you again for picking me up and for giving me a place to stay. I really appreciate it."

As Aiden smiled in response, his gaze softened. "Any time. I was happy to do it."

With butterflies fluttering in her stomach, Skylar said goodnight to her parents, then headed for the room where Aiden had put her bags. It shared a bathroom with Willow's empty room, so she didn't have to worry about hogging the bathroom while she took a long, hot shower.

She hadn't had time to take one after her flight from Miami to Vegas, as she'd focused on packing for her trip to Serenity. And once she'd realized that she wasn't going to have to rush back for her job, she'd taken the time to pack more than she might otherwise have. Which was why she had two suitcases instead of just one, like last time.

As she lay under the covers after her shower and getting ready for bed, Skylar realized that while her worry wasn't completely gone, it had lessened now that she was surrounded by people who shared her concerns. Though it had cost her her job, she didn't doubt for a second that she'd made the right decision to come to Coeur d'Alene to be near her family and Shiloh.

Exhaustion helped her fall asleep surprisingly quickly, and when she woke the next morning, it was nearly nine o'clock. It took her a minute to remember where she was, but once she did, she flipped the covers off and went into the bathroom to prepare for the day.

After going through her morning routine, she got dressed. She hoped that she'd get to see Shiloh that day, but she realized it might not happen.

When she left the room, she immediately smelled coffee and bacon. Venturing along the hallway that opened into the living area, she saw her parents and Aiden in the kitchen as if they'd never left it the night before.

"Good morning, darling," her mom said as she approached them. "How did you sleep?"

"Really well," Skylar said. "Better than I expected, to be honest."

"You were probably pretty tired after a long day of travel."

Skylar nodded, then thanked Aiden when he handed her a cup of coffee.

"Cream and sugar are on the table," he said. "And so is breakfast."

"Have you all eaten already?"

"Nope," her dad said. "We were just getting ready to sit down."

They all went to the table where there was a platter of bacon and eggs, along with a stack of toast and some fruit.

Once they were seated, her dad said a prayer for the meal, as well as everyone affected by Shiloh being in the hospital, but most importantly, Shiloh herself.

As they ate, her dad gave them the update he'd received from Charli just a few minutes earlier after Shiloh's doctor had come around. It seemed that her body was fighting an infection, which they'd narrowed down so that they could prescribe a more focused antibiotic instead of a broad spectrum one.

Unfortunately, it had meant that, since her immune system was compromised, they were discouraging visitors, aside from parents, for the time being. Skylar was disappointed, but didn't bother pointing out that she and Aiden were also parents. Charli and Blake knew that, so if they wanted them there, they'd be there.

When they finished eating, her mom started to clear off the table, but Aiden stopped her. "You took care of breakfast. I'll do the cleanup."

"I'll help," Skylar said, knowing that her parents would expect her to make that offer. Not that she was opposed to helping Aiden.

Together they cleaned the table, then Skylar loaded the dishwasher while Aiden washed up the pans they'd used to make the bacon and eggs. They worked in silence, though it wasn't a tense time like it might have been a few weeks ago. Things had definitely changed between them.

Or at least Skylar thought they had. Did Aiden feel the same shift she did?

Once the kitchen was all cleaned up, Aiden said, "Thanks for the help."

"You're welcome."

They joined her parents in the living room, where there was a large television on one wall. It was big enough that they'd probably feel like they were sitting in the front pew of the church.

"So, is Cole going to come home again?" Skylar asked as Aiden set to work getting the church service ready to stream.

"For sure if Shiloh needs the stem cell transplant," her dad said.

"I suspect he might show up even if she doesn't," Aiden added.

"I hope you're right," her mom said. "I can't tell you how great it was to have all my children close to home for that week he was here."

As the time neared for the service to start, Skylar's parents settled onto the loveseat, sitting close together. Skylar chose one end of the couch, and instead of going to the armchair, Aiden sank down on the opposite end.

When the musicians began to play, Skylar noticed that Peyton was once again on the drums. She'd taken to watching the livestream herself over the past few weeks, so she was becoming more familiar with the faces of the people who took part in the service.

After the welcome, the congregation stood for the singing, and when the camera panned out, she was able to spot several members of her family there.

She was surprised when, after just one song, Pastor Kennedy got to his feet and walked to a microphone that stood on the floor in front of the stage.

"I come before you this morning with a heavy heart as we received news through the night that Charli and Blake's lovely daughter, Shiloh, has once again been admitted to hospital. We have prayed for her before, and I'm asking you to join me in lifting her before the Lord once again. I'd like for a handful of people to join me here at the front to pray for Charli, Blake, Shiloh and their whole family, then I'll close."

There wasn't even a moment's hesitation before people began to move to join Pastor Kennedy at the microphone.

"Oh, bless that man," her mom said, reaching out to take her husband's hand. "And bless our church family for coming alongside Charli, Blake, and Shiloh."

As Skylar listened to people pray their hearts out for Shiloh's healing and wisdom for Charli, Blake, and the doctors, tears leaked from beneath her closed eyelids. She wiped at them, unable to believe how the prayers just kept coming. There was definitely more than a handful of people praying for her family.

Her heart heard those prayers and absorbed them like a thirsty plant drank up water. And with each prayer, her faith and trust in God grew. It was hard to understand God's purpose in allowing Shiloh to suffer. But amid that suffering, His people were rising up to support them.

The prayers weren't just for Charli, Blake, and Shiloh either. Jackson, Gareth's best friend, stood at the mic, and with a voice cracking with emotion, prayed for each member of Charli and Blake's family by name.

As her sniffles grew more pronounced, Skylar felt a wad of tissues being pressed into her hand. Looking up through tear-filled eyes, she found Aiden had moved closer to her and given her the tissues.

She mopped at her eyes, listening as Pastor Kennedy prayed after so many others had. There was emotion in his voice as well, and she knew part of that was because of his connection to their family.

As his prayer ended, the piano began to play the opening chords for *Great is Thy Faithfulness*.

Without opening her eyes, Skylar listened as someone sang the first verse, soon to be joined by the congregation.

Great is thy faithfulness, O God, my Father;
There is no shadow of turning with thee.
Thou changest not, thy compassions, they fail not;
As thou hast been, thou forever wilt be.

Great is thy faithfulness,
Great is thy faithfulness,
Morning by morning new mercies I see.
All I have needed thy hand hast provided;
Great is thy faithfulness,
Lord unto me.

Summer and winter and springtime and harvest,
Sun, moon, and stars in their courses above
Join with all nature in manifold witness
To thy great faithfulness, mercy, and love.

Pardon for sin and a peace that endureth,
Thine own dear presence to cheer and to guide;

Strength for today and bright hope for tomorrow,
Blessings all mine and ten thousand beside.

Skylar knew all the words, but there was no way she could sing them because of the tightness of her throat. Her mom and dad sang along, and even Aiden chimed in on the last verse and chorus. Like she had with the prayers, Skylar found comfort in the words.

"I am so grateful for this congregation," Pastor Kennedy said as he took his place behind the pulpit. "You have hearts full of God's love for each other. Thank you for lifting Shiloh and her family up in prayer. Thank you for the times you've lifted others in this congregation before Him as well. For the times we've interceded for our brothers and sisters."

Skylar wasn't sure if he was preaching the sermon he'd planned to, or if he felt led to speak in a different direction. The sermon certainly seemed to line up with what had already transpired in the service. Praying. Trusting. Believing.

When the service was over, they all just sat there in silence for several minutes. She glanced over at Aiden and saw him staring at the blank screen with a contemplative look on his face.

"Well, that was good for the soul," her dad said. "Not for the first time, I am so grateful for our church family."

"It's truly a blessing to have a Bible-teaching pastor and God-loving brothers and sisters," her mom agreed.

Aiden shut off the television, then said, "Anyone want another cup of coffee?"

"I wouldn't turn one down," her dad said as he got to his feet.

"Are you okay, darling?" her mom asked when it was just the two of them.

Skylar gave her a small smile. "I'm okay. I just... I've cried more over the past couple of months than I have in a very long time. Every time I think I'm cried out, there are more tears to come."

"There's nothing wrong with tears," her mom said. "We've all shed them during this time with Shiloh. I look at tears as silent prayers that God has no trouble understanding."

"Do you think Charli and Blake watched the service?"

"They might have. I know when Shiloh was in the hospital for treatment, Charli mentioned watching on her phone."

"I'm sure it will be encouraging for them to know that so many people are supporting and praying for them and Shiloh."

When her mom's phone chimed, Skylar picked up her own. There were no messages waiting for her, which wasn't surprising, but it was a bit disappointing.

She'd told her co-workers why she had to quit, and the only one who had expressed any sort of sympathy for the situation was Jack, the one pilot that she always liked to fly with.

Denise had seemed to feel like Skylar should just let Charli and Blake parent Shiloh and keep her distance. She hadn't understood why Skylar had felt so strongly about being there when she wasn't even Shiloh's mother.

But she was, whether she held the actual title. There was a physical tie from her to Shiloh that she couldn't erase. Charli also had a tie to Shiloh as her adopted mom, one that Skylar would never dismiss. Just like Charli hadn't dismissed Skylar's role in Shiloh's life.

"Here you go, my love," her dad said as he held out a cup of coffee to her mom.

"Thank you." She smiled at him as he sat down beside her with a mug of his own, then she leaned over to give him a kiss. "Love you."

"Love you too."

As a teen, Skylar hadn't understood what the affectionate interactions between her parents had really meant. She'd rolled her eyes and gotten grossed out about it.

But now, she appreciated them because they were just one of the many ways her parents showed that things were right between them. That their relationship was strong and able to weather the storms of life.

Aiden came from the kitchen with a tray that held two more mugs, as well as cream and sugar. He set the tray on the coffee table in front of the couch where Skylar sat.

"You didn't say if you wanted another cup," he said. "But if you don't, I'll drink it."

"Hopping yourself up on caffeine?" she asked.

He grinned. "Something like that. Or perhaps I'm just addicted to it a little bit."

"I'll happily take another cup."

He handed her a mug, their fingers brushing as she took it from him. He then held the tray so she could add cream and sugar to hers.

Since they'd had a late breakfast, no one was in a rush for lunch. Instead, they talked while they drank their coffee, then decided to go for a walk.

Skylar went to change her skirt for a pair of white cuffed shorts, which would be better for a walk. She pulled her hair up into a ponytail, then donned a pair of socks and slid her feet into a pair of runners.

Her ankle was all better, but she still tried to wear good shoes whenever she could now to make sure it stayed that way.

As they left the house, Aiden pointed them in the direction that would take them to a small park that had a path running through it. He and Skylar's dad took the lead, while Skylar and her mom followed.

"It's such a gorgeous day," her mom said as they walked down the sidewalk that was dappled with shadows from the shade trees growing in yards along the way.

There was a bit of breeze, causing the leaves to rustle and dance above them. They were heading into that time of year when early mornings and late evenings would become cooler until fall set in and they'd need sweaters and jackets as the leaves fell from the trees.

"It's a shame that they're cooped up in the hospital," her mom said. "This would be the perfect day to sit outside in the shade. The fresh air would probably do Shiloh some good."

It seemed no matter what they did, thoughts of Shiloh weren't far from their minds. That included when they stopped into a small ice cream shop that they came upon, and Skylar wondered what flavor Shiloh would have chosen had she been there with them.

Her dad treated them all to ice cream cones, then they continued their walk through the park. It was a nice way to spend the day, if only their reasons for being in Coeur d'Alene weren't so worrisome.

At some point, her mom joined her dad in the lead, so Aiden fell back to walk with Skylar. As they walked side by side, Skylar's fingers itching to curl around his, or to hold onto his elbow.

They hadn't gone on tons of walks, just for the sake of walking, when they were dating, but whenever they'd walked anywhere together, they'd held hands. Occasionally, they'd even walked with their arms around each other.

Skylar couldn't believe that she was missing that time. After everything that had happened between them, she shouldn't be even remotely interested in revisiting any part of it.

But the Aiden she saw now was the one she'd always imagined growing old with. Responsible. Caring. Willing to do for others.

If only he'd never gone away to college. Maybe then, they could have had that future.

But she knew that some kernel of how he felt when he broke up with her must have already been present when they were dating for him to buy into it so fully. It might have happened even if he hadn't gone away to college.

She'd never know because there was no going back in time. She could only move forward, accepting him as a friend without longing for something more.

If she wasn't the best for him nine years ago, she still wouldn't be the best for him now.

CHAPTER TWENTY-FOUR

Aiden was glad for a chance to get out of the house, and it was even better because he got the chance to spend some time with Skylar.

As they finished up their ice cream, they looped around to head back toward the house.

Though the circumstances that had brought them together that day weren't great, he felt a measure of peace after watching the morning service livestream and then going on the walk. It was so encouraging to know that there were many people who were praying and offering support to the family through this difficult time with Shiloh.

"I wish we could go see Shiloh," Skylar said.

"Me too," Aiden agreed. "But unfortunately, they probably won't let us visit her until they know for sure that her immune system is doing its job."

"Do you think that we're somehow responsible for her cancer?"

Aiden glanced over at her. "What?"

"Like maybe our genetics don't mix well, and somehow that triggered her cancer."

"I don't think so," Aiden said, though he honestly hadn't given it any thought. "This isn't like a genetic disease."

"But there are some types of cancers that are genetic," Skylar said. "Like breast cancer."

"Some variations of that, perhaps, but there are plenty of cancers that aren't tied to anything."

"Anything but bad luck?"

Aiden shrugged. "Something like that, I suppose. I don't think you should try to take the blame for Shiloh's diagnosis when no one is looking to blame anyone for it. Sometimes these things just happen."

"I guess I just want to know how or why she ended up with this."

"You and a lot of people who have loved ones diagnosed with cancer," Aiden said. "I remember reading on social media about a family who had a set of identical twin daughters and one was diagnosed with cancer as a pre-teen, but the other one wasn't. If it was something present in their identical genetics, both of them would have been diagnosed."

"It's just not fair."

"There's so much in life that isn't fair," Aiden reminded her. "Heart attacks aren't fair, and neither are boating accidents."

Skylar looked up at him and nodded. "Yeah. Those aren't fair either."

"You need to just accept that this has happened to our Shiloh and focus forward on how we can help her and Charli and Blake through it."

"You seem better able to cope with this than I am," Skylar said. "I'm struggling."

"If I'm coping better, it's no doubt somewhat attributed to what I've already gone through. I've learned that if I can survive the loss of a loved one—two loved ones, actually—I can survive this difficult journey with Shiloh. I'm not going to grieve her loss while she's still alive. I still have faith that, if her cancer has returned, God will use the transplant to heal her. Don't lose hope, Sky."

"I'm trying not to," she said, crossing her arms as she stared straight ahead. "But I just feel so helpless. And then I see that Charli and Blake feel the same way, and I'm left wondering who doesn't feel that way about this situation."

After a moment's hesitation, Aiden slipped his arm around Skylar's shoulders. He waited for her to pull away, but she didn't.

"God isn't helpless in this situation, and I believe He is guiding the doctors and those involved in Shiloh's care."

"I never would have thought you'd be the one trusting God like this."

Aiden chuckled but didn't move his arm, and she didn't move away from him either.

"I know, but you know you can also trust God. No one has a monopoly on Him."

She nodded. "I'm trying, but it's a real challenge. It's not that I don't have faith that God could heal Shiloh."

"What is it then?" When Skylar didn't answer right away, Aiden glanced down at her. "What is it you struggle with?"

"God could have saved your dad and Bethany. He could have prevented Shiloh from getting sick in the first place. So while I know that He can heal Shiloh, I also know that sometimes He chooses not to heal. Not to protect from death."

Aiden gazed down at the sidewalk they were slowly walking along. "Yeah. It's true that sometimes He chooses not to do what we think is best."

"And it scares me to think that might happen with Shiloh," she said, her voice tremulous. "I don't want to lose her even more than I already have."

Aiden rested his cheek briefly on the top of her head. "We'll just make the most of every moment we have with her and pray that we'll have a lifetime of moments ahead of us."

"Everything okay?"

Aiden looked up to find Skylar's parents standing on the sidewalk, watching them. Skylar stiffened and took a step away from him. Aiden let his arm drop from her shoulders.

"Just talking about whether God will heal Shiloh or not," Skylar said.

"Definitely a weighty topic," her dad replied. "We can discuss it more inside, if you'd like."

Looking around, Aiden realized that they'd made it back to the house. He led them up the driveway to the side door, then used the code to unlock it.

"Is there something else you'd like to tell us?" Cathy asked as they filed into the kitchen.

Skylar went to the cupboard and got a glass. "What do you mean?"

"You two seem pretty close," she said. "Have you decided to give things a second chance?"

Aiden caught Skylar's wide-eyed glance. "We haven't discussed that. We've just decided that having a friendship between us is probably a good thing, especially for Shiloh's sake."

"That is a good decision," Dan said as he took the glass from Skylar and filled it from the water dispenser, then handed it back to her. "But there's nothing to say God can't restore what was broken in the past."

Skylar wrapped both hands around her glass and took a sip, appearing to want to avoid responding to her dad's suggestion.

"Charli and Blake have successfully put the past behind them and forged a good, strong relationship," Cathy said.

"Their circumstances were different," Skylar told her. "And Charli's story isn't necessarily going to be mine."

"True. But it isn't necessarily *not* going to be yours either."

Aiden appreciated knowing that Cathy and Dan would apparently support them rekindling a relationship. However, it didn't seem that Skylar felt the same way.

He'd never come out and asked her to consider it, though. Maybe they should have a conversation about it.

But did he want to present her with the opportunity to outright refuse to consider a relationship with him?

Aiden understood why she might not want that. He'd hurt her tremendously in the past. It would require forgiveness on her part, and while it was possible she might forgive him, she would never forget.

She owed him nothing.

He owed her everything.

"Well, I think I'm going to go lay down for a little while," Cathy said. "Will you join me, darling?"

"You don't have to ask me twice," Dan said, bending to kiss her temple. "I enjoyed that walk, but I'd like to put my feet up for a bit."

Aiden watched them disappear down the hallway that led to the bedrooms, then turned his attention to Skylar. She was leaning back against the counter, her glass pressed to her lips. Her gaze was distant, and Aiden wished he could read her mind.

But since her parents had broached the subject, he thought that maybe he could see what she might be thinking. Although did they need the complication of trying to sort things out between them while the situation with Shiloh was up in the air?

Or would it be a good thing to face what was to come as a couple?

"Can I ask you a hypothetical question?"

Skylar's brown gaze swung his way, her brow furrowed. "What?"

"So, if I were to..." Aiden's voice trailed off, then he cleared his throat. "If I were to ask you out on a date, is there a chance you'd say yes?"

Her eyes widened, and she lowered the glass, reaching to the side to put it on the counter. "Why is that a hypothetical question? Are you not brave enough to just outright ask me?"

Her question stung because it was true. He'd stupidly thought that asking the way he had would make it easier to put it aside if she said that she wouldn't consider saying yes.

"You're right. I'm sorry." He paused, then said, "Do you want to continue this discussion or not?"

She considered his question for what felt like an eternity. "You can ask."

But there was no guarantee she'd say yes. He could tell that by her expression. Was she waiting for her chance to reject him like he'd rejected her?

If so, he could hardly blame her. Maybe she'd been waiting for this opportunity. And he'd give it to her, even if it meant getting hurt by her response.

He just hoped that once they opened this door that they'd be able to move forward without it negatively impacting things.

"Sky, would you go on a date with me?" He spread his arms. "I'm asking as the man I am now. The man who's learned from his mistakes, and who values and cares for the person you are now."

Her eyes narrowed, and Aiden braced himself for the ultimate rejection. His heart pulsed with pain, already anticipating what was to come.

But he held her gaze as he lowered his arms and waited for her response, whatever it might be.

"I need to think about it."

Aiden felt a spark of hope in the midst of the pain in his heart. "Really?"

She tilted her head as she crossed her arms. "To be honest, there's a part of me that wants to say yes. But there's a whole load of hurtful memories that make me want to have nothing to do with you in that way."

"I understand. I don't expect you to forget what I did to you," Aiden told her. "I just want you to know that I'm different now. I know what I did was wrong, and I am so sorry for hurting you the way I did. The way I treated you. The breakup. The pregnancy. I approached it all in the worst way possible, and I'm sorry. So very sorry."

Skylar looked into his eyes for a long moment, then dropped her gaze. "I believe you are, and I... forgive you. I know that's what

God wants me to do, and I'm trying to do that. But it's hard to ignore the memory of how shattered I was after you broke up with me. And then later when..."

Aiden took a step toward her, then stopped, putting his hands in his pockets. He had to give her time. She didn't totally trust that this time around, he would love and cherish her in the way he should have previously.

Was there a way to show her that?

"I need to..." She turned away from him. "I think I'm going to go to my room."

With that, she left him alone in the kitchen, nursing a heart that hurt but still held a kernel of hope. Until she gave him a final no, he would cling to that hope.

Aiden went to the fridge and pulled out the package of chicken he'd bought at the store the previous day. He prepared a basic marinade for it, then returned it to the fridge for dinner later on that day.

With that taken care of, he went into the garage and picked up a couple of tools to do some weeding. Taking care of the flower beds had been his mom's job. But since she was no longer living there, it now fell to him.

Aiden peeled off his shirt and left it on a chair on the deck, then headed for the large flower bed in the back corner of the yard. He had no idea what types of flowers were planted there, and he was sure he'd accidentally "weeded" a few of them in the time since she'd left.

He laid down the cushion his mom used to kneel on, then tackled the weeds that had sprung up in the past couple of weeks since he'd last worked on them.

With the sun beating down on his back and shoulders, Aiden prayed as he worked. For Shiloh. For Skylar. For Charli and Blake. For his mom and Willow. For anyone that came to mind.

It amazed him a bit how easy it had become to take the opportunity during these moments of solitude to pour out his heart to God. He knew there was a verse in the Bible about praying without ceasing, and it hadn't made sense to him as a teen.

He'd thought he didn't have the time to do that much praying. But now, he found that his day was filled with just one continual prayer from the moment he woke, when he started his day with a prayer of thanks to the Lord for giving him one more day. He didn't finish his prayer until he lay in bed at the end of his day.

Though he hadn't planned to do all the flower beds, once he started, it was easy to just keep going, working his way along the back fence. His mom loved flowers, so they were everywhere.

"You're going to get a sunburn, son."

Aiden sat back on his heels as he used the back of his gloved hand to wipe the perspiration from his brow. He looked up at Dan, who stood a short distance away, looking around the yard.

"You have a nice place here."

"Mom did all the flowers," Aiden said as he pushed up to his feet. He pulled off the gloves and dropped them on the cushion. "But now that she's not here, I get to take care of them."

"Looks like quite a job."

"It can be," Aiden agreed. "But I look at it as a way to get some sunshine, some fresh air and a bit of exercise."

Dan smiled. "That's a good outlook to have."

"It's one I haven't always had," Aiden confessed. "But lately, I'm trying to find the good in the difficult or the unwelcome things I don't necessarily want to do."

"Like weeding."

Aiden nodded. "It's not that I don't like yard work. But I prefer to use things that have a motor. Like the mower or the weed whacker. This kneeling in the dirt trying not to grab the wrong plant isn't so appealing."

"Well, it looks like you've done a good job, even if it isn't what you want to do."

"I'm going to grab a soda," Aiden said. "Did you want something cold to drink too?"

"Sure." Dan fell into step beside him. "That sounds good."

Dan veered off to sit in one of the chairs on the deck while Aiden went into the kitchen to get their drinks. He found Cathy and Skylar standing next to the counter, talking. Although their conversation died when they saw him, making Aiden a little self-conscious about the fact that he didn't have a shirt on.

"Been playing in the dirt?" Cathy asked as she gestured to her own shoulder.

Aiden checked one shoulder, then the other and saw what she was indicating. He didn't bother to brush it off since he was going to take a shower soon, anyway.

"Yeah." He opened the fridge and bent to pull out a couple of the cans of soda he'd put there the previous day. "Mom's flower-beds seem to contain as many weeds as they do flowers these days." Straightening, he lifted one of the cans. "Did either of you want soda too?"

Both women shook their heads, but Cathy said, "I'm going to get a glass of water and join you men outside in a bit."

"Sounds good."

Back outside, Aiden handed Dan one can, then set the other near the chair he planned to sit in. He went to where he'd dropped his shirt earlier and took a minute to pull it on before returning to where Dan sat.

"Did you and Skylar talk?" Dan asked.

Aiden cracked the tab of his soda, then lifted a brow at Dan. "Is that why the two of you disappeared earlier?"

Dan shrugged. "We figured it couldn't hurt for you two to have some time to yourselves."

"Well, we talked a little, but I'm not sure if it helped," he said. "In fact, it might have made things worse."

"I doubt that," Dan said. "Just have some patience with her. She isn't as apt to jump into things like she might have been as a teen."

Aiden had already come to the conclusion that he'd have to be patient. He had to let Skylar work out things at her speed, but at least now she knew that he had a strong desire to rekindle their relationship.

And he needed her to know that he wasn't looking for just some casual dating. He wanted that future they'd once talked about. The one with love, marriage, and kids. More kids. Ones that they could raise themselves this time.

The back door swung open, and the women appeared. Cathy had just sat down beside Dan when her phone rang. She glanced at the screen and murmured, "Charli."

She answered it, but rather than putting it on speakerphone, she lifted it to her ear.

"Hello, darling."

It was terribly hard to only hear half the conversation, especially since Cathy's side was limited to hums and one-word responses. They were left to have to decipher what she was hearing from her expression. She didn't look thrilled by what she was hearing, but she also didn't seem too upset.

Aiden's leg bounced as he lifted his can of soda to take a sip. Skylar was tapping her fingernails on the edge of her glass of water. Only Dan seemed calm and patient as he waited for his wife to finish the conversation.

When Cathy finally hung up, Skylar said, "Well?"

"Hang on." Cathy set aside her phone and picked up her glass to take a sip. "Okay. So Charli said that Shiloh seems to be responding to the new antibiotic, which is good news. Unfortunately, the doctors have seen some things that apparently concern them.

Shiloh will be having a full workup to see if there's a chance the treatment didn't work as well as they'd hoped."

"It's too soon," Skylar murmured.

"Unfortunately, there are times that treatments don't do what we hope they will," Dan said. "But that's why we wanted to be prepared for the next step if this first one didn't work."

Skylar bowed her head, but not before Aiden caught a glimpse of the pain on her face. He understood the pain, but he wasn't surprised by the news the way Skylar seemed to be.

"Listen, darling," Cathy said as she leaned to put her hand on Skylar's arm. "We are not without hope. God has provided a match for Shiloh, right in our own family, and I believe that there is a reason for that. So don't give up hope. We're not."

"I know. I had just hoped that her problem was something easily solved and not related to her cancer."

"And it might still be that. We just have to wait for the test results."

"Will we be able to see her soon?" Skylar asked.

"Charli thought you and Aiden could probably see her tomorrow, but she'll know for sure in the morning."

Aiden suddenly felt exhausted. The mental ups and downs and all arounds were wearing on him.

And if it was this bad for him, he could only imagine how bad it must be for Charli and Blake. He also hated to see Skylar so upset. It felt like he could do nothing to help anyone, and that was hard to accept.

The rest of the day passed quietly, with no more discussion about Shiloh's situation aside from praying for her at dinner.

When Aiden went to bed, he wished that he didn't have to go to work the next day. But if they needed him to come home during the day, he would. However, until they knew exactly what was going on, he needed to save his days off.

He could only pray that it wouldn't be necessary to use them.

CHAPTER TWENTY-FIVE

The house was quiet when Skylar left her room the next morning. It wasn't a complete surprise since she knew Aiden had planned to go to work, and her parents were going to run back to Serenity to deal with a few things before coming back later that afternoon.

Provided they were given the go ahead to visit Shiloh, the plan was to go once Aiden was off work. Her parents hoped to go to the hospital at some point, too.

Even though she'd woken up later, she still had several hours to fill until someone arrived back at the house. Thankfully, she had lots to do.

Something she was going to have to think about sooner rather than later was a job. She had some savings, but she didn't think it would last too long, given that she still had to get all her stuff moved from Vegas.

She had yet to tell anyone she'd quit her job, though she wasn't sure why she was keeping it to herself. Aiden had already expressed that he thought she should stay in the area. And her parents wouldn't be upset at all that she'd quit, hoping, no doubt, that that meant she'd move back to Serenity. Which, at the moment, appeared to be where she'd end up.

However, she had considered whether staying in Coeur d'Alene might be more beneficial. If Shiloh had lengthy hospital stays, Skylar would prefer to be nearby to visit her frequently. Yet, when Shiloh was not hospitalized, Skylar could still head to Serenity to visit her once or twice a week.

Skylar didn't necessarily think it was a good idea for her and Aiden to see Shiloh on a daily basis. Though they were her birth parents, Skylar felt like it was best they not be involved in her day-to-day life. Being in Coeur d'Alene would mean she was close enough to see Shiloh regularly, but far enough away that it wouldn't feel like they were encroaching on Charli and Blake as they parented Shiloh.

And her consideration of setting up her next home in Coeur d'Alene had nothing to do with it being where Aiden also lived. It really didn't.

She still didn't know what she was going to do about him asking her out on a date. Was it something he was really serious about? Or was he using it to gauge if she'd truly forgiven him?

Her heart had feelings for Aiden, but her mind wasn't entirely convinced about rekindling their relationship. At least, not just yet.

She'd asked for time, but she didn't know how much time she should take. Aiden hadn't pressed her for what she meant by *time*, which she appreciated, but she didn't feel like she could stretch this out for too long. It wouldn't be fair to him.

Looking through the fridge and the cupboards in the kitchen, Skylar was able to find plenty of food options for breakfast. She ended up choosing to have some granola and yogurt and a cup of coffee.

As she sat at the dining room table, Skylar hesitated a moment before bowing her head and praying. After giving thanks for the food, she also prayed for Shiloh, Charli, and Blake, along with the medical team involved in Shiloh's care.

While she ate her breakfast, her thoughts drifted to her conversation with Aiden about God healing Shiloh. Everything she'd said to him was a true accounting of the pain and fear she had that although God could heal Shiloh, He wouldn't. Would she be able to accept that?

It was amazing how Aiden had grown in his faith, despite the deaths of his dad and his sister and what was now going on with Shiloh. He hadn't let those events keep him from trusting God. She could definitely learn something from him.

After cleaning up her breakfast dishes, Skylar got her laptop out and did some research on job opportunities around the area. She included both Coeur d'Alene and Serenity, since she wasn't opposed to working and living in either place, though at the moment, she was leaning more toward Coeur d'Alene.

She didn't know exactly what she was looking for, but she figured that with her experience, a job in the hospitality industry was most likely.

Unfortunately, there weren't a lot of jobs that interested her. She did make note of the couple of possibilities she'd found, but she didn't fill out any applications. She didn't really want to be distracted by interviews or starting a new job until they knew what was going on with Shiloh.

With nothing else to do, she settled down on the couch with her phone to do some reading. She had a couple of books on the go and wanted to finish at least one of them.

Shortly after lunch, her mom called to tell her that Charli had let them know that Shiloh would be okay for visitors later. Skylar was thrilled to hear that, and immediately texted Aiden to let him know.

Aiden: *Wonderful news! I'm going to try to get off a little early. Hope to be home shortly after four.*

Okay. Would you mind if we went to a Build-a-bear store to get something for Shiloh before we go visit her?

Aiden: *I don't mind at all. We can go as soon as I get home.*

Skylar sent him back a thumbs up. She was trying to keep their interactions as normal as possible, and so far, he was also on board with that.

With still some time before Aiden would be home, Skylar went for a walk around the neighborhood, just for some exercise. Unfortunately, it left her a little sweaty, so she ended up taking a shower, then she got ready for the visit with Shiloh.

A little before four, Aiden texted that he was just leaving the office. Skylar made sure she had everything, with her shoes and purse waiting near the doorway.

When Aiden walked through the door, Skylar's heart skipped a beat. He greeted her with a warm smile that made her want to throw caution to the wind.

"Ready to go?" he asked.

"Yep." She slipped her feet into her shoes and grabbed her purse. "All set."

Aiden smiled. "Let's go get a bear."

He stepped out of the house and held the door for her, waiting until she'd joined him on the porch before locking up.

"So where are we going to build this bear?" Aiden asked when they were in the car.

"Unfortunately, they don't have the exact store I was wanting to go to here, but there is another place that does something similar."

"I think I know where that is," Aiden said when she gave him the name and address of the store.

It ended up being in an older part of town where some houses had been converted into stores. Most were high end boutiques and cafes. The stuffed animal store was sandwiched between a pastry shop and an antique shop.

"This looks interesting," Aiden said as they walked up the sidewalk to the small house.

It was a story and a half with a wide front porch. The front of the house was made up of two large bay windows that gleamed in the sunlight.

A soft bell chimed as Aiden opened the door, and almost immediately, a young woman wearing a flowy sundress appeared. She smiled when she saw them.

"Welcome to The Snuggle Studio, where every hug is custom made," she said as she approached them. "My name is Elena. How can I help you?"

"We'd like a stuffed animal for a little girl who is in the hospital with cancer," Skylar told her.

"Oh, I'm sorry to hear that about her." The woman's expression turned sympathetic. "Sadly, you're not the first to come for a snuggly for someone who is sick, and you probably won't be the last. Why don't we start over here?"

Elena walked toward one side of the large open area. After exchanging a glance, Skylar and Aiden followed her.

"We have a variety of animals you can custom make." Elena gestured to a display that was set up in front of the bay window.

Heavy damask curtains hung draped to each side of the window, and in front of it was an elevated platform which held a bunch of different stuffed animals at a tea party.

Smiling, Skylar reached out to grab Aiden's arm. "This is amazing."

"It certainly is," he said. "How are we going to decide?"

"I don't know." Skylar pulled him forward with her to more closely inspect the different choices of animals.

"I'm kind of a basic guy and think a bear would be fine," Aiden said as he pointed to one that was clothed in an old-fashioned dress and bonnet.

"Well, Shiloh already has unicorns, right?" Skylar said. "You brought her a couple from your mom and Willow."

"Yep."

"Charli said she's a big fan of dogs." Skylar turned to Elena. "Could we get her a dog dressed as an ice skater?"

"Certainly."

"Are we able to take this with us today?" Aiden asked.

"Yes. You just have to choose the color of dog and the skating outfit you want, and I will assemble it for you. We can also put an insert in it if you want to record something."

"Oh, that would be nice, but we'll have to figure out what we want to say."

"Well, while you discuss that, let me bring out our dog options and our selection of clothes for an ice skater."

"Should we sing a song?" Aiden asked when Elena had left them.

"What song?"

"Maybe *Jesus Loves Me?*"

Skylar hummed it quickly, then nodded. "I think that would be really nice."

"I'll just have you come over to this other side," Elena said, leading them to a room that was set up much more like a working area.

On a large table, she'd laid out an assortment of unstuffed dogs, as well as some skater outfits.

"I really like this white one," Aiden said. "It's unique, and it will match the unicorns."

"Plus, it's white like snow, so it goes with the ice skater theme."

"So white?" Elena asked. Skylar looked at Aiden, then they both nodded. "Now, on to the outfit choices. These are the ice skater options. I've also pulled a couple of our ballerina ones because they could also work for this. I'll let you look them over while I fill this little girl with fluff. Did you want to record a message?"

"Yes. We'd like to sing a song."

Elena smiled as she turned to pick up a small white box. She showed them how to record the song and how to play it back. "If you're not happy with it, you can record as many times as you like. It replaces the previous recording each time."

"Okay. Thank you," Aiden said as he took it from her.

"I'll leave you to do that while I fill the dog."

"Let's do the song first," Skylar said once Elena had gone into a small room at the back of the space. It had a large glass window, so she could still see them, but she probably couldn't hear them.

"Are you sure you remember it?" Aiden asked.

Skylar crossed her arms. "You're older than me, so I think that question applies more to you than me."

Aiden grinned as he lifted the small white box, then motioned for her to come closer. "We'll need to be close to this or it'll sound like I'm singing a solo."

"Let's rehearse first so we don't have to do a bunch of run-throughs."

Not surprisingly, they both remembered the song. Singing with Aiden reminded Skylar of the times they'd stood side by side to sing in worship services or with the youth group. Aiden had a nice voice, and hers wasn't bad either.

It took a couple of tries before they were certain enough that they wouldn't be messing it up. They sang the first verse and the chorus, then ended the recording with them both saying they loved her.

"I think that's perfect," Aiden said. "What do you think?"

"It's good. I hope she likes it."

"I think she's going to *love* it. I'm going to need to come back and get one for Willow."

"Yeah. I would have loved one of these when I was younger."

They turned their attention to the outfits, and after a brief discussion, they settled on a light blue tutu style skater outfit and a pair of silver skates.

When Elena returned, she carried the dog, which had gained even more cuteness now that it was filled out. "Everything ready to go?"

Skylar told her which outfit they wanted, then Aiden gave her the box. Working quickly, Elena inserted the box into the back of the dog, then showed them how it operated and how to change the battery and the message. Next, she put the outfit on the dog, then handed it to Skylar.

"This exceeds my expectations," Skylar said. "This has been so much fun."

Elena smiled. "I'm glad you've enjoyed it."

Over the next few minutes, Elena rang up the purchase—which came to a bit of an eye watering total—but Aiden didn't blink an eye as he handed over his credit card to pay. Skylar had intended to pay half, but she wasn't going to fight about it in front of Elena.

Aiden had added a special carrier as well, so that when Shiloh left the hospital, she had something to carry her in. Once the dog was all ready to go, they thanked Elena and left the store.

"That was an excellent idea," Aiden said as he pulled away from the curb to drive them to the hospital. "I think she's going to be thrilled with it."

"I think so too," Skylar said. "And I'll pay you for half of it when we get back to your house."

"I'd tell you you don't have to do that, but I'm not in the mood for an argument," he said.

"I appreciate that. Since it was my idea, if only one person was going to pay, it should be me."

"Halfsies is fine," Aiden told her.

Skylar had been braced for an argument, so it was kind of nice to not have that happen.

When they got to the hospital, Aiden parked, then they crossed the parking lot together to reach the entrance. It was bustling inside, and when they reached the elevator, there were several people already waiting.

The bell above the elevator doors dinged as the elevator arrived. When the doors slid open, a bunch of people filed out of the car.

Aiden rested his hand on Skylar's back and guided her into the elevator. As more people joined them, they shuffled to the side of the car, and Aiden stood close to her, keeping himself between her and the others in the elevator.

Skylar held the carrier containing the dog tightly in her hands. She couldn't wait to see what Shiloh thought of it.

"This is our floor," Aiden said, then led Skylar from the elevator.

When she and Aiden found Shiloh's room, Charli greeted them with a smile. "Hey, you two."

Getting up from the chair she'd been sitting in beside Shiloh's bed, Charli came to give them each a hug. She had an open book in one of her hands.

"Hi, Auntie Sky." Shiloh gave a little wave. "Hi, Uncle Aiden."

They approached the bed where Shiloh sat, her face wreathed in a smile. Skylar looked over at Charli and said, "Can we hug her?"

"Yep. Go right ahead," Charli said, waving towards the little girl.

Skylar set her bag on the chair, then bent to give Shiloh a hug. Though she wanted to hold her forever, she let go of Shiloh so that Aiden could hug her.

When he straightened, they exchanged a look, and Aiden nodded.

"We have someone else who would love a hug from you," Skylar said as she brought the carrier over to Shiloh.

"What's this?" Charli asked as she leaned close to Shiloh on the opposite side of the bed.

Skylar helped her hold the carrier so Shiloh could reach in and pull out the ice skating dog.

"Oh, wow!" Shiloh's eyes went wide. "A white dog, Momma. Look!"

"There's something special about this puppy," Skylar said, then showed her how to press the dog to play the recording they'd made.

Shiloh and Charli listened as the song played, a little tinny sounding, but Skylar thought their voices were recognizable enough.

"Is that the two of you?" Charli asked as she straightened at the end of the song.

"It sure is."

"That's amazing," Charli said with a grin.

"Since we can't always see you, we wanted you to have something that would remind you that we love you. If you hug the dog, it's like you're hugging us."

Shiloh wrapped her arms around the neck of the dog. "What's her name?"

"She's waiting for you to give her one."

Charli picked up the carrier and looked at it more closely. "You got this at The Snuggle Studio?"

Skylar nodded. "We went there before coming here."

"They are... not cheap."

"Whatever the cost, it was worth it," Aiden said. "Don't even think about it."

"Well, that was really nice of you guys. Thank you."

"Thank you!" Shiloh said, echoing her mom.

"What are you going to name her?" Charli asked as she sat down on the chair beside the bed.

"I don't know yet." Shiloh held the dog and made her dance a little, despite the canula still in her arm. "Maybe I'll see if I dream of a name tonight."

"That's a good idea," Charli said as she ran her fingers over the fur on the dog's head.

"Can we play a game?" Shiloh asked. "Maybe *Uno?*"

Charli went to the table and picked up the game. "How about you play with Uncle Aiden first, while I talk to Auntie Sky for a few minutes? Okay?"

"Yep."

With a glance at Aiden and Shiloh, Skylar followed Charli over to the small table and chairs on the far side of the room. She took the seat opposite her sister, but angled herself so she could still see the pair at the bed.

"I'm surprised that you came," Charli said, keeping her voice low. "Especially since we didn't know for sure how sick she was."

"Of course I'd come," Skylar said. "Now that she knows who I am, I feel even more drawn to be here during times like this."

"It would be easier if you lived here."

Skylar debated for a moment, then said, "Well, I will be soon."

Charli's eyes widened. "What? You're going to move back?"

"It seems likely," Skylar said. "I couldn't get the time off to come since I've taken so much time off already. So I quit."

"Oh, Sky." Charli reached out and put her hand on Skylar's arm. "I'm sorry you had to do that."

Skylar shrugged. "I'm surprisingly okay with it. I just need to figure out where to live and try to find a job."

"You wouldn't want to live in Serenity?"

"I'm not sure. My job prospects are probably better here."

"That's true," Charli said. "Have you talked to Kayleigh about this? There might be something out at the resort."

"I haven't yet. I don't want to impose on her just because we're sisters."

"What's family if we can't make use of those connections?"

Skylar chuckled. "Nepotism at its finest."

Charli leaned forward. "How are things with you and Aiden?"

"They're okay."

"Is there any chance of a romantic relationship between you two again?"

And wasn't that the question of the hour? "I don't know. Aiden wants that, but I'm not sure."

"Oooh. Has he said that?"

Skylar wasn't sure she wanted to tell Charli about what had gone on with Aiden over the past day, but she was going to find out one way or another. And she'd already told her she'd quit her job, so in for a penny, in for a pound.

Keeping her voice low, Skylar said, "He asked me out on a date."

"And you said no?" Charli asked with a frown.

"No. I haven't said no... yet."

"Don't say no, Sky. Give it a chance."

"I know that things worked out for you and Blake, but our situation is a bit different."

"What do you mean?"

"From what you've said, Blake didn't reject you because he thought he could do better than you. He ended your relationship because he thought he couldn't give you the life he wanted to. You don't have words he spoke emblazoned on your mind. Hurtful words."

"That's true, but Aiden seems different now. And he must be regretful for what he's done if he wants to try again."

"I'm not sure that my story will be the same as your story," Skylar said, though the words brought an ache to her heart. "I'm not sure I'm strong enough to try again."

"Maybe don't look at it as trying again," Charli said. "You're both different people now. Look at Aiden as the man he is now. Is there an attraction still there for you to him?"

Skylar glanced over at Aiden to see him laughing at something Shiloh had said. Oh, there was a lot that was appealing about who Aiden was now. His caring attitude toward his mom, Willow, and Shiloh was amazing. Even the way he took care of her.

But was it enough to offset the horrible memories?

She wasn't sure about that.

"What have you got to lose?" Charli asked.

"The friendship we've settled into," Skylar said. "We're getting along, and I think it's benefitted how we interact with each other and Shiloh. I don't want to risk losing that."

"I think that if it doesn't work out, you two would still be able to figure out how to co-exist with each other."

Skylar wished she shared Charli's confidence. "I'm still thinking about it."

Charli looked over at Aiden and Shiloh. "Don't wait so long that you lose out completely."

"If he's truly serious about wanting a relationship with me, then he'll wait until I can figure out how I feel."

Charli's dark brown gaze met Skylar's. "But he won't wait forever."

Skylar knew that was true, and when the thought of him giving up on her and moving on with someone else caused pain in her heart, Skylar knew that this wasn't about if she had feelings for him. She clearly did.

But were they strong enough to give her the ability to forgive and let go of the past?

CHAPTER TWENTY-SIX

Aiden waited until they were in the car on the way home from the hospital to ask Skylar about the brief snippets of the conversation he had overheard between her and Charli.

"Did I hear right?" he asked. "You quit your job?"

"Yes."

She didn't hesitate to confirm it, so it didn't seem like she was trying to keep it a secret. But if not, why hadn't she said anything to him about it?

"Is that really what you wanted to do?"

This time, her response was a little slower coming. "Well, I don't like being without a job, but it was the right thing to do. I need to be here, I think."

"Have you told your parents?"

"Not yet."

"Why not?"

"I don't know. Part of me feels that perhaps I was a bit irresponsible making that decision without having another job already lined up."

"It might be considered irresponsible if you didn't have a solid reason for doing it. Or at least I think you have a good reason to want to be here."

Skylar was silent for a stretch, then she said, "I never wanted to live here because it would be hard to see Shiloh and not be able to be her mother."

"And has that changed now?"

"Now, I've settled into my role as her aunt," Skylar said. "But since she also knows who I am to her, it feels like I should be closer to her. Especially with her health being so precarious."

"I understand the struggling with how to view her. I think I've come to a place of acceptance. I'll never be her father, but I can be someone who is still important to her."

"Yes. We're not just another aunt and uncle to her. She knows that as well as we do."

"Will you be staying with your parents again?" Aiden asked, wishing she could live in Coeur d'Alene, especially if she decided to give a relationship with him a shot.

"Probably. I really haven't thought it through too much, to be honest. A lot depends on where I find a job. If I get a job here, then it makes more sense for me to live here. Like you, I don't really want to deal with a commute, especially in winter."

"I'm sure Shiloh will be thrilled when she finds out," Aiden said as he pulled to a stop at a red light and looked over at Skylar. "When we spent time together after you left, she always talked about how she missed you."

A gentle smile crept onto her face. "I missed her a lot, too."

"Did you miss me?" he asked, half joking.

The light turned green, so he had to look away before she answered.

"I missed everyone," she said. "But yes, maybe I missed you a little, too."

"I'll take that."

"About the date," Skylar said. "Where exactly do you want this to go?"

The change in the direction of their conversation took him by surprise. But it was a direction he was happy to go in. It meant that she hadn't completely said no to the idea of dating.

"I'm not just looking for a girlfriend," Aiden said, deciding to lay it all out. "I want a wife. So if you do decide you want to go on a date with me, just know that I'm serious. No casual dating for me. I want this to be something headed toward marriage. If you're not interested in that, too, you might as well turn me down now."

"I don't mind that you're serious," she said. "I'm not looking for casual either." She gave a little huff of laughter. "Well, to be honest, I wasn't looking for anything."

"Have you chosen not to date?"

"Oh, I've dated," she said. "In fact, I'd just broken up with a guy when my mom called to let me know what was going on with Shiloh."

Aiden's stomach soured at the revelation. Of course she'd been dating. She was a beautiful woman who no doubt attracted the attention of many men. Including the rich ones who travelled on the private jets she'd worked on.

"Was it serious?" he asked. "Had you been dating long?"

"About nine months," she said.

He noticed she didn't say anything about the seriousness of the relationship, but nine months wasn't exactly casual. The breakup could be why she was hesitant to pursue something with him.

If the breakup had happened right before Shiloh's diagnosis, it had been several weeks already. Was that enough time for her to get over the guy?

"I didn't realize that when I asked you out," he said.

"Does it make a difference?"

"I think it does," he said. "Because if you're still getting over that guy, I understand why you wouldn't be interested in something with me. Just forget that I asked, and we'll continue on as we are. Friends."

Skylar was quiet, and when Aiden glanced over at her, he saw she'd turned her face toward the window so he couldn't see her expression.

"I still want a relationship with you," Aiden said. "But I don't want to be your rebound or for us to get involved when you still have feelings for someone else. That would doom the relationship from the start."

"I don't still have feelings for him."

"Okay. So if he showed up today and tried to get back together, you wouldn't be interested?"

"He already did show up, sort of, when I was in Vegas."

"What do you mean?"

"He started texting me again, wanting us to meet for coffee."

"Did you?" he asked. "Sorry. That's none of my business."

"I don't mind telling you, but maybe don't mention this around my parents. I don't really discuss my dating life with my family." When he nodded, she continued on. "No. I did not meet him for coffee, and he's now blocked on my phone and all my social media accounts."

"Was it a bad breakup?"

"Not really," she said. "He told me that he felt like he couldn't get past the wall I had built around my heart. That I was emotionally distant, and he didn't think we could have something long-term because of that."

"But then he changed his mind?"

"I don't know. And I didn't care, so when he texted me to meet up, I didn't have a problem telling him no."

Knowing she wasn't still in love with another guy brought a wave of relief to Aiden. She still might turn him down. But if she did agree to the date, at least he knew she was over her previous relationship.

He didn't like the idea of her dating other men. But since he'd also dated, he didn't really have any right to feel that way.

"Is there anything I can say or do to help put your mind at ease about us dating?"

"I don't know. I think it's something I just need to work on. Some of the things you said to me years ago were incredibly hurtful, and I struggle to get them out of my mind sometimes."

"I really am sorry for what I said."

"How will I know that you're really committed to a relationship with me, and that you won't drop me the minute another woman comes along who's prettier than me? Has a better personality? Has a better job? I don't want to be in a relationship that whenever a beautiful woman is around, I have to worry about losing you to her."

Aiden heard the pain in her voice and realized just how negatively his words and actions had impacted her. He could tell her that he hadn't meant them, but that wouldn't lessen the hurt they'd caused her over the years.

"You've told me about your dating life," Aiden said. "Let me tell you something about mine."

"I won't believe you if you tell me you haven't been dating," Skylar warned.

"No. I'm not telling you that."

"Not that I want to hear about the women you've dated."

"Well, babe, I didn't really want to hear about the men you've dated either."

"Fair enough." She waved her hand in the air. "Go on."

"When I was dating, I discovered I couldn't date women with dark brown hair and eyes."

"Well, they do say that blondes have more fun," Skylar said. "So it stands to reason that men would prefer them."

"No, that's not what I mean," Aiden said. "I couldn't date anyone that reminded me of you because no matter how attractive they were, they just didn't measure up to you."

"So only the blondes were pretty enough to distract you?"

Aiden wanted to sigh in frustration at not being able to express himself well enough. "No, again. I struggled not to compare every woman I dated to you, but at least the blondes were less of a physical reminder of you."

"How long ago did you date one of these blondes?" Skylar asked.

"It was back before my dad passed away," he said. "I haven't really dated since then."

"Why not?"

"Too many other things demanding my attention, including my move here to Coeur d'Alene and helping Mom with Willow."

Skylar was silent for a moment, then said, "If you were regretting the breakup, why didn't you try to contact me to work it out? Or to at least apologize? It wasn't like you didn't know how to get hold of me."

Aiden wasn't sure how to explain what had been in his mind back then without either digging a deeper hole or sounding like he was making excuses. Because depending on which part of those early years after the breakup he focused on, it could go one way or the other.

He wondered if anything he said would make a difference. Was she just dragging it out to make him pay for what had happened? He didn't really think so, though he certainly wouldn't blame her if she did.

The house came into view before he had a chance to land on an answer. However, he didn't want the conversation to end.

He pulled into the driveway and came to a stop. Before turning off the engine, he rolled down the windows a little. The day had taken on the gray shades of twilight, but it was still warm.

"I wish I could explain what was in my mind back then," Aiden said. "But all I can say is that I've matured enough to realize that what I did was wrong on several levels. I understand why you're wary of trusting me again. I get it, I really do. I can tell you that if you decide to give me another chance, I will treat you the way you deserve to be treated, and as God would want me to treat you."

"Like your dad treated your mom?"

Aiden smiled, remembering the times they'd discussed both sets of parents' relationships. "Yes. Like Dad treated Mom. Since my dad passed, I've tried to do a few of the things for her that he used to do."

"Like what?"

"She loves plants and flowers, and Dad used to bring her a new plant now and then. And in the summer, he'd pick up flowers for her to plant in her garden. She likes bouquets too, but definitely prefers something that lasts. So I've gotten in the habit of searching out rare plants that she might like to try her hand at growing. One of them was an orchid that has bloomed beautifully under her care."

"Do she still have it?"

"Yes. She very carefully transported it back to the house in Serenity." Aiden reached out to cover Skylar's hands with his own, where they rested in her lap. "Sky, spending this time with you has made me fall in love with you all over again. I see the tenderness of your heart as you deal with Shiloh and even with me. I admire the strength you had to give Shiloh up and then take a position on the periphery of her life. I know that wasn't easy at all."

"Maybe I'm just the easy option," Skylar said. "The one you already have a connection with. That you already know. The one that's here."

Aiden chuckled. "You may be many things, babe, but you're definitely not the easy option. And before you protest that, I want you to know that that is one of the things I love about you. I don't want an easy option. I want to be with someone who I know is going to work and fight for our relationship as much as I am. You are that person for me."

"If I don't feel the same way, how will things be between us as we deal with Shiloh?"

Aiden's hope for his chances with Skylar took a nosedive with that question. "We'll figure it out. I won't make things difficult for you."

Skylar turned one of her hands over so that their palms were touching. Warmth spread through Aiden as she sandwiched his hand between hers.

"I like the Aiden I've come to know since I came to your office," Skylar said, her voice soft. "Parts of you are still the boy I loved as a teen. But you've also changed from him. I worry you'll change again."

"Change is inevitable. For both of us. Our experiences in life change us. My prayer is that I will only change for the better in the years to come," Aiden said. "I feel like I'm more open to rebuke, and I'd be happy to have an accountability partner."

"Someone like Cole?"

"He'd be a good choice," Aiden said. "I know he'd have your best interests at heart, so if he came to me with concerns, I'd know they were really serious."

It felt a bit weird to be discussing things the way they were.

The first time he'd asked her out on a date, it had been preceded by some—or maybe a lot—of flirting between them. When he'd finally asked her out, she'd accepted without hesitation, and things had grown from there.

This time around, they were both coming with baggage. Lots of baggage. And since it was baggage that Aiden himself had packed, he now needed to have patience as he and Skylar unpacked it.

Discussion was needed.

These weren't things that could just be pushed off to deal with later. They would directly impact their relationship if they didn't at least try to hash things out. Because if they couldn't work through it, there was no chance for a relationship between them.

So while it wouldn't be even remotely a romantic start to a relationship, Aiden knew it was more important than roses or any other physical gift. This was him giving her the gift of understanding and patience. And it was as much a gift to him as it was to her.

Aiden wanted to think they were starting to build the foundation for something lasting. So the stronger it was, the better.

He just hoped that Skylar felt the same way.

"Can I have one more night to think about this?" she asked, her voice barely audible in the slowly darkening evening.

Aiden tightened his fingers around hers. "You can have as long as you need. I'm not going anywhere."

"I'm glad."

"I just realized we haven't had supper yet," Aiden said as he looked around. "And it looks like your parents aren't back yet. Do you want to go out and grab something?"

"Sure. I am a bit hungry."

After a brief discussion about their restaurant options, they settled on the one they'd always preferred as teens. And when they got there, they placed orders nearly identical to what they'd ordered back then, too.

By the time they got back to the house with the food, Cathy and Dan were there and greeted them with smiles.

"How did the visit at the hospital go?" Cathy asked as they joined Aiden and Skylar at the dining room table.

"It went really well," Skylar said, then glanced at Aiden. "Right?"

"Yes, I thought she looked good. Better than I expected. She even played *Go Fish* with me and didn't seem lethargic or anything."

"That is encouraging," Cathy said. "That means the meds are tackling whatever got her sick in the first place."

"Which could mean that her symptoms might be entirely attributed to the infection and not the cancer," Dan added.

Skylar lowered her burger without taking a bite. "Really? Is that possible?"

"It's possible," Cathy said. "But the test results will give us the answer for certain."

"But it is a very good sign," Dan said.

"Oh, that would be wonderful if it's something easily treatable."

"Hopefully, they'll get some of the results to Charli and Blake tomorrow."

"Will you be heading back to Vegas soon?" Cathy asked.

Aiden glanced at Skylar to see if she planned to reveal her plans to her parents. He wasn't sure why she hadn't said anything earlier. He'd still be in the dark if he hadn't heard that part of the conversation she'd had with Charli.

He hadn't planned to eavesdrop on what they were discussing, but that part of the conversation had been loud enough that he'd heard it without any concentration on his part.

"I'm actually not going back," she said. "Well, I'll have to go to pack up my apartment, but I'm not going to live there anymore."

"Really?" Cathy lifted her hands into the air. "What a wonderful answer to prayer!"

"What can we do to help you make the move?" Dan asked. "If you're going to stay with us, at least at first, you'll need to put your furnishings into a storage unit."

"Yes. I'll probably stay with you to start, but then, depending on where I get a job, I'll figure out where to live."

"Are you applying for jobs here, as well as in Serenity?" Cathy asked.

"Yes. I know that I probably should stick to hospitality jobs, but I've been thinking about also applying at some interior design places."

Aiden smiled at the revelation. Not just that she was serious about getting a job, but that she was looking at jobs in the field that once had been her career choice.

"Are you looking at getting back into interior design?" Cathy asked.

Skylar shrugged. "I thought maybe if I got a job as a receptionist or something similar, I could see if I still have an interest in it. Then maybe I'd look into going back to school. I don't know. I've changed over the years, so it's possible that I won't find it as interesting."

"Well, you know we'll support you whatever you decide," Dan said with a smile at Skylar.

"I'm just so glad that you're moving closer to home."

"So you'd be okay if I get a place here and not in Serenity?"

"Of course, darling," Cathy said. "An hour's drive is so much more manageable than a five or six-hour plane ride."

"When I wasn't able to get more time off to come home when Shiloh got sick, I knew that I needed to change my situation. If I move here, I'll be able to see her and not have to take time off, even when she's in the hospital."

"It sounds like you've put some thought into all of this," Dan said.

Skylar nodded. "I want this to work out, so I'm trying to make sure I'm thinking things through."

"So... is it just wanting to be closer to Shiloh that's brought you home?"

Aiden froze, then lifted his burger for a bite, curious about what her answer would be. He was watching her, so he saw when she glanced in his direction.

"No. That's not the only thing," she said. "But we'll see about the other stuff."

Cathy looked at Aiden and gave him a smile and a wink. "Well, we'll be praying for you. Both of you."

"Thanks, Mom," Skylar said, with only a slight edge of sarcasm to her words.

Aiden chuckled, then Cathy and Dan joined in, while Skylar just rolled her eyes.

It was nice to know he'd have the support of Skylar's family if she decided to give him another chance. He had betrayed their trust in him in the past, but that wouldn't happen again.

CHAPTER TWENTY-SEVEN

Skylar went through her morning routine before swapping her pajamas for a pair of shorts and a T-shirt. Though she hadn't slept very well, she'd still woken up early and decided to just get up.

In the kitchen, she found Aiden cooking something on the stove. He turned as she approached him and greeted her with a warm smile.

"Good morning, sunshine," he said, then turned his attention back to the stove. "Would you like a fried egg?"

"Thanks, but I'm not really hungry at the moment," she told him.

"You've never been one to eat breakfast, have you?"

"Not this early. I'll probably get hungry around nine or ten."

He turned with the pan and slid two fried eggs onto the plate that sat waiting on the counter. He also grabbed a couple of slices of toast from the toaster and put them on the plate.

"Do you have a kitchen downstairs?" Skylar asked.

"A small one. But since I brought groceries for all of us, I didn't put any of them downstairs." He pulled the carafe from the coffee-maker and poured some coffee into a mug on the counter. "Would you like some coffee?"

"That I could do with," she said. "But I can get it. You don't have to wait on me."

"I know I don't have to." He removed a mug from the wrought iron mug tree next to the coffee maker. "But I'd like to."

After he filled the mug, he handed it to her with a smile. "Cream is in the fridge, and sugar is beside the coffeemaker."

As they moved around each other in the kitchen, it occurred to Skylar that this could have been their life, if things had worked out.

But maybe there was a chance it still could be their life. If she was willing to give him a second chance.

That was what had disrupted her sleep. Wondering if she could really open her heart up to Aiden again.

The problem wasn't that she didn't love him. She did. The man he'd become was appealing to her, and because he'd already had a place in her heart in the past, it seemed like he didn't even need to work to get past her wall that other men had commented on.

But the thing Skylar struggled with was the fear of being hurt by him again.

When they'd been together in the past, she'd never felt insecure or jealous. He'd never given her any indication that he was interested in anyone but her, so she'd never worried about it. That was why it hurt so badly when he had basically said he wanted to break up so he could find someone better.

Sure, he'd said that both of them could find someone else, but she hadn't been interested in finding a guy who might be better suited for her. In her teenage mind, Aiden had been perfect.

So now, even though he'd said it wouldn't be an issue, she knew it would be something she struggled with. So how was she going to deal with it?

"Do you have plans for today?" Aiden asked as he sat down at the island counter with his food.

"I'm going to put in some applications, I think. They're mainly online, so I can do that from here. Might look around at apartments, too."

Aiden smiled. "So does it really seem likely you'll settle here instead of Serenity?"

"I think so," she said.

"I could ask around at the office to see if anyone knows if the interior design companies we work with are hiring."

"That would be helpful," Skylar said. "I'm not even sure if any-one will hire me with no sort of experience in the industry. Or even as a receptionist."

"You won't know until you try," Aiden said. "Are you planning to go see Shiloh when your parents do?"

"I thought I'd go when you do," Skylar told him. "Spread the visitors out a bit."

"I can swing by and pick you up when I'm done with work."

"Okay. Let me know when you're on the way, and I'll be ready to go."

Skylar could have gone with her parents, but she enjoyed going with Aiden. And she thought maybe Shiloh liked it when they came together.

They talked a bit more as Aiden finished his breakfast, then he got up to put his dishes in the dishwasher.

When he turned his attention to the pan he'd used to fry his egg, Skylar said, "I can take care of that."

He glanced over at her. "You don't have to. I made the mess."

"I know," she said. "But I don't have a lot to do today."

"Well, thank you." Aiden dried his hands on a dishtowel. "I appreciate that."

He picked up his laptop bag from where it sat on the counter, then took a step in Skylar's direction. However, he paused, a frown briefly crossing his face. If she hadn't been watching him, she would have missed it completely, as it was quickly replaced by a smile.

"See you later," he said. "Have a good day."

"You too."

Aiden hesitated again, then gave her one last smile before he turned and left the kitchen, heading toward the door. Skylar watched him go, then continued to stare at the door even after Aiden had closed it behind him.

She was grateful that he was keeping things as normal as possible between them during this time of uncertainty.

The more time they spent together, the more she saw great qualities in Aiden that she wanted in a boyfriend, and later, a husband. But would she be able to hold her fears in check? Or would she forever wonder if she was on the cusp of losing him?

She wasn't sure she could live that way. Always trying her best to keep him happy, even if it was at the expense of her own happiness. She didn't want fear to be the motivation for why she did things for him.

She didn't want to act a certain way or do things out of fear instead of love. How was she supposed to do that if fear was still present in her relationship with him?

At the end of the day, she did want a relationship with Aiden. Her heart ached with the love she held for him, but the fear was there, too. The better things were between them, the higher her fear of losing him would become. Could she honestly just take his word for things?

"Good morning," her dad said as he walked into the kitchen. "You're up early. Did you sleep well?"

"I slept okay."

"Has Aiden left for work already?" he asked as he filled a couple of mugs with coffee from the carafe.

"Yes. He left a few minutes ago."

"Are you coming with us to the hospital?"

"No. I think I'm going to submit some applications and look at what might be available for apartments in the area."

"So you're pretty set on staying in Coeur d'Alene?"

"Seems like the job I want is more likely to be available here," Skylar said.

Her dad nodded as he lifted his mug to take a sip. "I suppose that's true."

"Good morning, darling." Her mom joined them at the counter, giving Skylar a quick hug before walking to where her husband stood to take possession of the cup of coffee he'd prepared for her. "Thank you."

"Anything for you, my love."

As Skylar watched the affection flow between her parents, she wondered if they'd ever had moments of worry and doubt about the person they'd invested so much of their feelings into.

"Aiden gone already?"

Skylar nodded. "He left just before Dad came out."

"Did you talk to him before he left?"

"Yes," she said. "Why?"

"I'm just trying to figure out where the two of you stand in relation to each other. At times, tension seems high between you. But then, rather than it make you avoid each other, you seem to be interacting normally. I'm confused."

"Well, you're not the only one," Skylar confessed.

"Want to talk about it?"

Skylar wasn't sure she did, but she also could use some advice. However, she wasn't sure that she'd get unbiased guidance from her parents.

"Aiden asked me out," she said. "And he wants me to consider rekindling our relationship."

"I don't think you should rekindle things," her mom said, surprising Skylar.

"You don't? I would have thought you'd be on board with us dating."

"Oh, I am," her mom said. "I just don't think you should try to rekindle what you had. You're both different now. You've had experiences—some of them with each other—that have shaped you into different people than you were back when you dated before. So rather than rekindling, I think it's better to approach it as a fresh relationship."

Skylar could see the sense in what her mom said. Clearly, what they'd had in the past hadn't worked for Aiden, which meant, ultimately, that it hadn't worked for her either. If she viewed things in a new way, perhaps she could keep from thinking of how he'd been during the last weeks of their relationship and what followed. Perhaps...

"So you think I should date him again?"

"I think you should give it some good consideration before you dismiss it outright," her mom said. "I know he hurt you before, so you'll need to decide if you're willing to let that go or if the memory of that will constantly raise its ugly head."

"How do I let it go?" Skylar asked. "Honestly, it's what's holding me back. It's not that I don't want to leave that in the past, but I just don't know how."

"Have you prayed about it?" her dad asked, entering the conversation for the first time.

Skylar looked down at her mug, which was currently half full. "A bit."

"Praying is certainly the best first step," her mom said. "But then it's going to take a concerted effort on your part to forgive Aiden and move forward with him."

"What if he hurts me again?" she asked. "What if he finds someone he likes better after we start dating?"

"I don't think that will happen," her mom told her with a smile. "Aiden seems mature enough now to realize that commitment needs to be total and complete. Which means that once he's committed to you, he doesn't even give a thought that someone else might be better."

Would that be possible? Could she trust that his love would be strong enough this time?

"But you need to make sure that this is God's will first," her dad added. "And then trust Him to be with the two of you as you build a life together."

It sounded so simple when her dad put it that way. However, she wasn't sure how to determine if it was God's will.

Was the fact that she felt so unsettled a sign that it wasn't?

A pang of ache went through her heart at that thought.

"We'll be praying for both of you," her mom told her as she came to put her arm around Skylar's shoulders.

Skylar sat mulling over their conversation as her parents worked together to make themselves breakfast. She still wasn't super hungry, but agreed to a toasted bagel with blueberry cream cheese when her mom offered to make her one.

After they'd eaten, Skylar took over the job of cleaning up. Once everything was sparkling, she went to her room to get her laptop, then went out to the back porch, where there were some chairs and a table set up on the deck.

The day was forecasted to be hot, but right then it was pleasantly warm. Skylar sat down in one of the chairs and opened her laptop. She'd already done some preliminary research on companies that matched the kind of place where she wanted to work, so she continued to sort through which ones seemed to be a good fit for her. Not that she wouldn't apply to all of them if necessary, but she had some definite preferences from what she'd seen of their online presence.

Her parents came outside to join her at one point, but they didn't stay too long since they had told Charli they'd be at the hospital around lunch time. They planned to take food up to Charli and Shiloh.

Skylar tried to use her time wisely as she passed the hours until she got a text from Aiden saying he was on his way home.

She'd changed into a pair of white capris and a lilac colored blouse with tiny white polka dots on it. It was another warm day, so she'd pulled her hair was up into a ponytail and kept her makeup minimal.

Because she'd been keeping an eye out for Aiden from the living room window, she saw when he pulled in. Gathering up her purse and phone, she left the house, locking it using the keypad on the door.

Pushing his sunglasses to the top of his head, Aiden greeted her with a smile as she joined him at the car. "You look very nice."

"Oh, thanks."

He opened the passenger door. "Ready to go see Shiloh?"

"I am."

After she was seated, he closed the door, then strode around the hood of the car to slide behind the wheel. His arm bumped her as he shifted around to get his seatbelt latched.

He drove with a mature assurance now, unlike the reckless overconfidence of his teenage years. He no longer sped through yellow lights, barely making it before they turned red. Instead, he anticipated them, slowing down to stop just as the light changed to red.

It was just one more thing that revealed how he'd grown and matured over the years. He'd left behind the reckless bent he, Cole, and all their friends had seemed to have back then.

She'd found it thrilling then, but she definitely appreciated his approach to driving now better. Arriving safely at the destination was infinitely more important than the thrill of the trip there.

It didn't take long to get to the hospital, and soon, they were once again stepping onto a busy elevator. Once they reached the correct floor, Aiden stepped out of the elevator, then waited for Skylar to join him.

Shiloh was up and sitting at the table with Charli when they walked in. Skylar's heart lifted at the sight because it signified how much improved she was.

"Did Mom and Dad tell you the good news?" Charli asked as she hugged Skylar.

"No. I left before they got home." Skylar bent to hug Shiloh, then turned her attention back to her sister while Aiden entertained the little girl, passing on a joke from Willow.

"Yeah, they didn't leave that long ago," Charli said. "They were here when the doctor came around to give us the results of more of the tests."

"What did they have to say?"

"They said that the tests aren't showing any signs of relapse," Charli said. "So she's still clear."

"Why was she so sick then?"

"It was a bladder infection that got out of hand. Once the antibiotics kicked in, she started to improve almost right away. Her immune system is still compromised, and it will continue to be that way for a little while, so we just have to be on the lookout for any type of infection so that we can catch it before it gets to where she needs to be hospitalized."

"How did it get to that point this time?"

Charli glanced at Shiloh, a sad look on her face. "She was experiencing some pain, but she was scared to say anything. She didn't want to worry us, plus she was worried about what it meant."

"I don't blame her," Skylar said. "I think I'd worry too."

"Yes. We understand that, but we've had a talk with her to let her know that things will be better for her if she tells us right away when she doesn't feel well. Doing that might not mean a hospital stay if we catch problems soon enough."

"I imagine that is a good incentive for her."

Charli smiled. "It definitely is. And the other good news is that we get to go home tomorrow."

"Oh, that is wonderful news."

That news also meant that she would need to get her stuff packed up to go back with her parents to Serenity. With Shiloh out of the hospital, there was no reason for her parents to stay in Coeur d'Alene, and that meant that Skylar needed to move home with them since she couldn't stay with Aiden by herself.

"Did you tell Uncle Aiden the good news?" Charli asked Shiloh.

"I'm going home tomorrow!" Shiloh said with a beaming smile.

It was so good to see her in better spirits and in better health. It was something that Skylar was no longer willing to take for granted.

"That is the best news ever," Aiden said, lifting his hand for her to smack. "I bet you're excited to see your brothers and sisters and your dad."

As Shiloh nodded, Skylar wondered how hard it had been for Aiden to utter that sentence. It had firmly put Shiloh into a family other than his, which she was certain he still struggled with.

"Yes. We both miss Daddy," Shiloh said. "And I miss my bed."

"I miss my bed too," Charli said, pressing her hands to her lower back. "It will be good to be back home."

Skylar waited to feel regret that she'd essentially turfed her career over an infection. However, it didn't come. She was relieved that Shiloh was doing so much better, but she was also happy with her decision to return to Idaho.

Although, if she didn't find a job, she might feel differently.

"I'm going to go call Blake while you two are here to keep Shiloh company," Charli said as she picked up her phone from the table. "I'll be back in a bit."

"So, what are you doing here?" Aiden asked as he gestured to the table.

"I was coloring while Momma read a story to me."

"Oh, we've done that before," Aiden said. "Do you want me to read while you color with Skylar?"

Shiloh shook her head. "Auntie Sky reads better than you."

"Better than me?" Aiden pressed a hand to his chest. "What's wrong with my reading?"

Shiloh giggled. "Nothing. Auntie Sky is just better at voices and stuff."

"Okay. I'll accept that."

Shiloh turned to pull out another book from a bag that sat on the windowsill next to the table. "Here's a coloring book for you."

Aiden took it, and while he flipped through the pages, Shiloh picked up the book that was laying splayed on the table and handed it to Skylar. "This is the book Momma was reading."

Skylar took the book, noting that this one seemed to be about a girl and her horse. She'd never been a horse person herself, but it seemed that her daughter—niece—might be.

"Okay," Skylar said as she settled into a seat beside the table. "You color. I'll read."

The brief visits that she and Aiden had with Shiloh were soothing for the ache of giving her up that still lingered all these years later. And probably would still linger until the day Skylar died. Because regardless of how much time she spent with Shiloh, it would never be as much as she would have had with her had she never given her up.

But glancing up and seeing father and daughter—the man she loved and their child—brought with it a sense of calm and peace. Somehow, even without really trying, she'd found a way to accept that she'd never be a mom to the child she'd given birth to.

That development gave her hope that perhaps she could reconcile herself with the past she and Aiden had and leave the negative emotions there.

She might not be able to have Shiloh in her life in the way she would have been if circumstances had been different, but maybe she could have Aiden.

CHAPTER TWENTY-EIGHT

Aiden slid behind the wheel, then turned to Skylar. "Want to grab some dinner? Or is there some at home?"

"I think Mom and Dad were going out to dinner with some friends, so we should probably stop somewhere unless we want to cook a meal after we get home."

"Dinner out it is," he said with a laugh. "Up for some Italian?"

"Sure. Sounds good."

There was a restaurant that he'd found about a year ago, and he and his mom really enjoyed it. Even Willow liked to go there and order off their children's menu.

"I'm glad to see Shiloh so improved," Aiden said. "I'm not sure I'll ever get used to seeing her sick."

"Me, either. I suppose it's exacerbated by the fact that when she gets sick, she gets *sick*."

"Yeah. No simple colds for her."

They continued to chat about Shiloh, which then segued into a conversation about Charli and Blake's other kids, until he pulled to a stop in the small parking lot next to the restaurant. The lot was nearly full, so he wasn't surprised when there was a bit of a wait for a table.

"Must be a good place," Skylar murmured as they stepped into the small corner by the hostess stand, out of the way of other diners. "Smells delicious."

"Tastes delicious too," Aiden said.

When he noticed a few glances in their direction, he wasn't surprised. Given that he stood taller than most men and Skylar was beautiful, it was to be expected. Most people probably assumed they were a couple, out on a date, and he wasn't in the mood to do or say anything that would dissuade them from that assumption.

Skylar stood with her arms crossed, her shoulder touching the wall they stood next to. Her gaze was on the activity around them, and Aiden didn't pursue a conversation while they waited for their table.

Several groups left, so they ended up only waiting around fifteen minutes, which wasn't really that bad. The hostess led the way through the dining room to a small table set for two.

The next several minutes were spent looking over the menu and deciding what they wanted. It was easy for Aiden to decide. After eating there several times already, he had a few favorites. Knowing what he did of Skylar's taste, he was able to give her some recommendations. Apparently, her tastes hadn't changed much over the years as she took him up on his suggestion for lasagna.

While waiting for their main course to come out, they spent the time eating salad and fresh bread and talking about the people from his and Cole's class that he was still in contact with. Skylar hadn't stayed in touch with any of her classmates, but maybe that would change now that she was back in the area.

Aiden wanted to broach the subject of their relationship, but he held his tongue. He'd learned to be more patient over the past few years, but this situation with Skylar was testing him.

He was grateful that things were at least comfortable between them. She no longer looked at him with anger or distrust. But at the same time, she also didn't look at him the way she had when they were dating as teens.

He'd definitely cared for her then, too. However, looking back, he could see that her commitment to their relationship had been more than his was. She'd deserved to be loved and adored as much as she'd loved and adored him.

He might not have been willing or able to do that for her before, but he wanted a chance to do it now.

When their main course came, they were quiet for a couple of minutes as they dug into their meals.

"So, are you going with your parents to Serenity tomorrow?" Aiden asked. "I figure they'll be going home once Shiloh is released."

"I'm thinking about going back to Vegas, actually."

Aiden lowered his fork as he frowned at her. "I thought you were going to stay in the area."

"I am," she said. "But I need to go back and close everything up. I have an apartment there full of stuff, so I have to pack it up."

Aiden gave a huff of relieved laughter. "Oh. Of course."

She lifted her brows at him. "Did you think I'd changed my mind?"

"Uh. Maybe?" He shrugged. "I just thought that perhaps since Shiloh was doing so much better, you'd reconsidered your decision."

She shook her head. "I've already made up my mind."

"Your parents are sure thrilled at the news," Aiden said. "And the rest of your family will be too."

"Mom and Dad just want all their kids close." Skylar agreed.

"Are you going to need help with the move?"

"I don't know," she said. "I'm still trying to decide the best way to get everything here."

"Do you have a lot of stuff?"

"The usual amount, I think. Plus, my car."

"Can you rent a truck and tow your car?"

She gave him an exasperated look. "I'm not sure that I'm qualified to do that. Or that I'd want to."

"How far of a drive is it?"

"I checked last night, and it's around a sixteen and a half hour trip, with stops."

"You could do it one day," Aiden said.

"One looooong day."

"If you want, I could fly in, then drive the truck while you drive the car," Aiden offered.

Skylar sat back in her chair. "Really?"

"I wouldn't mind doing it," Aiden said. "But you might need more than me if we're packing up the truck, too. Maybe we should see if Cole wants to join us for a road trip."

Before she could say anything, Aiden pulled out his phone and sent a message to Cole. "Let's see what he says."

In the past, Aiden might have thought that Cole wouldn't make the time. But after his last visit to Serenity, he thought perhaps he might. And the idea seemed fun.

Aiden's phone rang with a video call, and after he answered it, he propped it up on a glass so that they could both see Cole.

"Am I interrupting a date?" Cole asked.

"Nope," Skylar replied. "We stopped for dinner after visiting Shiloh at the hospital.

"So you're moving to Serenity?" Cole asked, shifting in the phone's screen to look in her direction.

"I am," she said. "Or more likely, Coeur d'Alene."

"Why there and not Serenity?"

"There are more job options, so I think it will be better for me to be here."

"And it's closer to Aiden," Cole said with a wink.

Skylar sighed, but she didn't deny it.

"Could you spare some time for a road trip?" Aiden asked, saving Skylar from having to respond to Cole's remark.

"Depends on when we're talking about."

They spent the next half hour planning out when the trip would work for each of them. In the end, Cole and Aiden decided to fly into Vegas on Friday so they'd have Saturday to load the truck. Then they'd set out early Sunday for the long drive back to Coeur d'Alene.

Skylar was going to head to Vegas as soon as she could book a flight, so she'd have a few days to pack before the guys arrived.

While Aiden continued to chat with Cole, Skylar pulled out her phone. Her brow furrowed as she focused on the screen, tapping and swiping.

"Okay. My flight to Vegas leaves early Wednesday morning," she said, setting her phone down on the table. "So I'm going to be packing like a maniac until you guys arrive."

"Is that enough time?" Aiden asked.

"Yep. It will be fine. Since I won't be working, I'll have plenty of time to pack."

"Can't believe you succumbed," Cole said.

"Hey." Skylar directed a frown at her brother. "I have good reason for moving back. Maybe you should consider it yourself."

"Last I checked, they don't have a pro team in Serenity."

"You could take over for Jay coaching at the high school."

"Not yet."

Skylar smiled slyly at him. "Well, that's not a flat out no."

"I think we're all learning that the future isn't set in stone."

"That sounds amazingly philosophical coming from you," Skylar said.

"I'm not just a jock, you know," Cole retorted.

"No. You're a rich jock."

"Let's see," Cole said. "Canceling trip to Vegas."

Skylar laughed. "Fine. You're a philosopher and a pro ball-player."

"You bet I am."

Aiden smiled as the siblings interacted in such a familiar way. He had missed this, and he was glad that while other things had changed, the way the three of them could be together apparently hadn't.

He couldn't wait for Friday to come. Helping Skylar move back was something he was definitely on board with.

~*~

The next day, Skylar headed to Serenity with her parents, hoping that she could spend a little time with Shiloh that evening. Blake had come in to pick up Shiloh and Charli, and they were on their way out to Serenity as well.

She'd brought her suitcases with her, though she'd eventually need them back in Coeur d'Alene. Since she didn't yet have an apartment there, she would have to stay in Serenity for the time being.

Aiden had apologized for not inviting her to stay at his place, but Skylar hadn't been upset by that. She understood why he wouldn't do it, and she respected him for it.

During their last conversation about getting back together, she'd asked for another day. But with her decision to return to Vegas to pack up, it would have to wait. And she was glad for the extra time.

Something was holding Skylar back, and she wasn't sure what it was. She'd forgiven Aiden. Or at least she was pretty sure she had.

There was no doubt that she loved him. But was that enough?

He had become the man she'd always hoped to spend her life with, and she was confident that this version of Aiden wouldn't abandon her. That he'd be a rock in her life. Strong and unmovable. That kind of strength was appealing because there was a lot of uncertainty in their future, particularly when it came to Shiloh.

So why wasn't she jumping at the chance of getting back with him?

Even though she spent the trip to Serenity mulling that over, she still had no answer by the time her dad turned the car into their driveway.

She put her contemplations aside for the time being. There was still time for her to work through it, and maybe she and Aiden could have a talk on the drive back from Vegas.

Once in the house, she took her things up to her room, then returned to the kitchen to help her mom get them some lunch. It didn't take long, and soon they were seated at the table together.

Skylar felt a sense of calm that she hadn't the last time she was there. There had been a lot going on then. Uncertainty and worry. Not to mention her injured ankle.

But that was in the past now. Even the concern over Shiloh which had caused her to quit her job had eased—for the time being. And if there was a next time, she wouldn't have to make a mad dash from Vegas.

She was at peace with her decision to quit her job and return to Coeur d'Alene. It wasn't that she'd been unhappy in Vegas, but now that her future was headed in a new direction, she was glad to leave it behind.

As they were cleaning up after the meal, Skylar got a call from Charli.

"I was wondering if you wanted to come over for a bit this afternoon to see Shiloh."

"Oh, I'd really like that."

"Check if you can borrow Mom's car," Charli said. "If not, I'll come pick you up."

"Hang on, let me ask." She lowered the phone and looked at her mom. "Can I use your car to go to Charli's for a little while this afternoon?"

"Certainly, darling," her mom said. "Your dad and I are going to the store, so we'll be using his car."

When Skylar said she had a ride, Charli told her to come soon since it was likely that Shiloh would take a nap at some point that afternoon.

Her mom and dad waved off her offer to help clean up from lunch.

"You just go on," her mom said.

Skylar hugged her parents, then went up to her room to get her purse. When she came down, her mom gave her the keys to her car. "Have a good visit, darling."

"I'll be back in time to help you with supper," she said as she headed for the front door.

It wasn't long before she pulled up in front of a two-storey house. It wasn't super big, but it was on some acreage on the outskirts of town, which gave the kids lots of room to run and play.

"Hi, Auntie Sky!" The boys both greeted her enthusiastically as they gave her quick hugs.

She ran her fingers through their dark, wavy hair. "Hey, you two. How's it going?"

"They need haircuts," Charli said. "So I think that while you're here with Shiloh, I'm going to take them for that."

At Charli's instruction, Skylar walked through the house to the door that led to the large screened-in porch at the back of the house. It looked out over a yard that wasn't as manicured as her parents' or Aiden's, but it was large and held everything a kid could want, from a swing set with a slide to a treehouse.

At the far end of the porch, Shiloh sat cross-legged on the bench swing, a book in her lap. She looked up, and a smile lit her face when she saw Skylar. "Auntie Sky! I didn't know you were coming."

Skylar walked over to the cluster of rattan furniture that included the porch swing where Shiloh sat and bent to give her a hug and kiss. As she sank down onto the swing next to Shiloh, she said, "How are you feeling?"

"Better," Shiloh said as she put a bookmark into the book and set it on the chair beside her. "I don't like feeling sick."

"Oh, I understand that, sweetie," Skylar said. "Hopefully it won't happen again. But if you start to feel even a little sick, you need to tell someone. Once they know, they can give you medicine to keep you from getting worse."

"Yeah. That's what Momma said." Shiloh's shoulders slumped. "I just didn't want to bother anyone."

Shiloh's whispered words broke Skylar's heart. She shifted close enough to slip her arms around Shiloh. "You're absolutely never a bother to anyone, especially your mom and dad. We all love you and want you to be healthy, so we'll do whatever we need to in order to make that happen. We would do that for any of you kids."

"Even Willow?" she asked.

"Yes, definitely. Willow too."

The sadness slipped from Shiloh's face at Skylar's words, and she smiled at her again. It was a smile Skylar was so happy to see.

Skylar was glad for the opportunity to have this time with Shiloh. It was nice to be outside, in the screened in porch where bugs couldn't get to them, instead of in the hospital.

As they chatted, Skylar let Shiloh lead the direction of their conversation. They touched on a variety of different things, starting with the book she'd been reading. From there, they moved on to one of the nurses she'd had during her latest hospital stay. Then she told Skylar that she wished she could go skating with Lexi and Amelia.

After about an hour, Charli was back with the boys, and she sent them out into the yard to play in the sprinkler. Shiloh asked to go lay down for a nap, so Charli took her to her room, then returned to the porch with some water and a plate of chocolate chip cookies.

"I need chocolate," Charli said. "Desperately."

Now that she didn't have to worry about fitting into a uniform, Skylar didn't feel like she had to restrict her diet quite as much. "I wouldn't mind some myself."

They sat eating their cookies for a few minutes, listening as the boys yelled at the top of their lungs while chasing each other through the water.

"How are things with you and Aiden?" Charli asked as she picked up her glass, slanting a look Skylar's way before focusing on her sons again.

"We're getting along better," Skylar told her. "Certainly better than we did when we first saw each other."

"So you're friends?"

Skylar considered her sister's question. "Yes. I would say we're friends."

"That's good," Charli said. "And the prospect of more than friendship? Has anything more developed since we last talked about things between you and Aiden?"

"Not really." Skylar looked down at her hands. "We did talk some more, and I think I want to give him a second chance, but... I'm confused."

"How do you feel about him?"

"I... really, really like him," Skylar said, not wanting the first time she talked about her love for him to be with anyone but Aiden.

When he'd said he'd loved her in that previous conversation, her heart had about stopped. She hadn't been sure if he'd realized he'd said it, so she hadn't reacted at the time. At least outwardly. Inwardly, well, she'd been jumping for joy.

But yet she still hesitated to commit.

"When I see him now, I see the type of man I'd always imagined he'd become. Strong. Reliable. Added on to that, I see a gentleness in him I don't remember from before. Shiloh and Willow really bring it out of him."

"You do too," Charli said. "Though I'm not sure you see it."

Skylar nodded. "I do see it."

"Have you forgiven him for what happened?"

"I think I have. I can be around him without being angry at him."

"That's good," Charli said. "And have you considered your part in everything?"

Skylar shifted to look more fully at her sister. "What?"

Charli stared at her for a long moment before she said, "I understand that Aiden bears a lot of the weight of responsibility for what happened before. However, you also bear some of it."

Skylar narrowed her eyes at Charli.

"Just hear me out, okay? I've been thinking a lot about this since we talked, and I want to share my thoughts with you. What you do with them is up to you." Charli let her gaze drift to the boys. "I think that if you hope to make things work with Aiden, you need to shoulder some of the responsibility for your own hurt. Aiden shouldn't have to bear all of it."

"I need you to explain."

"I know you struggled with the fact that you got pregnant," Charli said. "And that giving Shiloh up hurt you a lot."

"Yes. That's true."

"But unless Aiden raped you, you were as responsible as he was for what you did that resulted in your pregnancy."

Charli's words shocked Skylar, not because they weren't true, but because they were. And she wasn't done yet.

"I believe you also need to acknowledge that the decision to give Shiloh up was entirely yours. You know that if you'd wanted to keep her, you could have. You would have had lots of support."

Skylar felt the truth of those words pierce her heart.

"I'm not saying that I wish that things had worked out differently, because I don't feel that way at all. I believe things worked out the way they were supposed to."

"So, what am I supposed to do?"

"I think you need to accept that you made decisions that would benefit you," Charli said, not pulling any punches. She lifted her hand when Skylar started to say something, feeling the need to defend herself. "You were entitled to make those decisions, and clearly, we have also benefited in a way we hadn't known was possible. I'm not getting after you for any of those decisions."

"Then what *are* you saying?" Skylar wasn't sure how she should feel at that moment. There was a mix of anger and sadness, along with some other feelings, bubbling inside her. One of them was going to spill out, and she wanted to make sure it was the right one.

"I'm saying that I think it's important that you free Aiden from some of the weight he carries for your unhappiness during that time, because it shouldn't all be his. Yes, he broke up with you in a way that was really hurtful, and his response to your pregnancy was bad, but you also made some decisions that have added to your unhappiness."

Skylar had never thought of it that way. Charli's words peeled back a curtain in her mind, and her heart hurt once again. Except, it didn't hurt for herself, this time it hurt for Aiden.

In her mind all these years, it was his fault that she'd had to give Shiloh up, and when they'd reconnected, she'd made sure he knew that. She'd thought she was too young—a couple of years younger than Charli had been—and not strong enough to be a good mom.

But Charli was right. The family would have supported her. She could have kept Shiloh.

"I don't want to upset you," Charli said. "But I think it's important that you talk to Aiden about this before you move forward. Don't try to build a relationship on the shaky past the two of you have. Sweep away all the regret and hurt and build your relationship on truth. And that truth should start with a very frank conversation about what happened nine years ago."

"You're right," Skylar said, then swallowed against the emotion that threatened to choke her. "I'll talk to him."

Charli reached out and laid her hand on Skylar's arm. "I would like nothing better than to see you and Aiden together, but I want it to be a lasting thing. And not just for your and Aiden's sake. I don't want Shiloh to watch her birth parents get together, only for them to fall apart at some point in the future."

Skylar shook her head. "I don't want her to see that either, and I don't want to live through that for a second time."

"So give yourselves the best shot by being honest about everything."

Skylar hadn't enjoyed hearing those truths from her sister. But now that she had, she knew that it had been necessary. That Charli had only been looking out for her best interests.

"I might have the opportunity to talk to him this weekend when we're on the way back from Vegas."

"Tell me about your plans," Charli said.

As she told Charli about what she was hoping would happen, Skylar had a confidence about the future that she hadn't had prior to their conversation. Because now she knew what she had to do. What had held her back from being able to fully commit to Aiden.

Unfortunately, the next few days were going to be busy, and she wouldn't see Aiden again until he arrived in Vegas. Suddenly those few days they'd be far apart loomed large.

Now that she was fully on board for a new relationship with him, she wanted it to happen right away.

CHAPTER TWENTY-NINE

Aiden reluctantly rolled out of bed, letting out a deep groan as the sound of his alarm sliced through the quiet morning. After shutting it off, he cast a glance toward the other bed, where Cole lay sleeping. In the dim light of his phone, all he could make out was a large, motionless lump beneath the crumpled blankets.

"Time to get up, bro," he called out, his voice cutting through the silence. "We've got to hit the road."

His muscles protested with every movement, a reminder of the previous day's exhausting efforts. He and Cole had spent hours lifting and hauling, their bodies strained from the relentless work. A few extra sets of hands would have been a blessing, but somehow, they had managed to accomplish the task on their own.

Cole had muttered a few times about how he should have just hired someone to pack everything up for Skylar. He'd even discreetly called up a couple of places to see if they had anyone available, but with such short notice, everyone had said they couldn't help.

"Ugh." Cole shifted on the bed, his arms breaking free of the lump of covers to stretch into the air.

"I'm turning on a light, so cover your eyes," Aiden advised.

After he'd switched on the lamp beside his bed, he shuffled to where he'd left his bag the night before.

"I could use a couple more hours of sleep. Or a long soak in a hot tub."

"Sorry, dude," Aiden said as he rummaged through his things for some clean clothes and his toiletry bag. "Neither is an option today. We've got a long drive to take care of."

"Why did we decide to do this all in one day?" Cole groused as he swung his legs over the side of the bed and sat up, rubbing his face before dragging his hands through his hair.

"I didn't take tomorrow off," Aiden reminded him. "So I've got to be back in Coeur d'Alene tonight."

"You should come work for me," Cole said, as he had many times before.

"Not gonna happen," Aiden said over his shoulder as he headed into the small bathroom to change and freshen up for the day.

When he came back out, Cole was on his feet at the small coffee maker, staring down at it. The aroma of brewing coffee grew stronger as Aiden returned the clothes he'd slept in and his toiletries to his duffle bag.

"Are you planning to grab breakfast here?" Aiden asked, referring to the breakfast offered by the hotel.

"Yes. I'm starving." Cole turned with a cup of coffee in his hand. "We can head down once I'm dressed."

While Cole got ready, Aiden made himself a cup of coffee. It wasn't the best he'd ever tasted, but it would help him wake up. After a couple of sips, he picked up his phone and sent a quick message to Skylar.

Are you awake? We're getting ready to head down for some breakfast.

It took a couple of minutes, but soon a reply came.

Skylar: *Yep. I'm ready. Just putting the last things into my bag.*

She'd turned the apartment keys in the night before, and as she'd stood looking at the empty space just before they left, Aiden had wondered if she would miss her life there. But once they'd left, she'd seemed fine.

They'd had dinner at a nearby restaurant after their long day of packing and loading the moving truck. But since they were all exhausted, they hadn't stayed up late.

Aiden hadn't had a chance to talk to Skylar about anything that wasn't related to the move in the time they'd been together. That was fine, however, because he was sure that he'd have lots of time with her during the long drive home.

Why don't you come by our room when you're ready?

When Skylar sent a thumbs up in reply, Aiden set his phone down and took his cup of coffee over to the window. Pushing back the curtain, he stared out at the scenery around the hotel.

The sun was still working to fully push back the darkness, but it looked like it was going to be a sunny day. Not his favorite type of day for driving, but it was better than rain or snow.

Cole had just come out of the bathroom when there was a rap on the door.

"It's Skylar," Aiden said when Cole gave him a questioning look. He went to open it, greeting her with a smile.

Though it was early, she didn't look as tired as he felt. The T-shirt and leggings she wore looked like they'd be comfortable for the trip ahead.

"Morning," he said as he held the door open for her to come in. She had a duffle bag on one shoulder and a smaller bag on the other.

"It certainly is," she agreed as she dumped the duffle bag on the floor next to his.

"Ready to get some breakfast?" Cole asked. "We should probably get on the road in the next half hour or so."

"I'm not super hungry, but I'll eat something, so I'm not starving in a couple of hours."

The three of them left the room and headed down to the main floor where the hotel had a small cafe style space that was set up to serve the breakfast. Cole headed directly to where someone was cooking what looked like eggs, bacon, and sausage.

Aiden and Skylar wandered by the other parts of the buffet before Aiden joined Cole. After ordering some eggs and bacon for himself, he went to where a toaster and a few varieties of bread had been set out. After making his choice, he put the bread into the toaster.

Five minutes later, the three of them were seated at a small round table in the corner of the room. It was only them and a couple of other people there so early in the morning.

Skylar had opted for a bagel with cream cheese and some fruit. Cole's plate was piled high with eggs, bacon, sausage, and some fruit.

"This is a pretty decent breakfast," Cole commented as they began to eat.

"It's great," Aiden said. "Lots of selection."

Cole had gotten another cup of coffee and took a sip. "Should keep us going for awhile."

They didn't talk much, focusing on their food, since they wanted to get on the road soon. Once they'd finished eating, they returned to their rooms to get their bags, then they checked out.

"I can drive your car for a bit, Sky," Aiden offered as they approached the part of the lot where they'd parked her car and the moving truck the night before.

"Sure. That works for me."

"Are you going to ride with me or Aiden?" Cole asked as he opened the door of the truck.

"Aiden," Skylar said. "Unless you want me to ride with you. I think the car will be more comfortable."

"No doubt." Cole pulled out his phone and held it up. "I've got a long audiobook I plan to listen to on this trip, so I'm fine on my own."

"Guess it's settled then."

Skylar unlocked the car with her fob, then handed the keys to Aiden. "You have your walkie talkie set to the right frequency, Cole?"

"Yep. I set them up when I bought them." He grinned. "I can't wait to use them. It'll be fun."

Aiden hadn't thought they were necessary, but then he realized it would be easier to just pick up one of the walkie talkies to contact the other vehicle rather than having to place a call on their phones.

Cole had picked a hotel along the highway leading out of Vegas, so it didn't take long to get onto the road they needed. They'd decided that Cole would lead and set the pace in the truck, and they'd follow in the car.

As they left Vegas behind, heading north, Skylar let out a long sigh. Aiden glanced over at her. "Everything okay?"

"Yep. It's just weird to think I'm closing this chapter of my life so completely."

"What do you mean?"

"Well, I'm not just leaving Vegas, where I've lived for the past few years, I'm also leaving behind the career I've had for almost a decade."

"Did you work private jets that whole time?"

"No. I started out working on commercial flights."

"Which did you like better?"

"I would say the private ones," she said. "It was less stressful to only have to deal with a handful of people rather than a whole plane load of sometimes...ofttimes... cranky people."

"Do you have any regrets about this change in your life?" He knew she was sacrificing a lot, so he figured she'd have some regrets about having to make these changes.

"No," she said, without any hesitation. "It's time. I've had the chance to see parts of the world I wouldn't have otherwise. I've experienced independence living on my own, in a city where I didn't know anyone. I'm not leaving here wishing I could do more."

"I'm glad."

She was quiet for a minute, then said, "I'm ready for what lays ahead now. I'm ready to make peace with the past and to look forward."

Aiden's heart lifted at the statement. "That's a good outlook to have."

It was on the tip of his tongue to ask if that included a second chance for them. But he kept the question to himself. He'd told her that if she needed time, she could have as much as she needed.

Thankfully, his ability to be patient had grown over the past several years. He'd had to learn to be patient in dealing with people on the projects at work. And though she was an angel most of the time, there were moments when Willow tested the limits of his patience, forcing him to dig deep for more.

Still, being patient with Skylar was the hardest thing in the world. But he needed her to see that he was as good as his word.

"Have you had any responses to your applications?"

"Yes. One company called me to set up an interview for Wednesday."

"An interior design place?"

"Yep. I haven't applied to places that aren't interior design related. I figured that I'll save those to apply to if I've exhausted these places with no luck."

"How about a place to stay?"

"I haven't looked around too much. Until I know what my salary is going to be, I'm not sure what my budget is for rent."

Aiden told her a bit about what he knew of the different areas in Coeur d'Alene as he followed Cole down the highway.

The landscape was quite different from the verdant surroundings of his Idaho home, yet the desert terrain near Vegas had its own charm. Distant mountains loomed, shrouded in a hazy glow under the intense sunlight.

He didn't think he'd enjoy living in the stark, hot environment of Vegas, but apparently Skylar had liked it enough to remain there for several years.

Skylar shifted beside him, and when he glanced over at her, he saw that she'd angled herself to face him more fully. "Are you able to drive and have a conversation at the same time?"

Aiden gave a huff of laughter. "I thought we were already doing that."

"A *serious* conversation."

At that comment, he instantly sobered. He had mixed feelings about having a serious conversation with her, presumably about their future, because it could go either way. She hadn't given him any indication over the past few days of what she was thinking.

"Yes. I can have a serious conversation with you while I drive," Aiden said. "In fact, there's nothing I want more."

"Nothing?" she asked.

"Okay. I'd like for Shiloh to be completely healed," he said. "But having a serious conversation with you is right after that for what I want."

"Yeah. Me too."

Bringing up Shiloh seemed to cast a shadow over everything. Aiden disliked that every time he thought of Shiloh, her cancer came up in his mind too. He wished he could associate her with only positive thoughts. However, sadly, he had no recollections of a time with her that didn't involve her illness.

"So what did you want to talk about?" Aiden asked.

"I had a conversation with Charli the other day that helped bring some clarity to things in my life and how I've dealt with stuff that's happened."

"Is that a good thing?"

"Yes. Very good. I think it's necessary for me to face those truths in order to move forward."

Aiden pulled out to pass a slow-moving trailer, following not far behind Cole, who had also passed the vehicle.

Once they were back in the right-hand lane, free of the slower traffic, Skylar said, "I owe you an apology."

Aiden glanced over at her. "Say what?"

"Ever since the day of our breakup, I've blamed you for the unhappiness in my life. I blamed you for the fact that I had to give Shiloh up to Charli and Blake."

"That's understandable," Aiden said, not quite grasping what she was getting at.

"Going back to that summer before we broke up, I made the decision to sleep with you," she said. "Because of that, I also have a responsibility for the pregnancy that resulted."

What she said made sense, but he still felt that he bore more of the responsibility for what happened. He'd slept with her, knowing that he wasn't as committed to their relationship as he'd been in the past. And definitely not as committed as she'd been.

"Then, I got pregnant with Shiloh and gave her up, feeling like I had to because you weren't with me."

"Raising her on your own would have been difficult," Aiden said.

"But realistically, I wouldn't have been on my own." Skylar fell silent for a moment. "I would have had it better than a lot of other single mothers who manage to do it on their own. My family would have helped me, just like they helped Charli. I didn't *have* to give her up. But I told myself I did, and it was because you weren't there."

Aiden was not sure how to respond, but it seemed perhaps she didn't need responses from him yet.

"Talking to Charli helped me to see that in all of this, I wasn't taking responsibility for my own unhappiness and the decisions I'd made. I was putting all of that on you. Blaming you for everything that happened back then."

She hadn't been the only one blaming him. He'd blamed himself.

"You aren't to blame for everything," she said. "You made some mistakes, and so did I. Though I'm coming to understand that giving up Shiloh wasn't one of them. It was truly best for her to be with Charli and Blake."

"I feel like my mistakes were worse than yours," Aiden told her.

She reached out to put her hand on his arm, making Aiden wish he could concentrate on her rather than on the road. Maybe he wasn't able to have this conversation while driving after all.

"We can both take responsibility for what happened back then, but I think it's time that we both forgive each other and ourselves."

"Yes. We should." Aiden glanced over at her again. "But can you do that?"

"Right now, it almost feels easier to forgive you than to forgive myself."

"Yeah. I agree."

"But I want us to do that, because I agree with Charli that we need to build a strong foundation. And in order to do that, we need to bulldoze the old foundation that we had. Bulldoze and clear it all away to make room for something new. Something strong because of our love for each other and our faith in God."

Aiden's heart swelled with the knowledge that she wanted a relationship with him. "But the pieces will all still be there. We won't forget."

"True, but we can use them to remind us how far we've come. And of the mess we make when we wander off the path God wants for us."

"So you're willing to make that effort?" Aiden was all in, but she needed to be all in, too.

"I am." Her hand tightened on his arm. "I've been scared to risk it again. But now that I've changed how I view the past, I've realized that there will always be a risk. The only love that doesn't require a risk is God's love. So, in loving you again... in loving anyone, really... I'm taking a risk. Even loving Shiloh comes with the risk of heartbreak."

Aiden nodded. "I've already experienced that, having lost two loved ones."

She rubbed his arm gently. "I'm sorry you had to go through that."

"Thanks." He cleared his throat. "Even though I understand there's a risk, I also want you to know that I will do my best to show that you can trust me. I don't want to hurt you. I never want to do that again."

"I don't want to hurt you either," Skylar said. "But I'm sure I have with some of what I've said to you since we've reconnected."

Aiden couldn't deny that, but he also felt that he'd deserved it.

"So I'm sorry about that."

"You don't have to ap—"

Skylar's fingers tightened on his arm as she said, "Stop." He glanced over to see her glaring at him. "You have apologized to me for what you felt you needed to. Now, let me do the same."

"Okay. You're right."

Skylar gave a little chuckle. "I never would have thought I'd be asking someone to let me apologize to them like this."

Aiden tossed her a grin. "Yeah. It feels a bit crazy."

"It does."

"Well, I forgive you," Aiden said, looking at her briefly. "Just as you forgave me when I apologized."

Suddenly he felt something press against his shoulder and realized that Skylar had leaned forward to rest her cheek on his upper arm. "Maybe this would have been a conversation better had out of the car."

"Why?"

"I want to give you a hug," Skylar said. "But I can't."

"I'll take an IOU until we get to our next stop."

Skylar straightened with a laugh. "That works."

Keeping one hand on the wheel, he took hers with his other, wanting to have physical contact with her. "So where do we go on our first date this time around?"

For the next few hours, they discussed not only their first date but also their future together as a couple. This was a conversation he had been eager to have for some time, and it brought him a sense of relief and hopefulness.

They'd been on the road about three hours when the walkie talkie crackled to life.

"Let's pull in up here," Cole said. "Need gas and would like to stretch my legs."

"Sounds good," Skylar replied into the walkie talkie. "We'll follow you off."

Five minutes later, they were pulling up to the pumps at a truck stop just off the highway. Before he did anything with the gas pump, Aiden got out of the car and circled around the hood to open the door for Skylar.

Once she was on her feet outside the car, Aiden took her into his arms and picked her up, spinning her in a gentle circle before setting her down. "Just had to do that."

As he kept his arms wrapped around her, the world seemed to fall away, leaving just the two of them in a universe of their own. The rumble of engines. The smell of oil and gas. The murmur of voices. None of it was present in that moment between them.

Standing there, wrapped in each other's arms, time seemed to slow. The scent of her hair, a delicate blend of jasmine and vanilla, enveloped him, drawing him closer as if to merge their very hearts together. He felt the soft rise and fall of her chest against his, a gentle rhythm that spoke of life and love intertwined.

He pulled back slightly, just enough to gaze into her eyes. Those eyes that had once looked at him with anger, hurt, and disappointment now shimmered with unshed tears of joy and forgiveness.

"I never thought..." he began, his voice barely above a whisper, thick with emotion. "I never dared to hope that we'd be at this point in our lives again."

She smiled, a small, tremulous thing that spoke of her own disbelief and wonder. "Neither did I," she admitted, her fingers moving to cup his face, thumbs gently stroking his cheeks. "But here we are."

He leaned into her touch, savoring the softness of her skin against his. His heart swelled with gratitude, threatening to burst from the sheer magnitude of the second chance she had granted him. He vowed silently to himself that he would spend every day proving himself worthy of her love and trust.

With a bright smile and a sparkle in her eyes, Skylar gazed up at him. "I love you, Aiden."

"I love you too," he said, lowering his head to kiss her but then pulling back. "I'd rather our first kiss not happen beside gas pumps."

Skylar moved her hands from his cheeks to clasp them behind his neck. "I don't mind where we are," she replied.

"In that case..." Aiden leaned in and gently kissed Skylar's lips. At first, it was a soft touch, reminiscent of the many kisses they had exchanged over the years.

Yet, as the kiss lingered, it felt different... new...

Within the warmth of their embrace, the tentative hope Aiden had had for a future with Skylar gave way to the assurance of what was to come as they built a life together.

As they held each other, Aiden's mind wandered to the possibilities that lay ahead. He imagined lazy Saturday mornings, the sunlight streaming through their bedroom window as they lingered over coffee and shared dreams. He pictured holidays spent with both their families, the laughter and love filling their home as they created new traditions together.

Skylar's gentle breathing against his chest grounded him in the present, even as his heart soared with visions of their future.

Their journey hadn't been easy. Years of hurt and betrayal had nearly derailed their chance at happiness.

But God had other plans, gently guiding them back to each other when they had least expected it. Now, as they stood entwined in this moment of quiet joy, Aiden felt a peace he'd never known before.

Their tender moment was interrupted by the sound of a throat clearing nearby. Aiden and Skylar reluctantly broke apart to see Cole standing there with an amused smirk.

"As touching as this reunion is, we should probably get moving if we want to make it back tonight," he said, gesturing to the gas pumps.

Aiden nodded, feeling a flush creep up his neck. "Right, of course." He turned to Skylar with an apologetic smile. "I'll fill up the car."

Skylar went into the store to get some snacks as he pumped the gas. Soon, however, they were back in their seats, ready to continue the trip.

As he pulled back onto the highway behind the truck, Skylar reached over and laced her fingers through his.

"Ready for the next leg of the journey?" she asked, giving his hand a gentle squeeze.

Aiden smiled, his eyes were fixed on the road ahead, but his heart was full of love for the woman beside him. "With you? I'm ready for anything."

As they drove on, following Cole in the moving truck, Aiden felt a deep sense of peace. Whatever lay ahead, he knew that God would lead them through it, just as He'd already led Aiden through some of the most difficult times in his life.

But this time, he'd have Skylar by his side.

EPILOGUE

Skylar left the bathroom and sank down on the edge of the bed. She still had to make it, but there was something more pressing on her mind at the moment.

A glance at her phone revealed she had one minute and thirty-eight seconds left to wait. She set her phone on the nightstand next to her side of the bed. Her gaze went to the large, framed photo that stood there beside her glass of water, and a small stack of books that included her Bible and a notebook, along with her tablet.

The photo reflected one of the happiest days of her life. The day she and Aiden had gotten married. The smile on her face reflected the joy she'd felt on that early spring afternoon when they'd said their vows in front of a small gathering of friends and family.

They'd gotten married just eight months after they'd decided to give their relationship a second chance that day at the truck stop.

Aiden had known from the start of their relationship that they would end up married, so he'd proposed on Valentine's Day with a beautiful ring. Two and a half months later, they were standing in front of Pastor Kennedy, pledging their love and lives to each other.

Teenage Skylar would have been appalled by the brief engagement and the modest wedding that followed. Back in those days, whenever she'd envisioned her wedding—which was often—she'd pictured a grand event with all her friends serving as bridesmaids, and Layla and Amelia as her flower girls.

Her dress was going to be breathtaking, made of satin and adorned with lace. Aiden, along with his friends, would look dashing in tuxedos.

When they'd decided not to wait the year it would have taken to plan a big wedding, Skylar realized it wasn't all that important. She was at the point in her life where she was more eager to begin her life with Aiden than she was to have an extravagant wedding.

Even though the wedding had ended up being quite simple, Skylar wouldn't change a single detail.

Charli had been her matron of honor, while Cole had been Aiden's best man. And of course, Shiloh and Willow had been flower girls. Charli and Blake's two sons had been the ring and Bible bearers.

Looking down at her hand, Skylar smiled, remembering the moment Aiden had slid each of the rings onto her finger. First, to make her his fiancée. Then, to make her his wife.

Her gaze drifted in the direction of the bathroom. Would she soon discover that, just six months after their wedding, he might have made her a mother?

Her stomach was in knots at the thought. She hadn't told Aiden she suspected she might be pregnant, even though she was confident she was. Her period was almost two weeks late, which was not usual for her at all.

Though they had used birth control, they hadn't exactly been overly careful with it. So would she be surprised to see a positive on the test that was sitting face down on the bathroom counter? No. She wouldn't be.

What did surprise her was the knot of anxiety that had immediately taken up residence in her stomach when she'd first allowed herself to consider that she might be pregnant. Even now, her mind said she should be thrilled, but she wasn't.

She wouldn't be *un*happy if she was pregnant. She was just... worried. Anxious. Scared.

When the timer on her phone went off, Skylar snatched it up and turned it off. She stared into the bathroom, reluctant to go and see if her suspicions were correct. Maybe she should have told Aiden what she suspected, so he could have been there with her.

But she wasn't sure she was ready to tell him how she was feeling. It probably wouldn't make sense to him, because, honestly, it didn't make sense to her.

"Just do it," she muttered, clutching her phone in her hands. "Get up, march your butt in there, and *look* at it."

When her butt stayed firmly seated on the bed, Skylar let out a sigh as her shoulders slumped. She just couldn't seem to motivate herself to face the news head-on.

Sitting there and not knowing wouldn't make her less pregnant if the test was positive. It was just putting off the inevitable.

"You can do it," she told herself. "And you're not going to be alone this time. Even if it's positive, Aiden's not going anywhere. Not this time."

Still, this moment was dragging her back to the last time she'd taken a pregnancy test. The emotions of that time had come roaring back with a vengeance, catching her completely off-guard.

Given how well things were going for her and Aiden, she hadn't thought that memories of that time would still impact her. Or at least not to the extent that they were.

Getting up, she put the phone back on the nightstand and began to pull the bedding into place. She did her side, then Aiden's. Taking her time, going from side to side. Sometimes he helped her, but he'd gone in for half a day's work, while she'd taken the whole day off so she could have a slow morning before the upcoming busy weekend.

When her phone chimed with an incoming text, she tossed the navy blue throw pillow she'd been holding onto the burgundy bedspread and went back to pick up the phone.

Aiden: *Just checking in. Are you up? I tried not to wake you before I left.*

Yep! I'm up and just made the bed, so no crawling back into it for me.

Aiden: *I'm glad you got to sleep in a little. I'll be home around twelve-thirty, then we can head to Serenity for the program.*

Did you want me to make you a sandwich or something to eat before we go?

Aiden: *A sandwich would be great, love. Thank you. See you soon. <3*

Love you.

So now the clock was ticking. She either had to check the test, or put it away to check later.

She tossed the phone on the bed and turned toward the bathroom. Check the test, take a shower, get ready for the day, then make sandwiches for their lunch.

Taking a deep breath, Skylar headed to the bathroom. She'd left the lights on, so there was no way to avoid seeing the test on the counter.

She hesitated in the doorway, but then made herself step up to the bathroom vanity. The test lay exactly where she had left it, taunting her and causing her anxiety.

She reached out and picked it up. Then, without giving herself time to hesitate, she turned it over and stared down at the little screen that proclaimed that she was pregnant.

The air was sucked from her lungs, and her heart seemed to completely stop for a solid two seconds before it began to race.

She was pregnant.

They were going to be parents... again.

Only this time, they would keep the baby.

"Okay. It's positive."

Skylar stared at it for a long moment before she turned and stripped off her clothes and climbed into the shower.

Tears fell unchecked as she struggled to not be angry with herself for not being over the moon with the news. As warm water spilled over her shoulders, she rested her hand on her belly and tried to focus on the fact that within her body was a new life.

A precious new life.

That was what she needed to focus on.

Please, God, help me with my emotions.

By the time she got out of the shower, Skylar felt marginally better. Rather than dwell on the pregnancy test, she turned her attention to choosing her outfit, then doing her hair and makeup.

She settled on a pair of camel colored pants with a tapered leg and paired them with a turtleneck, which was a couple of shades lighter than her pants, and she planned to wear a burgundy blazer to top off the outfit, along with a fall colored scarf.

They were going to Serenity early because it was the fall festival weekend for the town. They planned to help the church set up for their part of the festival, and then have a family dinner at her parents' place.

But first, she had to decide what to do about her new knowledge. Tell him now, or tell him later?

She had just put the finishing touches on their sandwiches when Aiden arrived home from his half day at work, but she hadn't figured out what to do yet.

"Hello, babe," Aiden said as he came to give her a kiss.

Skylar leaned into him, prolonging the kiss for just a moment. As they stepped apart, Aiden gave her a smile. "You look gorgeous. I think I need to change into something to match you."

"You have a sweater that would work," Skylar said as she filled a couple of glasses with water. "But you look just fine the way you are."

He carried the glasses to the dining table where the plates with their sandwiches and some chips waited. Once they'd both sat down, Aiden held out his hands for her to take, then said a prayer of thanks for their food.

"Are you okay, babe?" Aiden asked as he finished his sandwich.

"What?"

"You seem a little distracted," he said. "I know my meeting isn't exactly the most interesting news."

"Oh no, it's not that." Skylar reached out and took his hand. "You know I enjoy hearing about your projects."

"Then what is it?" Aiden asked. "I feel like there's something bothering you."

Over the months they'd been together for the second time, he'd proven to have an acute sense of her moods. She usually appreciated it, but right then, she wished he'd been a little less in tune with her.

His blue gaze held hers, filled with concern that reminded her that he loved her and would do anything in his power to make things right for her. She needed him to know because he would help her come to grips with the news and the emotions that it had stirred up.

Standing up from the table, she said, "I'll be right back."

Aiden's brow furrowed. "Okaaay."

Returning to the bathroom, Skylar picked up the test. After a moment of wondering if it really was the right time, she decided it was.

Back in the kitchen, she found that Aiden had cleared their plates from the table and was putting them in the dishwasher. He straightened and turned toward her as Skylar neared him.

She came to a stop in front of him, then reached for his hand. Aiden didn't resist her action, which made it easy for her to press the pregnancy test into his palm.

"What's..." Aiden stared down at the test, his eyes going wide as he saw the message in the display window. He looked up at her, shock on his face. "You're pregnant?"

Skylar nodded. "Yes. I took the test this morning."

A smile grew to take over his entire face. "This is amazing!"

He stepped forward and took her into his arms, lifting her off the floor as he spun in a circle before setting her down. "Oh, Sky, I love you so much, and I can't wait to raise this baby with you."

The words helped settle something inside her. His excitement was in direct contrast to how she'd felt, but she was glad he'd reacted the way he had.

"What's wrong?" he asked as he cupped her face in his hands. "Aren't you happy?"

She blinked rapidly, willing herself not to cry. "I'm... not sure how I feel."

"This is a good thing, babe," Aiden said. "A wonderful thing. I've wanted to have a family with you. A child that we could raise."

"I just feel... guilty?"

Aiden frowned. "Why?"

"It seems unfair that we're together now, and able to give this baby what we couldn't give Shiloh. What if she gets upset because her biological sibling will have us as parents, but she doesn't?"

"I think she'll be excited," Aiden told her. "She's asked when we're going to have a baby, and I've never gotten the feeling that she was upset by the idea. The opposite, in fact."

Skylar knew he was right. But would Shiloh still feel that way once the baby was there?

"And even if she does have feelings about it and even if she's upset, we'll work through it. She's a strong little girl who is confident in Charli and Blake's love, and in ours as well. We'll talk to Charli and Blake about it before we tell her so we can approach it in the best way possible."

Aiden pulled her into his arms and wrapped them tightly around her, grounding her and reminding Skylar that this time around, she wasn't on her own.

"Everyone is going to be thrilled, babe," he murmured. "And I'll be with you through this, every step of the way. This won't be like Shiloh's pregnancy. You're not going to be alone."

She knew that. Had known from the moment she suspected she was pregnant. And yet, hearing him say the words finally broke the knot of anxiety she'd been carrying.

"You're entitled to how you feel, and I don't blame you at all," Aiden said.

Skylar moved back enough so that she could look up into his face. "I want you to know that I'm not mad that I'm pregnant. I don't even wish I wasn't. If you had asked me a month ago how I'd feel about this news, I would have told you I'd be ecstatic."

"So what happened?"

"I don't really know," she said. "When I first suspected I was pregnant, I started to feel kind of anxious, and then, when I took the test today, all sorts of emotions took over."

"I'm sure it was hard to not remember the last time you took a test and the months that followed."

"I guess that must be what happened," Skylar said with a frown. "But I don't like how I'm feeling. I want to just be happy about this baby."

"You will be," Aiden assured her with a gentle smile. "Just give it a little time. Since we probably won't be telling anyone right away, you'll have some time to work through it all. And I'll be right there with you."

"Thank you," Skylar said as she leaned into him. "I love you so much."

"I love you too." He bent down to press a kiss to her lips. "And you're going to be a wonderful mother. I just know it."

Some of his excitement had rubbed off on her already because for the first time since realizing the possibility that she might be pregnant, she also felt a small spark of excitement. And she was confident that it would grow.

~*~

Aiden bent down close to Skylar as the doctor finally lifted the baby and laid him on Skylar's chest. "You did such a great job, babe. You're amazing."

It had been a long labor, but Skylar had been a trooper, never issuing a word of complaint even when she'd clearly been flagging.

"He's here." Skylar looked up at Aiden. "We did it."

"*You* did it," Aiden told her. "You did all the hard work. I love you."

He pressed a kiss to her temple, his love for her overwhelming him. Together, they gazed down at their little boy.

"Welcome to the world, Miles Albert," Skylar whispered. "We're so happy to have you here." Her eyes drifted closed as she cupped his small head. "Thank you, God, for our precious baby."

As he watched the woman he loved cuddle their son, Aiden could only thank God for the journey He'd brought them on to finally be at this moment. Together, and building a family of their own.

It hadn't taken long for Skylar to sort through her emotions following the revelation that she was pregnant. And they'd had a few weeks to savor the news, just the two of them, before sharing it with the family.

As Aiden had told Skylar, Shiloh had been *thrilled* when she'd learned they were pregnant. He was sure people outside their close circle of friends and family would wonder how they made it work. Being so close to the daughter that had been given up for adoption.

He probably wouldn't have been able to believe how they'd worked it out if he wasn't living it himself. It hadn't always been easy, but when everyone involved wanted what was best for Shiloh, it was easier to put aside their own wants.

Shiloh's fight with cancer had brought another dimension into the situation, but thankfully, she'd been clear for the past year. But that had only come about after a stem cell transplant from Cole shortly after they'd gotten married, when they discovered that her cancer had come back.

He was so grateful that God had allowed the procedure to be a success, and he could only hope that she would stay in remission for the rest of her life.

"Should I send out the news?" Cathy asked.

Both their moms had been there for the duration of the labor, and Aiden was so thankful for their support. Willow was having a sleepover with Shiloh, and Charli and Blake had promised to bring them both to the hospital once the baby had arrived.

It was the middle of the night, however, so that visit would be a few hours later.

"Yes, please, Mom," Skylar said as the nurse came to take the baby.

After giving Skylar another kiss, Aiden followed the nurse so that he could take some pictures of his son. It felt like he'd waited his whole life for this moment, and as he stood there, love filling his heart for Miles Albert, he felt such a sense of longing for his dad. He would have loved the little boy who was his namesake.

His mom joined him, and together they watched as the nurse weighed and measured the little boy before putting a diaper on him and wrapping him up.

"Here you go, Daddy." The older nurse handed him the swaddled baby. "You can take him back to Mommy now."

Aiden didn't hesitate to return to Skylar's side. He settled on a chair next to her bed, and the two of them began their lifetime of loving their son.

A few hours later, Charli and Blake showed up with the girls. They hadn't brought anyone else, since that would have been a bit too much for her small hospital room.

"Where's the baby?" Shiloh asked when she walked in with a stuffed animal in her hands. "I can't wait to see him."

"Right here, sweetie," Skylar said, gesturing to the small hospital bassinet beside her bed.

Aiden had had the chance to spend some time with his son while Skylar had taken a shower and had changed into the cozy pajama set she'd spent so much time trying to find.

Shiloh immediately scooted around the bed to where Aiden stood next to the bassinet. "Oh, he's so cute!"

Willow joined Shiloh, while Charli went to Skylar and bent to give her a hug. Blake held out his hand to Aiden. "Congratulations."

"Thank you," he said. "It's been an amazing experience."

Blake grinned. "The arrival of a child is truly a miracle."

In Aiden's mind, this moment was indeed a miracle. Given how he and Skylar had ended things all those years ago, he never would have seen a way for them to have a future together. Let alone a child.

And while it hadn't all been easy, it had definitely been worth it. The grace Skylar had offered him after how he'd treated her never ceased to amaze him. He owed it to her—to both of them, actually— to do what he had to in order to be the husband she needed. And also the father that Miles would need.

Without his faith in God and the incredible support of their family, it might have seemed overwhelming. However, he was eager to embrace this new chapter in their lives and was hopeful that their small family would continue to expand.

And the best part of all of it was that he'd be doing it with Skylar, the woman who'd been strong enough and brave enough to give him a second chance at love with her.

~*~ The End ~*~

Other books by
Kimberly Rae Jordan

ABOUT THE AUTHOR

Kimberly Rae Jordan is a USA Today bestselling author of Christian romances. Many years ago, her love of reading Christian romance morphed into a desire to write stories of love, faith, and family, and thus began a journey that would lead her to places Kimberly never imagined she'd go.

In addition to being a writer, she is also a wife and mother, which means Kimberly spends her days straddling the line between real life in a house on the prairies of Canada and the imaginary world her characters live in. Though caring for her husband and four kids and working on her stories takes up a large portion of her day, Kimberly also enjoys reading and looking at craft ideas that she will likely never attempt to make.

As she continues to pen heartwarming stories of love, faith, and family, Kimberly hopes that readers of all ages will enjoy the journeys her characters take in each book. She has no plan to stop writing the stories God places on her heart and looks forward to where her journey will take her in the years to come.

www.ingramcontent.com/pod-product-compliance
Lightning Source LLC
Chambersburg PA
CBHW030406180626
46812CB00005B/1939